Jaz Davison (writing as J. A. Zarifian) is an award-winning stage director and actor. She has been by turns a daughter, a sister, a cousin, a mother, a divorcée, an aunt, a widow, a lover, a godmother and an éminence grise. No one remains unchanged after meeting her. This is her first novel.

Dedication

For my father (or "Mister Century + Four")
– sorry it took so long, but I think they get it.

J. A. Zarifian

ONCE UPON A MOUSE

With 12 Full-Colour Illustrations by
Daniel Cabuco

AUSTIN MACAULEY PUBLISHERS™
LONDON • CAMBRIDGE • NEW YORK • SHARJAH

ISBN 9781787105096 (Paperback)
ISBN 9781787105102 (Hardback)
ISBN 9781787105119 (E-Book)

www.austinmacauley.com

First Published (2018)
Austin Macauley Publishers Ltd.
25 Canada Square
Canary Wharf
London
E14 5LQ

Acknowledgements

Thanks to the many people involved in this project:
— to my agent Linda Langton, for the belief;
— to the staff at Austin Macauley for making it real;
— to the Town of Solihull for welcoming and inspiring me;
— to all those who befriended this stranger in a strange land, especially to Liz Morris, her family and dogs—sanity achieved;
— to both the Knightsbridge Theatre (Los Angeles, USA) and the Crescent Theatre (Birmingham, UK) for letting me hone my story-telling craft through Directing and Performing;
— to Wanda Raven, for being my bull-sh*t meter;
— to Bonnie MacBird, friend, mentor, advisor; and
— to a host of others for being inspirational to both my life and my words: Amy Ball, Jon Mullich, Donna McManus, Jayma Mays, Adam Campbell, Jen Chang, Brad Upton, Kurt Engstrom.
— Finally, to Daniel Cabuco, your art astounds me, and to see what my book has inspired in you humbles me. Working with you has been a true artistic meeting of the mind and heart;
— to my amazing supportive family—my children, Diana and Casey, and my sister and brother, Shelby and Raymond;
— to William Goldman, for the writings that inspired a girl of 17 and continue to challenge and enthrall her; and
— to my Aeolus—my all.

Chapter 1
The Beginning

"It was enough to make the cow go mad."

An odd thought indeed, and one with bad ramifications for life on a farm, but Danni thought it still.

Danni, being a mouse, didn't completely understand the complexity of her thought, but had had it nonetheless. For all she cared, the cow could jump over the moon, as it was wont to do – and let the little dog laugh himself silly. But right now, what with her dish and spoon gone, Danni didn't much care about the everyday occurrences on the Farm. Or in the town. Or anywhere.

"That damned Farmer's Wife!"

Another thought was also tumbling over and over in Danni's wee head. This thought she understood completely. Not that her cousins weren't nothing but trouble – being partially sighted and all – but they were the only family she had left. After her Mother had died in the clock incident, living with the trio had its benefits: company for only. Still, she had grown tired of being the grain and cheese winner of the hole.

But she did feel it was a bit her fault. She hadn't said anything when they'd called to her, at her, for her. She had just sat on the plank of wood running between the walls and watched them with her soft brown eyes. They'd bumped into things and each other several times before fleeing out of the hole and into the house. They couldn't help not being able to see but, bless their little hearts, did they have to be stupid?

Danni shook her head in wonder, closing her eyes and sighing deeply. Everyone seemed to do things that seriously defied logic, as if they'd all been given a script or programmed or brainwashed, doing things that would either put them in danger, or kill them or, in polite society, have them locked up. Good thought, that last one – and Georgy Porgy and Wee Willie Winkie should be the first two on the list.

But when she'd heard the sickening thunk on the wood floor and three agonisingly short squeaks, her little heart raced faster than usual – mouse heartbeats averaging 500 to 600 per minute, and that was just at rest – and she forced herself to peek out of the hole.

Gouging the floor was the carving knife. And three bottom halves of what were her cousins, their tails still in spasmodic motion.

A magician with a blade, that Farmer's Wife, but to what end? Nailing handicapped mice, well it didn't seem sporting. Seemed bad form, truly. And the more Danni considered it, the madder she got.

Barely thinking, she scurried out of the hole, taking her Mother's old route to the clock. She had silently vowed never to do it, but she was drawn – it was, after all, the shortest, safest way to the highest place. On her periphery, she saw that the Farmer's Wife was preparing for the inevitable clean up – a small broom and pan near the slaughter site – and she heard the sound of water being poured into a tub. Then Danni was inside the clock.

Dark though it was, there was never a feeling of being closed in. The gold of the pendulum, bells and chains gave off a dull glitter but in an expansive way. Danni jumped to the lowest weight and hurried up the chain, a trick of the trade her Mother had shown her – why did the action seem so natural to her, when she had never before done it alone? Pushing that thought aside, she was soon at the top, in the box that contained the very works of the clock.

Her Mother had often shown Danni how to enter the clock, not only as it was what her Mother did (and Danni would be expected to do the same when her time came), but it was also a place of safety in time of need. Her Mother had taken great pride in this "trick-of-the-trade," which was another inexplicable thing to Danni. "But why?" she would demand, only to hear her Mother say patiently, "Danni, it is the way of things, sometimes you just have to act on Faith." This seldom comforted Danni, but her Mother was so kind and gentle that Danni felt she ought to at least try to accept this thing called "Faith", whatever it was, even though not doing so seemed more sensible.

At the top of the mechanism, at the far side of the face of the clock, was a hole. It was there since Time Immemorial. Why was it there? Another curiosity that her Mother just took on Faith, but it would prove very helpful today. The hole led to the top of the clock and a grand view of the room. Even the cat, when it wasn't just fiddling around, but was instead making an attempt at chasing the mice of the house, knew better than to try to ascend this clock.

Firstly, it was smooth wood on three sides and had equally smooth glass in the front. There were no good footholds for the kind of jumps that would be needed to get to the top, and the one time the cat had considered an attempt, the Farmer's Wife had twigged it immediately and knocked the cat silly for even having the thought – and the cat did not forget this. It was shortly after that clubbing that the cat started murdering the violin. Somehow it had a soothing effect on the Farmer's Wife. Another thing Danni could not fathom – they called it "music" – rubbish!

Atop her perch, Danni saw the Farmer's Wife make her approach, carrying the tub of water and a mop. Danni could see a small stream of water coming from the base of the tub. "Still not mended properly," Danni silently chided. The Farmer's Wife put down the tub and balanced the mop against the wall. Danni averted her gaze as the Farmer's Wife swept up the remains of her cousins. Danni looked again after hearing the pan and broom set down. The virago was struggling with the carving knife now, wiggling it gently back and forth so as not to leave too big a gap in the wood. It gave suddenly and the Farmer's Wife rose unsteadily, very close to the clock. Then Danni struck.

She jumped straight onto the Farmer's Wife's head, landing with a slight thump on the bonnet. The Farmer's Wife went suddenly stiff at the feeling, her head giving a decided shake. Danni had grabbed onto the white fabric and let gravity work. She rode the bonnet down the Farmer's Wife's forehead until she was completely in the woman's line of vision. The Farmer's Wife was now totally rigid as even the head shake had stopped. Her eyes grew wide and her mouth took on an "O" quality. Quite abruptly, Danni squeaked out:

"Murderer!!"

...and leapt onto the Farmer's Wife's ample bosom, skittering up and around her back.

Suddenly galvanised into action, the Farmer's Wife let out a scream that became a bellow as she reached around for Danni, and the bellow became a scream yet again as the woman had forgotten that the hand attempting to reach and swat was still gripping the carving knife, which now pierced into her own shoulder. She jerked the blade out and fell back into the clock which teetered slowly away before rocking back over and crashing onto the bloodied shoulder of the Farmer's Wife.

Danni had already scurried down the harridan's back, onto her skirt and had made a calculated leap to the rug on the floor before turning back to look at the chaos in her wake. Her jaw dropped slightly at the sight of the inert figure on the floor, the huge box of the clock cracked in places, the glass front shattered before her, shards so very close indeed, some as large as the carving knife itself. Danni had no idea how they had missed her.

Suddenly, from the remains of the clock came a loud, off-pitch gong which made Danni jump...

the Farmer's Wife opened an eye...

Danni wasted no time in running from the room towards the open back door where she collided with fur.

Shaking her little head to clear it, she found herself looking up into the panting face of the little dog. Only now, Arnie wasn't laughing.

"What's happened in there, Danni?" the dog asked, and a slight grin began curling up the edges of his mouth.

"Clock fell." she squeaked out.

"You run up it?"

"Yeah."

"Your Mother'd be proud."

"What?"

"Well, up until the clock falling part..."

"But..."

"How'd you make it fall? Tiny thing like you..."

"She chopped up my cousins!"

The dog shook his head. "That again…" he muttered.

"AGAIN?" she said. "This defies logic," she thought.

"Oh, it happens but… not the clock falling…"

"She knocked it over!" Danni yelled.

The dog looked perplexed. "She wouldn't."

This stopped Danni for a moment. Of course she wouldn't. The Farmer's Wife loved that clock. She had even danced a jig [more insanity] when she realised that Danni's Mother no longer clambered up there.

The little dog stared at her. "Danni… tell Arnie what's happened."

For the first time, Danni began to feel uneasy. What had she done? Behind her she could hear the Farmer's Wife attempting to move. So could Arnie, and his look did not convey any sort of humour.

"Arnie!" she implored, "I got mad at her for killing them, it wasn't right." The dog just blinked his deep brown eyes.

"I jumped her." Danni whispered. There was a pause which seemed an eternity as Arnie took in this revelation. Then a moan came from inside the house. Arnie lowered his head. His shoulders began to heave unsteadily, his breathing uneven. Danni looked around, not knowing what to do or where to go, and when Arnie lifted his head and she could see his eyes watering, and…

…he let out a long, raucous laugh, at the same time that…

…the Farmer's Wife let out a scream about mice, about a particular mouse, about Danni! – cursing her, wishing her blade could find a home cutting off Danni's tail.

Then Danni saw Arnie abruptly suppress his laughter into low chuckles.

"Get on my back." Arnie stated simply.

Danni stared. In the distance, she saw the Farmer had stopped work and was looking towards the house.

"On my back, Danni, NOW!"

She wasted no time, climbing up and grabbing onto his collar. Arnie made a good show of pretending to see something scurry by, then made a few jerky movements before tearing off towards the field. Behind them Danni heard the Farmer's Wife shout, "That's it, Dog!! Go get it!" The wind in her face blew tears from her eyes as she whizzed past the Farmer. He only noticed Arnie, though, since Danni's fur was a similar colour up by the dog's collar, where she was barely hanging on for dear life.

"Liza?" The Farmer called as he got closer to the house. "Whatever is the matter? What's happened to you?"

"Oh, Henry…" She moaned, but Danni and Arnie were too far away to hear any more.

Chapter 2
The Grasshopper, Jon...

Arnie finally began to slow as they passed a series of trees. Danni could not remember ever being this far from the house; she could scarcely recall leaving it. Almost all of her knowledge of things had come from what she'd heard and the opinions she had formed from them. Now she sensed her size deeply and tried not to tremble.

Arnie stopped by a rock and knelt down a little. She took this to mean to jump off, which she did. The rock was cold beneath her feet.

"I can't bring you back, Danni." he told her. "Nothing like this has ever happened. We'll expect new blind mice, I'm certain, but..."

Danni's brows furrowed and she asked; *"New* blind mice?"

Arnie nodded. "But this has never happened..." he tried not to laugh again, "funny as it was..."

"New blind mice." This time it was a statement. "But that doesn't make sense..."

"Of course it makes sense," Arnie sniffed, "it's the way it's always been."

"Just because it's the way it's always been doesn't mean it makes sense!" the mouse roared.

Arnie shook his head. "Where do you get such ideas?" Somehow Danni could tell it wasn't a real question and that Arnie was not expecting an answer. "And what do you really know of sense?"

Danni opened her mouth but stopped. She *was* young. She had not been farther than the main house of the Farm. No one else really shared her opinions. But it just *felt* wrong. She shook her head.

"I guess I'll have to think about that." she conceded. "It just doesn't seem logical."

Arnie cocked his head and his grin came back. "Big word." He looked around. "You should be safe here for the night. There's coverage above and the roots are open enough in that tree there for you to hide and spend the night. I'll come in the morning and bring some food..." he drifted off as his grin gradually vanished.

"What am I supposed to do, Arnie? I mean, if I can't go back?" she asked. She again felt very small and very vulnerable.

"I don't know..." he admitted, then perked up suddenly. "Maybe we'll have an idea in the morning! Maybe Elsie will have an idea..."

"You're going to ask the cow?"

The dog looked at Danni sharply. "Have you jumped over the moon?" Danni blinked. "I thought not."

Danni looked around herself hesitantly. Arnie softened his gaze and his tone. "It's the best I can do, Danni. I've never really been an idea dog." Danni could see the truth in this. Arnie brought his nose close to her and snuffed gently. Danni put her paw on it, not bothered by its dampness.

"Thanks, Arnie." she said softly.

"See you in the morning." he replied and started back across the field, pausing once to look before heading off at a gentle trot.

Danni watched for a long time. Even after she could see him no more, she watched. The day was waning. Night would be coming on. She looked about her surroundings. The roots Arnie had mentioned did look safe enough, so she scrambled down the rock and went to them cautiously. She stepped over a long line of ants, not wanting to disturb their progress. Each of them carried something (useless things, as far as Danni could tell) as they made their way industriously across the ground – the pebbles and divots must have seemed like boulders and chasms to them! – heading in cadence towards their anthill.

Danni had seen ants work like this at the farmhouse, assembly line like through the cracks in the floor boards and the joins in the walls, always heading back to their home, their hill, where ever ants go with their stuff. Never stopping, barely pausing, in some unheard rhythm, dutifully continuing their path. She could see the sense. Soon enough the weather would change and everything they needed would be all but impossible to get. She saw similar behaviour in the Farmer and his Wife in the ways they took care of themselves, their farm and the farm animals.

"Now this was logical," she thought, even if it meant giving credit to the Farmer's Wife.

But now she noticed something else. A *sound*. A sound that matched the rhythm of the ants' progress. Steady, not quite a drumbeat, but something of a sort of syncopation, and a sweet sound at that. As quickly as she noticed it, it stopped. And the ants stopped too. Briefly. Then they began to move again, but it wasn't in the same sort of synchronised fashion. There was almost a panic in them. They moved not unlike her cousins before they fled the hole and Danni suddenly felt a horrible pang of guilt. She opened her mouth to speak and the sound began again.

The ants again synchronised their steady gait to the ant hill. And in they went. The sound continued even after the last ant had gone into the hole. Danni looked around for the source of the music, for that's what it really was to her now, a sweet melody. She looked at the shifting grass, the branches of the fruit trees above her, the grasshopper, the reeds off in the distance, the leaves of a nearby bush, the small grasshopper, the…?

His back legs oscillated in a smooth motion, the grasshopper's eyes were closed and the sounds were most certainly coming from him. Danni moved closer and the music stopped. The grasshopper's legs had stopped moving and he had opened both eyes to stare at Danni. Then his legs grew tense and Danni knew he was about to…

"Please don't go!" she called out. "Please don't jump."

The grasshopper regarded her cautiously.

"Were you making that music?" she said softly.

Still with caution, the grasshopper nodded. Danni couldn't help herself, she smiled. The grasshopper tilted his head and almost seemed amused.

"That was lovely…" Danni said, finally.

The grasshopper nodded. "Got anything to eat?"

"Beg pardon?" She said, a little too boldly.

"Got anything to eat? Simple question. The ants take all the good stuff…"

"Well, couldn't you get it yourself? I mean… like now…?" she said, with a hint of irritation.

"Hey," the grasshopper drawled, "I'm an artist. Haven't you ever heard the adage, sing for your supper?"

"No," said Danni, getting quite irritated.

"Socialist," retorted the grasshopper.

"That's the opposite of…"

"Conservative…"

"… no…" said Danni again.

"Capitalist!"

"…I don't think…"

"Bourgeois…" (In a regal tone, mind you.)

"…That's pretty much the same…" began Danni.

The grasshopper leaned back on his hind legs indignantly. "Have you heard of the starving artist?"

"I think I've heard the phrase…"

The grasshopper bowed. "C'est moi."

Danni looked at him askance. The grasshopper remained nonplussed.

"Look," he said, "I make music. I don't have time to go about and hoard like the ants you paid so much attention to. I ply my wares and I depend on the kindness of those moved by my sound."

"That doesn't seem very wise." Danni stated.

"Of course it's not wise, I follow Intuition, not Judgement. Didn't I say I was an artist? Maybe I would be doing something else if I were wise, but not being wise I don't have many options."

"You could take a day off playing and collect some food to put away. The winter is coming, you know, and it would be good to have a store of food set aside…"

But the grasshopper was waving her off. "Yes, yes, yes of course it would be good… it would be lovely… perfect…" he suddenly looked deflated, "… but I can't stop."

Danni watched for a moment. "But you have."

He bored a stare into her. "Mice think you can pick up food just anywhere!!" he harrumphed. "You have to know where to look, dontcha? Besides, I've been doing this most of the day… You think this is *refreshing*

15

for me? That I can just, oh, I don't know, do laps after this? Creating is very difficult." Again, he seemed to sag. "But it's what I do. What I do best."

Danni became thoughtful. She couldn't quite follow the logic, but she did understand the idea of doing what you did best. Even though she didn't see the logic in her Mother going to the clock every day, she could clearly recall her Mother's sense of pride when she returned, the feeling, it seemed, of a job well done. She looked at the grasshopper differently now.

He sensed the difference and cocked his head: "You have any place to stay?"

Danni shook her head. "I was told to try the roots of that tree, they seem…"

"Yeah," he interrupted, "that would be good, but not here… one of them houses a snake – I don't think you want to meet him – and the other one a very large spider. I *know* I don't want to meet her…"

Now it was Danni's turn to feel deflated. Arnie seemed so sure she'd be safe, but then Arnie had admitted he wasn't much of an idea dog.

"…but…" the grasshopper continued.

"But?" Danni repeated hopefully.

"… on the other side of the tree, there are a few places a little higher up… well, they've been good for me so far. And I think you'd fit."

Danni looked at him curiously.

He shrugged. "Sometimes 'artist' is synonymous for 'sucker.' Besides, you did like my music."

"I really did…" she said, relieved to have a place for the night.

"Don't lay it on thick, rodent. I may be an artist-slash-sucker-slash-unwise, but I don't like to be pandered to." He led the way to the other side of the tree and asked, "What's your name?"

"Danni…"

"I'm Jon."

"Nice to meet you, Jon…"

"Nice to meet you, Danni. Do you have any food?"

Chapter 3
...and the Queen Ant, Celina

Danni awoke slightly disoriented. She was curled up into herself so she only saw her stomach and front paws one over the other and she was very hesitant to lift her head. She listened carefully and when she heard nothing untoward, she lifted her head slowly to observe the darkened hole she had come to the night before. There was a shaft of sunlight just peeking in giving her the impression that the sun was coming up. Stretching herself and giving herself the requisite shake, she approached the opening cautiously to peek out.

She could hear Jon before seeing him. He was yelling off in the near distance and she followed his voice. "... greedy Capitalist pigs!" she heard.

"We're ants" came a feminine reply, which made Danni stop for a moment. "In this case, it's the same thing!" Jon barked out.

Danni continued onward to the voices and found Jon on a hard patch of earth. Near him, atop the ant hill, was an uncommonly large ant (or ULA).

"Jon...?" Danni tested.

The ULA saw Danni and suddenly took wing. Danni's eyes grew wide as the ULA flew in her direction and then back towards Jon. "Is that supposed to be your muscle?" It asked Jon.

Inwardly, Danni took pride – she was, after all, a mouse – to be looked upon as a strong-arm of sorts... and yet, she wondered if the ULA meant it in a derisive manner. She hurried over to them both.

"I'm a mouse." she started.

"Thank you, Captain Obvious." it intoned.

"That doesn't mean you ought to be rude..." Danni said, with as much muscle as she could muster.

"If you'll excuse me, I'm having a discussion with the Artist?" and the ULA turned back to Jon. "We, you and I, have been over this many a time before, *crass*-hopper. We, the ants, appear to be doing the work. You, the *not*-ant, appear to be doing precious little other than rubbing your legs together in a fashion most unbecoming to an unattached bug... so no, We, the Queen, really don't think there is any 'excess food' here for you, the common or garden variety pest. In fact, there is no excess. At all. Ever.

The Queen looked at Danni, then back to Jon and explained with withering sincerity: "One has many duties, but One's *chief* responsibility is the welfare of these ants. Ants. Note that. You are, pardon my mentioning, a completely different order, family, genus and species. But we do appreciate your asking." And with that the Queen Ant flew back to the ant hill.

Jon watched her departure. Actually, Danni was pretty certain he wasn't really looking after the Queen, he just didn't seem to want to turn to face her just now. Danni didn't know what to say and, for once, she chose to follow the feeling and said nothing.

After a pause, and without turning, Jon said: "I've been working on something new, Danni, would you like to hear it?"

"Yes, Jon, I really would."

And he jumped onto a nearby rock – sunnier and more comfortable than the hard place from where he had been speaking to the Queen – and, after a deep sigh, began to move his back legs together and play. The sound was lush and lovely and sweet and Danni almost closed her eyes to truly hear it clearly in her head, but her attention was suddenly diverted…

…by the ants coming from the ant hill. Even though this tune was of a more gentle, almost melancholy nature than the one from the day before, she noticed that the ants were keeping time with it in much the same manner as they had when Danni first saw them.

She watched their progress for a time before she finally turned to Jon and coughed. The music continued and so she coughed again. This time she added; "Jon…"

18

Begrudgingly Jon stopped, it was obvious he was coming to a place that he felt was a grand moment in the piece and he did not look too pleased about being interrupted. He glared at Danni, who was watching the ants.

They were moving about in the same awkward manner Danni has observed the previous day, much like her cousins' behaviour before departing their hole…

"Play, Jon!" she demanded.

But Jon was feeling rather abused and pouted: "Stop, Jon. Play, Jon. Stop, Jon… I am not a machine, you know, I happen to be…"

"An artist, yes I know, now play!!" And the quickness in her tone made him continue, grudgingly, but continue he did, until he became lost in his own reverie.

And the ants moved again in their synchronised manner as they sought out more food, more winter supplies to safely store away, deep beneath the ground. Danni's eyes widened. Quietly she moved away from Jon and went to the ant hill. She selected a random small hole, stared down it for a moment and then called: "Hello? Hello?"

She looked back at Jon to be certain he was well into his playing. He was. As she turned back to ant hill, she continued: Hellooo? Your Ineffable Hugeness, Hell… Oh…!" And she stopped abruptly, with the Queen Ant hovering imperiously before her face.

"Yes, Mouse?" The Queen had an icy tone.

"My name is Danni." the mouse replied.

"Well how nice for you."

"You really oughtn't be so hostile…" Danni started, "considering what Jon is doing for you and your 'precious' clan…"

"We're a *colony*, if you don't mind…" The Queen interrupted, "and the last We knew, that grasshopper was just making a load of noise…" Danni looked over her shoulder and called sharply: "JON!"

The grasshopper stopped again.

Stopped in a huff, you might say: "You are really becoming annoying…"

"Look at your cla… uh, colony now…" Danni said softly and the Queen Ant watched in growing horror as her ants moved about pell-mell, with no real direction, almost in a panic.

Danni turned to Jon: "Sorry, won't bother again…" And after a moment, Jon started up again. The ants found purpose in their movement again and returned to their work in an orderly way. Danni looked at the Queen Ant who was watching carefully.

"That wasn't just a fluke…" she said slowly in a very subdued voice, "…was it?"

"Doesn't seem to be." Danni replied. "Seems they move when he plays and stop when he stops. And not just stop, they lose sight of what they are to do." She looked at the Queen Ant cautiously. "So… maybe he isn't just 'doing precious little'…"

The Queen Ant looked at Danni... "Celina..." she said. Danni gave a shake of her head but the Queen continued, "Our name is Celina."

Before they could say another word, they were startled by a strange sound. Their attention was drawn by the little dog running across the field making small unintelligible noises.

"We're going to just hazard a guess and say he's with you." Celina intoned. Danni nodded.

"Could you just keep him away from our ants down there? Can you do that?"

"Do my best..." Danni replied and scurried over the rocks, cautiously jumping over the ants and settling on another hard patch of ground between the approaching Arnie and the ants. After a bit, Arnie finished his approach and she saw the reason for the unintelligible noises: the dog dropped a small sack on the ground in front of Danni. He panted for several moments, looking at the mouse with a huge grin the whole while.

"Danni..." he gasped out, while panting and grinning – not easy, just you try it!

"Arnie." she greeted and when the dog tried to speak again she said: "take your time."

The little dog took in several more gasps of air and then sneezed. In the distance, they both heard:

"Creating here!!"

"Sorry, Jon," she called back.

Arnie cocked his head. "Making friends already?"

"You could say that..."

"That's good! Did you sleep well?"

"I found a comfy hole," Danni began, and Arnie looked so pleased and proud of himself that Danni found she had no heart to tell him it hadn't been in any of the places he had recommended. She looked at the sack and Arnie's attention was also drawn to it.

He started in recognition. "Oh! Yeah... for you..." he nuzzled it closer. "Best I could do..."

Danni approached the sack which was wet from Arnie's slobber and looked inside. She smiled. "Some grains!" she yelped in happy recognition.

Arnie nodded but looked contrite. "They're a little damp..." he apologised. Danni nodded as she touched a few pieces. "...had to push them in with my nose..."

Danni delicately raised her hand up from the sack. "I think I'll let them dry in the sun." She smiled. Patting his nose was one thing. She wondered how she might wash the grains without ruining them.

"I'm gonna have to get back, Danni..." he said gravely. She looked at him. "It was pretty bad last night. Never seen her in such a state... and you know how that makes him... Even Precious noticed. It actually put that cat off playing last night, it did." Slowly Danni nodded. "And Elsie had nothing either. I think she was distressed by the whole thing... couldn't chew her cud like usual... hope the milk doesn't sour... What are you gonna do?" he asked.

20

Danni shrugged. "I dunno…" She admitted. "I guess I'll have to explore a little and see. Or maybe stay here." She found that she was shaking a little. "I don't know." She looked up to see Arnie smiling at her. That made her tremble even more. "What?"

"You always were different, Danni. I think you'll be fine. You could go to town, you know, it's not that far down the road over that way…" He indicated over her shoulder, beyond the trees. "I'm sure there'll be something for you over there…" She looked at him with a raised eyebrow. His smile shrank slightly to a grin. "Well, maybe not *sure*, but… it's worth looking, huh? And who knows? In a few days, she might have settled down and forgotten… After all, she never used to remember your Mother climbing the clock until it struck one. Between you and me, I don't think she really remembers the clock!"

Danni understood what he was saying, but the whole clock workings had her a little stymied.

"Thank you, Arnie. You really have been a big help." The dog looked down in quiet embarrassment and pawed the ground slightly.

He suddenly brightened and looked up at her: "I'll bring grain whenever I can, okay?"

"Just don't get into any trouble!" Danni warned. Arnie nodded. He leaned in and snuffled her lightly. Danni hugged a section of his snout before stepping back to look at him, "Bye, Arnie." she said with a slight catch in her throat.

"Bye Danni. You know… I know I laughed… but what you did was also really brave. Remember that."

And with that, the little dog turned around and went dashing back across the field. Danni felt her eyes moisten up slightly and she rubbed at them with her paws.

"You gonna eat *all* that?" Celina was beside her looking at the sack. "We mean… one is sure you're hungry but that really is a *lot* of grain… and didn't he say he was coming back?"

Danni regarded the Queen ruefully. Suddenly Celina smiled. Really! It so took Danni by surprise that she let out a small laugh herself.

Celina went on in all seriousness: "We have a small group of worker ants ready to take these out to a sunny spot to dry them… well… and clean some of them… most of them… all one needs is you're okay… okay?"

Danni regarded the Queen carefully. "What about Jon?"

The Queen looked down for a moment then looked back at Danni. "We really didn't know that what he's been doing has been so helpful…" she explained. "We mean, one is used to dealing with what's in front of one, what the intake has been and needs to be, how much one's workers do…" She looked over at Jon. "We just never realised that something one couldn't see…" she stopped.

Danni nodded: "I guess sometimes it's not about what you can see." Even as she said it, the words seemed strange.

"We suppose you are right." allowed the Queen.

"So…" continued Danni, with just a hint of muscle.

"The Grasshopper deserves a share of the stores."

Celina went happily back to her duties and Danni looked off towards the grasshopper. He was lost in the reverie of his music. Her brows furrowed slightly. Maybe this was what she was supposed to do: go out into the world and open creatures' eyes to one another. Maybe she was supposed to be of help this way.

Well it was certainly better than sitting around in the farmhouse, keeping away from the Farmer's Wife, or going up and down that clock for no real reason. She felt a momentary twinge of guilt. Going up and down that clock had made her Mother so happy. But as she looked from Jon to Celina, who was now directing another group of ants to empty out the contents of the sack Arnie had brought and set the grains in the sun to dry, the guilt subsided. Knowing that Jon would be taken care of because he was earning his way and knowing that she had a hand in it made her happy. She didn't have to have the *same* happiness as her Mother… so long as she was happy, she knew her Mother would have been as well. She went over to the Queen and said: Should we tell him together that there will be a new arrangement?"

Celina looked at her: "Good idea… but not until break time, Danni. He may be doing a good thing, but we have a schedule to run here." Danni nodded and climbed up on a nearby rock to watch Jon and the ants while they worked and especially to just listen to the marvellous sounds that came out because of that work.

******

It was later that afternoon, after Jon and Celina had come to an agreement as to what sort of share he could expect from the ants through the Winter months as well as what was to be expected of him to earn that share, which Danni had brokered fairly between her two new friends. As evening approached, Danni was drawn to look off in the direction beyond the trees.

Arnie had told her the town was that way and she began seriously to consider the option. Moving quickly up the nearest tree, to as high a branch as she could manage without fear of falling, she looked off in the direction he had indicated. And sure enough, very far off, she could see the tops of many buildings, as if a congregation of farm houses were packed all next to each other. But there were spaces in between and other things that Danni could not quite make out, in spite of her excellent vision, along with the hills, mountains and many trees.

She could, by looking closer to where she was, make out a road which meandered its way towards the town. There was also a river which ambled near the road, crossing it from time to time, opening up to make a larger expanse of water and then closing together again. It seemed in places almost as if it could be jumped over from Danni's vantage point. With all the trees and bushes that grew beside the road, Danni felt certain she would have adequate hiding areas should the need arise. With a little nod of satisfaction to herself, she climbed back down the tree and found Jon waiting for her.

"You going someplace?" he asked.

Danni nodded. "I think I'm going to head toward town." Jon nodded slowly, but with very little enthusiasm. "Are you alright?" she asked. Jon continued to nod, but a frown was fixed on his face.

After what seemed a very long time he said: "I appreciate what you did, Danni." And then there was another pause: "Because of your eyes and ears, you saw something that neither Celina nor I had noticed." Another pause hung in the air between them: "Is that why you're going?" Danni looked confused so Jon continued. "...To look and listen for other things?"

The little mouse pondered this. It did seem that that *was* what she was doing. At the same time, she knew there must be something else. She just hadn't placed her paw on it completely. But as she looked at Jon's searching gaze, she smiled and nodded.

"I suppose so." she replied. "I know I can't go back to the farmhouse."

"You could stay here...?" Jon ventured.

Danni nodded again. "It would be nice." she smiled. "And maybe I'll come back. But I do have to go and look." Jon nodded with a little more enthusiasm, then grew suddenly serious.

"You won't lose your way, will you?" he asked.

"All I really have to do is listen for some extraordinary music and I'm sure I'll find my way back." They both nodded, and smiled at each other until a sharp voice broke their quiet.

"Hey! Artist! Break time is over. We have work to do!" Jon looked sideways towards Celina and then turned his look to Danni.

"There is something innately wrong about forcing art." he mused. "But... a bug's gotta eat."

"Bye, Jon." Danni offered.

"See ya, Danni." Jon replied and turned to hop back to the rock they had all deemed best for his ministrations. He paused for a brief moment, took in a breath, and began to play. It was bouncy and joyful and perfect for travelling. Jon looked over at Danni and gave her a wink, then settled himself again, eyes closed, as he continued his tune.

Danni watched the ants for a moment, happily moving about, gathering their stores and taking them back to the ant hill. She turned and took a step when Celina floated before her.

"We don't get a goodbye, is that it?" the Queen asked seriously.

"I didn't want to..."

"Don't give me that. Royalty has feelings too, you know. Just say goodbye, curtsy and be on your way." Danni smiled.

"Good bye, Celina..." She said, and gave a little bob – curtsying and mice were not mutually compatible – then started down the rock.

"Better," she heard behind her. "Work on the curtsy." Danni found herself smiling for quite some time as she worked her way to the road and then along it.

Chapter 4
The Thorny Situation

Though she did stay to the side of the road – and well covered by the underbrush and shrubs – Danni was still able to see the many new things all round her. Not that trees, shrubs and rocks were new, but these were different, not ones she had seen day in day out, through a window or a quick jaunt outside the Farmhouse. The wild berries alone were making the journey easier to enjoy. She hadn't seen much in the way of other creatures, the birds were always about, but they never had much to do with her as they were too busy with their own lives to have even bothered with a little mouse ambling along. Still, she felt as if a purpose had been attained. With a light heart she continued down the road, every now and again taking a moment to sit near a rock and watch the river as it coursed alongside. She found herself thinking how beautiful the water was. In this free form with its constant motion, the sunlight all but dancing on the ripples, it enchanted Danni. And the sounds! The gurgling and churning noises, as it passed over rocks or just pushed its way along, were very calming and relaxing. ...As was the wind gently rushing through the leaves of the trees. ...And the gentle howling in the distance made her feel...

...howling in the distance?..?..

... howling!?...

She pulled herself up short and listened again. The howl became a cry with a guttural tone, somewhere deep in the throat of whatever creature was spewing it forth. Then a pause for what could only be a breath before the din would start up again. Danni shivered at the sound; it was wretched and haunting all at once. But she also knew she must find it, see its source, see if there was anything she could do.

She started in the direction of the shrieks, stopping and starting as she went. A squirrel came darting by and almost ran over Danni before pulling up short and staring down at the little mouse.

"I'd go the other way, mate," the squirrel offered, "were I you..." he looked Danni over carefully. "Especially if I were you." and he darted off.

Danni wished she didn't feel as curious as she did, she wished she could just turn around and follow the squirrel, she wished she were back by the tree roots with Jon and Celina, she wished she were still in the Farmhouse, she wished her Mother were still alive, she wished… but, instead, she pushed past a bit of underbrush and saw where the unearthly sounds were coming from.

A good-sized, golden coloured cat was lying on the ground, on its side, but all Danni could really see was its back, its rather large head and its smooth tail. Suddenly there was an intake of breath and again the moaning began, deep in the throat of the cat and with a warbling violence that struck Danni as quite odd. Even the cat at the Farm never made noises quite as demonstrative as this creature. For a moment she wondered if this beast was also, like Jon, an artist and this was its form of expression. She shook her head… she could almost be certain that, unlike Jon, this din was going to get the poor thing nowhere. Danni skittered to the bottom end of the cat, its tail making strange jerking motions, not the gentle swishes Danni was used to seeing from the Farm cat. As she got closer to the front of the animal, she could see its back paw and stopped.

Blood was caked on the pad and onto a large section of the golden fur. And as she looked closer, she could see there was a thorn in the pad. From the looks of it, it went deep into the pad. Danni looked down at her own front paws. She could do something about this. She looked around. There was a good-sized rock not far from the cat and behind it was a tree, its roots open and maze-like. Beyond that was brush. If need be, she could make a dash for the cover. Slowly, she edged over to the rock and climbed up. She could now see the cat in its stretched-out, pained and very sad state.

"Excuse me…" Danni started.

The cat howled again, piteously.

"Sorry…" she tried again.

The cat rolled slightly on its back and moaned for all it was worth.

"I'd just like to…"

Again an uproar that could only be linked to violent murder.

Danni sat back on her haunches, her mouth open in disbelief. She shook her head, then took in a deep breath. "HEY!!!" she shouted with all her might.

Birds that had not already fled the scene now did so. The cat angled its head towards Danni and turned a pair of golden eyes onto her. For a moment, Danni froze. Was this really a trap? Was the cat actually hale and hearty and ready to leap on her from its sad position on the ground?

The cat lifted up its injured foot ever so slightly and with one of its front paws seemed to point to it. It took in a great sigh.

"Ouch." it said simply, and it laid its great head back down again.

"Oh really?" the mouse drawled. Either this was a very badly laid trap or the cat was totally without guile – or stupid – but Danni really wasn't certain.

"Pain…" the cat whined.

Stupid, Danni determined.

"Really hurts…"

"Excuse me!!" Danni said sharply. And the cat stopped whining and looked quizzically with one eye on the mouse. "Thank you." Danni continued. "I would like to help you, but I don't know if you've noticed, being in such pain and all, that I am a mouse...?"

"Sarcasm really isn't necessary..." the cat intoned.

"What?" said Danni, sarcastically.

"I am fairly well incapacitated, I think you would have noticed that, what with my being flat out and all..."

"I think you might have noticed that you've scared away half the forest with your crying..."

"I was calling for help!" the cat said indignantly. "However others see it, that is what I was doing and it certainly didn't make you run off so I must have been doing it well." Danni pondered this for a moment. Not stupid. Maybe just ignorant.

"How do I know you won't eat me?" Danni asked. The cat was back on its side and eyeing Danni in a disquieting way.

"How do I know you're really here to help me?" it asked. "How do I know you didn't set that thorn out where I wouldn't see it? It's possible that you knew that as I tried to pull it out with my teeth it would only push it in farther. How do I know you're not just inwardly gloating and putting on a good show of pretending to be frightened? Hm? Hm?"

Danni went back to voting for stupid. And somehow this gave her a belief that the cat might not hurt her. "Look," Danni tried, "I will do what I can to help you, but I need your word that you won't hurt me... or... eat me... or play with me until you kill me... or..."

"Really you have covered all the bases..." the cat said. "I promise on my mother's grave."

Danni started towards the cat's paw but stopped suddenly. "She *is* dead and buried, right?"

The cat turned a laconic stare onto Danni. "She is dead and was buried, just not very well buried." Danni gave a nod and moved towards the injured front paw. She reached up and before she could touch the thorn the cat gave out a whining wince.

"I've not touched it yet..." the mouse complained.

"Are you sure? Because it just throbbed..."

"Look, do you want me to do this or not?"

"Yes, of course I do, I just... well... you will be gentle?" the cat asked. Its frightened face was close to Danni, its great golden eyes filled with an anxious sadness. Danni reached over and patted it just under its golden chin.

"I will really, really try." she said. "I can't promise that it won't hurt, but I do think it will be better once it's out," the cat nodded and laid back down. Danni could sense it was tensing up. "Do try to relax... I think it will be easier for me if you do... try to think of something else...?"

The cat seemed to give a nod and Danni turned to examine the thorn. It did seem to be well into the cat's foot, but Danni knew her paws would be able to grasp it better than the cat's teeth ever could.

She looked carefully to see the angle of the thorn and the best way for it to be moved. Then, with a small intake of breath, Danni grabbed the thorn and pulled.

It popped out so suddenly that Danni was thrown backwards and emitted a small cry. She shook herself and stood up just as a squirt of blood came shooting from the cat's paw straight onto her. And as quick as that, she couldn't see a thing… and then she heard the cat start to move.

"OH!" Danni heard that outburst from her left and so she headed blindly to the right – straight into a large paw! She tried to go back to the left, but really ran aimlessly about until she felt herself being swept up by the paw! She now worked frantically to clear her sight, and succeeded just in time to come face to teeth with a large cat's mouth. Danni tried to duck and wriggle, but she was still struggling vainly when she felt the rough, sharp tongue of the cat lick across her. Then again, and again. She closed her eyes tightly. Another lick, and another. Then nothing. Silence.

When Danni finally worked up the courage to open her eyes, she saw that the cat was putting her back on the ground. Then the cat began to tend to its own foot, licking it in much the manner it had just licked Danni. Danni looked herself over to spot any damage. There was no trace of any blood. In fact, she was cleaner than she had been since leaving the farm. Aside from her face feeling mildly scraped, she had to admit that her fur really had never looked better.

"Sorry…" the cat got out between licks. "I didn't know it would do that…" (More licks) "I really am embarrassed…" (Licking still) "I mean, here you are helping me and what do I do? Bleed all over you! Are you all right?" this last was said with full attention being paid to the mouse.

Dumbstruck, Danni could only nod. The cat appeared to smile and looked back to its foot. Danni's heart rate was slowly coming down from the thousands to its normal triple-digit value.

"Seems to have stopped now," it said, a decidedly grateful tone to its voice. "I should probably let it be for a bit… maybe get some mud on it… oooh, I hate water… still…" It looked back to Danni. "I'm Leo," he said, then waited patiently, looking at Danni.

Finally realising what was expected, the little mouse replied: "I'm Danni."

Leo's smile grew broader. Danni thought it rather ominous. "Thank you, Danni. I am in your debt."

"When you smile like that, do you know that you look like you're about to pounce?" Danni asked, trying to sound casual.

The cat's smile faded slightly. "Luck of the draw," he said. "It's no wonder some find it rather hard to trust me. They either can't tell what I'm thinking at all or they just think I'm about to set on them." He shook his great head. "It's just the face," he said. "I really do appreciate this," he continued.

"Glad I could help." Danni replied.

"I mean, I was calling for quite some time…"

"I can imagine…"

"And no one would help…"

"No, they all ran off…"

"But I knew that eventually someone would!" he said, suddenly absurdly cheerful.

"Oh?" Danni questioned.

"Oh yes. I was absolutely certain they would."

"Really…?" – scepticism in her voice.

"Positive," said Leo, triumphantly.

"But you still made an almighty fuss!"

Leo looked at Danni indignantly. "Well it still hurt," he huffed. Danni wasn't about to argue with this. "Is the river very far?" Leo asked, looking around.

"Just over there," Danni pointed.

"I try to stay well away, but…"

"Why?" Danni asked. She couldn't imagine not wanting to look at the river and hear its song.

"Erm, I'm a cat, Danni." Leo tried. "Pretty much all of us have a major issue with water. Drinking is fine, drinking is lovely, but anything else…" he moved anxiously on his front paws. "Just thinking about it makes my paws itch. I like to stay near, though. I always like to be near, it's good to be nearby for a drink." He looked down at his injured paw. "But with this,

I'll have to get closer," and he gave a heavy sigh. "Will you come with me?"

Danni shrugged slightly. "Sure," she said.

Leo smiled, but not as broadly as before. There was something more assuring in this softer smile. Leo began to walk, nursing his front paw as he moved, and Danni kept pace easily. "Just beyond the trees over there," she told him and they moved along in companionable silence.

Danni climbed up a fallen tree and looked over at the river again. Rainbows were flickering in the water as it slid under the sunlight. She heard Leo sigh and turned a look on him. He was scanning the river bank anxiously and then, suddenly, his face relaxed, and Leo began to move forward. As he did, the anxiety seemed to return. "What?" Danni asked. Leo jutted out his chin toward a section by the river. It was in the shallows, not much movement and many little rocks to stand on. The area was slightly muddy, without a lot of pooling.

"I just look for the places that have less water and more dry," he acknowledged and slowly started that way. Gingerly, Leo set his poorly paw onto the mud, wincing as if he were laying his whole body down in something vile. His paw was jerking up and down, not wanting to go into the mud, but being over-ruled by himself in a bitter battle of will. He looked over at Danni, sheepishly. "This is embarrassing..." he said, "I really can be a hopeless baby sometimes..."

Danni found it odd... to be aware of ones shortcomings and yet be unable to really do anything about it. She found herself nodding in what she hoped was a sympathetic fashion but felt it lacking. Finally, Leo hopped away from the muddy ground and sat on some dry leaves.

"Suppose I ought to let this dry a bit..." he offered. "So... where are we going?" The question so took Danni by surprise that she let her mouth drop open. Leo's great golden eyes were full of anticipation, staring back at Danni.

Finally, the little mouse got out: "We?"

Leo grinned. "Of course 'we'. 'We' as in 'us' – not 'wee' as in 'tiny' or 'whee' as in 'hooray' or..."

"...or 'We' as in royalty," interrupted Danni. "I understood the word, I don't follow the logic."

"Oh," Leo explained: "Well... just before I got the thorn in my paw, I had come to a fork in the road... didn't you notice it?" Actually, Danni had not, so she shook her head. There could have been a one-man band and she wouldn't have noticed it what with Leo carrying on as he had been. "And I believe that this is where one actually chooses."

Danni was very confused. "Actually chooses?"

"Well," said Leo, matter-of-factly, "I am a firm believer that everything happens for a reason and that we have a path to follow..."

"...and that therefore things are pre-ordained?" Danni asked hesitantly.

Leo gave a small nod. "If you like." he conceded. "But there are times when we come to a fork in the road and we need to choose which way. Sometimes one way looks very easy, and most times that would be the path one would choose. Only it turns out that it leads you to nothing of value, in fact it sets you back! And the other path, while it looks a little dicey, might just be the one to advance you and bring you closer to your real goal."

"And what would that be?" the mouse asked, not masking her scepticism.

"Well, that's part of the journey." Leo replied happily. "You see, I was planning on one way and then I found myself with a thorn in my paw. So I wasn't able to continue, right?" Danni conceded this. "And then you came along and helped me. So you see, if the thorn hadn't gotten into my paw, I would have been long gone and we wouldn't have met under such circumstances. In fact, we might have met as adversaries, which could have ended badly – for you. But we didn't. And you helped me so there must be a reason we should be together and I plan on seeing it through until I have a clue what that reason is."

"Do you always find out what the reason is?" Danni asked.

"No, actually…" Leo said. "Or at least, not yet. But, I am rather young and I think sometimes that kind of wisdom comes with age."

"You don't look that young…" Danni ventured.

Leo shook his great head sadly. "I've always been big for my age." But before Danni could ask any more about this, Leo said: "Of course, the fork in the road isn't always a literal one."

"Where did you learn all this?" Danni found herself almost demanding.

Leo seemed a little perplexed. "I don't know," he said simply. "I suppose I've always been this way. Born this way, if you really think about it."

"You're saying that even if something looks easy and comfortable, it's wrong."

Leo clarified: "Not always wrong, but if you have a choice…"

"And everything happens for a reason?" said Danni sceptically.

"Oh yes."

"But you don't always know what the reason is…"

"That's right!" said Leo brightly.

Danni's reply dripped sarcasm. "And somehow you knew that I would come along to help you."

"Well, now that's not completely true…"

Danni softened. There might still be some sense of logic to the cat.

"I said I knew 'someone' would help me."

Danni sagged slightly, and shook her head in disdain and adjusted her opinion: *he's **beyond** stupid.*

"And that someone was you." And Leo sat back smugly and that provoked Danni even more.

"That doesn't make sense!" Danni exclaimed. "How can you 'know' something like that, based on no sort of physical evidence? Things happening 'for a reason' but 'we don't know what the reason is'. That's an intangible! And 'pre-ordained existence'? Pah!"

"I didn't say pre-ordained," Leo stated simply, "you did. I said we all had a path to follow. And I also said it wasn't a literal path or a literal fork in the road. But this non-literal fork in the road is where you make your choices, for good or for ill!"

"And again, I say this doesn't make sense..."

"Have you always lived in the forest?" Leo asked simply, but with a firm edge to his tone.

"No..." Danni was slightly taken aback.

"I didn't think so." he sniffed. "But now you're here. Why?"

"Well, I had to leave the Farm..." she stated.

"Had to?" he said, probingly.

"Well, I scared the Farmer's Wife."

"So?" said Leo, relentlessly.

"So it's no longer safe for me there..."

"Why?"

"What? Why what?" said Danni, weakly.

"Why did you scare the Farmer's Wife?"

"Oh. Well, I got mad..."

Leo raised an eyebrow, but said nothing. Danni went on speaking very rapidly: "She killed my cousins, they were blind! I thought that was wrong so I called her a murderer and jumped on her back. I didn't know she was going to stab herself with the carving knife! Then I ran out and Arnie the dog helped me escape to the edge of the Farm and then the next day he told me I couldn't come back!" The words all flew pell-mell out of her. She was a little breathless and more than a little aggravated at being made to recall.

"Didn't see that coming, did you?"

"Huh?" said Danni, completely at sea.

"Her killing your cousins?"

"What? How could I..."

"And you having to leave, why couldn't you just hide in your hole or your home until it all blew over?"

"Well, no, that would have been too dangerous..."

"More dangerous than venturing into the forest?"

"Oh well, that's different..."

And then Danni had to stop. How was it different? She had always been a bit afraid about the areas beyond the Farm. Her Mother had always told her to stay to the house. But she hadn't blinked when Arnie told her to climb on his back and took her out to the edge of the Farm. She looked at Leo who was smiling gently, like a cat that had swallowed a...

"You had a fork in the road," he said simply. "And from what you're saying, there was nothing out of the ordinary to make you aware that you were about to make a change. So you had no tangible evidence to give you reason to believe you were about to change how you lived your life? It just happened. But you sure don't seem too upset about it... in fact you seem like someone who is following a path right now."

"Well, I am heading to town..."

"Not a literal path, Danni." Leo sighed.

"Can we just agree to disagree?" Danni asked.

Leo smiled again: "If you like."

Danni nodded. Leo's discussion was giving her a headache, and she was glad for a little quiet.

"So we're going to town?" asked Leo. "*So much for quiet,*" thought Danni, but she just looked up at the cat. Leo stared placidly back, smiling that smile.

"What do you eat?" she finally asked.

"Don't worry about that, it won't be you."

"But you eat things *like* me…" Danni squeaked.

"Actually, I prefer things cooked…"

"What?" And Danni thought the old saying *out of the frying pan, into the fire* seemed all too real.

"I am not from the forest either." Leo informed her. Danni looked at the cat, and tried to remain calm.

It seemed Leo had some kind of story to tell as well. Whether or not Danni would hear it remained to be seen. Or heard, actually.

"Are we going to town?" he asked again. Danni pondered this. She had wanted to go to town, but now the prospect of such a big bustling place was weighing on her. Then, as she had never been to town, she wondered if it really was as she thought. Her confusion was becoming palpable. "Well…?"

"Oh stop talking." Danni said a little too abruptly. She wasn't happy with the way her mind was working. She had been through a great deal in the past two days and now, having to dissect it was becoming too much. She didn't want to delve. She knew very well that she was doing the right thing, moving on as she was. There was no reason to question what she was doing or why. There were circumstances that had taken her from where she was and had put her here. That was all there was to it.

And now this feline was giving the impression that there actually was more to it all. How certain he had been of someone coming to his aid. Everything happening for a reason. The idea of lives being pre-ordained. A fork in the road. Paths.

"I used to eat mice." Leo said suddenly. Danni froze. Slowly, she turned to look at the cat, to see it as it really was a predatory animal, and she the prey. But Leo looked forlorn. Almost ashamed.

Danni sat, looking up at the golden cat, and the words came from her mouth before she could stop them: "Do you want to talk about it?"

Oh how she wished she could take those words back, and say,
"*just kidding,*"
         "*let's get a move on,*"
                  "*time's a wasting…*"
                           What was she thinking?

She was furious with herself, and had looked away from Leo in shame. When she looked back, she saw him staring at her. Sad. Wrestling with something in his great head. Hesitant. And just as suddenly, Danni wanted to know. "You don't… have to tell me…" She said slowly, with "but I want you to" deeply embedded in the tone. Leo nodded.

32

"Maybe I should…" He turned back to the river. "Hold on…" he said softly, "I need a drink." and he went onto a rock that was well away from the flow of water, but easy for him to bend over and lap up. He did this for a time. Almost as if he might never drink again. Finally he raised his great head, his eyes closed for a moment, and then he turned and approached Danni.

"There was a man… an old fellow… and he brought me to his home along with a rooster and I believed I was to be kept there with his three sons. He gave me to his youngest son. I don't know what it was all about, there was much grumbling between the lads… the man had next to nothing and he seemed to believe that the rooster and I and some scythe were going to get the boys some kind of income. I'm not the sharpest knife in the block, Danni, but I could not come up with any kind of job that would involve all three, you know?

"Me and the bird, maybe, but add the scythe and I was clueless. The lads then decided to go their separate ways, and the old man had said something about going far away, but…"

Leo paused and shook his great head, "Danni, I really believe in strength in numbers, you know? One is just so lonely and… against others… futile…" He stopped for a moment, his eyes clouded over in the memory.

"…Anyway, the eldest went off with the rooster and after a time, came back with a donkey and all the gold this donkey could carry… and donkeys are pretty strong, let me tell you. But the rooster was gone. The second brother went out with his scythe. And after a time he came back with a horse laden down with gold. Bigger animal, more gold. And again, no scythe."

Leo hesitated: "I suppose you can see where this is going?" Danni blinked. She hadn't heard someone tell her a story in a very long time and she was a little captivated by Leo's tale. She shook her head and thought for a moment.

Finally, it dawned on her: "It was the youngest son's turn, and that meant you…?"

Leo nodded, sadly. "I mean, I liked the kid. He wasn't the best keeper… I think he was hoping for more from his dad, but he wasn't mean or anything… still… next thing you know, he picks me up and off we go. And I don't know where, but we go around a *lot*. And I see loads of other cats… and every time I think, hey, we're gonna settle down! Then we're off again. He takes me on a *boat*, Danni… I mean, it was all very well and good, but I was terrified, and I was beginning to think he was gonna just dump me. I mean, the others, they must've sold their things… and got too good price for them, didn't they, so they must've fleeced the person who bought them, you know?"

Danni did have an idea about what he said. She remembered vividly the tellings of a young man down the road who traded his cow for beans and how everyone at the Farm thought him a great dolt. She wondered for a moment what had become of him.

Leo's narrative broke her reverie: "So we get to this island. And it seems they have been over-run with mice. Well, mind you, we didn't have much money to begin with, so I hadn't been getting nearly the rations I was getting back where we lived, so I was hungry. And I scrambled down and got me a mouse. And then another... Seems the King of the island saw this. I'm not quite sure, because I was eating, you know? Next thing you know, the Lad is handing me off to the King, he goes off with all the gold a mule can carry and I'm in the palace and there are mice *everywhere!* I guess I went into a sort of frenzy, sorry, y'know... well, after all that... I'm thirsty. But I've eaten so many that I'm raspy and nothing comes out but a meow... which I thought was very clear, but suddenly all these people are running around as if they think I'm gonna eat *them*! I mean, come on! These are people! So they leave me alone in the castle and I'm just so thirsty! I'm crying out for a drink..."

Leo suddenly stopped and looked sheepishly at Danni. "If you thought I was noisy before, well... I guess it was worse. Because some young man is there asking me to leave. Danni, all I wanted was some water. I didn't get all high and mighty and ask for milk or cream or anything, heck, I couldn't even talk! All I could get out was a meow! So the guy gives a little nod and he dashes off..."

A shadow seemed to cross Leo's face for a moment, then he went on: "They started shooting at me. I was in the castle, it wasn't a very big one, but still... so I had a little protection, but the walls started coming down... I got out, but I guess they didn't know, because they just kept shooting and shooting until there was nothing left of the place. But I was on an island, Danni... and I was the only cat. No way was I gonna blend in... So I had to find a way to get on another ship to get back to where there were more cats... and I did... but there was a storm... the boat went sideways, hit some rocks... I held onto a piece of wood and I finally got to shore... but, oh my... truly put me off water, you know? And put me off mice. Put me off wanting to deal with people, too... for a while."

Danni waited for a moment, but the cat didn't continue. "For a while?" Danni asked. The cat regarded Danni carefully.

"People started being nice to me," he said simply. "Giving me leftovers and such..." there was another pause. "I just don't worry about eating, okay?"

Danni narrowed her eyes at Leo: "What aren't you telling me?"

Leo sighed. "You don't believe what I say about paths to follow..."

"Well..." Danni wanted a real answer, now.

"You don't. And you don't believe what I say about how everything happens for a reason..."

"Well..." the mouse insisted.

"Or forks in the road... so I am going to keep this last part to myself for a bit, if you don't mind." And with that, Leo was silent.

Danni was struck by this outburst. She had listened intently, she had made every effort to really hear Leo's story, she was very taken by it, it was a sad tale and even sadder in that there seemed no reason for him to have been treated so unjustly, both by the youngest son as well as the King and all the people of the island. No reason.

"But you said everything happens for a reason!' she blurted. "How can there be a reason for that? That whole story you told me! What can the reason be for that?" At that, Leo levelled a stare at her and Danni felt increasingly uncomfortable.

"I learned caution from that, Danni." He finally said. The mouse blinked. The cat smiled. "Whereas, you seem to be very judgemental..." Leo said gently.

Danni bristled. She had heard that before, and she still saw nothing wrong with that. You make a decision and then you are prepared. You are on your guard and know what to expect, how to interact with others, who to avoid, who to befriend... but this time, she heard it differently. After all, she had helped a cat! She looked up into Leo's golden eyes. They were gazing down at Danni gently, with a hint of amusement. Finally, she simply asked: "Is that such a bad thing?"

"I would think it would serve you well... but I think you might miss other opportunities. You didn't see the fork in the road."

Danni found truth in this. If she hadn't already made the judgement that helping others was her calling, she might have just run the other way after seeing Leo was a cat. But now, she was discovering that she had an innate curiosity to look into things before judging them. Maybe this curiosity could work for her as well, if she could let the judgement stay aside. She shook her head and looked at Leo.

"Shall we press on?" Leo asked. Danni smiled and nodded. "Would you like a ride?" the cat asked and leaned over slightly so Danni could jump onto his back. Danni sat just above Leo's shoulder blades and the cat started a slow walk.

"Leo..." Danni murmured.

"I'll tell you the rest, Danni..." the cat assured. "Just not right now." And somehow, this comforted the little mouse.

Chapter 5
A Simple Traveller

He was a "foot-travel" man. He just didn't like to be dependent on anything else, be it animals or carts. And he was used to carrying things, though it did make him a little bent and worse for wear, but he kept at it. He knew what he did was of great importance and so he continued.

He hadn't travelled the road for some time. He had meant to, but he knew he would have to wait a time for things to settle. Still, he was well aware he probably should have been this way sooner.

He was a repair person, he claimed. He could fix most anything. He travelled simply, with his tools, supplies and sleeping gear, and had spare else. He made a little money, enough to get by and set some aside, and he had specific places he would always go. He'd also hear of other places of interest and he'd head over there as well until they also became familiar and specific. By rights, he was a very simple man. Ordinary. Nothing stood out about him. He did what was needed and moved on. People liked that about him, how he seemed to know when to show up and when to depart. And he liked that about himself.

He turned down the path to the farm house. He'd hoped all was well with the little mouse. After her mother had died he thought for certain that she would come with him, but she was too young, he'd assumed, so he left her there with her cousins and figured he would let some time pass before coming back and seeing if maybe she had changed her mind. She was a special mouse, was little Danni. And he knew that most certainly. The way she saw things, the way she could see the logic of a situation, even at so young an age, she could tell at a glance when something was amiss, when people weren't behaving rationally, or when they were doing things that just seemed wrong. A good, sensible head on her little shoulders had Danni.

He saw the house ahead. The dog barked out a warning that soon turned into a greeting. It loped up to the man and continued with the barks until the woman came to the porch and shielded her eyes from the low-lying sun to see what the dog was going on about. And she smiled.

"Stop it, dog!" she called out.

"Oh, no worries," the man called back, "I know he knows me... he's just telling you I'm here!" Then the man noticed her arm in a sling, bound close to her body. His brows furrowed.

"Liza, what's this?" he asked, his voice full of concern, and the Farmer's Wife pulled a face.

"Stabbed myself in the back, Simon. Can you believe it?" Actually, he could, but he kept up the concerned look.

"Tell me..." he said in that inviting way of his.

"You come in for some lemonade and I will... Henry will be here soon and I know he'll want to speak to you. That bucket is in need of a proper mending." Simon nodded.

"Well, I'll sure fix it up, Liza. You wouldn't let me really tend to it last time... that clock took up most of my time..." The Farmer's Wife looked curious now.

"Clock?" she asked as they came from the porch into the kitchen. Simon put his pack down near the door and sat at the kitchen table. Liza reached for the pitcher of lemonade near the sink. She made a face of pain as she went to get a glass, forgetting her circumstance and trying to use the other bound-up hand. "Damn that mouse..." she cursed.

Simon was suddenly very alert. The Farmer's Wife had no idea that Simon had a special interest in Danni and he wanted to keep it that way, but her sudden curse made him go a little cold. She poured the lemonade and took careful pains to put the pitcher down before taking up the glass with the good hand, then turned a small, wan smile to him and gave him the drink. "Sorry, Simon..." she apologised.

"No need," he said gently, taking a small sip, and repeated, "no need... but what happened?" And she began to tell him of the blind mice and their demise. And then how another mouse jumped on her and startled her so that when she tried to slap at it she had forgotten about still holding the carving knife and landed it in her back.

"Luckily it wasn't too deep..." she mused. "I think... but it's still sore. Henry's bound me up like a trussed turkey here to keep me from using it. And wouldn't you know, three more mice show up the next day! Blind as bats, but they're there..." she looked about the floor.

"I know it..." Simon leaned in slightly. "But the *other* mouse?"

She brightened slightly. "Oh I think the dog got it. Well, he took off after it like a shot, I tell you! All the way across the field out there. Not sure though. You know, most animals like to show off their prizes... but if he didn't get it, he must have scared it off good. He goes off every morning and checks, I think. Just to be sure. He's a good protector, that dog."

Simon looked over to the porch and saw the dog lying down placidly, gazing simply at them both. Then he sharply turned his head to the side and stood up, letting out a sharp, happy bark.

"That'll be Henry..." said Liza and got up to go to the door. Simon now drained the glass. Maybe Henry would know more. He turned and looked into the front room. The clock was gone. He turned back in time to see Henry amble in, give his wife a little kiss and then observe Simon. A smile creased his weathered face and he strode, hand extended, to the man. Simon took it and they shook hands heartily.

"Simon," Henry smiled.

37

"Henry," Simon greeted. "Now what's all this about your poor Liza?"

Henry shook his head. "Well, you know I wasn't in the house at the time, Simon, so I really only have what Liza tells me, but my, it was a mess."

"I still don't know where all that wood and glass came from but..." Liza started to say and then Henry patted her on her good shoulder, encouraging her to sit back down.

"Never you mind about that, dear..." and he patted her hand soothingly, giving Simon the smallest of concerned looks.

Taking the hint, Simon said: "Liza tells me that bucket is not truly fixed, Henry... I really should take another look at it."

Henry gave a small nod of thanks before replying. "Yes, that would be grand. I put it out in the barn... dear, will you be all right?"

"Of course I'll be all right... you go tend to that and I'll see to supper. You will stay, won't you, Simon?"

"I would never miss out on a chance of getting some of your cooking, Liza," Simon complimented. Seeing the woman blush, he gave a smile and followed Henry out the door, grabbing his pack as he went.

"Henry..." he began, but was cut off.

"She doesn't even remember having a clock, Simon. And I can't tell her otherwise. So we don't speak of it, but it concerns me. It only happened a few days ago, but she just has no recollection. It's as if it was never there."

"But that was her pride..."

"...And joy, I know!" Henry shook his head. "She did have a crack to her head. At least, I think there was something of a bump, but the bump's gone down now and she still..."

"...and the mouse?" Simon got out as they approached the barn. Henry nodded.

"Oh, it was actually the *little one* that done it. The little one from out the brown one that used to run up and down the clock?" Simon felt a chill. "Least, that's the one I think it was, haven't seen it since." And with that, Henry brought up the bucket. "Here we are." and handed it over to the traveller.

Simon had wanted to mend this thing for the longest time. The way the husband and wife would be at each other about getting it fixed had a tendency to get on Simon's last nerve, what with Henry telling her there was a hole and Liza giving him suggestions, and it was like a bad song that you couldn't get out of your head.

"She said the dog got it..." Simon mused.

"Oh I don't think so..." said Henry, shaking his head. "Dog wouldn't hurt a fly."

"She thinks he goes off in the morning to be sure it isn't coming back..."

Henry let out a little laugh. "Well, now he does go off in the morning... sometimes has a little sack, too..." he smiled. "But knowing the dog, he's probably trying to find it and bring it back..." he broke into another laugh and Simon joined him.

"You let me tend to this, Henry," Simon assured. "I'm sure I can have it repaired before supper."

"Will you need me?" smiled Henry, but he knew the answer and had already started out of the barn.

"No, no, you finish up whatever you were doing and let me really get to work here." Simon watched him go, then, pulling out his heavy mallet, turned his attention to the bucket.

Chapter 6
Doyle and his Cart

While it seemed town was close from a tree-top view, Danni and Leo found that it was actually farther. The sun had begun to set and the two were quite tired from their walking. Danni wondered if staying close to the river had been such a good idea, that maybe it twisted and turned more than they thought. She hadn't said anything, but the darkness of the forest was beginning to frighten her a bit. The trees were very thick in this section. They even seemed to connect over the water and she wondered if she would be able to see the moon when it rose, if it hadn't risen already.

"Maybe we should get closer to the path…" she pondered aloud.

"Oh, it's just over there," Leo indicated with a nod of his head. But the light was fading fast and Danni could not make it out, though she had felt her eyes to be very sharp. Leo stopped suddenly. Danni could feel her heart racing.

"Wh… what…?" she asked as the cat backed up awkwardly. "Leo…?' The cat was making strange movements and, being on its back, Danni could not glean as to why. "Leo…?" she asked again, more sharply.

"Awwwwww…" Leo began and Danni edged closer into the cat's neck. "Ew…Wet."

The mouse sagged. "What?" she demanded.

"Wet…" Leo all but moaned. "Must be a bog… ew…" he shook his feet as he maneuvered himself back towards a dry area. Danni shook her head, feeling very silly for letting her fear get the better of her. It was the dark creeping in that gave her pause, she knew it now. Then off in the distance she saw a flickering light.

"Leo…" she started.

"I hate wet feet," the cat moaned. "And with the sun gone down I can't properly dry them."

"Do you see that?" she asked, wanting to know and also trying to divert the cat's attention from his whinging. The cat turned its great head to look where Danni indicated. He sniffed.

"Looks like a fire," he said and suddenly brightened, "Oh that could be better than the sun!" and he began towards the light.

"But wait, couldn't that also mean people?" Danni was trying to be cautious, but Leo seemed to have different ideas.

"Exactly." he smiled. "And when there's people, there could also be…"

The sudden thrashing in the bushes near them sent Leo to dash to the side and Danni fell to the ground. She darted her head this way and that and began to creep over to the moist area they had left. No human would want to be in the wet, she hoped. She moved herself well under a bit of the muddy grass and watched with fear-filled eyes. "Danni?" she heard Leo whisper, but the thrashing was getting closer. "Danni!" he cried a bit louder.

"I'm hiding, Leo," she whispered back, "Can't you just be quiet!"

And the thrashing broke through to the slight clearing they were in and the tall shadow of a person loomed above them. She couldn't make him out at all, but she could tell he was carrying something, a shovel or spade or some sort of tool. Then he began to step closer to her and she shook violently. She saw him raise the tool high and then bring it down with a thud. The earth around her shook, the wet crowding in closer. He pulled the spade out and again, another thud on the other side of her, and the earth again shook, the wet cramping her. And then another thud behind her. Danni's breath came in short stops and starts as she felt the ground above her shift and the spade slid in above her, barely missing her head! Then it was lifted up and Danni could once again see the trees around her – she was uncovered! Her hiding place being lifted away from her.

She began to dart away then froze with fear, realising she had almost been beheaded. She stared up at the looming shadow who had stopped his lifting and began to lean down towards her. The gentle face of a young lad gazed down at her with obvious concern. He clucked his tongue in his mouth as he took in a short gasp of air.

"'Wee sleekit cow'rin' tim'rous beastie…'" he got out when a sudden yowl behind him made him startle up and an instant later he himself was crying out and turning, dropping the spade and going about trying to reach behind him. As he turned sharply, Danni saw Leo firmly attached to the lad's back and it was all she could do not to laugh. "Get off!" he called, "Leave off, I've not hurt it!"

Finally Leo cried out: "You alright, Danni?"

The little mouse skittered to a fallen tree and climbed up onto a branch jutting up towards the sky that could not be seen. "I'm okay!" she yelled and Leo disengaged himself from the lad's back, gracefully landing on the ground and jumping up on the fallen tree to inspect Danni for himself. It was the lad's turn to be frozen in place now.

"I'm sorry," Leo said softly, "I thought you had a better grip…"

Slowly the young man turned around to see the unlikely pair on the fallen tree, his eyes wide as saucers and his mouth beginning to shape itself into an "O".

"Did you…" he stammered, "… did you…"

Danni was suddenly overcome with a surge of anger. "What did you call me?" she cried out. "A, a … 'wee beastie'?"

"…You're…" he said, still stammering.

"'Cowering'?" interrupted Danni.

Leo tried to lean in to stop her but there was no use. He looked up almost apologetically at the lad.

"…talking…" the lad finally got out.

"'Timorous'!?" Danni all but screamed. "What part of the country are you from anyway?" she demanded.

"You talk?" came the full sentence.

Both cat and mouse stared up at the lad. Poor gormless thing, they both thought. "You both talk?" he asked again.

Leo shook his great head and Danni raised an eyebrow, "Of course we talk!" she all but shouted. Leo gently touched her little shoulder with part of his paw.

"Danni," he began and the mouse turned her furious gaze on him. "You're yelling."

"Well he almost killed me!" she said even louder.

"But you're fine…"

"But he almost killed me!" she said again, but not quite so loud.

"But you're fine…" Leo repeated, softer still.

"And then he called me names!!" she got out.

"But you're…" began Leo in his softest voice.

"No, no, no!" the lad said suddenly and found himself kneeling on the ground to be closer to the two amazing animals he was now with. "It's a poem!" The two animals turned a stare at him. He blinked at them, coughed slightly and started, "'Wee, sleekit, cow'rin' tim'rous beastie, O what a panic's in thy breastie! Thou need na start awa sae hasty, Wi' bickering brattle! I wad be laith to rin an chase thee, Wi' murd'ring pattle!'" he stopped, proud at his memory, and looked at them both. Danni leaned in slightly to Leo, who was doing the same back to Danni.

"Did you get that?" she asked.

"You have a 'breastie'?" asked Leo hesitantly.

Danni shrugged. "What language is…"

"I'm truly sorry…" the lad said. "Wait, that's another line from the poem, but really, I am. I was just getting some peat to dry out for later…" He shook his head, then: "I'm talking to animals," he murmured in disbelief.

"I'd say you're trying to have a conversation, actually," Leo replied.

"Is your back all right?" said Danni to the lad.

"I think so…" and again he shook his head. "Wait. Are you two with each other?" Leo and Danni exchanged a look that spoke of their mutual concern for the lad's sensibilities.

"Considering that I just ran through a bog to leap on you with claws extended to keep you from hurting my friend here…" Leo explained quietly. Danni held back a smile: Leo had said 'friend'.

"But…" interrupted the lad.

"Yes, yes, cat, mouse, we know." Leo was beginning to feel the damp quite keenly, and subtly changed the subject: "Yeah, yeah, it's sort of new for us, too, – look, is that your fire over there?" Inadvertently, the young man looked behind him then, remembering where he had come from, turned quickly back to the two animals.

"Y…yes… the fire… uh…" he stammered out. "Would you like to…"

"Lovely," Leo finished. "Lead on. Danni, on my back…" and the little mouse jumped onto the back of Leo's neck. "Got a name, lad?" the cat asked. "And don't forget your thingy there…"

"Doyle," the lad introduced himself, gathering up his spade and the cut bit of peat, then he started to move though the bushes from where he had come, holding onto the branches to make it easier for the cat and his charge to pass as well.

"I'm Leo and the mouse you almost killed is called Danni."

"I am so sorry…" Doyle said to the mouse. Danni couldn't really look at him, she was still both scared and a little excited over the whole ordeal. They walked on. "I've… really… I've never met talking animals… before."

"Ever tried to talk to one?" Leo asked.

"Well… no…"

"All right then. I don't know about Danni here, but I know I'm not a big conversation starter with people. They usually end up telling you so much more than you really want to know…"

The fire was small, but inviting, a ring of good sized rocks circling it to prevent spreading and there was a device that spread across it so as to hang a small pot from which steam was rising.

Leo eyed the pot with a small grin. "Smells good…" he ventured.

"It's stew." Doyle pronounced. "Would you like some?" Leo's grin faded to a solicitous gaze.

"That would be wonderful, are you sure?" Leo was starting to dry out, and that was making him more gracious.

The young lad nodded and turned to go towards a nearby shadow. As they got closer, Leo could make out a four-wheeled cart. There was a large tarpaulin covering the top where Doyle lifted up a section and dug out another plate and a muslin bag. Leo moved to a rock to let Danni off and the two sat watching the young fellow.

"Are you all right?" Leo asked Danni in a quiet voice. The little mouse looked at him, her composure coming back slowly.

She nodded. "That was scary…" she breathed out.

A hedgehog passing by didn't even stop as he sniffed and said: "Try getting walloped by flamingo-wielding royalty," and continued on. Both cat and mouse watched the little animal depart before looking back at each other. Leo's grin returned as he watched Doyle work. He felt very lucky indeed, but then, he felt pretty much always taken care of. He looked over at Danni and could see that the little mouse did not share his feelings as she was eyeing the lad suspiciously. Leo almost shook his head; if he had been in the mouse's situation, he might be thinking the same. But then he stopped himself. Must be a reason, he thought, as he watched Doyle spoon out some stew on two plates and put one before Leo.

"It's pretty hot," he said. Leo nodded and Doyle turned his attention to the bag, producing a bit of cheese and a small bit of carrot. He placed them before the mouse. "Is this enough?" he asked gently.

To Danni it was a banquet. The cheese was bigger than half her body and the carrot about the same. She inwardly chastised herself for distrusting the boy, but was still feeling hesitant as she looked up at his kind blue eyes.

"It… it's quite a lot, thank you, I don't know if I can finish it…" she said sheepishly.

"Eat what you can, all right?" Doyle told her, running his hand through his tangle of dark, wavy hair. "I can save what you don't eat for another time… I mean… if you like…"

Leo watched the two of them and understood that they were dancing around each other, the boy for almost hurting Danni and the mouse for judging him. It was an awkward pause though. He looked down at his dish.

"Well this looks excellent," he said, attempting to change the mood. Doyle smiled in relief.

"Thanks," he said, "you sort of have to make do on the road."

"Yes," Leo agreed and put his head down to the plate. It did smell good.

"It got dark quite suddenly, though…" the lad ventured. The mouse and cat looked at each other. They hadn't noticed any strangeness in the passing of the day, but then they were deep in the forest where it had seemed fairly twilight for a time. Still, it wasn't that far from where they were to where Doyle was. The lad continued, "I was well over the hill back that way on the path, and there was a mist at the top of the hill, you know, a low-lying fog. I went into it and… well it was all I could do to see in front of me, but I could tell when I'd reached the top of the rise and the hill began going down, when you're guiding a cart that's easy… then the fog broke and I was in this forest…" He looked slightly perplexed for a moment. "I thought I was going up a familiar hill, but…" he trailed off. Danni could feel her hesitation about the lad begin again.

Leo sighed. Again with the telling you more than you really want to know. "Well, maybe you were supposed to end up here." Leo said in a definite tone.

Doyle turned a surprised look at the cat. He smiled. "What, you mean like fate?" he asked.

Danni sniffed. "You see, Leo thinks everything happens for a reason."

"Really?" Doyle asked.

"I do." Leo nodded between bites of the stew.

"Optimistic thing, aren't you…?"

"I guess I was born this way…" he offered.

"Every day will turn out well?" Doyle asked.

"Pretty much…" said the cat.

"Follow the path and don't stray…"

"Exactly…" said Leo.

"Help will turn up if you need it…"

Leo looked at Danni and smiled. "Yes indeed…"

"Even though you have no indication how…?" interrupted Danni, but Leo just told her softly: "*He* gets it…"

"Sounds like you were born of Faith…" said Doyle. And Danni gave him a sharpish look.

44

"I was, indeed!" Leo exclaimed, "That was my mother's name!"

Now Danni looked sharply at Leo. She put down the bit of carrot she had been chewing. What did they know of this? And how was that Leo's mother's name? That was the thing Danni's Mother always spoke of, how Danni needed to act on it, be aware of it, trust it... but she had never explained it! And now these two were talking about it as if it were an old friend. Danni's suspicions were aroused again and she eyed the two creatures carefully. What *did* she know about them? The lad, precious little, but Leo had been friendly and kind and... to what end...? She was beginning to feel very apprehensive indeed as she wondered where she could run to or if she really even needed to.

"My mother's name is Hope." Doyle was saying. Leo nodded.

"Something you always need." Leo added and licked some of the gravy from his whiskers. "Gets you through the hard parts..." He turned his great head to observe Danni and immediately noticed the tension permeating from her. "Danni...?" he asked, softly. "Are you all right...?"

"What...?" she hesitated. Would they tell her the truth? Would they tell her what it really meant? Or did they actually know each other and they were playing her for a fool? She looked down at the carrot she found she could no longer eat. "I... I'm tired." she half lied. Whatever they were up to, she found she felt as if she had to stay with them for the nonce. She didn't feel safe out on her own, though she only felt a *bit* safer where she was. She was small and felt her size again. But now she found she was also feeling somewhat behind... slow... stupid.

"Shall I wrap the rest of this back up?" Doyle was asking. She nodded, dumbly. Doyle looked at her and then at Leo who gave a little shrug. Doyle wrapped the little bit of cheese and carrot into a small cloth and then put them back in the muslin bag. He took Leo's dish and his own and placed them into a bucket of water. Carefully, he took the pot off the rack and placed a cover over it. "Would you like to sleep under the cart?" Doyle asked Leo. "It would be relatively covered, I mean, unless you like to sleep outside...?" He took up a blanket and a cushioned mat which he placed on the ground near the fire. "Sometimes I sleep under the cart, but..." he looked up and saw stars between the branches of the trees. "It looks like a nice night." He went back to the cart and took out a book before going back to settle onto the mat. Carefully, he removed his shoes, gingerly touching one of the leather tongues that appeared worn and loose. He set them beside him. Leo began the cleaning portion of his evening, licking his paw and rubbing it across his face.

"I'm going to have to do a bit of tidying first..." he said between licks. "But I think it's a fine night too... Danni?"

"I..." she began. "I think I'll go to the cart." she said listlessly. The front wheels had wood covers just above the tops of them and she felt it a relatively safe spot, she would have a covering over her, be up high and would be able to notice most anything untoward around her. She began to sprint over and climbed up the wheel spoke with great agility. Once on the top of the wheel, she turned a few times and settled herself down, her nose under her arm, her eyes watching Leo and Doyle. Leo was watching Doyle as well, as the lad began to look studiously at the page before him. Feeling his stare, Doyle looked over the top of the book and met Leo's gaze.

"Book," he said blankly. And blank was the gaze back from Leo to Doyle.

"Of course it's a book…" Leo replied unconvincingly and blinked.

"Sorry," came the sheepish response, "I said, I've never talked to an animal before… I don't know what you really do or don't know…" Blink. "Just rhymes and fables and stories…" Doyle said, in an embarrassed tone. Leo sat up a little straighter. "My mother would read them to me…" Doyle offered by way of explanation. "I mean… it's the only book I have… I…"

"Stories?" Leo asked. "You know stories?" Doyle nodded. Leo walked over to him. "Tell away…" the cat said, sitting in front of him. Doyle moved from his reclined position into a cross legged one and opened his book. He flipped through some pages and stopped, smiling.

"Okay…" he began, "The Elves and the Shoemaker," he pronounced, laying the book in his lap. "There was once a shoemaker who through no fault of his own had become so poor that at last he had only leather enough for one pair of shoes. At evening, he cut out the shoes he intended to begin upon the next morning, and since he had a good conscience, he lay down quietly, said his prayers, and fell asleep." Leo stood up and moved closer to Doyle, sitting on top of the book. Doyle smiled and gently moved the cat back to the place in front of him. "In the morning, when he had said his prayers and was preparing to sit down to work, he found the pair of shoes standing finished on his table. He was amazed and could not understand it in the least. He took the shoes in his hand to examine them more closely. They were so neatly sewn that not a stitch was out of place, and were as good as the work of a master hand…" and again, Leo climbed up onto the book and reclined, this time looking up at Doyle expectantly. Again, Doyle smiled before taking the cat up and placed Leo on the ground before him. Leo cocked his head slightly but said nothing as Doyle began again…

"Soon afterwards, a purchaser came in and, as he was much pleased with the shoes, he paid more than the ordinary price for them, so the shoemaker was able to buy leather for two pairs of shoes with the money. He cut them out in the evening, and the next day with fresh courage was about to go to work. But he had no need to, for when he got up, the shoes were finished, and buyers were not lacking. These gave him so much money that he was able to buy leather for four pairs of shoes. Early next morning he found the four pairs finished, and so it went on. What he cut in the evening was finished in the morning, so that he was soon again in comfortable circumstances and became a well-to-do man." Leo slowly began another approach, placing one paw on Doyle's leg. The two looked at one another and Leo smiled. Doyle nodded and lifted the book from his lap to continue reading. Leo's smile faded.

"Now it happened one evening not long before Christmas, when he had cut out some shoes as usual, that he said to his wife, 'How would it be if we were to sit up tonight to see who it is that lends us such a helping hand?'

The wife agreed and lighted a candle, and they hid themselves in the corner of the room behind the clothes which were hanging there. At midnight came two little naked men who sat down at the shoemaker's table, took up the cutout work and began with their tiny fingers to stitch, sew and hammer so neatly and quickly that the shoemaker could not believe his eyes. They did not stop till everything was quite finished and stood complete on the table. Then they ran swiftly away." The book was again back in Doyle's lap. "The next day the wife said, 'The little men have made us rich, and we ought to show our gratitude. They were running about with nothing on and must freeze with cold. Now I will make them little shirts, coats, waistcoats and hose and will even knit them a pair of stockings. And you shall make them each a pair of shoes.'" and as Doyle took in a breath, Leo was again comfortably seating himself on the pages of the book and looking up expectantly at Doyle.

The lad sighed. "Leo..." he began, "why do you keep sitting on my book?" The cat blinked.

"Is it me you're talking to?" he asked.

"Well, yes, of course."

"Then I should be where your attention is..."

"Well, I won't be able to finish it if you keep sitting on the book..." protested Doyle.

"Oh, it's called *The Book*. Well, it is so very comfy..." the cat said and shifted slightly.

"That's as may be, but I can't finish the story if you sit on the words." Leo got up immediately and looked down at the book, peering with extreme caution.

"Ohhhh..." he cried out sadly. "I think I've smushed them!" Doyle looked down, "No, they're fine. There's nary even a wrinkle on the page."

"But look at them!" Leo was very concerned, "They're all flattened!" He anxiously looked up at Doyle, "Did I do that?"

"No, no..." Doyle consoled him without really understanding why. "See, those are the words and I need to see them to read them to you."

"Read?" the cat asked.

From her place on the wheel, Danni had raised her head. "Read?" she asked.

Perplexed, Doyle looked from one to the other. "Yes, read the words of the story..."

"Words are what you *say*..." Danni started.

"Yes," Leo agreed. "When you tell a story, you use words..."

"Well, this one is written down," the lad said, a bit defensively. Leo looked warily at the Comfy-Book. Danni climbed down and quickly skittered over to get onto Doyle's knee and look at the comfy-book-thing in his lap. Sure enough, there were flattened squiggly things all over the section that was visible. Danni looked at Leo who looked at Danni. Together they turned their gaze to Doyle. He looked at them for a time, trying to figure out just what they were having a difficulty with. And his mouth dropped open. "Don't you know how to read?" he asked. Again, Leo looked at Danni who looked at Leo. And again, they both looked to Doyle.

"Maybe we do if we knew what that meant," the mouse said honestly. Doyle shook his head, admonishing himself.

"I'm sorry... I really am sorry..." he started. "See, these things here," he pointed to the squiggles, "they're words... what we say? Someone wrote them down so that once we know what order the words go in, we can read them and tell a story... or write them ourselves, or read letters or signs or..." Both animals stared.

"Why don't you just *tell* the story...?" Danni asked incredulously.

"Well, I guess because there are so many, people wanted to have them written down as they couldn't commit them all to memory."

"Why not?" Leo asked.

Doyle looked at him in confusion: "Well... because there are so many!"

"Well it seems you have to memorise a lot to do this reading thing..." Danni ventured, looking into the book. "And written? You mean, make those things yourself?" she pointed to a group of squiggles.

"Well, no, these are printed by a printer... writing by hand is..." and he stopped when he saw the two animals staring blankly up at him, "...different..."

"So there's *another* way of doing this?" Leo asked. Doyle nodded. Leo shrugged and smiled. "Seems to me easier to memorise the story..."

"Especially when we all know it," Danni said. Doyle jerked his head to the little mouse, "And not as a story, I mean, everyone knows that's what the shoemaker said happened to him last Christmas. How his wife made clothes for these 'mysterious' little men and they put them on and then were so pleased that they ran away..."

Leo was nodding. "What did he say they said? 'Now we're boys so fine and neat, why cobble more for others' feet?'"

Danni nodded now. "I understand it happens around every Christmas time... somehow, peoples shoes all start to have problems, some of them just mysteriously disappear... so they have to go to the shoemaker for another pair, I mean, the weather can be dicey... only, I think he does it himself. Living off others misfortunes and blaming it on some fictitious mystery people... Scandalous."

Leo and Danni nodded together on this and looked up at Doyle who stared at them again, open mouthed. He shook his head.

"But..." the lad started, "the story says they never came back...?"

"Oh, so shoes are supposed to last forever?" Danni chastised. She looked over at Doyle's own shoes just beside them. "I guess yours were made by some other kind of shoemaker?" Leo was making a grab for the loose tongue when Doyle moved the shoes out of harm's way.

"No, shoes don't last forever, but this is just a *story*!" explained Doyle.

"No, *that* is an actual event." Danni sighed and shook her head. "Really, you would be amazed at the things that can go on around here." And for emphasis she turned to Leo, "Am I right?"

"Well, I'm not from this exact area..." he started.

"You knew about the shoemaker!" said Danni emphatically.

"Well, that was big news…"

Again Danni shook her head. "And that man going around kissing all the girls and then running off whenever the other fellows appear?" she asked.

Leo paused for a moment as recognition set in and he nodded. "Oh, him… yes, that really does seem a bit odd…"

Danni went on: "…And what about the man in the nightgown going to everyone's house to see if their children are in bed?"

"Well, children do need a set schedule…" said Leo tentatively.

Doyle looked from one to the other as recognition of his own began to hit. "Wee Willie Winkie!" he exclaimed. "And Georgy Porgy!!"

Without missing a beat Danni nodded and said: "Ought to be locked up, should those two!" But Doyle was shaking his head and began turning the pages of his book swiftly.

"Georgy Porgy, pudding and pie, kissed the girls and made them cry, when the boys came out to play, Georgy Porgy ran away." He looked up and beamed at the two. They stared back. He looked back at the book. "Wee Willie Winkie runs through the town, upstairs and downstairs in his nightgown; Rapping at the window, crying through the lock, 'Are the children in their beds? For now it's eight o'clock'."

Danni's brow was furrowed deeply when he looked over at her and with it his smile faded. "What are you saying?" she asked. "What are you doing? How do you do that?"

"Do what?" said Doyle, even more at sea.

"Make them all come out sounding similar near the ends." And now it was Danni's turn to be a little at sea herself.

Again, Doyle simply smiled. "It's a rhyme!" he explained. "Just like before, when I was quoting the poem to you?"

"Yeah," Leo started, "what do you mean by that, what's a poem?"

Doyle was now furrowing his brow, but then, as he had never spoken to an animal before and if they didn't seem to even know what a book was, then why should they know about poetry or rhymes? The best he could think to say was: "Some people have a talent for putting words together to make it rhyme, or sound similar at the end like you said, Danni."

"Why?" Danni asked.

"Why what?" Doyle countered.

"Why make it do that?" Doyle was stymied for a moment. Why indeed. Some people thought it sounded nice… it made his mother happy… and it did take a lot of talent to be able to come up with rhyme schemes. And… Why did people do that? Finally, he said: "Some people find them easier to remember when they come out like that. And some people find them more pleasant that way…"

Now, both the mouse and cat were looking at him in a way that could only say they didn't really believe him. He brightened for a moment. "Some people say that they are ways to remember history. That sometimes these rhymes were written about monarchs and social things… almost like a secret code."

"Why would being sick be a secret?" Leo asked.

"Sick?" asked Doyle, not following.

"Cold." said Leo.

Doyle shook his head. "Not cold, code… I guess you don't know that word either…" he thought for a moment. "Have you ever wanted to say something to someone but you didn't want anyone else to know?" Both the cat and the mouse had to nod at this. "Well, a code is a way of doing it without anyone else knowing!"

"So it's where you go to tell them in private?" said Danni.

Doyle released a sigh. "No…" he sighed. "I'm sorry… usually codes are written symbols… and if you two don't really know about those… I guess I don't know how to explain the other…"

"Wait…" Danni interrupted. "Symbols? You mean, like when you aren't supposed to go somewhere and so someone leaves a rock or something that indicates 'don't go'?"

Now Doyle brightened. "Yes, like that, only a longer message, I guess… see sometimes even when people say something, they are actually saying something else… underneath."

"So what they are saying is not what they mean?" said Danni disapprovingly.

"Or it means something else as well as what you think it means," countered Doyle.

Oddly, this made some sense to the little mouse. Still, she couldn't quite grasp it. She shook her head. "So… sometimes someone says no and they mean yes?"

"That's too simple, I think… and gets you in trouble. At least, my mum says so."

"Well, can't you give me an example?" she all but demanded.

Doyle looked at her in all seriousness. "Danni… I will try. I'm afraid I don't have the example right at the tip of my tongue, but will you let me think about it?" Danni sat back on her haunches. This was odd.

Her Mother always told her not to think about things that couldn't be explained. And some of the things she *could* explain made no sense – "a large animal took bites out of the moon!" Rubbish! How did the bites come back, then? And no one would acknowledge the lack of logic… Except… wait a moment… there had been someone… Except… her brow furrowed deeply as she tried to remember who the "except" was. There *had* been someone who agreed with her, or at least gave her the impression that the way she thought was rational, and that it was the rest of the world that was not being sensible. Why couldn't she remember who…?

"Will that be all right, Danni?" Doyle asked, shaking her from her attempt at remembering. She looked at the lad, with his clear blue eyes and shock of wavy dark hair. His face was full of emotion and concern as he leaned in towards the mouse.

Slowly Danni nodded. "All right..." she said, her concentration not quite gone. There was still someone lurking in the back of her mind and she could not grasp anything other than it was someone who agreed with her. And that was a little different from someone who wanted to explain it to her. Danni liked to learn. So long as the learning made sense and wasn't locked in allegories, like a moon-eating animal. She smiled, slightly. "All right." And with that, she scurried back to the wheel, climbed it quickly and assumed the same position she had when she first alighted. But she seemed to feel better about being there. Indeed, she looked over at Doyle who had stretched out on his mat and was absently scratching Leo's well exposed stomach. Leo's face was a mask of reverie, and with a little contented sigh, Danni closed her eyes and waited for sleep.

Chapter 7
The Fruit, the Fox and
What's Under the Tarpaulin

Danni could feel a sort of swishing motion that seemed to come from somewhere above her. It gave her the impression of the Farmer's Wife slapping at a hanging rug to get the dust out, only much gentler. Still, it began to confuse her as to why this would be occurring, so she opened her eyes. The sun was coming up, the trees were sparkling green, the grass had dew and a golden length of fur swung down past her line of vision and then up out of sight. She stood on all fours. She was still on the top of the wheel, so that was all right. All seemed to be as it was the night before and then… the golden length of fur passed by again, going the other way. Danni leaned over as far as she dared and could see a section of Leo's hip and part of his front paw hanging over the wheel cover; the swishing length of fur was his tail. She surmised that Leo had climbed to the top of the wheel cover sometime in the night and this thought made her smile.

She stretched the stiffness out of her little body and looked around. The fire was out and Doyle was still sleeping beside it. He was on his side, facing her, his eyes closed in a relaxed way and his mouth opened just slightly. There was something very different about him, but she could not place it. She hadn't met many humans; she'd heard about them, seen some from a distance, but Doyle was different. Aside from his youth, Doyle had a quality that she wasn't sure about and this puzzled her. She prided herself on being able to assess situations, individuals.

She felt comfortable with him, especially in the way he spoke to her about the rhyme thing. He didn't start to tell a story about it, he stopped and said he would think about it before he could tell her. Well, he was either going to come up with a story or he was really going to talk to her about it. One way or the other, she would have a better idea about this thing he was talking about or about him and whether or not he was to be trusted. Satisfied, she looked around and scrambled down the wheel.

She liked walking about on the dew-laden grass. Sometimes it was so heavy she could actually sip the water from it and it tasted so sweet to her. She walked to the other side of the wagon and looked around. There was a path before her – Doyle must have just turned off it the night before.

Off to the side, near the path, but very high up, she could see some grapes hanging from a vine that seemed to be suspended between two trees. It was an odd sight, but not unheard of. The grapes were a beautiful deep purple and Danni began to crave one. She scampered over to the tree, stopping occasionally and taking care to look about her before starting up again. She scrambled up the tree, clinging to the thick bark, until she found the connection point of the vine. Carefully, she moved onto the vine, angling herself above a bunch of grapes. She went to move for one and stopped cold.

A fox was directly beneath her, licking its mouth with a long pink tongue and waving its fluffy red tail in the air. Danni shifted back slightly, finding coverage behind some leaves. The fox was pacing beneath her, looking up hungrily. Presently, it sat back on its haunches and jumped. Danni stifled a scream. The fox was a good jumper to be sure, but the vine was well out of its reach. Still, it tried again. Danni felt pretty certain that it could not reach her but she was now beginning to wonder if it really was her the thing was after. She looked up to see if there were another animal, maybe larger and more visible, hovering above. Nothing she could spy. And there certainly was nothing below her but the grapes. It tried again to jump and landed a little awkwardly.

"Damn grapes…" Danni heard the Fox curse.

"Grapes?" Danni said it aloud, without thinking. The Fox looked up.

"Talking grapes?" it asked.

Danni peeked out from behind the leaf.

"Oh." said the Fox, quite dejected. After all, talking grapes would have been quite something.

"What are you trying to do?" Danni asked.

"Not that it's any of your business, but I was hoping to have some of these grapes. I have heard that the season has been a good one and so I thought I might try them. Of course, looking at them now, I think they are probably awful…"

"But foxes don't eat grapes." Danni said simply.

"I beg your pardon?" the Fox was slightly appalled at the presumption.

"Well, you do eat all sorts of things, that's true, but I believe your staple is meat."

"I like berries!" the Fox said defensively.

"These aren't really berries." Danni advised. "*You* don't eat them."

"I most certainly *do*!" the Fox insisted.

"Have you ever had one?" Danni asked.

The Fox's face fell. "Well… no," it admitted. "And I don't think I will… well, bother it, if you want to try them, fine, but they look sour to me… and maybe you're right… I probably would hate them…" and it began to turn its back on Danni.

"Hold on…" Danni said. The Fox turned a look up to the mouse. "I didn't say you'd hate them. I'm asking if you're going to make that kind of snap decision without even being able to try one."

"I can't get to them. So why not?"

Danni slid to the bunch of grapes and loosened one then dropped it to the Fox. It landed with a gentle thunk on the grass.

"There. Try it." the mouse offered.

The Fox gingerly nosed the fruit then took it into its mouth and bit. "Ooh…" it called out, "There are seeds!" Danni rolled her eyes. "Oh it's juicy… I thought it would be…" continued the fox, looking up at Danni.

"Could you please… maybe… send down some more?"

"Will you make me a promise?" asked Danni, who was inexplicably feeling very brave.

"Anything…" said the Fox.

"Promise me you won't dismiss something just because you can't get to it! Just because you don't know anything about it doesn't mean it should be hated."

The Fox pondered this. "But then I would have just wanted them all the more…" it said. "And that way I wouldn't have been disappointed."

"Oh, so you've never been disappointed before?"

The Fox pondered this as well. "Well. Yes. I suppose so… I mean, I'm sure everyone has at one time or another."

"Exactly. And that doesn't mean you have to go around despising things just because you can't have them. And sometimes… if you ask nicely, someone might help you get what you want." And Danni gnawed on the top of the vine until the whole bunch came loose and tumbled down to the Fox. It gave a little leap of joy.

"Oh but this is a feast!" it called and smiled up at Danni. "Thank you." it said. "And I *do* promise. Oh, I can share these back at the den!" And it gathered them up in its mouth gently, looked up at Danni again, winked and then darted off up the path before cutting across into some bushes.

Danni smiled as she watched it go. She pulled a grape from another bunch and took a satisfied bite from it. The juice squirted everywhere and Danni laughed as she slurped and chewed.

"Danni!?!" she heard. The call was sharp and frightened. "Danni?!"

"I'm here!" she called back and scrambled down the tree, darting across the path and towards the small encampment. Leo was on top of the cart, looking about frantically. "I'm here, Leo!" she called again and the cat saw her, took a step forward and disappeared.

"LEO!" Danni cried as she climbed up the cart wheel and wrangled her way to the top. A section of the tarpaulin had slipped and she could just see the top of Leo's head and then his front paws.

"Danni?" he tried.

"I'm here, Leo."

"I can't get out."

"I can see that…" she suppressed a grin. She looked over towards the fire ring and saw Doyle's mat was unoccupied, with the blanket tossed to one side. "Where's Doyle?"

"I think he went to get more water." said Leo. "Maybe wood. Some more peat. I don't suppose you can help me get out?"

"Thorns are one thing, Leo… I don't think I can lift you…"

"It's lumpy down here…" he complained and shifted slightly.

The tarpaulin suddenly moved a bit, jostling Danni slightly. "Don't move, Leo, the cloth is moving too… I think you being tangled in there and me being tangled in there as well would not be good…"

"But…"

"Where are you two?" she heard Doyle call. Danni turned to see him coming through the brush with the bucket, sloshing some water as he walked.

"We're over here," Danni replied. "Leo seems to have taken a tumble…" she indicated the cart and Doyle went slightly pale. He put the bucket down swiftly and came quickly to the cart.

"Don't move, Leo…" he said softly, calmly. Danni was alerted to his manner. He wanted to keep Leo from getting agitated, but why…? "Danni, why don't you move off the tarpaulin?" again, gently, but determined, and Danni shifted to the wheel cover. Doyle then assessed where Leo was and positioned himself very carefully. "Leo, would you mind if I lifted you by the scruff of your neck?" he asked.

"Oh that is a bit undignified…" the cat intoned, dryly. "But I really don't care, Doyle, I'd just like to be out of here."

Doyle took the cat as he described and lifted him up from the tarpaulin and away from the cart. Just as he cleared the cart, he lost his footing slightly and fell against its side, unceremoniously dropping Leo to the ground. The cat landed without incident but there was a loud snap from the cart. Danni turned to look, imagining a section of wood to have broken.

A section of tarpaulin appeared gathered now, as if a large hand were holding it from within. Only it was not a circle of fabric, but a line. It was most peculiar to see and as Danni looked a bit closer she thought she saw the gleam of metal. Doyle let out a sigh and lifted the tarpaulin. Under it, Danni saw a myriad of metal things, some shiny, but most old and rusty. There was a chain and as her eyes drifted to follow it, she saw a closed section of heavy metal in a half-circle almost, but part of it seemed to be attached to the tarpaulin and another part of it had a small circle of light metal just off-centre, smaller than the heavy half-moon that was holding the fabric. Somewhere in her mind she knew this thing was something to be feared.

"I thought I had it upside down," Doyle was saying. "I couldn't get it to close, and I was very afraid it just might do that on its own…" He pushed down on a section that looked like a large spoon to Danni and some of the half-moon opened a little, showing a collection of what looked like pointed teeth. It was now open enough for Doyle to tug out the tarpaulin before releasing the pressure on the spoon part and letting the half-moon section of metal close again.

He surveyed the damage done to the tarpaulin and sighed again. "I'll have to stitch this up…" he said, mostly to himself, but Danni was looking at the metal object and backing away slightly. She could now see that the half-moon section was connected to another half-moon section and that there was a pattern that brought the two halves together like an angry mouth. "You were very lucky, Leo..." Doyle said to the cat who was placidly cleaning his front paws and ankles. Leo looked up at him curiously and then smiled.

"I know." he replied simply.

"What is that thing?" Danni asked, instinctively shivering.

"A trap." Doyle said, and by the way he said it, Danni could tell he liked the thing about as much as she did. "Some people lay them out to trap animals. It's horrible. I found this one, but I couldn't get it to close. So I just put it in the cart to take back to the mongers."

"Mongers?" said Danni still unable to look away.

"Iron mongers. They sell things, but they're always on the look-out for more metal to melt down and use to make other things. It's how I help make some money. I try to collect the old things and take them back. They give me pretty good money for it... still... if I can get any of these off the ground, I think I've done a bigger service."

"Leo was on that?" she whispered.

"I don't know... he may have just been near it, but still... I didn't want to risk it so..."

"He said he was sitting on something lumpy..." said Danni, and Doyle let out a short, dry laugh. He moved the tarpaulin so Danni could really survey the items beneath. They were of various sizes and shapes, all of some kind of metal; she recognised a few, but certainly not all. Still, looking at the array before her she could understand Doyle's laugh. Everything there would feel lumpy. She looked up at the lad with a serious face, however, and asked; "There's nothing else here that could hurt him, is there?" Doyle smiled at her.

"Nor you," he said softly. "I hadn't expected guests, Danni. Or I would have done more to make it safe." Danni smiled in spite of herself. "Now, mind, these are all metal and so there is a danger regardless, if you're not careful, but nothing like that thing. So no climbing onto it, I should think..." this he said also to Leo, who looked up in bemused silence.

"There's a ledge right here," he said as he pointed to the front of the cart, "that could be used as a seat when I'm pulling it." He looked the two animals over. "Not that you two would add much weight to it." he looked over to the long handles. "It would be grand if I had a pony or a donkey to harness to it, then I could sit up there myself. But until I can get one of those, it's just me." He turned back to Danni and Leo. "And you two. And I don't know about either of you, but I am feeling a bit hungry."

"There are grapes right across the path!" Danni blurted out.

Leo looked up at her admonishingly: "So that's where you were..."

"I just wanted a look around..." she explained. "I gave some to a fox... I would have tried to bring some, but you were calling for me..."

"A fox?" Doyle asked. Danni nodded. "Weren't you afraid?"

"No... well... at first, but it just wanted some grapes..."

"Right across the path?" Leo asked. Danni nodded.

"Wait..." Doyle stopped. "There was a fable about a fox and some grapes..." He went to his book and looked into it. He turned a few pages, a puzzled, quizzical look on his face. "Huh…" he gave a small grunt. "Could have sworn it was in here…"

"Are we going to get some grapes?" Leo asked.

Doyle looked up from the book to the two animals before him. He smiled. "I think that's a grand idea. I can look for the story later." He put the book back by his mat then took a basket from the cart and turned to Danni. "Will you lead on?" he asked with a slight bow and sweeping his hand out in the direction of the path. Danni took the lead, careful to be sure she stayed in their sight lines, and led them to the grapes.

Chapter 8
Not a Laughing Matter

"Do you want any more eggs, Simon?" The Farmer's Wife asked. He looked up at her from his plate with a satisfied smile.

"Oh no, no, no…" he replied. "Goodness, you give a body enough to last the whole day!"

She smiled at the compliment and continued bustling about by the stove.

The Farmer took in another mouthful then spoke: "That bucket is better than new, Simon," he told the man. "Nary a bead of water coming through."

"Well, I should hope so… Now you mind it well, Henry…"

"Will do, will do…" he sopped up some of his egg yolk with a biscuit. "And I noticed you tended to the ladder in the barn."

"Well, I was there…" he smiled.

"And the hen house! That fence was getting the better of me… I've been lucky nothing's carried the hens away!"

"Well, I noticed that, too…" Simon demurred. Henry shook his head, a smile spreading across his face.

"Is there anything we can give you? I know you don't like money, but there must be something you're in need of?"

"I've already packed some of my preserves for you, Simon," Liza said, "and put together a packed lunch as well."

"Both of you are always too kind." And inwardly, he was sorry he couldn't ask for the mouse. But then… he turned back to the room where the clock had been and saw it. The violin. "You know…" he started, "that violin…"

"Oh, take it!" Liza said without a thought. Henry looked a bit more concerned. "Now Liza, you know how the cat likes that thing…" he looked at Simon, "Sometimes he plays it quite well…"

But Liza was shaking her head. "Hasn't touched it in days…" she said. "And the sad thing can't even catch any of the mice in the house, why give it a reward for doing next to nothing?"

There were times, Simon thought, when Liza had sensibilities he wished would last a bit longer than a moment.

"And if it will do Simon some good…" she turned a smile on him, "do you play Simon?"

"No, actually…" he admitted. "But I know someone who does…"

Liza gave a bigger smile. "Lady friend?" Simon looked down. The moment had passed. Liza took his downturned face to be an admission. "See, Henry? Oh let's give it to him. Maybe someday he'll come by with his friend and she can play!"

Henry looked into his wife's open, happy face. He loved seeing her like this and it had been some time since she had given him such a smile. "All right," he conceded and got up from the table to fetch the violin. He brought it and the bow over to Simon, who smiled appreciatively at both of them.

"Thank you," he said sincerely, and gingerly touched the instrument. "Well, I'd better get moving if I'm to make it to my next stop!" he declared, and pushed away from the table. "I'll just get my pack together…"

"Off again…" Liza mused from the window over the sink.

"Well, I never stay more than a…"

"Oh, not you, Simon… the dog. Gone off over the field again," she chuckled. "Silly thing…" and she gathered up the dishes. "You get yourself together, Simon, so we can give you a proper good bye." and with that, Simon went to gather his pack, which was already set to go and, wrapping the violin in some cloth, attached it carefully to his pack.

When he came out of the barn, both Liza and Henry were waiting for him on the porch of the house. He sauntered up to the two, his hand extended to Henry. They shook firmly, a small similar smile on both their faces. He turned to Liza, who had a teary smile for him. She pulled him to her in an awkward hug, he was cautiously aware of her arm and back, and he pulled away with a smile for her and a pat on her good shoulder. With a wave, he began down the path, which ran almost parallel to the field. He turned once to wave at them again, as they were waving still, and then he continued on and didn't look back.

He went alongside the field for a bit, looking over into it as he went. Once he was certain he was out of view, he took the cloth containing the violin off his pack. He set it on the ground and, raising his boot-clad foot up in the air, brought it down with a sickening crunch and twang as the strings came undone from the fret. Two more times he stomped on the instrument before he lifted it up, tightened the rope around it so nothing would fall out and, promising himself he would find a good place to dump it later, he continued down the path until he saw what he was really looking for.

The little dog had set down the sack and was looking about the area carefully. He sat for a moment and scratched himself when the noise to his left made him turn. Simon smiled at the dog, who wagged his tail.

"You making sure the mouse isn't coming back, then?" Simon asked. "That's certainly what Liza thinks." The dog chuckled low in his throat and looked at Simon. "That's what I thought," Simon said. "You helped her escape. Brought her out here, did you?" The dog nodded. "But she's not showing herself… maybe she's moved on…?"

Again, the dog nodded, and then suddenly, he spoke to Simon: "She said she was going to maybe have a look around… but I think she's headed for town. She always was different, I mean she never really did fit in… still… I said I would bring grain whenever I could…" and the dog trailed off as his attention was diverted by a melodious tune nearby.

Simon had unhooked his mallet from his pack quietly and raised it high in the air.

The dog didn't have a chance to make a sound.

Chapter 9
Rhymes with a Reason

Leo liked sitting up on the seat on the cart. It afforded him a good view of all around and still let him chat with Doyle and Danni. The little mouse, however, seemed to prefer sitting atop Doyle's cap, a funny looking thing that had a short brim in front only, but was made of a comfy fabric which was also easy for Danni to hold onto. The lad was also very good about letting her know when he was going to take it off, affording her more than enough time to jump on his shoulder or the seat behind by Leo. But it was never for long, and soon, Danni would hop back on and listen to the sounds of the forest and Doyle humming some song she'd never heard.

He had what he called canteens along the cart, which he had filled with water and was therefore able to slake Leo's erratic thirst. There were times when the cat would be in an unreasonable panic over the water situation, feeling that not travelling by the river was a bad idea, but once Doyle had shown him the canteens and made sure the cat had his own little cup to drink from, Leo seemed to calm down. Danni remembered his story and she felt sympathetic towards him. She couldn't really recall something that might have scarred her as much as this one incident had scarred Leo. She tried to put herself in the cat's situation, but the best she could do was feel badly for him. But even then, being so high up, looking out over the countryside, seeing the trees and the clouds scudding by, all put Danni is such a good humour that she found it hard to feel bad for any great length of time – even for a friend.

It was beautiful. Everywhere she looked brought new things to see. Sometimes Doyle would stop to investigate something shiny in the underbrush, but would usually come away with nothing. Every now and then he would uncover something: a short length of chain, a cuff, and once the sharp part of an axe without its handle. He would diligently add these things to his cart and they would continue. It was disciplined, she decided. But not without the same lightness of heart that her Mother had shown.

He would often hum and marvel at things he saw himself. And then, suddenly:

"Danni, about what I was saying before…" he started. "I still haven't come up with a good one for the code part… but most of the time, the rhymes are, well they're called Nursery Rhymes because they are usually read to small children… it's a means of bonding, getting closer… it's also a way to start to understand language… like the way my mum used to move my hands when she'd sing one to me: 'Pat-a-cake, pat-a-cake, baker's man'…"

He had stopped the cart and begun clapping his hand together to a beat he made as he spoke the words. "… 'Bake me a cake as fast as you can. Pat it and roll it and mark it with a B, and put it in the oven for baby and me', and she would trace the shape of the letter B and then tickle my stomach."

Danni had moved down from his cap to his shoulder to look at him. He was smiling with a faraway look in his eyes. Suddenly they sparkled as he spoke again: "Oh but there was another. And though I don't really know if it's true, some people said this one meant something altogether different: 'A Ring, a ring of roses, a pocket full of posies, Ashes, Ashes, all fall down.' Whenever children would recite that one, they were usually in a circle holding hands and they would walk in the circle for the beginning and when the last part would come, the 'all fall down' part, they would let go of their hands and tumble down." He smiled as he remembered and looked at Danni who was regarding him sceptically.

His smile became a grin. "I know, it was a game and we were small… but," and here his voice took on a softer, more urgent tone, as if he were sharing some forbidden thing with her: "Some people said that the rhyme was about the plague. When you caught the plague, there would be a rose-shaped ring on your body. And 'pocket full of posies' were flowers that people would wrap up and carry with them to smell so as to not notice the sick around them. and 'ashes', well, they would have to burn the dead and their clothes and everything so as to stop the spread of the disease… then 'all fall down'… would be… well, when the person would die." Again he looked at the little mouse who was staring back at him.

"Read to small children, was it?" she asked. Doyle gave a slight shrug and nodded. Danni shook her head. "You'd think they'd have nightmares." He laughed at this and nodded. He took the cart handles up and proceeded again.

"Oh there's another one…" and he began to sing, "'Rock-a-bye baby, on the tree top, when the wind blows the cradle will rock, when the bough breaks, the cradle will fall, and down will come baby, cradle and all.'" he glanced at Danni sideways.

"That's awful." she sighed. "Well, not the tune, that's kind of pretty…"

"Yeah, see a lot of these are put to a tune of some kind to help you remember them better… they also help build your memory skills… there's a grand one for remembering numbers…" he stopped walking for a moment as he screwed up his face in thought, closing his eyes as he did. "'One, two, buckle my shoe; three, four, shut the door; five, six, pick up sticks; seven, eight, lay them straight; nine, ten, a big fat hen…' I think it goes on… I can't remember all the rhyme… but I can count higher, I assure you!" he laughed then, a hearty one that Danni could feel rumbling through his shoulder.

"And some rhymes may be a code for a historical event. Like Mary, Mary, quite contrary… some people think it's about Queen Mary, or

Bloody Mary, King Henry the Eighth's daughter, but it could also be about Mary, Queen of Scots. Bessy Bell and Mary Grey are more about Queen Mary and her sister, Queen Elizabeth, Henry's other daughter." Danni looked curiously at the lad. She had heard talk of kings and queens and emperors and the like, but never with names like those. She couldn't even recall names. She looked at Doyle again. He was lost in a reverie, humming to himself. And the humming began to take the form of words…

"Three blind mice… three blind mice… see how they run… see how they run… they all ran after the Farmer's Wife, who cut off their tails with a carving knife, did you ever see such a thing in your life as three blind mice?"

Danni couldn't move. She sat on his shoulder like a small statue, staring up at his happy profile and waited. He knew. *He knew*. The Farmer's Wife must have sent him. Danni didn't think she was that important, really; and maybe what she had done was bad, even wrong, what the Farmer's Wife had done really was worse… but to send someone after her, a little mouse… what was the point of that? After all, Danni couldn't do anything to hurt the Farmer's Wife, could she, really? Well, aside from make the woman stab herself in the shoulder. And fall into the clock. Which fell on her and broke pretty much to pieces. But it really had been an accident, Danni hadn't meant for all of that to happen.

"Something wrong, Danni?" Doyle asked, seeing the rigid figure on his shoulder. The little mouse jumped hearing her name. She couldn't jump to the ground, it was too far. She looked back at Leo on the seat. He was smiling lazily, his eyes closed to the sun. Had he not heard Doyle? Had he not heard the song and recognised what was being said? "Danni?" Doyle began again, and he stopped walking. Leo's eyes opened and a yawn stretched his mouth to enormous proportions. His teeth were incredibly pointy and sharp looking.

"It was an accident!" she found herself crying. Doyle looked perplexed, but the little mouse continued. "I didn't mean for her to get hurt… but it was wrong to kill them! She shouldn't have killed them! And they didn't run after her, they couldn't, how could they, they were blind! Please don't hurt me… I didn't mean for her to get hurt, but I'm not sorry…. I'm not…"

Doyle gently gathered the little mouse into his cupped hands. The motion and the movement put a panic into her, but he was making a shush sound, much like the breeze through the trees, and little clucking sounds with his tongue and one finger gently caressed Danni's wee head. In spite of herself, Danni was beginning to calm, in fact she was almost sleepy. Doyle had leaned back against the plank where Leo was seated. The cat stretched himself and placed his front paws on both of Doyle's shoulders, peering over one to see Doyle gently handling Danni.

"What's wrong…?" Leo asked.

Doyle gave the cat a look. "Dunno… I was singing a rhyme and she suddenly panicked."

Leo cocked his head: "Rhyme?"

Doyle nodded: "About the three blind mice…"

"Oh…?"

Doyle muttered on: "…you know… about the Farmer's Wife cutting off their tails…"

"Did you know her cousins?" asked Leo.

"Who, the Farmer's Wife?"

"No… Danni's cousins… they were blind… right, Danni?" said Leo.

From her comfortable place in Doyle's hands, Danni nodded. Doyle stopped caressing Danni's head. Danni looked up and remembered what had frightened her so.

"Right?" Leo asked again. "That's why you left the Farm to come to the forest, right?" Slowly, Danni nodded. "There were three of them, were there? I don't remember you saying how many…"

Doyle looked at Danni cautiously, concern furrowing his brow. "*This couldn't be happening,*" he thought to himself. It was odd enough being with animals who could talk, but to find out that they were somehow *living* the rhymes and stories he had been brought up on… it was almost too much. He looked around. The terrain was nothing like he had been around before and he knew he had started off in a direction familiar to him. Over to his left there was a large castle that appeared to be jutting alongside the hill that had been previously in front of them. Not the size of Warwick Castle, but still, tall and turreted. And over to his right, before the other hill they had passed, was another castle. Rounder perhaps, darker, certainly, but nicely appointed. Castles were not that close together as he could recall.

The mouse began to tremble and Doyle let his attention turn back to her. She was staring up at him with such terror that he didn't know what to do or say. He tried to smile, look reassuring. And the mouse began to cry.

"Did she send you?" she finally got out. "You're not taking me back there, are you?" and she suddenly hiccoughed loudly. Leo was moving his paws back and forth on Doyle's shoulders, agitated at his friend's distress.

"No, no, no, no, no…" Doyle soothed. "Danni, I don't know this person… I don't… I only know this as a rhyme."

The mouse looked up at his blue eyes. They were filled with concern, sadness even, they were pleading with her for understanding. But it seemed so ludicrous. How could a part of her life be a little song?

"Danni…" Doyle said, softly. "I don't understand this either… but I would not hurt you. I wouldn't want anything to hurt you. And I know Leo feels the same, right, Leo?"

The cat looked suddenly alert at the mention of his name: "Of course not… no… Danni you helped me… I would never… I owe you, remember?" he turned a look at Doyle. "You really don't know the Farmer's Wife, do you?" Doyle smiled.

"No," he sighed out. "I know a few farmers, and I have met their wives, but they all have names… Mrs Morris; Mrs Taylor; Mrs Raven… and none of them have ever gone after mice, let alone blind ones!" he smiled, but it was half-hearted. "I am confused, though…" he told them. "This is not a place I am familiar with. But for whatever reason, we are together… and I think that the only way for me to find out just what is going on is to stay with you two. I am very puzzled, but somehow you both seem to make sense, at least."

Danni sat up a little in his palm. She made sense! Doyle thought she made sense! Then something struck her. "Confuzzled." she said. Doyle looked at her quizzically. "Well, you're confused and puzzled, so..." Doyle let out a laugh that rumbled through him, Danni could feel it from his hands and she saw that Leo felt it from his shoulders.

Leo gave an appreciative nod. "Good laugh there, Doyle..." he complimented.

"Great word there, Danni!" Doyle said to the mouse. Now Danni smiled. "Shall we continue on?" he asked them both. "Still a bit further we can go before stopping for lunch, eh?"

Both cat and mouse nodded, Leo leaned back from Doyle's shoulders to sit back on the seat and Danni scurried up Doyle's arm to his left shoulder, where she sat back on her haunches, one paw on the collar of Doyle's shirt. Doyle took up the handles of his cart and began down the path.

"Doyle..." Leo started, "I think I'm thirsty..."

Chapter 10
La Belle Pleut

It was not long after that the rain started. Gently at first, a refreshing drizzle that landed on them like the dew of the morning. But after a time, it began to come down harder. Doyle seemed used to this type of change in weather and he pulled his cart off the road near two standing trees, encouraged Danni and Leo to get under the cart, tugged out another tarpaulin and fashioned it to fit from over the section where the handles started to about three feet from their end and tied it off on both trees. The effect was a roomy, covered sitting area that still afforded them the opportunity to see out. Sections of the tarpaulin drooped over the rope, giving the rain a place to drip out and not fall too directly in their space. Once finished, he took off his stockings and shoes, carefully seeing to the loose tongue and seeing they stayed in a dry spot, brought out some food and the three ate quietly, watching the rain splash around them.

"Rain like this..." Doyle started, "it could stop and start all day; it could clear up at a moment's notice, or it could go harder. Here's hoping it's not the latter." Danni looked up at him, expectantly. "Well, if it did," he continued, "we really would be better inside somewhere, you know? And the only places I've seen are those two castles..." and he indicated both to the left and to the right of where they were sheltering.

"Castles?" Leo asked between licks. He was trying furiously to clean off the rain and get back to a semblance of dry.

Doyle nodded. "One on either side." he marvelled. "Very odd..."

"What, that there's only two?" Leo tried, "but that's an even number."

Doyle cocked an eyebrow, "Only two? No, of course not... that there are two so close together... I... I'm not used to that..."

Leo shook his great head and smiled: "Sounds like you're from a not too picturesque place, Doyle."

Doyle felt a bit defensive suddenly. "I used to live in London..." he said. "We moved before the war... Dad had been asked to manage a factory in Birmingham, so we moved up there... but he didn't like the city too much... it's very industrial, you know... he wanted me to grow up in a more pleasant spot... a few miles off was a smaller town... it's funny, because if we were still in London, it would be the sort of place they would ship me off to. Mostly the rich people lived there, you know, the owners of the mills and factories... but there was a place for us in Solihull... but then dad died... accident at the factory... and mum and I had to go to a smaller spot... It's like a farm, but we really don't have much... some chickens and ducks, but we grow all our own vegetables, we live off it fairly well... still... she gets a pension from the factory... It's a nice town... a sweet town... but we don't have castles popping up around hills..." he looked again. "In fact... we don't really have hills like these... these are more like mountains..." his voice trailed off and there was silence but for the rain's song on the tarpaulin and the ground outside.

"I've heard of London." Leo said finally.

Doyle looked at him and chuckled. "Were you there to see the queen?" he asked in a gently mocking way.

Leo looked at him in all seriousness. "No, but I heard about a cat that did that... seems silly to go that far just to scare a mouse... I really think it was just a story, some animals just do like to brag... see what they can get from it..." Doyle stared at Leo for a bit. The cat looked at himself and then back to Doyle, before asking: "Did I miss a spot?"

"Where *am* I?" Doyle finally asked.

Leo brightened. "Here," he said happily.

Doyle pushed on, not wanting to brush the cat off, but he really was in something of a quandary now. "Yes, Leo, I know that... but just where is here?" He looked back up the path they had come down. "And where is my home...?"

"I had a feeling you weren't from around here..." Danni finally spoke.

"Really?" Leo asked, not quite dripping with sarcasm.

"Of course... I mean, look at how he's dressed... have you ever seen a fellow with a cap like that?" Doyle reached protectively for his brown wool flat cap.

Leo studied it for a time before shaking his head: "You have a point... they either have the brim all the way around, and farther out than his, or no brim at all... or a brim and a kind of point at the top... and then there's feathers on many..."

"You certainly seem to spend a lot of time looking at hats..." Danni interrupted. The cat appeared miffed. "Well you asked..." he harrumphed.

Danni went on. "And then there's his trousers..."

Doyle looked at his brown tweed trousers. They were worn in places, but his mother had always stitched them up so as no trace of wear showed unless it was a close inspection. His shirt was not so lucky, it was well frayed around the wrists and collar, but it had been his father's and his mother had taken it in a bit for him, knowing that he would use it for work and not be concerned with his growing out of it. There was a simple brown jacket in the cart, if he felt the need to look more respectable going to other people's homes and seeing if there were any iron to be had. He had his better clothes at home. Home.

Danni was continuing: "I've only seen trousers that tie... some of them have buttons... but not like those." There was no response. "Leo?"

Leo just shrugged, "I think I'll keep any further fashion commentaries to myself, thank you." he intoned, his nose clearly out of joint. The mouse shook her head slightly, and there was an awkward silence.

"What year is this?" Doyle interjected. Both animals gazed in confusion at him.

"*This* year." Leo said, simply, then raised his eyebrows in the hopes that he hadn't sounded too obvious but also that its obviousness was nonetheless present.

Doyle shook his head, "No..."

"Well what, as opposed to *last* year?" said Leo.

Doyle was getting testy, "...No..."

"Or *next* year?" said Leo, just as testily.

Doyle's patience was waning, "The number!" Again, confusion gazed out from their eyes to Doyle. "The year number, you know." And now a deafening silence reigned.

"*I* know it to be 1941," he told them. "12th of March." They both blinked. "That doesn't mean anything to either of you?"

Leo swayed slightly, his tail making the jerky swishes that Danni now knew meant he was either in pain or perplexed. Danni contented herself with rocking back and forth slightly on her back legs. It wasn't that she was afraid of the burgeoning situation, she was just uncertain as to where it was going, how it would ultimately affect Doyle and, in turn, affect her and Leo. Leo, on the other hand, suddenly needed to relieve himself, noticed that the rain had not really abated, and was determining when he could leave the conversation without appearing too rude and go to the far end of the cart and take care of his duty. As for Doyle, he could not put his finger on it... why he felt he ought to be terrified; not knowing where he was and in the company of two creatures who not only had no concept of the current date or year, but were in fact animals who could talk, and how he had managed to stumble upon this inexplicable place...

Surprisingly, he was somewhat calm. Only somewhat because he was beginning to feel a bit of a thrill at the idea that he was on some kind of adventure on which no one else had been. A thought suddenly passed through his head and he pinched himself. Pain. Not asleep. Not a dream. But even if it really was, which could explain away a great deal, it was not a dream like any he'd had before and he found himself enjoying it immensely. With a sudden smile, he looked at Danni and Leo, who were looking so perplexed that he almost burst out laughing. But his smile alone seemed to ease them and some of the visible tension left their bodies. "I suppose I am just going to have to see where this leads." he pronounced.

Leo sighed. "Oh that's lovely, if you'll excuse me, don't want to be rude, need to... you understand..." and with that he went to the far end of the underside of the cart.

Danni was not so pleased. "What do you mean?" she asked, "'see where this leads'?"

"Just what I said, Danni."

"But aren't you curious? Aren't you concerned? Aren't you upset you might never get back? Aren't you angry?"

Doyle looked thoughtfully for a moment, on his own and at the mouse. "I am pretty certain that I'm *all* of those things, Danni. But I don't see *the use* of some of them." The little mouse let her jaw drop open. "I'm not you, Danni, I guess I think things differently."

"*No use* for them?" she sputtered.

"Not really…"

"But…"

"Danni, what *use* would being angry do? Storming about in a huff? What good would that do in answering any questions I might have, and yes, I have quite a few, but getting angry, or staying angry… well, I don't think you or Leo would want to travel with someone like that, would you?"

Grudgingly, the mouse could see the logic, but she was not going to let go yet. "But where you come from! What about that? What if you can't go back?"

"Again, Danni, I could whinge and complain, but it won't get me home. And I haven't exactly explored all the options of trying to do that, have I? Who knows? If I start back down the way I came, I just might find my way back, but in the meantime, I thought you and Leo wanted to go into town?"

"But what have *we* got to do with it?" she demanded.

"I thought I was helping you get there." Doyle said simply. "So I suppose I am curious, I do want to know more about this place, and I am concerned, I think you and Leo are both very nice and I don't want anything untoward to happen to either of you. I don't know how well I can see to that, but I would like to try. In the meantime, I think I will hold off on the upset and angry part and hold on to the curious and concerned part."

Again, she could see the logic, but she didn't quite grasp why he wouldn't want to know more about his situation. Of course, he had asked them questions and they had told him all they really could so it would be a bit silly to keep asking the same things of someone who had no more knowledge. That would be insane, asking the same thing and expecting a different answer. And he seemed so calm about it all. Danni wanted to be infuriated but found she couldn't. In the end, she gave a little nod. It was not totally comforting, but somehow it seemed all right. Doyle looked off into the forest.

"The rain is not letting up too much," he said quietly and crawled closer to the cart where he had a shovel tied under the little seat. "I'll dig a little trench, keep the water from coming in here too much." and he found Leo sitting close to his shoes. "I suppose those aren't like ones you've seen either, eh?" he asked.

Leo was startled to realise he was being watched. "Hm? What? No…" he rambled and then nodded. "No, I guess not. I mean. They are *shoes*, that I will give you." He leaned in to Doyle conspiratorially. "Steer clear of the far left wheel, will you? Sort of… left me mark…" he looked down.

Doyle nodded for a moment until realisation crept in and he took in a slight gasp of recognition. He patted Leo on the back. "No worries, Leo…

70

perfectly natural. At least, you tidy up after yourself." Leo grinned up at him and Doyle scratched him under the chin. Leo's eyes closed for a moment, lulled by the touch. After a quick scratch to Leo's ears, Doyle started back to the work at hand. "Need to make a little trench…" he mumbled and undid the shovel.

Danni was looking back toward the path. She climbed up to the top of one of the wheels and looked about. To her left was the tall castle, with several turrets shooting into the sky. It looked beautiful, but seemed empty… almost too quiet. She looked to the right to see the rounder castle. It was darker, but Danni could see that this was due to a vast overgrowth of bushes. She could see well with her sharp eyes, but she could not quite tell where the bushes exactly began, only that they were certainly crowding over the area where the entrance would be. She shook her head and sighed. Another one of those strange things that she just couldn't understand or justify. She turned her sight back to the turreted castle when, below her line of vision, off in the near distance, she saw a flash of colour and movement, then nothing. Her brows furrowed. She turned back to see that Doyle was making slow progress with the trench and that Leo was making do, dozing directly beneath the little seat on the cart. She smiled a bit at that, he was well protected from the rain by the tarpaulin.

Another flash of movement and a dart of colour took her back to looking out before her. Curiosity getting the better of her, she darted down the wheel and started back to the path, shooting over into the underbrush towards the trees where she had seen the movement. It wasn't an animal, she was certain of that, and maybe it would be a human that could answer some of Doyle's questions. Even if he were going to be lax about the whole situation, it didn't mean she couldn't put out a little effort. After all, he had been feeding both her and Leo, as well as keeping them safe and escorting them to town. It was the least she could do. She could avoid the heavy rain by staying in the underbrush. After a bit, the rain seemed to be slackening. When she looked up however, and she saw how tightly the trees were connecting together, she realised the branches were making a canopy similar to Doyle's tarpaulin; only not keeping out quite as much rain. Then she heard the sound. Gentle, soft, sad…

Someone was crying.

Danni went through another bit of underbrush and found a very small clearing with a felled tree cutting across it. And sitting on the tree, with her back to Danni, was a girl in a blue dress, her curling red hair falling down her back, her head and body heaving gently with soft sobs.

Danni started out across the clearing, stop-starting as her Mother used to do when she would head to the clock. Danni never saw the need for the motion, but now, not wanting to alert the girl or frighten her, the stop-start seemed the best way to go, moving in time with the sobs, stopping on the intake of air and starting again when the sound would come out. She was on the fallen tree in no time, far enough away so she could not be reached but near enough to be heard. She looked at the girl and realised she was probably a young woman, not a child. Having not been around many people, Danni had to only assume this, but the way she was crying was not like tantrums she had heard children would fall into, this was the sound of someone very, terribly sad.

"I'm sorry…" Danni tried after the young woman took in a small amount of breath. A second intake came as she turned to see where the sound had come from, her eyes immediately lighting on Danni. Somehow, her wide amber eyes became even larger and her small mouth made a lovely "O".

Even though she had been crying, and Danni could see it had been for some time, she was lovely. Her skin was pale and smooth and her hands, which had been covering her face, were small and delicate, much like the rest of her, sweet and lovely in her pale blue dress."I'm sorry," Danni said again, hoping that she wouldn't scream. Many women seemed to scream when they saw a mouse. Or so she had been told. The small beauty closed her mouth, still watching Danni carefully. "Can I... can I help?"

Again her amber eyes filled with tears and she brushed them away carelessly. "Oh I wish you could..." she got out, her lilting voice had a childlike tremor to it and she let out a sigh. "I wish someone could."

"May I ask what the matter is?"

"It's a long story," she said.

Danni asked honestly: "Is there a short version?" The lovely thing let a smile cross her face at this. Her large eyes smiled along. Her hands clapped together in a release of tension. Danni was spellbound by her beauty.

"I'll try," she said softly. "My father travels a great deal – business, you know – and every time he goes he asks my sisters and I what we want him to bring back. They always seem to have something in mind, but... I just want him to come back, you know? But I know he knows that, so I ask for a flower or something simple. Well, he found a rose at a castle and he was going to bring it to me but... a beast lived there..." she looked over her shoulder at this, off to the left of where they were. "He said he would kill my father for taking the rose, but my father explained that he was only getting the rose for me. So the beast said he would let my father go and if I came of my own free will that my father would be spared, but I would have to stay with him... well, of *course* I had to take my father's place..."

"Excuse me..." Danni interrupted, "but did you say he let your father go?"

"Yes. So that he could say his farewells to me and my sisters and come back for his punishment or to bring me."

"So he got away," said Danni, thinking that would be the end.

"Away?"

"From this 'beast'?"

"The beast let him leave, yes."

There was a pause as Danni shook her head, "I'm sorry... so he got away, but then he went back and took you with him?"

"Yes. Of my own free will."

Again the little mouse shook her head. "Why?" she asked.

"Well I couldn't let father go on his own and be killed..."

"No... I mean *why* did he go back at all? He was *freed*! He was *let go*... he didn't *have* to come back!"

The beautiful young woman sat up a bit straighter. "Of course he did!" she said indignantly.

Danni narrowed her eyes and looked at the young woman sideways. "Why?" she asked again, almost certain of the answer.

"Because..." and Danni joined in with the young woman's reply, "... He gave his word." The beautiful woman nodded her head, her burnished

73

curls bouncing, and her amber eyes filled with earnestness. "And you know how important that is…" she finished.

Danni sighed, "Not really, but you humans certainly seem to think so. Even if it means someone's death or someone being made to stay where they don't want to be."

"I would think you would understand…" she said to Danni, "being a magical mouse and all…"

Danni startled at this. "Who said anything about being magical?" she asked. "Well… isn't that why you're here?" said the young woman, brightly. "To help me? I've often heard of people in need finding aid in little magical creatures… like you… who appear from nowhere… at just the right moment."

Danni shook her head. She was beautiful, this lovely thing before her, but Danni was not certain just what went on between her ears. "If I can help you, I will… but I am not magical. I'm just a mouse. There is no such thing as magic."

The young woman sat back in shock at this. "No magic?!" she cried, and truly sounded appalled. "But every night, there is a lovely supper ready for me in my room… and every morning as soon as I wake, a lovely breakfast! And everything I could imagine and wish for, I find all throughout the castle! When my father left me, the beast said he could pack as much as two trunks could carry and the trunks never filled! You don't think that's magic?"

"No. I call that servants doing their jobs properly," said Danni, matter-of-factly.

"But I see no one!"

"When they are doing their jobs properly, you shouldn't." Danni wasn't certain how she knew this, whether or not she had heard it from someone, but it seemed correct.

The lovely creature paused at this and slowly, with great deliberation, nodded.

"So how *did* you come to be here?" Danni asked, trying to cut to the chase.

The young woman shook her head slightly, bringing herself from her reverie for the moment. "Oh… yes… well… as you might imagine, he has a horrible temper…"

"This 'beast'?"

"Yes… Who else?" and then, taking a deep breath, she gave the shortest version she could: "Well, he came to my room again, to chat, and just before he left he asked me the same question, again… and when I said no, he just flew into a rage! I was so frightened! Once he started down the hall, tearing at the tapestries, I just ran… and… here I am…"

"But why?" Danni asked.

"Why what?"

"…Are you sitting here?"

She took a small bite of her lower lip, "Because, I am indecisive."

"Of what? Whether or not to sneak back and get a fast horse?"

She shook her coppery curls, "Whether or not to go back."

Danni put one paw to her head which hadn't stopped shaking, dumbfounded. Finally she looked at the young woman. "May I ask you two questions?"

"Of course," she smiled, and leaned a little closer to Danni.

"What's your name?"

"Belle."

"*Stands to reason*," thought Danni. "Belle," she said aloud, "what was the question this 'beast' asked you?"

Belle sat upright again, looking over her shoulders, tremors of fear reverberating through her. "He... he asked me if I would marry him!"

Danni nodded. "Go back home, Belle." she told her.

"He isn't that bad, though, you know..."

"Go back to your father..." Danni insisted.

"I mean, except for the bouts of temper, he really is kind..."

"Don't become a statistic, Belle..."

"What does that mean?"

All Danni knew was: "That's what happened to my mother the day she died!"

"But how can I prevent something I don't understand?"

Danni couldn't remember who first called her mother a statistic, but she did know it was a sharp, cruel word. And she knew Belle was in danger. "Don't go back!"

"He has never done anything to *me*, you know..."

"Why are you justifying this?"

"And he has made sure I got everything I desired..."

"Belle!" Danni finally shouted. The lovely amber eyes gazed down at Danni. "Please. Listen to me. Go back home. Leave. I'm sure your father misses you. Just as I'm sure you miss your father. This 'beast' will get by... seems he's been doing quite well, if you really look at it... it's not like he's going to die or anything! You've been there long enough. You know your father wouldn't want you there if you were unhappy, would he?"

Belle worked her mouth for a moment in thought. "No..." she said, somewhat unconvincingly, "no..."

"Can you get home from here?" Danni asked, almost certain that Doyle would help her find her way.

"Oh yes... really, it's actually quite close... just behind the dark castle," she said, pointing to her right, "You know... the one overrun with thorns?"

"Thorns!" Danni thought. Now *that* was a new one.

"Danni!" was suddenly shouted from behind them. Belle jumped slightly.

"It's all right," Danni calmed, "That'll be my friends. I left without telling them. We could help you back to your father's house, if you'd like?"

Belle shook her lovely head. "No... no... thank you. I suppose I must do this myself." She smiled hesitantly. "Thank you, Danni. You're very sensible... for a non-magical mouse."

"You're very beautiful..." Danni blurted.

Belle nodded simply. "I've been told." she said without guile or conceit. And she turned and left the clearing.

"Danni!? Are you all right?" Doyle called again.

Danni turned on the log and called back: "I'm here! I'm coming!" but before she could leave the log, Doyle burst through the bushes into the clearing. He was a little unkempt, the rain must have stopped, but his hair dripped water lightly at the ends, his waves somewhat straightened. His blue eyes were wide and his breathing was slightly laboured.

"Oh..." Danni started. "Oh I am sorry... I should have said something..."

"You should have..." Doyle agreed. "But you're all right?"

"Yes," she replied and Doyle put his hand beside her to climb on, after which he placed his hand to the opposite shoulder so Danni could alight there. "I am sorry..." she repeated. Doyle gave a nod and started back the way they had both come. There was a silence between them that Danni was certain meant she hadn't been forgiven. She felt awfully uncomfortable and tried to think of the right words to really let Doyle know how sorry she was when he spoke.

"I thought you were mad at me..." he said softly, not looking at her, "and decided to run away..."

Danni's mouth dropped. That was the furthest thing from the truth! She put both her paws on the collar of his shirt. "Oh no, Doyle!" she said emphatically. "I just saw something! I... went to go see what it was... and to see if it was someone who could help you... you know... figure things out...?" she drifted off.

Doyle stopped. He put his hand out for her to step on, which she didn't do at first, as they were still not at the cart, but he gave his hand a little shake so she understood he meant for her to be there. She stepped on sheepishly. He brought her forward to look him squarely in the face. "I think it might be best, Danni, if we thought of ourselves as a team. Do you understand me?"

"Like a group?" she asked.

Doyle nodded. "That has a common goal. That works together. That helps each other. That relies on each other and talks to each other. What do you think of that?"

"I'd like that very much, Doyle." And she did.

He put his other hand up to her paw, extending one finger to her. "Shake?"

Danni smiled and placed her paw on top of his finger, which he moved up and down slightly. Doyle smiled at the mouse and moved her back to his shoulder. They started back towards the cart.

"Was it?" he asked.

"Was it what?"

"Someone who could help?" Danni looked over her shoulder back towards where she had left Belle.

"No..." she said, "I think she was having a hard enough time figuring out her own things."

Chapter 11
Castles, Castles Everywhere

The rain having stopped, their lunch having been eaten, the three travellers set forth again down the path. Danni could not help but look at the castle to the left of the path. She knew that Belle had come from there and Danni began to wonder just how horrible this beast really was. Belle had said she felt well taken care of, but Danni still felt justified in telling her to leave. Danni actually felt a bit angry at the beast for keeping Belle there… hoping she would finally relent to be his bride, it was awful. She turned to look to the right of the path and saw the other castle. They were getting closer now so she could make out that the tangled mass of darkness was in fact thorns. Huge thorns. She had never seen a thorn bush of such size. And what kind of buds were growing on it? Going up towards the castle, there were buds – huge buds – on all the sections near the path and they appeared almost metallic. It was so terribly odd and Danni couldn't help but stare…

"Oh my…" she breathed out suddenly.

"What is it?" Doyle asked.

On the seat behind Leo, released a sleepy purr.

"Those aren't buds, they're people," Danni whispered.

Doyle looked at her and then turned to focus on the castle himself. "Is that a thorn bush growing all around that castle?" he asked and then he, too, saw what Danni had mistaken for buds. Armoured men, who must have been trying to get through the bush, were splayed out, skewered to sections of thorns, some wrapped around by the tendrils of the thorns, some held aloft, but all, quite dead. Some looked as if they had been there for many, many years. Making the sight all the more incongruous were the flowers just beginning to blossom… such loveliness amid such a grotesque scene was almost too hard to gaze upon. "Maybe we should keep going…" Doyle said finally though he, like Danni, could not quite avert his eyes.

Then, the sound of approaching hooves made it easier. Startled into action, Doyle pulled over to the side of the path as a horse and rider began to plunge along from behind. Seeing the suddenly appearing cart caused the white horse to falter and rear up, but the rider was skilled and calmed the animal swiftly. He saw Doyle ahead of him and called out: "What ho!"

Doyle removed his cap. The rider was like none he had ever seen before. His cloak was thrown carelessly over one arm and coloured a rich burgundy. It looked as if he were wearing a very short dress of a similar coloured, edged with gold ribbon, and his legs were not covered with a sensible pair of trousers, but with black tights. His shoes appeared to be made of velvet and looked more like pointy-toed slippers. But it was his hat that caught much of Doyle's attention. More like a ladies work bonnet, it was also of burgundy velvet, close fitting around the man's head, but billowing out somewhat on top, with a white feather attached to one side and spilling down the back. His straight blond hair fell to his shoulders and his pale face gazed down at Doyle with anticipation.

His mighty horse pawed at the ground. "Good morrow, my lad," the oddly attired man called out. "Know you the way to the castle?"

"Erm…" Doyle managed.

"Which one?" Danni asked.

The rider stared harder at Doyle and saw Danni. He took in a gasp and, pulling a sword from a scabbard that had not been noticed until it was unsheathed and sparkling in the sunlight, he dismounted abruptly. Doyle took a step back, Danni clung to his shirt collar and Leo, who had been jerked from his slumber, arched his back and hissed, spitting as well for good measure. The rider swung his sword full circle and then pushed the point into the ground and fell to one knee, both hands on the sword's hilt. He gazed with deep brown eyes up at Danni. "Are you a fairy who's taken animal form?"

Danni looked at the young man. He was smaller now that he was on the ground, she could see he was not much taller than Doyle, but he had the build of one older – not by much, but certainly older than Doyle. Not averting her gaze, she tapped Doyle on his neck and whispered: "Is he serious?"

"He has a sword, Danni, so I think he is." The mouse shook her head. First she's 'magical', now she's a 'fairy', maybe it would have been better to stay at the Farm and let the Farmer's Wife kill her. These people were not normal. Leo took the moment to curl up and go back to sleep.

"I'm a mouse," she informed him.

The young man studied her. "So it is." and he stood up, the sword going back to its sheath. "I search for the castle containing the Princess Briar Rose." Everything he said seemed to be a proclamation.

Danni waited. "… Because…?"

He looked at the mouse curiously. "Because I am the Prince and that is what I have set out to do…" he looked Doyle over. "Is this your pet?"

"No…" Doyle got out. The fop was royalty. This explained much.

"Look, Prince whoever…" Danni started.

"Prince," he interrupted.

Danni was taken aback: "Prince?"

"Yes."

"What's your name?"

"I am the Prince," he insisted.

79

"I got that... Prince Who?" The Prince looked confused. "What do people call you?"

"'Your Highness'."

"What do your parents call you?"

"'Son'."

She shook her head. This was going to be a long day, getting on with it might be the best course of action. "There are two castles," she said. "I have been told that the one over there..." she indicated to the left of the path, "contains a beast. The one over here..." and she pointed to the dark castle, "contains a lot of death."

The Prince stepped back slightly. "What mean you, death?"

"There really aren't many kinds other than no longer living," Danni tried, "But look for yourself... up that hill."

With a one-handed flourish, he removed his hat, while his other hand hovered above his eyes in a nicely turned-out 'looking' position. "Yes, I see a castle... I see massive thorns... some appear to be flowering... some appear to have.... dead people...?" He took another step back.

"At least, he has good vision," Danni sighed. Doyle grinned.

"Well. I suppose I must go forth..." The Prince announced, albeit, not as emphatically as before.

"... Go forth...?" Danni repeated.

"To the castle," he indicated wanly.

"... Because..." she began, and as the Prince looked at Danni, she could see that he was becoming hesitant, so she continued, "...because you like the idea of being skewered on an overgrown thorn?"

"Not really, no..."

"Then maybe you and Nelly Grey here ought to go back from whence you came?"

"His name is Rupert," the Prince said, "and maybe I should at least make a go of this..."

"Doyle, how many dead people did you count up there?" Danni asked.

Doyle stammered at first then: "I didn't count, Danni, but there were an awful lot..."

She looked back at the Prince, her paws upturned, her eyebrows raised as if to say, 'See?'

The Prince toyed with his hat for a moment, gazing up at the castle hesitantly, trying to work something through in his head.

"Look..." Danni tried again. "I understand that a lot of people do a lot of strange things around here, from what I have seen, and no, it hasn't been a lot, but it's enough to make me wonder for the sanity of the world, and yes, you *are* a Prince..."

"*The* Prince..." he interrupted

"*The* Prince," she conceded, "and as *The* Prince, don't you think you owe it to your parents... your people... to, I don't know... stay alive?" There was a pause.

Leo yawned, stretched and turned around, curling up in the opposite direction and falling back asleep. The Prince observed this and suddenly one eyebrow arched. The corners of his mouth turned up slightly. "You have lied," he announced.

"I beg your pardon?"

"You say you are not a fairy in animal form."

"I'm not," Danni insisted.

"And yet you warn me of the treacherous road ahead..."

"Anyone could see that..."

"I could not see the castle before I came into your presence, and yet now I see it plain as day, because the veil has been lifted from my eyes."

"The *hat* was lifted from your eyes..." Danni explained.

"This is not the castle I seek, dutiful fairy, is this what you are trying to tell me?" and the Prince smiled.

Danni could not afford to let the opening go by. "This is *not* the castle you seek..." she got out.

"I should continue down the path?"

"You *should*! You should just continue down the path."

"Mayhap the true castle I seek is but a short league farther?"

"Mayhap less than that."

And with that, the Prince bowed deeply, stood erect, replaced his hat and remounted his steed. He looked fondly at Danni. "I thank you, disguised fairy," he proclaimed, "whose identity shall remain hidden... I thank you for your wisdom and shall now be off." And with a shout, he pushed his heels into the horse's sides and the animal bolted on, heading down the path with swift ease.

Doyle watched their progress for a moment: "What just happened?"

Danni all but shouted at him: "I keep telling you, there are lunatics around here!"

Doyle shook his head. "There's something wrong..." he began.

"Him thinking he should go up to that death trap, *that's* wrong!"

"No, Danni... it's something else... I know it..." said Doyle slowly.

"Hey Doyle..." Leo called, his attention now focused on the path ahead.

"Yes, Leo?"

"I see something shiny."

"What? Where?" said Doyle, looking in the direction of the cat's gaze.

"Just up a few yards... and to the right..."

"Me, too..." said Doyle, taking up the cart's handles, starting up the path, and then stopping again where the item was just visible. He knelt down, moved away some brush and pulled it up. It was a single metal glove from a suit of armour.

"I think this will fetch a pretty penny," Doyle said softly. And he laughed, as he took the glove to the back of the cart and placed it under the tarpaulin. And then with another laugh, "... this is *not* the castle you seek..."

He looked at Danni and Leo. Leo grinned. Danni looked down the path the Prince had ridden. Then Doyle abruptly said, "All right, all right, let's keep going down the path." And as they set off, he smiled at his friends, "Maybe it'll come to me as we go."

81

Chapter 12
Memory

As they trudged along, Doyle could not escape the fact that something was niggling at his memory. It all seemed so strange and yet familiar, the scene being played out, but with the wrong end of the stick coming up. He went over in his mind the day's events as well as those of the day before.

He knew the low rise he was travelling over yesterday had seemed strange, but sudden heavy fogs were normal in the hills around Solihull. The day had already been overcast when he had set out, but days like that were common enough, especially in the early spring. It had been unusually quiet, which was a mixed blessing because quiet was often followed by a bombing. That was a concern. He knew well enough to stay away from the cities, too over-run with people, buildings and smoke, so his outings concentrated to the south and east. He could be gone on his forays for several days at a time, sleeping out under the sky, and he had promised his mother not to go much farther south than Wooten Wawen since the bombings.

The Coventry bombing had been only four months ago and he could see the effect on his mother. He knew she was becoming more and more apprehensive of his leaving on his iron-finding excursions, but she did her best to jolly it up. They both knew that what little he found would bring in that something extra they would always need, for there was always something that needed mending, or that needed to be bought. She was not one to coddle or over-care. Even after his father had died, she pressed on because it was what needed doing, and for Doyle's sake primarily. They were open with one another, Doyle being very companionable and his mother also good company. Still, the concerns of everyday life during wartime managed to have many on edge, and Doyle knew he was quite lucky to have a mother like his. Her name, as he had told Leo, was Hope, and she did exemplify that without relying on it solely. She impressed upon him the value of hard work as well as that of well-earned play.

They had been relatively unscathed so far, in Solihull, aside from a rare scattering of bombings in the fields near Elmdon, the whole town appeared to be untouched. But never did they all think it could last. It seemed everyone was being hit, but the farther north of London, the rarer it seemed to be. The German planes seemed to want to get *back* over the channel and going too far north would certainly make doing that more of a rarity. Still, the planes could be getting better equipped. The Germans could be making them stronger, with larger fuselage for more petrol to attack farther inland. Warwickshire had all the appearances of safety, but since the attack on Coventry and the destruction of its Cathedral… Doyle only knew what he had heard from people of the town so he could not surmise what the rest of the country really felt, but there was an air of fear. Still, the radio broadcasts from Churchill and, of course, King George, did rally spirits greatly.

Doyle had a fierce sense of pride when he thought of his King and, of course, the Queen. People had encouraged her to send the princesses out of the country, for their own protection, but she had staunchly refused, saying that they would not go without her. She would not go without the King and he would not leave his people. This had been a grand assurance to all, that if there was fighting on the home front that needed doing, all could be assured that the Royal family would be there as well. Doyle's mother would often recite the poem the King quoted on the first Christmas broadcast of the war.

And Doyle himself had committed it to memory. "I said to the man who stood at the gate of the year: 'Give me a light that I may tread safely into the unknown.' And he replied: 'Go into the darkness and put your hand into the hand of God. That shall be to you better light and safer than a known way.' So I went forth and finding the hand of God, trod gladly into the night. And He led me towards the hills and the breaking of the day in the lone east. So heart, be still: What need our little life, Our human life to know, If God hath comprehension? In all the dizzy strife Of things both high and low, God hideth His intention.' And again, Doyle felt a sense of calm about his situation.

His mother had always loved words. Since he was small, she read to him: the Bible, Shakespeare, Chaucer, old poetry, just to let him hear the lilt of the language. The nursery rhymes and fairy tales that followed only encouraged his own desire to read for himself and he was a voracious reader. His father had also loved books so they had a fairly large and varied collection, save the one or two volumes that had to be sold to make ends meet. Even at times of war, a rare book was something for which the right buyer would pay a fair price. The book he kept with him was one from his childhood, but one he enjoyed going back to time and time again, as a reminder of a more carefree existence; but also, the resonance of the stories would hit him, sometimes in a different way, and he always came away from them feeling safe and secure. He knew he carried them because of that – for when he was away, it was nice to have the book to turn to and feel the security he would normally feel at home…

…the book!…

…he stopped walking so abruptly that Danni had to grab his collar to steady herself and Leo almost tumbled from his seat.

"Wha..?" the cat got out.

"Doyle!" Danni admonished and looked all around to see what ever could have made him stop so.

Doyle bent under the cart handles and went to the back of the cart, not even removing Danni, who clung tightly with both her paws as she watched the earth get closer to her and then felt the sickening rise of her stomach as she was brought back up to Doyle's standing position. She tried to say something but found it best to keep her mouth closed and try to calm her rising tummy.

Doyle pulled back a section of tarpaulin and found his book. Leo had regained his balance and composure and was stepping carefully along the side of the cart to where Doyle and Danni were, but he could see that the little mouse was a bit the worse for wear from the abrupt shifting.

"What's the matter, Doyle?" Leo asked, placing a paw on the lad's shoulder. "Step off, Danni, I think you'll thank me for it." The mouse weaved slightly but made it across Leo's leg and onto the cart. The stability felt grand and she leaned into the cat who took his leg back off the lad and now had Danni securely between his front legs and chest.

"The stories..." he muttered, turning the pages.

"Look," Leo tried to calm, "let's find a spot to camp, pull together some fire wood, make a little ring, maybe have a little dinner, then we can have a story..."

"That's not it, Leo," Doyle spoke softly but urgently. "Remember this morning? When Danni found the grapes?"

"Those *were* good grapes, Danni..." said Leo.

"I think there's more..." the mouse offered.

"There are," Doyle confirmed, still turning pages, "but do you remember how I had said there was a story about a fox and grapes?"

"Yeah," Leo remembered, looking down at Danni, "that could have been very dangerous, Danni..." the mouse burrowed into the cat's chest a little deeper. Had she done something wrong?

"Well, I couldn't find it and I still can't find it..." Doyle said, looking up. "I remember it though... it was how a fox saw some grapes and tried to jump for them and jump for them and once he realised he couldn't reach them, he gave up and huffed off, believing that they must be bad or sour..."

"That's what it said!" Danni blurted.

Doyle looked at her. "What?"

"It said they were probably awful, or sour, so I gave it one," said Danni, hesitantly. "It enjoyed the grape so much it wanted more, but I made it promise not to make a snap judgement about things, not to hate what it knows nothing about..."

Doyle's brows knitted together, "You did...?"

"It didn't agree right away, because it thought it would just be disappointed until I asked if it had never been disappointed before. Well, of course it had, and when I said how sometimes if you asked nicely you might get some help, it agreed and I sent a bunch of the grapes down to it. It was very grateful."

"That was very nice of you, Danni," Leo complimented. Doyle nodded, "It was... but now the fable is gone."

The two animals looked at the lad. "Fable?" Leo asked

"It means, literally, fabulous. They're morality stories, stories with morals. You know, where what has happened is summed up in a single sentence as a lesson. In this case it was…" he shut his eyes for a moment to think and chewed his lower lip. His blue eyes opened again as he recalled: "'It is easy to despise what you cannot attain.' You see, the fox was going to go away thinking that… but somehow when you intervened…"

"Well what that Fox was thinking was wrong!" Danni shot out defensively, "I mean, wasn't it? That Fox hadn't even tasted those grapes and was going to go off thinking those grapes were sour, maybe telling others… those grapes might have gone bad on the vine because of it…"

Doyle looked at the mouse calmly. "I know, Danni, I know what you're saying, and in any other situation I would applaud your determination to help the fox, in understanding and in letting it have some of the grapes. But this place…" he extended an arm to encompass all around them, "there is something very different about this place, not just for talking animals and oddly dressed men on horseback…"

The animals looked up at him. "I believe I *told* you this place is peculiar," Danni intoned.

Leo nodded. "Yep. She has been on about that…" the cat concurred.

Doyle shook his head. "There's a story about a slave who takes a thorn from a lion's paw, sound familiar?" They looked at him blankly.

"It's like you two!" Doyle implored, "and how you met!"

"Erm… sorry to break this to you, Doyle," Leo confided softly, "but I'm a cat."

"Yes, but your name also means lion and, well, you are big enough to be a lion cub…"

The cat nodded and smiled, "I have big bones."

"But I'm a mouse and I really don't think that can also mean 'slave', even where you come from."

"There is also a story about a lion letting a mouse go and the mouse comes back to help the lion."

"There really *are* a lot of stories where you come from, Doyle, that must keep you very busy…" Leo mused with a happy smile. "…they sound very entertaining…"

Doyle was beginning to get worked up now, he knew he had a point and was struggling to get to it. "And this prince…"

"*The* Prince," Leo corrected.

Doyle slammed one hand on the open book and exploded. "There are *more*, you know, really there are. But *this* one was heading to the castle of Briar Rose!"

Leo sniffed. "I've never heard of it, but then we don't seem to be big on names…"

"Exactly!" Doyle shouted. "Because fairy tales are typical. They need to be typical so people reading them can place *themselves* in them! They're… fantastical, but plausible! They are not real, but acceptable! They're food for hope…" at the mention of his mother's name, Doyle stopped, not knowing what to do next.

He looked down at the book and began to turn the pages again. "There was a story… 'Briar Rose, or the Sleeping Beauty'… about a Princess who is cursed by an evil fairy to die on her fifteenth birthday if she pricks her finger on a spinning wheel… but another fairy tries to soften the blow by saying that she would only sleep for a hundred years…"

Danni looked up at Leo. "Now *that* sounds like something that would happen around here…"

Doyle looked at the mouse. "Well, yes Danni, it would have. But I think you just sent the prince who was to wake her off on a different adventure!"

Danni's mouth dropped open and anger rose to the top of her head. "So I should have let that fellow go up to those thorns and just die?"

Doyle was still turning pages… he didn't remember so many being empty. There were blank spots mixed in with the nursery rhymes as well. One gap got his attention immediately. "Wait…" he whispered, "…'Hey Diddle Diddle'. Where's 'Hey, Diddle Diddle'?"

Leo eyed him with concern and spoke to Danni, "Was it too hot today, do you think that was it? I mean, I didn't notice it but…"

The lad looked at both of them, "You know: 'Hey, diddle diddle, The cat and the fiddle, The cow jumped over the moon… The little dog laughed to see such a sight And the dish ran away with the spoon.' It's gone."

Suddenly Danni felt light headed. Very light headed.

Doyle had turned his attention to the blank spaces again. "And so's 'Hickory Dickory Dock!'"

Danni's little mind was working feverishly: fiddle had sounded like diddle… so dock… must match up with… what?…

And then the word came to her: *Clock!* Her mouth felt very dry as she said it. "Something about a clock…"

Doyle nodded. "'… The mouse ran up the clock. The clock struck one, And down he run, Hickory dickory dock.' I know it, but it's not here," he said and slapped the book. "I learned it from here!"

The clock struck one. It only struck one. It never struck anything else but one.

"*She* run…" Danni corrected softly.

Doyle turned a look of confusion onto the mouse. "No, I'm sure it was *he* run…"

Danni shook her head vehemently, "She. She was my Mother." And then Danni slowly felt everything go dark around her.

Chapter 13
Out from the Shadows and into the Night

There were noises in the dark. Soft and distant and no need to really pay attention, but she felt she ought. *No one is too poor to pay attention.* Where did that come from? She knew that, but from where? Everything was moving and nothing was. It seemed as if waves were flowing over her, but she was certainly not wet, not floating. Were there voices? As much as a part of her wanted to care, she allowed herself to sink deeper into the dark
and hope the
quiet would
come back.
And she saw
her Mother's
face... the
trace of a
smile...
...and a
...sickening...
...thunk...
...!   on wood...

******

Danni startled awake so suddenly that Leo, sitting before her and gazing down at her, jumped straight up and let out a howl. Quickly trying to regain his composure upon landing he called out: "Whoa, yeah... Doyle! Her eyes are open!" and stared back at Danni. "That was frightening...well, that and you fainting." Doyle put down his small axe and set aside the piece of wood he had been chopping before rushing over to the pair.

Danni was looking all around her, peering into the dark. But then she realised that it wasn't like the dark from which she had just been roused. It was mostly just night-time, and she was not far from a lovely fire, dancing light and warmth falling over her. She found herself on a small pillow, sinking into it, actually, as it was of down feathers. Her mouth was still very dry and she looked up into the expectant faces of her friends.

"Do you want some water, Danni?" Doyle asked, bringing forward a small thimble.

"Why didn't I think of that?" Leo mused dejectedly. Danni let Doyle put the thimble to her mouth and she drank gratefully.

"Are you all right?" Doyle asked.

"Oh I should have asked that…" Leo admonished himself.

Doyle smiled over at the cat. "Leo, you have been watching over Danni as diligently as a soldier. I should think you would take much pride from that." Leo puffed slightly, looking away.

"You… you were watching over me…?" Danni finally spoke.

Leo jerked his great head back to the mouse, pleased that her first words back were to him. "Yes," he blurted, "Just like Doyle said… like a soldier…"

"If you were a pot, you would certainly *not* be boiling," Doyle smiled. The animals looked at him. His smile drooped a little. "It's… from an old adage… watched pot…, never boils…, never mind… how are you feeling, Danni?"

Leo poked her lightly with his paw and looked at Doyle. "She feels the same…"

Patiently, Doyle nodded. "Are you all right?" he asked again.

The little mouse took stock. She was still a little thirsty, she was beginning to feel hungry, but she also still felt a little dizzy. That might be the thing to go with first, she decided. "I'm a little dizzy still," she said softly.

Leo began to rock back and forth on his legs and looked anxiously at Doyle. "You said she'd be okay?" he almost whined.

Doyle gave Leo a scratch along his neck. "And she will be," he assured, looking back at Danni. "You've been unconscious for a fair bit of time," he told her, "we thought it might be best to just set up camp and tend to you."

"I thought it was tend to her and then set up camp?" Leo injected.

Doyle smiled at the cat gently. "Yes, Leo," he said, "I stand corrected." This made the cat sit up a little taller. Danni had to smile; while she didn't like worrying her friends, she certainly found Leo's concern endearing. "Do you remember what happened?"

Leo shook his head. "How can she remember what happened, she fainted?"

"I meant before she fainted, Leo…"

Danni admired how patient Doyle was with Leo. She would have lost her temper well before this last interjection, but Doyle was very calm and even. She liked that.

"Do you?" asked Doyle again.

Danni startled a bit, remembering she had been asked a question. "Oh, yes, sorry…"

"Don't scare her, Doyle…" Leo admonished.

"I'll try not to, Leo…"

"You were saying a poem…" she tried.

"A nursery rhyme…" Doyle corrected gently.

"Don't pick on her, Doyle..."

For Danni it was too much. "Please, Leo, I'm all right!" she said loudly. The cat sat back slightly. She could tell he was miffed. "I'm sorry, Leo... I'm not used to being so tended to..." and she tried a smile. This appeared to mollify the cat, who nodded almost sagely. She looked at Doyle. "Was that a for-real nursery rhyme? I mean, you didn't just make that up...?"

Doyle nodded. "It was for real..." he told her. "I've known that one since I was very little."

Danni looked away. It was all so very confusing. And the other one, the one about the farm cat, the cow and Arnie.

"Danni... do you remember what you said?"

She nodded. "My Mother used to run up the clock at the Farm... I never understood why, but she would always do it... twice a day... and then the clock would strike one and she'd come back down. But one day she didn't. They told me the clock struck her. She had always wanted me to do what she had done, always wanted me to come with her and learn... I just never saw the reason for it, you know? And she'd never tell me the reason... why it was so important, just that it was to be *done*... so I moved in with my cousins and never really dealt with that clock again. Until I jumped on the Farmer's Wife. Then the clock fell and shattered..." she stopped for a moment.

What had Arnie said...? "She didn't remember..." she whispered. "Who didn't remember?" asked Doyle and Leo together.

"Arnie, Arnie said the Farmer's Wife didn't remember the clock... how could she not remember the clock? She loved that thing."

"Arnie?" Doyle prodded.

"The little dog at the Farm! He helped me escape. That was your other rhyme, wasn't it? The little dog who laughed? Arnie laughs, Arnie loves to laugh... especially at Elsie, the cow. But the cat cannot play the fiddle to save his life, not really..." she paused. "Why are they gone?" she asked. "Are they really not in your book anymore?"

Doyle shook his head. "I looked through it pretty carefully," he said, "and I couldn't find them... or Sleeping Beauty... or Beauty and the Beast... I can't seem to find the Grasshopper and the Ants, either..."

Danni took in a small gasp, "Was... was that a fable...?"

"Yes. It was about a grasshopper who did nothing but sing and make music all summer so he had nothing to eat when winter came. And when he asked the ants for some of their grain they said that if he had worked as hard as they had, then he wouldn't need to come to them... 'The idle get what they deserve' was its moral."

Danni was afraid to speak. Jon hadn't been idle. He had worked very hard with his music and it had helped Celina's ants. She just pointed it out to Celina. A coincidence. It was a coincidence. These were stories Doyle had, they weren't real life. It was very strange, admittedly, but... Danni stopped.

Did she have something to do with all this...? She shook her head. "I don't understand..." she said, a petulant edge to her voice.

"Hey…" Doyle said gently. Danni looked up at him. He smiled. "I don't either. Maybe it's because of that fog I went through. Maybe it's some exciting mystery, and we three get to be Sherlock Holmes and figure it out."

"Mystery…?" Danni asked.

"Where's Sherlock's home?" Leo wanted to know.

With a smile, Doyle shook his head. "It's a person, Leo, a detective, someone who solves crimes… or mysteries, which means something beyond understanding, Danni, well, and other things, but that is the meaning I'm going with for this. Look… let's have something to eat and think about getting some rest." He knew Danni needed no more aggravation.

Something was going on with Danni and he knew that prodding might just seal her up altogether. If he was going to discover any more about her, he was going to have to go slowly and carefully. He liked Danni, and inwardly he knew that she knew more than she was letting on. But he was also considering the fact that she might know more than she even really understood. He would have to let her ponder all this.

"Could we hear a story?" Leo asked.

"Well…" Doyle looked at Danni. She seemed lost in her own thoughts.

"Please, please, please, please, please?" Leo begged. "I promise not to sit on The Book."

Doyle couldn't help but laugh. "We'll see how we all feel after we eat," and he went to the fire to tend to their meals.

Chapter 14
The Story of Justice Served

Once they had supped, and had cleaned and put away the dishes, Doyle removed his shoes and sat on his cushioned mat near the fire, his blanket to one side, his book on the other. And Leo sat beside the book, next to the down pillow where Danni was resting. Leo had not let her do much whilst Doyle prepared the supper, and had kept a careful eye on her as well to be certain, but now he looked expectantly at the book and then at Doyle. Doyle turned a gaze in Leo's direction and the cat smiled widely. Doyle's laughter was again deep and resonant. He looked at Danni.

"Do you mind if I read a story aloud?" he asked her. Leo's smile drooped slightly as he looked hopefully at Danni. She couldn't disappoint the cat.

"It might be best if you did," she said dryly. Leo smiled again and, with his paw, he pushed the book closer to Doyle.

"I've got it, Leo, I've got it," he chided the cat gently and scooped the book up, turning the pages until he was settled. He cleared his throat: "'The Goose Girl.'"

******

There was once an old Queen whose husband had been dead for many years, and she had a very beautiful daughter. When she grew up, she was betrothed to a Prince in a distant country. When the time came for the maiden to be sent into this distant country to be married, the old Queen packed up quantities of clothes and jewels, gold and silver, cups and ornaments. And in fact everything suitable to a royal outfit, for she loved her daughter very dearly.

She also sent a waiting-woman, a creature lovely of face, to travel with her and to put her daughter's hand into that of the bridegroom, for the Queen was unwell and too old to make the journey herself. Each woman had a horse. The waiting-woman's horse would also carry all the treasures. The Princess' horse was called Falada, and it could speak when spoken to.

When the hour of departure came, the old Queen went to her bedroom and with a sharp little knife cut her finger and made it bleed. Then she held a piece of white cambric under it and let three drops of blood fall on it. This cambric she gave to her daughter and said: "Dear child, take good care of this. It will stand you in good stead on your journey." For a parent's blood given in protection was a powerful talisman indeed.

Then they bade each other a sorrowful farewell. The Princess hid the piece of cambric in her bosom, mounted her horse and set out to her bridegroom's country.

When she had ridden for a time, the Princess became very thirsty and said to the waiting woman: "Please get down and fetch me some water from the stream in my golden cup. I must have something to drink."

"The cup is packed deep with all the treasures," the waiting woman countered. "If you are thirsty, dismount yourself, lie down by the water and drink." And she added, "I didn't choose to be your servant..."

So in her great thirst, the Princess dismounted and stooped down to the stream and drank, since she could not have her golden cup. The poor Princess said, "Alas!" And the drops of blood answered: "If your mother knew this, it would break her heart."

The royal bride was humble, so she said nothing but mounted her horse again. Then they rode several miles farther, but the day was warm, the sun was scorching, and the Princess was soon very thirsty again.

When they reached a river, she called out again to her waiting-woman. "Please get down and give me some water in my golden cup." She had forgotten all about the rude words which had been said to her earlier.

But the waiting woman answered back more haughtily than ever: "The cup has not risen from the bottom of the sack like cream in a pot of milk! If you want to drink, get the water for yourself. I won't be your servant."

Being very thirsty, the Princess dismounted and knelt by the flowing water. She was most distressed and now a bit fearful of her waiting woman. She cried, "Ah me!" and the drops of blood answered: "If your mother knew this, it would break her heart."

But while she stooped over the water to drink, the piece of cambric with the drops of blood on it fell out of her bosom and floated away in the stream, but she did not notice this in her great fear. The waiting woman, however, had seen it and rejoiced, for by losing the drops of blood, the Princess would now become weak and powerless. She dismounted her pack horse and when the Princess was about to mount Falada, the waiting woman said, "By rights, Falada belongs to me. This jade will do for you."

The poor Princess was obliged to give way. Then the waiting woman ordered her to take off her royal robes and to put on her own mean garments, and finally, she forced the Princess to swear before heaven that she would not tell a creature at the court what had taken place; that if she did not swear, she would be killed on the spot. Terrified, the Princess swore. But Falada saw all and marked it.

The waiting woman then put the real bride on the pack horse, mounted Falada, and they continued their journey.

There was great rejoicing when they arrived at the castle. The Prince hurried towards them and lifted the waiting woman from Falada, thinking she was his bride. She was led upstairs but the real Princess had to stay below.

The old King looked out of his window and saw the delicate, pretty little creature standing in the courtyard. So he went to the bridal apartment and asked the bride about her companion who was left standing in the courtyard, and wished to know who she was.

"A servant girl from the castle sent along with me for company. Do give the girl something to do to keep her from idling."

But the King had no work for her and could not think of anything. At last, he said: "I have a little lad who looks after the geese. She may help him."

The real bride was sent with the boy to look after the geese.

But the false bride had more things to tend to and she said to the Prince, smiling prettily, "Dear, I pray you, do me a favour."

He answered, "Anything I will gladly do."

"Let the blacksmith be called to cut off the head of the horse I rode. It was beastly to me on the way to you and angered me so." The false bride was afraid that the horse might speak of her treatment to the real Princess, so she pleaded her case most believably to the Prince so that it was settled and decided that the faithful Falada had to die.

When this came to the ear of the real Princess, knowing she could not stop what the false bride had asked without breaking her oath, she promised the blacksmith a piece of gold if he would do her a slight service. There was a great dark gateway in the town, through which she had to pass every morning and evening while tending the geese. "Would he place Falada's head in the gateway so that she might see him as she passed?"

******

"What?" Danni squeaked. "No really, what? Is that what it actually says?" She clambered off the pillow and onto Doyle's arm to look at the book for herself. "Where does it say that?"

"But Danni... you don't read..." said Doyle, as Leo adjusted his head onto Doyle's knee, and soaked up all the commotion.

The mouse turned a glare up to the lad. "There's no better time to learn than the present. So, where does it say that?" And Doyle showed her the section, reading it again carefully, placing his finger under each word. "What's that squiggle at the end? Is that a word?"

"It's a question mark, Danni, to let you know it's a question. Like this dot, is a full stop, it lets you know when you've reached the end of a sentence. And this is an exclamation mark, when something being said has much meaning to it, it's a method of showing excitement, or anger or joy."

"Well then I'll be using a bunch of those!" she exclaimed. "How could she do that to her horse? Her horse was the only one who could fix things! Her horse knows the truth!"

Doyle was pleased at how well she was following the story, and even happier that it seemed to be one she didn't know. He saw how carefully she studied the words as he spoke and pointed them out. He gave a slight nod though, as this part had always bothered him when his mother read it to him, but he remembered what she had told him and after finishing the story how it had made sense.

He told Danni: "Sometimes in a story a sacrifice needs to be made so the truth really can be found out. Sometimes in life, we need to sacrifice something to really grow."

The little mouse snorted, "That doesn't make sense..."

"Let me continue and I think it will."

Danni settled on Doyle's arm. "Fine," she grudgingly conceded. "But I'm sitting right here and I'll be watching!" And she turned her attention to the letters before her, willing them to make sense in her mind. She was engrossed by the image of the real Princess kneeling to drink, with the doomed Falada beside her, and the waiting-woman watching imperiously from her jade. Danni forced herself to concentrate on the letters. She poked Doyle's arm. "Go on!" He pointed to where they were starting and, placing his finger beneath each word, continued to read.

******

The blacksmith promised to do what she wished, and when the horse's head was cut off, he hung it up in the dark gateway. In the early morning, when she and the little lad went through the gateway, she said in passing, "Alas, dear Falada, there thou hangest." And the head answered: "Alas! Queen's daughter, there thou goest. If thy mother knew thy fate, her heart would break with grief so great."

They passed on out of the town and right into the fields with the geese. When they reached the meadow, the Princess sat down on the grass and let down her hair. It shone like the night sky, the sun shining out stars upon it and when the little lad saw it, he was so delighted he wanted to pluck some out. But the Princess called to the wind to catch the lad's hat and set it flying so that he would have to scramble for it until she could put her hair back up properly. And sure enough, a strong wind sprang up and blew away the lad's hat, always just out of his reach until the Princess had finished combing her hair and had put it back up again so that he could not get a single strand. This made him very sulky and he would not say another word to her. And they tended the geese till evening when they went home.

Next morning when they passed under the gateway, the Princess said again, "Alas, dear Falada, there thou hangest." And Falada answered again: "Alas! Queen's daughter, there thou goest, if thy mother knew thy fate, her heart would break with grief so great."

And again, when they reached the meadows the Princess undid her hair and began combing it. When the lad saw this, he ran to pluck some out but she again called to the wind to catch the lad's hat and set it to sailing. Sure enough, the wind tossed his hat and he went far over the meadows after it, returning to the Princess after her hair was all put back again and he was not able to pull out a single strand. And they tended the geese till the evening.

When they got home, the lad went to the King and bade him not to make him tend the geese with that Goose Girl.

"Why not?" the King asked.

"She vexes me every day!" And the old King ordered him to tell what she did to vex him. So the lad spoke freely of passing under the dark gateway with the geese and how the Goose Girl would speak to the horse's head hanging on the wall and how the head would answer her. He continued to tell the King of what had happened in the meadow, and how his hat would mysteriously take flight. The old King listened intently then ordered the lad to go out with the Goose Girl one more time and to let all transpire as it had.

The next day, the King placed himself behind the dark gateway and heard the Goose Girl speaking to Falada's head and heard the horse's response. He also followed her out into the field and hid behind a bush. And with his own eyes he saw the Goose Girl and the lad driving the geese into the meadow. Then after a time, he saw the girl let down her hair, which danced like moonbeams in the sun. And before the lad could get too near, the girl called to the wind to help her and off went the lad's hat so he had to run after it. The old King observed how she did comb her hair and put it back up before the lad had returned. There upon he went away unnoticed, and in the evening when the Goose Girl came home, he called her privately to a room and asked why she had done all those things. Frightened that she had been observed, but knowing well her behaviour to the King she spoke:

"I may not tell you that, nor may I tell any creature, for I have sworn under the open sky. And if I had not done so, I should have lost my life."

He pressed her sorely and gave her no peace, but he could get nothing out of her. Then he said: "If you won't tell me, then tell your sorrows to the iron stove there." And he went away. She crept up to the stove after making certain she was alone and began to weep and lament, unburdening her heart to it and said; "Here I am, forsaken by all the world and yet, I am a Princess. A false waiting woman brought me to such a pass that I had to take off my royal robes. Then she took my place with my bridegroom while I have to do mean service as a goose girl. If my mother knew it, it would break her heart."

The old King had gone to the room beside and stood by the pipes of the stove and heard all that she had said. Then he came back and told her to go away from the stove. He caused royal robes to be put upon her and her beauty was a marvel. The old King called his son and told him he had a false bride – she was only a waiting woman, but the true bride was here, the so-called Goose Girl.

The young Prince was charmed with her youth and beauty and grateful for the wedding was only two days away. The next day, a great banquet was prepared to which all the courtiers and good friends were bidden. The bridegroom sat at the head of the table with the false bride on one side and the true Princess on the other, but the false bride was dazzled by the other's beauty and brilliant apparel and did not recognise her.

When they had eaten and drunk and were all very merry, the old King put a question to the waiting woman: "What does a person deserve who deceives his master?" The false bride answered: "No better than this: he must be put stark naked into a barrel stuck with nails, and be dragged along by two white horses from street to street till he is dead."

"Then that is your own doom," said the King, "and the judgement shall be carried out!"

When the sentence was fulfilled, the young Prince married the true bride, and they ruled their kingdom together in peace and happiness.

******

Doyle let the book close gently. He could tell from Leo's contented purring that he was asleep. Danni, however, hadn't moved.

"Danni?" Doyle called. The mouse turned to look up at him. There were tears in her soft brown eyes. "Oh Danni…" Doyle started, concerned.

"That was beautiful," she said.

"What was, Danni?"

"You were right. There was nothing she could have done to save Falada, but Falada *did* end up helping her. The poor girl… she was only doing what she was told… she made a vow and she kept it. I don't think I could have done that… how horrible for her, how degrading… all because she had been raised to be kind and humble and, oh, that horrible woman! She got what she deserved all right! And handed it down herself! What a wise King to know she would fall for that," she stopped and looked up at Doyle. "Thank you, Doyle," she said with such earnestness, such sincerity that the lad was almost moved to tears himself. He smiled down at her.

"You're welcome, Danni," he said softly, putting the book down. "Now maybe we should take Leo's lead here and get some rest? You keep the pillow." He moved his arm so she could easily jump onto the downy thing. Then, cautiously, he slid to lie down so as not to disturb Leo. Taking his blanket, he balled it up loosely and rested his head on it. Danni waited until he was finished with this before she circled once, twice, thrice, and then curled up, and settled with her nose tucked under her front paws. She sighed contentedly and drifted off to sleep.

Chapter 15
Step Forward, Step Back and
All Tumble Down

Leo could feel warmth on his belly before he became aware of anything else. It felt good and sunshiny and he opened his eyes slowly to gaze upside-down at Doyle working at the fire ring. As he was about to smile, the upside-down shape of Danni appeared directly in his line of vision, staring at him with eager eyes.

"You're awake!" she called and Leo turned over quickly, more from the start than any eagerness to wake up. "Doyle's got some eggs!" she announced. "I don't really like them, but we thought you might, he's putting some cheese on them as well, you do like eggs, don't you Leo?" Someone was well rested, he thought, and whilst he felt relatively caught-up on his own sleep, he certainly had no place for the kind of exuberance Danni seemed to be displaying.

"Eggs are good…" Leo replied and set to his morning clean.

"Leo…" Danni began.

"Yes, Danni?" Leo got out between licks.

"Why do you clean so often?" The cat stopped mid-lick and stared at the mouse. This kind of inquisition was not usual.

"You are Danni, right?" She smiled at him.

"Of course I am," she replied.

"Well… I think you clean fairly often as well, don't you?" he tried. "I don't think I'm inordinately clean-conscious… but I do like to be tidy… hairs in place and all…" and he gave a lopsided grin. The mouse nodded.

"I have food if you're hungry," Doyle called to them. Leo looked at the fur remaining to be sorted. It would have to wait. His belly growled as he breathed in the smell of the food and he moved over by the fire ring. Doyle had already placed Leo's plate on the ground and the cat sat and pondered it for a bit. This was nice. It hadn't been this consistently nice for some time. Not since the Dame. What a kind soul. Wonderful woman. He looked over at Danni, contenting herself with a bit of cheese and carrot, and Doyle, tucking in hungrily at his plate. Then Leo took up a bite of food himself. Oh, yes, Doyle was a bit of all right as a cook.

"Danni, what do you think about what I said before?" Leo asked. Danni looked up suddenly, some bits of cheese still on her whiskers. She quickly slid them off and into her mouth as she considered the question.

"You've said much, Leo, what in particular are you talking about?"

"Things happening for a reason... forks in the road..." Danni thought for a moment, chewing on a bit of carrot.

"I'm still not quite certain about it all, Leo, truthfully," she admitted, "but I can see that it means much to you... and I am not going to doubt things that have happened to you to make you feel this way." Leo nodded as he ate more of his egg and cheese. He would have to be certain to have his toilet far away from the group today. Maybe tomorrow, as well.

"After I came back from the island, and that horrible boat trip, a wonderful thing happened."

Danni looked at the cat, putting down her food. She knew this was what he had promised and she didn't want to miss a thing.

"I was lying there on this beach... the waves coming in and out and I really didn't have the strength to move, when a pair of the most gentle hands I have ever known scooped me up and held me to a soft, warm body. A towel was wrapped around me and slowly, I began to feel warm and toasty and more like myself. I was still very groggy, mind you, and the saltwater of the ocean was all over me, I was so thirsty, but I found a saucer before me with fresh water, and oh it was so cool and refreshing, and there were little tit bits and sweet meats for me to eat... I began to think I had died and was imagining all this... when I saw her face."

"Her...?" Danni was enthralled.

"She was old... but she was well-off... she had a lovely home, near the sea shore, but not so near that it was uncomfortable, you know? I was really quite lucky that she had found me, she didn't go down to the seashore that often anymore – she herself had said that something drew here there that day. And people would come by asking her aid – she was very sensible she was – and would help them all recognise that they could fix their problems fairly well on their own if they just looked inside themselves... she was something like you, Danni," (the mouse felt some pride in this) "so people saw me, and knew she had taken me in, and they were kind, almost as kind as she. After a time, I moved on, mind you, she had other cats, they would come and go, but people always seemed to know which ones had been with her... people seemed to know me wherever I went..." and he grew wistful for a moment.

"They would see me and ask, 'Is that the Dame's cat?' and someone would tell them yes, because as I said, Danni, I didn't want to say much to people, I mean, I saw what it was like for my lady, she was forever listening and helping. But because of her, I was well tended to, and I believe all the suffering I'd had, well, the Dame made up for it. She brought me back and gave me luck, and let me deal with people again. I mean, I didn't want to be owned, mind you, I wasn't going to go off with a human unless I really wanted to, and, well, until recently, I wasn't really meeting up with any humans I wanted to spend more than a few minutes with…" he looked up at Doyle, who had been watching the cat and listening intently.

Doyle smiled at him. Leo returned the smile. "There is always something, Danni…" continued Leo. "No matter how bad things get… I just believe that there is always something… better."

Danni looked at her carrot. Everything was going around in her head, not in the dizzying way it had yesterday, but it was shifting, that she was certain of. "Is that Faith…?" she asked quietly.

Both Doyle and Leo looked at the mouse. They could tell this was something big for her, they both sensed that this was something she had been holding in deep and they both hesitated so they could respond as thoughtfully. Leo looked over at Doyle, sensing the lad might have a better turn of phrase. Doyle saw the look in the cat's eye and took in a breath.

"Faith means many things, Danni… but I guess a simple definition is… complete trust." Danni thought about that. Leap of faith, her Mother had said… a leap of complete trust. That made sense.

Leo continued: "I've always thought of it as a firm belief in something for which there is no proof."

"A sincerity of intentions," Doyle injected.

"A duty to one's promises," Leo added. Danni let the words fall over her and she considered them all. One aspect bothered her.

"But how could your mother be named Faith?" she asked Leo. "And yours be called Hope?" Doyle smiled at her.

"Well, I've already said how Leo also means lion… some words mean other things… and sometimes people – or animals – might use them for naming their children." This puzzled Danni.

"Then, what does Doyle mean?" The lad grinned at her.

"Well, it certainly doesn't mean anything as wonderful as Hope or Faith… I'm not sure why my parents named me that, Danni… but I like my name, do you like yours?"

"Well, yes, it's my name. I don't think it means anything else, but I like it fine, she said quickly. She had never really considered it, actually, never really occupied her time… or had it? Not wanting to dwell there, as it was making her feel uncomfortable, and after all Leo had said, and how they both had explained things so carefully to her, it seemed best to let it go… for now.

Danni gave herself a shake and smiled up at her friends. "Shouldn't we get cleaned up and started?" she asked. Doyle gave a nod and gathered up the plates, placing them and his little pan in the bucket. Danni had finished her cheese and moved her carrot onto the piece of muslin Doyle used to wrap it up with. Leo went back to the task of cleaning himself.

******

Both Danni and Doyle were pretty much finished with their work, and Leo with his fur, when they heard it. A soft whistling down the path up which they had come. Doyle had just packed the last thing into the cart and took Danni up onto his shoulder. Leo made a swift leap onto his little seat.

He was a tall man, maybe not much taller than Doyle, but he was slender and that gave the appearance of greater height. He was by no means skinny, but he was certainly not brawny. His hair was very dark, almost black, and long, the crown section held in the back by a band so that the rest of his hair was free and wavy, more so than Doyle's, and tumbled just past his shoulders. He had a tall, crooked stick that he seemed to be using as he walked, not relying on, but something he might need on more rough terrain. He was simply dressed, with a large pack on his back, some of his gear dangling from it, and when he saw the cart he stopped. A broad smile crossed his lips, and his dark eyes crinkled with the size of it. He had a hat in his hand, it appeared he had just been adjusting it to place back on his head, but he kept it off. His smile had a crooked quality to it, and he tilted his head slightly as he looked Doyle over.

"Hello," he greeted simply, no pretension, no rush, a faint melody in his lilt. "I don't usually see many people on this path, not this early."

Doyle paused for a moment. "We were just heading off," he admitted.

The man looked about by the cart. "We?" he asked, his smile not wavering, it's crooked quality still there. He made no attempt to close the distance between them.

Again, Doyle hesitated. "My friends and I," he indicated Leo with one hand and a slight nod to Danni on his shoulder.

"Oh, of course," the man replied as if it were the most natural thing in the world. "Nothing better than animals for friends. I'd like to have a cat and mouse as company. That would pass the time. My name's Simon," he said, again simply, no pretence to his tone. He seemed a foot –traveller, perhaps a seller of small goods, but there was certainly something about him – and Doyle could not for the life of him tell if it was good or ill. He went for caution.

"I'm heading to town," Simon announced, "I hear there's a fayre on the way, a real Festival… are you heading that way?" and with that, he took a few small steps towards the group.

"To town, sir, yes," Doyle replied.

"Festival?" Leo piped. Danni turned to the cat and shushed him. Leo looked away, pretending to be interested in a passing butterfly. Still the man smiled, and shook his cocked head amiably.

"Seems one of you might be interested in…" and he stopped, fixing his gaze on the mouse, his smile vanishing. The mouse was eyeing him suspiciously and he knew that look. "Danni?" he whispered. The mouse's eyes widened. "Danni, is it you?" he asked louder.

Doyle took a protective step back making it easier for Danni to jump to Leo should she choose to. The mouse was aware of this but she couldn't help staring at the man. Words and phrases came out at her... clever... sensible... quite the logical mind...the clock... he fixed the clock...

"You fixed the clock..." she said softly.

The smile came back to Simon's face. "You clever, clever thing," he called out. "You remember, of course you remember, smart thing like you, how could you forget? What are you doing out here?" and he stepped a little closer.

"Simon...?" she tried. And flashes came to her. His face, looking down at her, gently picking her up to place her on top of the clock as he worked, how the bell made the whole casing shudder. Listening to her as she complained about this or the other at the Farm, talking to her about other things he had seen around the countryside, and sharing her opinions, encouraging her opinions... her Mother had been none too pleased, but it had kept Danni occupied. And he had talked about taking her with him when he left, a sensible mouse like her would be an amazing companion, but her Mother wouldn't let her. And he left, promising to come back and visit, but then her Mother died and she was left with her cousins and a clock she couldn't be bothered with. "You never came back..." she breathed.

He nodded, looking deeply troubled. "I know, I know, it was hard to get back your way... but I was trying to this time..."

"Did you stop at the Farm?" Danni asked apprehensively – did he know?

He nodded. "And the commotion there! I'm sorry for your loss, Danni, I didn't know about your mom, I'm very sorry..."

"It was just after you left... I kept expecting you to come back, but..." she told him and again he nodded gently. "Did she tell you?"

"Who?"

"The Farmer's Wife?"

"That you were the cause for her arm being in a sling and a chunk of her back being torn up? Yes she did. I knew you must have had your reasons though."

"She killed my cousins," Danni explained.

Simon nodded again. "I heard. But you know, three more mice turned up not a day after you left!"

"Blind?" Danni was incredulous.

"As bats. And the strangest thing... the clock is gone and she doesn't even remember it!" Danni looked up at Doyle for a moment, but the lad was still cautiously studying the newcomer.

Simon went on, "Henry said she'd hit her head as well, but he said once he cleaned up the mess, she didn't even mention it! Just went on about you jumping her and then taking off across the field, the little dog chasing you."

Danni shook her head. "No, no, Arnie was helping me! I was on his back! I told him what had happened and he made sure I got away."

Simon nodded. "I thought as much... and look at you, here you are!"

Danni nodded and smiled. "This is Doyle," she said, patting his neck.

The lad gave a smile now and put out his hand. Simon took it in his own and gave it a firm shake. "Pleasure, Doyle," he said genuinely. Doyle gave a slight nod.

"And that's Leo," Danni introduced, "I'm sorry I shushed you, Leo." This did not completely mollify the cat and he eyed Simon lazily.

"Pleasure, Leo, what a beautiful coat of fur you have," he complimented, perking the cat slightly. "And goodness... your eyes are the colour of gold nuggets." Leo was hooked.

"Thank you," Leo replied as if he heard it all the time.

"Was everything all right when you were at the Farm?" Danni asked.

"Well aside from the clock and you being gone, all seemed right as rain." and he stopped himself. He looked at Doyle seriously. "I'm sorry, son, am I keeping you? I certainly don't want to be in the way of your travels..."

"Well, we were about to start off, sir..."

"You'll walk with us, won't you Simon?" Danni invited. "You don't mind, do you, Doyle? I haven't seen him in ever so long," she looked up at him with her pleading brown eyes and Doyle could only nod.

"You're sure?" Simon asked, "Maybe you'll let me pull your load every now and then? I don't want to be in the way."

"That would be nice, sir," Doyle replied. "I have it for now."

"This is so strange," Danni sighed. "We were talking about Faith and Hope and I was really thinking about it and... you came. What do you think, Leo, she called back to the cat, "is that what you might call a 'sign'?"

"You just might," the cat admitted. It certainly was an odd turn of events and, it seemed, a very pleasurable one for Danni. And better than the Prince fellow. At least, this man was dressed sensibly.

"And I'm sure you've had your fair share of adventures?" Simon asked.

Danni nodded. "Meeting Leo was quite an adventure," and she told Simon about her encounter with Leo and how they had met Doyle. She talked about meeting Jon and Celina, and the fox, and her encounter with The Prince.

Simon was shaking his head in disbelief. "Some things never change, eh?" he muttered. "Some of these creatures just don't have the sense that God gave a fly." And Danni nodded. Simon understood her chagrin, her annoyance. "Common sense, right Danni?" Again the mouse nodded. "Did you hear about that old woman?" Simon asked.

Danni shook her head. He continued, "Who swallowed a fly?"

"I thought it was a spider," Leo tried.

Simon called back to the cat, "That was to catch the fly."

"Why eat it to begin with?" Danni exploded. "I'm telling you, with people like that no one is safe! What an example."

"Oh you don't have to tell me," Simon chimed in.

"I mean, what if children hear about this? They might try it themselves... What happened to her?" she asked.

Simon said: "She died, of course."

"Well I hope that's an end to it," Danni pronounced.

Simon let out a laugh, short and staccato. Leo cocked his head. "I doubt that." Simon continued, "It would take much, much more to put an end to all of this," he said, swinging his arm for emphasis.

Doyle marked this, but said nothing. They rounded a bend in the path and stopped. From their vantage point they could see an open field with tents in the distance, flags flapping in the wind atop them. There were many other small carts and a roped off enclosure of sorts, with bench seats around sections and to one side there were various kinds of animals in stalls, paddocks and pens.

"Is that it?" Leo asked, his golden eyes wide. "The Festival?"

"Sure looks like it," Simon smiled. "Still a bit of a ways off. I'll need to stop off there. I've been told about a few people I know who set up down there. Gonna see if they need any repair work… you never know what kind of work you might find in that sort of surroundings – things always have a way of breaking."

"Especially if people don't tend to them properly," Doyle agreed.

"Yes," Simon drawled, looking out over the field. He started walking again and Doyle fell in beside him. Danni had scurried to Doyle's other shoulder to get another look at the tents and carts, the flags flying in the breeze. The tents were of many different colours, as were the flags. Danni could not recall seeing so many different colours and all in one place. It was remarkable.

"Will we be able to stop there?" she asked Doyle. He looked at her fondly. "If you'd like, Danni."

******

And two children tumbled down the small hillside into the path before them.

Simon jumped ahead of Doyle, who was already pulling the cart to a halt; Danni grabbed onto the collar of his shirt to avoid tumbling to the ground but Leo almost lost his footing on the seat, grabbing onto the wood with his front claws fully extended, his back ones grabbing futilely at the air. Doyle quickly helped to right him then turned to see Simon admonishing the children. They were two scruffy things, a boy and girl, small, with round faces and matching blue eyes and blond hair, both dressed for what appeared like more than a day out.

"Hey, hey, hey, here now! People are walking here!" Simon bellowed out forcefully.

The two children righted themselves, each in turn helping the other so it was barely a moment before they stood side by side, staring solemnly up at the others.

Looking in their faces, Doyle could see they were not much more than eight, maybe ten if they were small for their ages, but he could also see that they were brother and sister, so close in looks were they.

"We're all right, Simon," Doyle said firmly. "But they look a bit knocked about..." He moved slowly towards the children with a smile. Simon let out a small sigh and took a step back. "It's all right," Doyle comforted. "Are you both okay?" The boy pointed to the girl.

"She said ve should go..." he announced.

The girl turned a stare at her brother as her mouth dropped open. "Za house vas talking!" she called back to him.

"It vasn't za house, ve vere *eating* za house."

Doyle took a small step back. Were these German children? How had they gotten there and where were their parents? He shook his head slightly, this could be very bad, he thought. "Where are your parents?" he asked a little stiffly.

Both children stopped at this, turning to look up at Doyle, their blue eyes filled with tears. "Zey left us out here," the boy said as the girl released a pent-up sob. The boy put his arm around his sister which calmed her a little. "Zis is za second time..."

"What?" Doyle asked.

The two children nodded. "It vas our step mutter..." the boy continued. "Papa vould not do zis on his own. I vas able to get us back za first time, I had a lot of little stones zat I would put down und ven za moon rose ve vere able to follow zem back home. But za second time..."

"He used bread crumbs," his sister interjected miserably.

He shrugged his little shoulders. "It vas all I had, zey took us out so suddenly..."

Doyle blinked. "What are your names?" he asked quietly, knowing the answer. The boy stood a little taller. "I am Hansel und zis is my sister, Gretel."

"Of course you are," Doyle said before he could think.

"Ve vere hungry!" Gretel cried out, "und ven ve saw za house..." her voice faltered.

"It vas made of bread und cake und za vindows vere spun sugar..." Hansel told him, his eyes wide at the memory. "But she said she heard it talk... und she moved away so suddenly, I ran after her und zen ve both fell... here..."

His sister looked up into Doyle's face. "It vas talking about us nibbling at za house!" she cried. "I vas scared."

"And that's the most sensible thing so far!" Danni called out.

The children looked at Danni and their mouths dropped open simultaneously. "A magic mouse..." they said together in abject awe.

Danni shook her head. "No. But if it helps you, fine. What are you thinking, eating a house?"

They looked at each other. "Ve vere hungry...?" they tried.

"So you're going to fill up on sugar? You need some real food! And let me tell you, if a house starts talking to me, I go. And I go fast. Who knows? It could be some sort of trap!"

The children gasped and held each other. "But vere do ve go? Vat do ve do?" they asked in unison.

Simon stepped forward. He held out his hand and spoke gently. "Here, "he said, "it's a sixpence..." To Doyle he murmured, "I found it by a stile a few miles back," and to the children he continued, "there's a fayre down the road... you can probably get something good to eat and maybe ask someone to help you find your father..."

They looked at the money in his hand. "It's a little crooked, but it's still good," he told them gently, ever so gently.

Hansel took it up in his hand and looked at it as if he had never seen so much, Gretel did the same. "Maybe if ve get somesing ve can take back, step-mama von't be angry vis us...?" he said to his sister.

"Maybe ve vill be better on our own..." she replied and nudged him, looking up at Simon. They both said: "Sank you", and Hansel gave a little bow while Gretel gave a small curtsy. They turned, took each other's hand, and skipped down the path.

******

Doyle stared after them, watching until they disappeared from view.

"Very rational, Danni!" Simon told the mouse. "And very well put... you've really become quite a convincing speaker," he praised. "You always had such intelligent opinions, but it seems you have grown into expressing them so much better!"

The mouse smiled shyly. It was so nice to hear the compliments, and then the way Simon beamed at her, she felt very good indeed. But she could sense Doyle's hesitation. "What's the matter, Doyle?" she asked.

His brows were furrowed and his mouth was set in a firm line. He was starting: "They were..." when Simon interrupted him: "Lost and a little silly," he finished.

Then Simon added: "Seemed like they could become smart kids, I mean, that was pretty bright, using pebbles as a means to find their way home... seems they have a bit more growing up to do though..." and he smiled over at Doyle. "Shall we press on?"

Doyle looked at the man. His face was alight with a smile, but there was something in his demeanour that told Doyle not to say anything else. And he listened to that. With a nod, he took up the handles of his cart and started.

"Danni?" Simon asked, "Would you like to ride on my shoulders for a bit? It would certainly make me happy?"

The little mouse smiled, her eyes as wide as they could be. "Oh yes!" she cried, stepping back and forth on her paws in anticipation as Simon put his hand close to Doyle's shoulder so she could jump onto it. Suddenly she turned to Doyle. "It *is* all right, Doyle, you don't mind?"

Doyle looked at Simon's hand. It was long and slender, not the real hands of a worker, and they were almost delicate. He could see they had some wear marks, callouses and a scar or two, but he was struck by the delicacy of them. His mother had said of his own hands that they were like those of a pianist, but Simon's were certainly different, and he couldn't deny they were more delicate.

He looked at Danni, staring imploringly at him and he smiled. "Of course not, Danni, you haven't seen your friend in quite a while." The little mouse just about flipped with joy as Simon brought his hand to the opposite shoulder and Danni alighted there.

Yes, Doyle thought again. There certainly was something about the man. And Doyle didn't like it at all.

Chapter 16
Into the Corners We Go

Of course, Simon had known it was Danni. He had found them before they had even awakened, having moved almost non-stop since leaving the farm, and stayed back far enough so as to make his appearance seem serendipitous. Still, he had to play his cards close to the vest, he needed to be certain she would remember him and that he could win her over again. That she hadn't really forgotten him was a blessing and he was grateful not to have to jar her memory, especially in front of the others. The others. That was the one rub. But it was only a boy and a cat – Simon felt fairly secure in being able to overcome that obstacle. After all, she had just met them and he had a history with the mouse. The boy looked different, though. As if he didn't quite fit in with everything around him and that had Simon puzzled, but not too concerned. After all, look at what she had done since leaving the farm! Dealing with the Grasshopper and the Ants, the Fox and the Grapes, Sleeping Beauty's Prince and now Hansel and Gretel.

She was amazing in her handling of it all, how simply and directly, letting logic dictate but also relying on the fact that she was an animal. There was something about the logic coming from a mouse, tiny but so assured, that inspired others to think about what they were doing and truly consider her way as being better. He could tell there were other things she was not saying, but he knew she would tell him when the time was right and she felt comfortable. Still, it all seemed even easier than he could have hoped, and he chastised himself for not coming back sooner. But he knew that his time away had only given Danni a better perspective on everything: the seeds had been planted for her displeasure with life here, and her logical mind could not accept, nor empathise, with the people and creatures around her. He had hoped, and now that he was back -- he was delighted to see how well those seeds had grown.

He hadn't wanted to go, but he felt called, like someone being called from a deep sleep, and he knew he had to leave the place, the odd little fairytale land he had stumbled upon which he had never believed existed, and once he had found it, had set about in a single-minded determination to eradicate it totally.

In actuality, this place was a lie – this place and what it represented. He was certain that what remained was only still there because of die-hard hold-ons that couldn't come to grips with the fact that even with a politically correct wash thrown on them, fairytales were beyond outdated. They were alive only so cartoons could be made of them; giving false hope to little girls and boys.

They were pie-in-the-sky fantasies designed to keep children as children, fearful and uncertain, never growing up. He had known that for as long as he could remember, even though he hadn't been exposed to them as a child the way some had – no, but he saw the way children of his peer group dealt with them. Fearful and apprehensive of dark shadows and monsters; never really knowing that the worst monsters were *always* lying there inside themselves. And of growing older to become tormentors, like the evil step-brothers and step-sisters who would go to untold lengths to make sure the simple, sweet innocent stayed in his or her place in the background. He saw how it really was: that people grew to hate. To discourage. To knock down.

And he knew that many of these people were that way because they had believed in these stories and these *stories* had let them down. There was no strong prince. There was no pliant princess. And if he could make them gone, eradicate them, make the ideal of them gone, eradicated the memory of them, how much better things would be. Not watered-down versions, cleaned up so the violence was out of view, so the fear was swept away… If they were gone altogether, if they were wiped clear and erased from where they began, the Great Eradication!, how much better, how much easier, simpler even, he could make it for others.

Since he began, he had managed to move some along so that now several were missing, but he had remembered them; meeting up with them and moving them into another direction, so that when he looked in his book, they were gone. The stories were gone. And when he came back, he saw that no one remembered them anymore, though historians claimed "some" stories were lost to the annals of time. He knew. He knew they were gone because he had worked it, he had made it so. But there were still more, and he knew that with Danni's help, he could send it all spinning out of control so that the fairytale people would be deep into their own concerns and not into those of their respective fairytale, which just might keep them from ever really surfacing anywhere again. There was a chance, and he had to take it.

He had to be cautious. The cat was a side-issue. Obviously from a lesser known tale that was on the verge of being forgotten or he would still be where he was needed and not with Danni. The boy was just a boy, but looking at him Simon could tell he was not from this place. Somehow he, too, had managed to find a way here, but Simon wasn't sure to what purpose. If it was akin to his own, all the better. If it wasn't, Simon knew he would have to be calculating and subtle and not give himself away. Sowing the seeds of discord and separating Danni from them would be his last choice – that could draw more attention than needed – but separating them was what he might need to do, regardless of the boy's business here. He knew he did not have a great deal of time. It was always erratic, his coming back, he knew how to get here, but sometimes he was thrown back to his own place before he could really finish things, so he knew he had to work efficiently. He wasn't certain he would have another opportunity and that uncertainty led him to feel that he needed to complete all his efforts this time around.

Mentally he ticked off what he knew. Hey, Diddle Diddle was gone. Hickory Dickory. With the bucket mended he hoped that would not be something he would have to endure again. His book showed that the Grasshopper and the Ants was out, as was the Fox and the Grapes. The Sleeping Beauty seemed to be gone, Danni had seen to that, but he would have to be certain. And now Hansel and Gretel. But he had noticed that Beauty and the Beast seemed to be missing. Danni had said nothing about that. Maybe it was the boy. Or maybe Danni was holding something back. Either way, he would find out. It wouldn't be hard.

******

The little mouse was thrilled beyond words. It was coming back to her, even though he had only worked on the clock for a short time, she knew how good she had felt when Simon had been around.

One day he was just there at the farmhouse, working on some things. He had dropped a nail, it had rolled under the floor boards down near where she and her Mother lived. It wasn't very big, but it was an obstruction in their living arrangements. Her Mother had gone out and Danni knew she would be dismayed at having this thing in the middle of their home. She knew she couldn't just put it in her cousin's area, they would trip over it and make a holy row about it all. The more she stared at it and wondered about it, the angrier she got until she took it in her paw and worked her way to the hole at the side of the wall closest to the area where it had fallen. She saw the large figure of a dark-haired man looming over a chair and tacking down some cloth onto it. A series of the same nails lay before him within easy reach. It seemed that he was being careful, but when the mallet came down, he let out a loud cry, the mallet falling to the floor and upsetting the nails in the process. One rolled off a bit of a ways and Danni could see how the one she was holding had ended up in her home. She shook her head.

"You could be a little more careful!" she admonished. The man turned, dark eyes wide, to see who was chastising him. When he saw no one, he went back to bending his thumb back and forth to assess the damage done by the mallet. "I'm down here!" Danni called again. She didn't like being ignored and though her Mother would probably scold her for speaking to a person, she was just angry enough not to care. And she was close enough to the hole that she could nip back in if it started to look a little dicey.

The man turned slowly towards the voice and even more slowly, he focused on the tiny mouse standing by the hole where the floorboard met the wall. She held one of his tacking nails and looked so angry and defiant he about burst out laughing. But he kept his face straight, seeming to know that he needed to meet her seriousness with equal seriousness.

"So you are," he replied. "I'm afraid I'm not a very good upholsterer."

"I didn't mean your thumb," the mouse told him and held up the nail, "I meant your equipment." And she tossed it down so it rolled a bit towards him. He could see the effort it took for the little thing to throw the nail and he wanted to applaud her, but he knew he must stay nonplussed.

"Now how did you get that?" he asked.

"Hole in the floorboard over there," the mouse pointed and sure enough, he saw that near where he was working, there was a separation between a section of the wood planks. He could patch that.

"I'm sorry," he said simply. "I'll look out for that."

"You could use a dish," the mouse told him.

"Beg pardon?" She rolled her eyes at him as if he were deaf.

"You," she said, pointing to him "could use" she made some kind of gesture that he took to mean work, "a dish!" she made another gesture as if she were eating from a bowl the way a person would. Then she held up her paws and raised her eyebrows as if to say "See?"

He had wanted to laugh at her, but what she'd had was a good idea. And he could put the dish on the other side of his nailing so if the mallet fell again it wouldn't accidentally hit the thing. He smiled at the mouse.

"That's very clever." he told her. The mouse stopped and stared at him. He looked around to see if there was something else about the room that would cause her to be so still all of a sudden. Nothing. "What?"

"What did you say?" she asked softly.

"I said that was very clever."

"Does that mean stupid?"

"No," he said, setting the chair to one side and turning his full attention to the little thing. "It means the exact opposite. It means mentally quick or resourceful, intelligent, which is a pretty big word for very smart. I use nails a lot, but most of the ones I usually work with are longer so I can keep them in my mouth while I work, a few at a time, and use them as I need them, then get some more from a box I have. But these are so small, well, my fingers just get pricked all the time reaching into the box, so I figured I'd put a few on the floor. A dish would keep them all central and still spread out so I could get to them easily and not worry about getting more holes in my fingers than I need to."

"Why would you need to?"

"That's very smart, too..." he said ruefully. "What I said was what's called 'a turn of phrase' and some people might take it to be funny, but you're right. Why would I want that? I should have just said 'getting any holes in my fingers' and been done with it." He smiled at the mouse. "You think very logically," he proclaimed.

"Does that mean smart or stupid?" she asked again. She certainly seemed fixated on how she was perceived.

"Neither, actually, it means capable of reasoning or of using reason in an orderly fashion. Or formally true or valid. But it is usually used in reference to someone who would be thought of as smart."

"I'm smart?" she asked.

"Well. I've only just met you, and I may not be the best judge, I mean, *I* didn't think of putting my nails on a dish, but I think you are smart." The little mouse gave a very little smile at this, but her shoulders sagged slightly. "You don't hear that too often?" he asked.

"Usually the opposite," she replied. "I'm always being told that I'm either silly, or boring, that what I say is just wrong, that I don't understand, where do I get such ideas... That little dog outside laughs when the cow jumps over the moon, did you know that? First off, why the cow does it is just beyond me and whenever the dog laughs he's just encouraging her! And my cousins... they insist on running out of their hole and all around the house!"

"Well... they are mice aren't they?"

"They're partially sighted!!" she shouted. "They could be considered blind! Are they *trying* to get killed?"

Simon had cocked his head at the tirade and smiled broadly.

And Danni had felt pleased then, that she had found a kindred spirit. Even more pleased now to be spending time with him again.

******

Doyle knew it was best to keep his counsel to himself. He had always been told to be respectful of his elders, but not to take all they said at face value. His parents had raised him to know that while people for the most part were basically good, there were some who held a different view and that it was best to steer clear of them, and even though someone might be your elder and deserving of your respect, they truly might not have earned it, so keep the problem to yourself and bring it home where it could be discussed and assessed.

But he couldn't get home.

And he began to think of all the reasons why he couldn't just up and excuse himself right now. His mother would be getting very nervous, with his being gone two nights! The longest he had been was two, and who knew how much longer this ordeal was going to take. Town had seemed so much closer than it really was and Doyle was beginning to doubt if they were actually going in the right direction, or if they were taking a road that circled round one of these unknown mountains or tree covered paths and had missed the way altogether. He could turn back... after all, he was just going to see Danni and Leo to town, see what other bits of iron he might locate, and then head back from whence he came. He was fairly certain he would find the way, and now that Simon was here, Danni had someone she knew and relied on...

That was just it. Danni knew him, relied on him...

But Doyle didn't trust him. And for this he kept his counsel.

The man fed into Danni's judgemental statements. He encouraged her, applauded her, and even seemed to feel the same way. It seemed so narrow. As if no one else was allowed their own feelings or business without either of them making a judgement and calling them down for it. Even if what was being done seemed senseless, if the people they were encountering somehow really were from fairytales and Danni was setting them on a different path, Doyle was not certain, but it seemed that this might have bad ramifications.

He was disturbed by this turn of events, especially as they seemed to be getting close to some kind of understanding about what was going on around them. And Danni making her own little leap of faith in grasping the word and what it might mean to her. He still was not sure exactly where he was, but he was becoming more certain that it was nowhere near his real home. Soon, he felt, he was going to need to draw from his own stores of faith and somehow he would have to find the strength to follow this thing through to whatever end there might be and then hope he could find his way back home.

******

Leo observed the group before him from his vantage point of the little seat on the cart. He closed his eyes, turning his face up to the sun.

A big ball of yarn would make everything pretty much perfect.

Chapter 17
A Trip to the Fayre

The fayre was well under way when they managed to turn one last bend in the road and come to an entry point. Music was playing and the smells of different foods being roasted were enough to make even a fully-fed man feel hungry again. Judging from the foot traffic, the local town wasn't far away. And it seemed that it was a far more populated area than Doyle had previously visited.

Simon had been pulling the cart for a time, Danni still on his shoulder. They had talked the time away, Danni mostly, about how she had managed with her cousins, the inanities of farm life, but precious little about what had happened on the road with Leo and Doyle, aside from how well they had gotten on. Doyle marked this and wasn't sure if Danni just hadn't wanted to say anything or if she was waiting for a time when he and the cat were no longer in earshot. He had hoped it would be the former but feared it could be the latter.

Simon indicated a section where people seemed to be leaving carts and the like – it was in the shade of several large oak trees and many other carts were already about, so it appeared safe enough. Doyle nodded amiably and they pulled off the pathway to secure their spot. Doyle got his jacket from under the tarpaulin and tucked his book in the inside pocket, then put the jacket on. Leo jumped down and circled the cart, assessing for himself where it had been placed and, finding it passable, he rejoined the group.

"Did I park it well enough, Leo?" Simon asked with a smile. The cat looked up at him curiously for a moment.

"I think you did a fine job putting the cart where it is, Simon, yes," and he smiled politely, uncertain what Simon had really meant by the word, 'park'. Doyle marked this as well. While Simon quite looked the part of a working man, neither his voice nor his words really fit in with this strange place. Doyle had noticed a strangeness, but now Leo's hesitation made him think it certain that this man, who seemed so comfortable walking the paths and chatting with Danni, was as much a stranger here as Doyle himself.

"Would you like me to carry you, Leo?" Doyle offered, seeing all the different animals roaming about, he wasn't certain how well they would all get on.

The cat smiled up at Doyle. "Tempting, Doyle, but I've been on that seat for quite some time, I thought leg-stretching time was in order, you know?"

At that, Doyle turned his attention to the different parts of the fayre – the tents and booths and the people milling about – while he straightened the jacket collar around the back of his neck. "But you see all the other animals…" Doyle continued, looking around them he could see many types. He looked back at Leo who was staring curiously up at him.

"They have their business, Doyle, and we have ours," said Leo firmly.

Doyle nodded at this, a little hesitant and disbelieving, but he would keep an eye. Off to one side he saw a man with a large tray in front of him and leather straps attached to the tray that he had hoisted over his shoulders. On the tray was a varied selection of all sorts of pies.

And Simon approached him. "Let me taste your wares," he said, simply. The pie-man looked at him.

"Simon, is it?" he asked, a smile on his face, and Simon nodded. The pie-man gave a little laugh and asked, "Show me first your penny!" Reaching into his pocket, Simon pulled one out and placed it in the money dish on the tray. The Pie-man was obviously confused for a moment as Simon lifted off a pie of his choice.

"I see the straps are holding out," he observed before taking a bite of the pie.

The Pie-man's attention was turned to the shoulder straps. "Oh yes, yes, fine work you did. Suppose if you hadn't I'd be looking at you a bit cross, eh?"

The two men laughed and the Pie-man's attention was diverted to another customer. Simon broke off a bit of the crust and offered it to Danni. Gratefully she took it and nibbled. He knelt down and offered a piece of the meat to Leo. The cat made short work of it and then took a moment to clean his mouth.

"Would you like a bite, Doyle?" Simon asked.

"Thank you, sir, but no. I'd like to see everything there is on offer, actually," said Doyle, as he made a mental note to check his book later. Privately. Simon gave a nod and turned his attention back to the pie.

Doyle looked about himself, marvelling at the scope of it all. There seemed many different stalls all selling different goods: foods, lovely trinkets, ribbons, tools; there were larger tents where clothing was being shown and areas in the back of the tent where one could try the item on in privacy. Off to one side was a make-shift stage, some sort of production being readied; there were paddocks where animals were being cared for and possibly sold off; and nearer to what would be considered the centre was a much larger tent where inside a wood floor had been laid down for dancing. Dotting along the edge of these places were smaller tents where the people who worked there could stay in the evening.

"You look as if you've never seen anything like this, Doyle," Simon said.

The lad nodded. "Not quite like this, sir" he agreed, "But it couldn't have just been set up…"

"Of course not," said a woman just beside them. She held a small tray of sweets which she proffered to both Doyle and Simon, who happily popped one in his mouth. Seeing Doyle hesitate, she smiled "A sampling," and cocked her head to indicate over her shoulder, her pretty pink bonnet bobbing along with the motion. "You can buy them there… if you like." He nodded and took up a small bite.

"You were saying…?" he urged the woman as he ate the small sugared wedge.

"It was set up a few days ago for the King, of course," and she pointed beyond the large dancing tent where, in the distance, there was another castle, this one large and tall and white and lovely. Doyle couldn't help thinking that they seemed to pop up like weeds. "He is encouraging his son to marry, so in the evening there is the Festival, with food and dancing and merriment in the large tent for all those eligible to meet the Prince. But during the day, there is merriment and joy for the rest of us from the nearby towns."

Doyle looked at the tent and stopped chewing for a moment. Festival. Prince to marry. He smiled – it was the only thing he could think to do to as his mind raced and he didn't want to let on where his thoughts were going. "Impressive…" he said, noticing Simon watching him. "Then when *did* this start?"

The woman was anxious to please, and more anxious to talk about things other than the sweet treats on her tray; "Well, as you can imagine, it's taken several days to set up, but the fayre began yestermorning so the first night of the Festival was last night. Oh and it was lovely… beauties from all across the country, music like you've never heard and the food!" she sighed.

"If we stay, I should think it would be quite a spectacle to see…" Doyle murmured and turned to move on.

"Oh yes…" the woman breathed. "Maybe she'll come back…"

Simon wasted no time. "She?" he asked almost dismissively, but quickly none the less. Doyle stopped but barely turned around.

The woman nodded. "The Maiden in Gold. When she appeared, the prince would dance with no other. But she left so suddenly, some might say she disappeared. No one knew who she was…"

Doyle was anxious to leave the spot, scanning the tents and carts and stalls he saw his out. "Danni," he called to the little mouse, still perched on Simon's shoulder. "I see a cheese stall… Come with me?" and he extended his arm towards Simon's shoulder,

"That sounds lovely…" Danni uttered as she leapt onto Doyle's hand before Simon could say a word. Then she looked back at the man. "Are you coming, Simon?" she asked politely.

"Not just now, Danni," he smiled, "I think I want to chat with this lovely young lady a bit longer. You three go ahead, I'll find you!"

Doyle was not sure if he really wanted to be separated from the man who he somehow knew would question the woman about the Maiden in Gold. But Doyle knew to whom she was referring.

Cinderella! It had to be.

He was still so deep in his own thoughts he had barely noticed Danni chatting away by his ear.

"... I don't know what you would call it, meeting up with Simon like that... but it certainly has me reeling!" Excitement was pouring out of her. Doyle couldn't help but be pleased at her tone; it was nice to have her so happy. But his apprehensions did keep him from enthusing too much.

"It must be quite a treat for you," he smiled.

"Oh, it's more than that..." she gushed. "I don't know... Leo, what would you call it?"

The cat's attention was pulled from a child swinging a stick with a toy bird attached, making small bird-like noises as it spun in the air. "Hm? Well. I suppose you could call it a miracle," he mused.

Danni nodded at this. That's it, she decided, that's what this was, a miracle. She didn't hear Leo follow up with "Or a fork in the road..." but Doyle did and he looked down at the cat slowly, meeting those large golden eyes that locked into his. Leo knew something, Doyle thought, and while it might not be along the lines of where Doyle's mind was going, the lad could tell that Leo, too, had some reservations about this Simon.

Standing before the cheese stall, they saw many sumptuous selections. The smell was a mixture of glorious and awful, the usual reaction from Doyle's nose, but he could see other people having something of the same issue. Danni scoured the offerings hungrily. She had never seen such varied choices before: the smooth creamy colour of cheddar she was familiar with but the crumbly one with the purplish streaks had her confounded. The small rounds were amusing and, while still small, they would be quite the handful for her. She looked at the little card in front of it and the squiggles on it... She studied them intently, remembering some of the words she had watched Doyle read from the story the night before. He had made certain sounds from each of them and she could recall many. Slowly she sounded it out: "Guh... oh... ay... tuh... sss..." she tried.

Astonished, Doyle jerked his head at the little mouse and saw that she was in fact staring at a card before one of the cheeses. Slowly he pointed to a card. "Do you mean this one?" he asked quietly. Danni nodded. "The Goat's cheese?" Again, but with some excitement, Danni nodded. "Danni, you read that. You sounded it out and read that."

"It says 'goats'?" she asked. Doyle nodded back to her. "Would I like that?" she asked.

"Well," he explained, "it's soft, so it's not easy to hold onto like the cheese I've been giving you, it might get messy, but it is tasty..."

"What about that one?" she asked, pointing to the crumbly one with the purplish streaks. She looked at the card before it and studied the squiggles: "Buh... ull... eh.... ugh..."

117

"Bleu…" he told her, hardly able to contain himself. It was amazing. The mouse was amazing.

But she looked somewhat perplexed. "That's how you write blue?" she asked.

"Oh no, no…" he replied quickly. "I suppose that's the hard part about reading, sometimes some words sound like others but are spelt differently… in this case that is the French word."

"What's the French word?" the mouse asked, looking at the other cards to see what began with 'Ff.'.

"No, Danni… I mean, it's the way the French would spell blue."

"What are the French?" she wanted to know.

Doyle was taken back. He had forgotten that they didn't always understand things he spoke about. "Not, what, Danni… who. The French are a kind of people."

She contemplated this. "So, they look different?"

"No…" he ventured, "they're from a different place…"

"Like you?" Doyle smiled.

"I suppose so, to you, yes…"

"Erm… down here?" Leo reminded. "Trying to pay attention here too…"

"And to you, Leo… anyway, bleu cheese might be considered very strong…"

In the end, they agreed on some gruyère. Danni had tried to sound it out but found her stomach wanted to eat more than her mind wanted to read. Hesitantly, Doyle handed over some of the coins in his pocket, not certain at all what the man behind the cart would say.

The cheesemonger looked at Doyle curiously, "You only wants this bit, right?" he asked, holding the parcel of cheese wrapped in white paper. It wasn't a small piece, but it wasn't too large either, and Doyle knew that a piece that size at the cheese shop back home would be twenty or thirty pence at least. Doyle nodded. The man looked at the coins again and took up one. Doyle was more than a bit stunned to see it was a farthing. He waited for a moment then brought his hand back, putting the coins in his pocket. He took the parcel proffered by the man and thanked him, turning around and moving away in something of a daze. Did money even really have a worth here? And that the fellow hadn't even questioned it.

He was still mulling this over, when he heard Leo call: "Are you planning on sharing that?"

"Oh, yes…," he said, as he was startled from his reverie. Looking about he saw the stump of a tree just off to the side of some of the carts. Leo saw it too and headed over, jumping up casually and sitting to one side, leaving more than enough room for Doyle to sit as well. Opening up the package, he gave a nice chunk to Leo and a smaller bit to Danni and took a piece himself.

There were more people milling about but it still was not over-crowded by any means. The town must not be terribly large and still, as it was early in the day, he figured many people just hadn't pitched up yet. But what

118

actually drew his attention were the animals. Walking along beside people, or casually on their own, many of these were natural enemies to the other and yet, they barely paid heed. Or they looked as if they were acknowledging the other with a polite nod. Some were even exchanging words. Finally he asked of his friends, "Do the animals always get on?"

They looked up at him, Danni having moved to his lap where she helped herself to another crumble of cheese. "With what?" she asked back.

"Well. With each other."

The two animals shared a look. True, they were considered enemies, Danni had always been told to watch for the farm cat, but had never really seen the farm cat do any harm to any mouse, only to the violin. For his own part, Leo's only thought was that animals only caused problems for other animals when one was actually a human who had been bewitched or enchanted. The main problem the animals had weren't with each other, but were mostly with humans.

The cat looked up suddenly: "There *were* the two Kilkenny cats," he announced. "Once they got at each other all that was left were nails and tails. Ugh."

Danni nodded and shuddered at the thought. "Oh," she remembered, "The lion and the unicorn!"

"What?" Doyle asked sharply, but Leo was nodding his agreement with Danni: "Oh, that was a terrible row…"

"They went at it hammer and tongs and all for a coin…" Danni sighed.

"Coin?" Doyle was flummoxed.

"A crown," Leo explained.

"But the Lion and the Unicorn are the symbols of Great Britain," Doyle interjected.

Danni and Leo were lost in their own remembering. "And people kept giving them food, hoping they would leave until they finally just chased them out of town…" Leo chuckled.

"I understand they caused quite a ruckus…" Danni mused.

"Lots of damage…" Leo agreed.

Doyle could wait no longer. "'The Lion and the Unicorn were fighting for the crown, the Lion beat the Unicorn all around the town. Some gave them white bread, some gave them brown, Some gave them plum cake and drummed them out of town,'" he recited. The animals stared at him.

"How do you *do* that?" Leo marvelled.

Danni was less impressed: "You know, Doyle, if I didn't know better I'd think you were a terrible show off."

"No, it's a nursery rhyme, but it's like one of the ones I told you about, Danni, that means something else. The Unicorn is the symbol of Scotland and the Lion is the symbol of England. The two countries are connected but they were separate…"

"How can something connected be separate?" Leo asked, sitting back on his haunches and putting his paws together and slowly bringing them apart.

"They both had their own governments and their own crown! Not the coin, but their ruler, their king… or queen… When Mary, Queen of Scots was vying for the throne of England, she pledged for a peaceful union…"

"Did she get it?" Danni asked.

"No… not really…" Doyle hesitated and decided it best not to go into the beheading. "But when Elizabeth, The Queen of England, declared Mary's son, Prince James of Scotland, to be her successor and he took the throne, he announced his intention to unite the two countries. He wanted everyone to treat the two countries as a united one, but the parliaments could not agree on a structure. There were at least three other attempts to try and unite them but it wasn't until 1707 that both parliaments came together and everything worked." He looked at them both, pleased at his memory for history.

Then Leo said: "That's great, Doyle, really good. But couldn't they keep their battles back where they're from? I mean, why drag it here and make a mess for us to pick up?"

The lad looked at the two of them. He wished he could make them understand that they were all connected, that things that happened here also had a place back where he was from. But the cat and mouse gazed up at him quizzically, both waiting for his response and wondering why he had brought it up in the first place. Finally, Doyle sighed and shook his head.

"I don't know…" he admitted and waited a moment. "It is nice to see animals getting on so… Shall we continue?" he asked and wrapped the cheese back up, putting it into his jacket pocket. Danni scurried back up to his shoulder and Leo leapt delicately off the stump. Back to the carts and stalls they went, observing and commenting and taking in all the new sights and sounds. They stopped at a cart filled with ribbons of every colour imaginable. Danni had never seen such pretty colour up close. She had seen rainbows, she had even seen them in the farmhouse when the sunlight shone through a window in a particular way, but these were all before her to look at and, if she wanted, to touch.

A young man beside her was doing just that. He lifted up a bunch of blue ribbons but then put them down again in favour of a bunch of pink ones. Then he would put those down in favour of red ones, all the while a look of perplexed consternation on his handsome face. He shook his head.

"Can't decide?" Danni asked.

Slightly startled by the sudden intrusion, the young man looked over at Doyle's shoulder and, upon seeing the mouse, he let out a nervous laugh. "I am no use," he admitted. "All these colours are so beautiful, and they would all suit her well…"

"A surprise?" Danni continued.

"Oh no… she was very specific," he admitted, "but she didn't come, so she doesn't know all there is on offer… and if I don't make a decision soon, I'll be here way too long…" he smiled at the mouse. "She wants to come to the fayre tomorrow, you see, but she wants some new ribbons, thinks it will make her more presentable…"

"For a dress…?" surmised Danni.

"Oh no…" the man went on, "for her hair… her bonny brown hair…" and he seemed lost in the memory for a moment, as he fingered the deep green bunch he now held. Danni coughed and his attention was again diverted to her.

"What colour did she want?"

"Blue," he replied and indicated the many different shades of blue before him.

Danni looked at Doyle, who was watching the exchange going on between them, a look that somehow crossed confusion with a desire to interrupt. Danni looked at his eyes, then set her sights to the blue ribbons before them. "Those," she said abruptly, pointing to a shade that were very like Doyle's eye colour.

The man took up a bunch and looked at Danni curiously.

"Well," continued Danni, "the sooner you get back, the sooner you can tell her of all the other choices. She'll probably want to get some others, but if you keep wondering and pondering you won't get back for some time and she will probably be cross to be kept waiting."

This made sense to the young man, he knew his lady well, she would be worried and then angry were he to be too late. And who knew, maybe if he got home swiftly enough, gave her the ribbons and told her of the others, she might want to come back today. They could watch the Festival and maybe dance themselves. He drew out some money and paid the woman in charge of the cart.

"Thank you," he said to her, then turned to the little mouse, "and thank you." Then he waited until…

"Danni," she blurted, after a bit.

"John," he introduced, "Johnny… if I can get these to my lovely Julie, then I might persuade her to come back with me later. Thank you again!" he said and tipped his hat then made off in haste through the crowd.

Danni watched him go before looking up at Doyle. "He was nice," she decided. Doyle nodded, but The Bunch of Blue Ribbons might also be gone.

"Doyle!" he heard and looked for Leo. The cat was standing by another stall and indicating with his great head for them to come over. Before Leo was a display shelf which, once Doyle and Danni got to him, Doyle could see had leather-bound books on them, the bindings tanned to various colours.

"It looks like yours!" Leo pointed out with pride at a book that was, in fact, a twin of Doyle's own. He took it up and opened it. The pages were all blank.

Doyle smiled down at Leo. "It does look very much like it, Leo, only this one has no stories in it… it's to write stories of your own… or draw pictures… or use as a diary…" The cat appeared disappointed. "But you know…" Doyle continued. "I might be able to write some of my own… maybe even about you two." The cat puffed up at this; Danni, too, stood a little straighter.

Doyle took the book up and showed it to the salesman and, holding out his coins again, the salesman took up five pence. Doyle nodded and brought back his remaining coins and his new book. Craftsmanship seemed worth more than food. He knelt down and showed the book to Leo, who rubbed the edges with his chin and smiled up at Doyle. Danni scrambled down his arm to get a better look at the item. Doyle opened it to show them both the blank pages and she touched an open page almost reverently. Squiggles were going to go there, she thought. Squiggles that made words and words that made a story. And some of that story would be about her. She looked happily from Leo to Doyle then scrambled back up his arm to her post on his shoulder. Doyle tucked the book into the other inside pocket of his jacket and stood up. Looking at his friends he said: "Shall we?"

Eager nods were made and they continued about the fayre.

Chapter 18
A Searching He Will Go

He was searching impatiently. He circled the area of the Festival and beyond, knowing full well that this Golden Maiden would be coming from an area where there was a hazel tree. And a grave. He also knew that it might not be well marked and that a well-to-do home should also be near enough to it. The woman selling the sweet treats had pointed out where she first saw the Maiden in Gold and the direction in which the prince had run off after she had disappeared.

He hadn't searched long when he saw two white doves soaring in the sky. A moment later they landed.

On the top of a hazel tree.

Near enough he saw a sturdy structure, the large stone manor of a well-to-do person. And a broken pigeon house.

This was the right place. Looking back to where he had come from, Simon could tell it was not too far away from the large tent, and he could casually venture this way again, later. Maybe this time *with* Danni.

******

The day drifted on. There had been a stage show about a beautiful maid who longed for true love and the twelve men who desired her. She gave the men a series of tests to prove which of them was the best choice, giving a rose to the ones who had passed and letting leave the ones who didn't until the very last test made her reveal her choice. The audience drew much merriment and while Doyle liked how involved the audience got, he wasn't too sold on the show.

A small band of players took to the stage with their instruments and were playing some lovely music when Simon finally showed up. Danni had become a bit anxious, was trying to keep it to herself and enjoy the time, but she brightened considerably when she saw Simon and he joined them on their chosen bit of grass.

"Beautiful day," he sighed as he sat beside them. He had a small bag of apples which he shared, Doyle took one and gave it a quick once over before taking a bite. Danni scurried over to Simon, climbing up on his leg as Simon bit into his own apple, then gave a piece to Danni. She nibbled at it, delighted. Doyle looked at Leo.

"Do you eat apples, Leo?" he asked.

"If it's food, I'll try it," Leo acknowledged and Doyle bit off a piece of apple and placed it before him. The cat licked at it, appreciating the tang and put it in his mouth, chewing awkwardly, but he grinned, "Nice…" he garbled and continued chewing. Doyle smiled at the cat and his enjoyment.

"We're going to have to move the cart," Simon told them. Doyle looked at him, "Oh?"

The man nodded. "Seems the carriages and coaches and such that are bringing the finer people this evening are to be parked over there. They've said anyone who wants to stay can move their things over to that side of the field…" he pointed off, not too far from where the cart was.

Doyle could see that other carts were already being moved there and that a large fire ring was being put together. "Should we go now?" he asked.

"Not before we pick up something nice for dinner, don't you think?" Simon smiled. "Should we get something already cooked or see what we can find to cook ourselves?"

Danni looked over at Doyle. "You must be tired of cooking, Doyle, let's get something from the stalls!"

Doyle smiled back at the mouse. "*You* must be tired of what I've been giving you!" he teased.

"There *were* sausages…" Leo mused. "And thick-cut bread…"

"And roasted corn!" Danni piped in.

Doyle laughed at the two. "I guess it's been decided, then!" and he stood up, digging into his pocket for his coins.

Simon also rose, Danni skittering to his shoulder. "Oh no, Doyle, I'll get them…" he offered.

"That's very kind, Simon, but I really can pay…"

"Well, then let's go in it together…" the man suggested. "I can go pick everything up and meet you back at the cart."

Doyle found this agreeable and pulled out his coins. "How much do you think you'll need?"

Simon eyed the money carefully and picked up a shilling. "This'll do," he said. "I can bring you back change." Doyle was anxious to see what that would look like so he nodded.

"May I come with you?" Danni asked solicitously, still perched on Simon's shoulder. For a moment, Doyle felt horribly protective. But the Festival wasn't due to begin for some time, and this way he still had time to discuss all with Leo.

"I thought you were!" Simon laughed and the mouse smiled with a bit of relief. "Shall we?" Simon asked her gallantly.

"To the stalls!" Danni called and waved back at Doyle and Leo as she and Simon made their way to the food. Doyle watched, a mix of emotions playing across his mind. Danni and Simon blended in with the crowd before he looked down at Leo.

The cat was staring up at him fixedly with a raised eyebrow. "I don't like to be judgemental, Doyle," Leo began, "but who *is* that man?"

"I know…" he concurred, "I *thought* you had noticed…" and he reached into his jacket pocket.

"Noticed? *Noticed*? Let's just get him a sign that says 'Hi, I don't belong here' so he can get on with it…" the cat spluttered, raising a paw for emphasis. "He just blusters his way in and people are either too polite to say anything or too stupid to pay attention!" Then cat sagged and shook his great head, "But Danni thinks the world of him!"

"I know…" Doyle agreed.

"How can she be so smart and not see?"

"Sometimes people with opinions as strong as Danni don't always see what goes against what they believe…"

Leo nodded. "Yes… *people* can have a one-track mind sometimes…" before he exploded, "but Danni is a mouse and I thought that being an animal she would have a bit more sense! All she talks about is sense! And being sensible! And… I'm sorry, Doyle, *you* being people and all, but…"

"I think you're right, though…" Doyle shrugged, "but as you also said… this could be a fork in the road." Leo looked up at Doyle sadly. He knew it was true and there was nothing he or Doyle could really do or say, because it would be up to Danni to decide which fork she would take.

"Do you think she'll go off with him… permanently?" the cat breathed, almost wishing he could take the words back. Doyle had been thinking it as well. He knew any decision would have to be Danni's and the best thing he and Leo could do was not push the issue should it come up but he did want to just shake the little mouse and get her to open her otherwise sharp little eyes.

"We'll cross that bridge after we've burned it…" Doyle said softly, "I'm also concerned about the stories…" and he stood up.

Leo was perplexed. "What? What?" he stammered.

"Leo, some of the stories were missing, remember? I told you?" The cat looked up and nodded and Doyle began to head towards the cart, Leo following at a gentle trot. "If I'm right, and I really hope I'm not, there are going to be several more missing and I don't know how Danni and Simon are doing it, but I think they are responsible!"

The cat grabbed at Doyle's leg with open claws and, feeling the needle-like things in his shin, the lad stopped. "Wait, wait, wait…" the cat stuttered. "You think Danni is taking them out of your book?"

Doyle got down on one knee to face Leo. "No, no, no, Leo, not 'taking' them… they're, well, just disappearing. She is talking to the people and the creatures that are archetypes in the stories I've been reading you, and then something happens to them. I know you and she think I'm just reading a written account of what you all know has happened around here – but where I come from, Leo, these are called Fairy Tales and Fables and Nursery Rhymes I grew up on them and I love them. And I don't know how I got here or why, but since I did, the stories in my book are just disappearing! Pretty soon it'll be as blank as the new one I bought today! And the people and the creatures Danni and Simon have been talking to? They are the very characters from the stories that are missing!"

125

The cat thought about this. "But she was surprised to find some of them missing!" he pointed out and Doyle nodded.

"Yes... so I'm wondering if Simon had anything to do with those..." and he lifted up the book. "Here... if I'm right, the story of Hansel and Gretel will be gone and so will The Bunch of Blue Ribbons – Danni had something to do with that one... and Simon with Simple Simon." He opened the book and looked for the titles. Finally he stopped turning pages. Nowhere.

"Are they gone?" Leo whispered.

Sadly, Doyle nodded. "But if I'm really right, Simon is going to try and do away with Cinderella as well," Leo looked at him quizzically. "The Maiden in Gold that the sweets lady talked about?" Recognition fell over the cat. "Well, she's a story too, Cinderella, about how being good and kind and devout even during times of great testing will bring good fortune to you." He thought of the stage show they had seen and realised the story was also a test for the prince, to see if he deserved Cinderella and if Cinderella deserved to get married. It was all so very complicated and he shook his head. One thing at a time. He looked at Leo. "We have to be very quiet about this, Leo, we have to watch and be careful... we can't keep them separated, that might look too obvious, and we don't want to make her angry with us by thinking we don't like or trust Simon..."

"But we don't..." Leo wanted to be sure.

"No we most certainly don't... but we have to stay aware and see if we can figure all of this out... Swear?" and the lad held his hand out to the cat.

Leo looked at the extended hand. He knew this was important, to be asked to swear was always important. He placed his paw on top of Doyle's.

"Swear," he said. And meant it.

Chapter 19
Simon from the Sky

Simon tried not to appear concerned and was a good enough actor to pull it off, but as he held the coin in his hand his mind reeled with the possibilities and none of them were good.

A shilling. The boy had a shilling. And it had been minted in 1939. English. Could he have gotten it from someone here? How could that be? But looking at the boy, he knew there was something amiss, that the boy didn't belong, but had he slipped in here like Simon? And from sometime in the 1930s? It was a completely different world there let alone here, and while Simon had now had plenty of practice assimilating himself into this world whenever he arrived from 2005, he was woefully short on his resources when it came to dealing with a boy possibly from England who would easily be in his 80s back where Simon was from.

Had the boy been in an accident? A bombing? Was the war going on where he was from? Was that how he had gotten here? But how did he bring money? His own money! Simon had never been able to bring anything except his book, somehow the book was always there. Once he'd become more familiar with the place he began to earn the little money he might need for food and things, but even then he had never needed much as he was usually paid in food or things he could use further on his travels.

Simon remembered the first time he had ended up in this place. It had been during one of his first trips to the hospital. He wasn't certain why he had been taken there, but he knew it had to do with the voices in his head. It was really the one voice that was so insistent that they cared about – and when they had tried giving him a shock of some sort he remembered falling back, far back and finally landing on grass, but so softly and gently, it was as though it had happened in slow motion. He had looked around and was amazed at the lush greenery and the people walking about, none of whom really paid much attention to him. Watching the way the people moved and spoke to one another, he soon realised he was dressed in a similar fashion. He had wondered if he were dreaming, but when he pinched himself, there was pain, so either the dream world had managed to bring in sensation or he really was someplace else. It didn't take him long to realise that where he was corresponded with the fairy stories he had heard tell of from his friends, the kind that movies were made from, the kind that had been taking quite a drubbing where he came from for their violence and fantastical qualities... of murder and enchantments and evil and monsters; of good triumphing over evil; of all the things people now know are not true.

If Simon's mother had been lax in most parenting skills, at least she had not exposed him to those foolish stories. She had been a drinker, had imbibed a few drugs in her time, and was given to roaming, but had pretty much always put a roof over Simon's head. Simon's father had a bit more of a fairy tale feel to his life, roaming free and loose, believing in things that could not be seen nor proved, trusting in... something.

Father. The word had little meaning, just a man dropping in and out of Simon's life like a skipping stone, sometimes taking him with him, other times leaving him alone for long periods of time, until he deigned it time to return, happy and boisterous and not wanting to hear the ramblings of a child left fearful in the dark. Simon had climbed into himself at an early age, recognising what was expected of him and delivering as well as he could but noting everything and keeping each issue separate from the other -- all the pains and the few moments of happiness, categorising them trying to find a formula for repeating them. He would write these theories down whenever they came to him and knew if he could get someone to publish them, people would recognise them and see he was not only in his right mind, but had the answers for all they were going through.

Charming and affable, he had many friends that he kept at arm's length, but who were still admiring of him enough to want to help when he had an issue, be it with another friend, a school setting or something more formal like the police or the hospital.

He could be in the fairy tale world for what seemed like days and when he was suddenly pulled out, like sliding down through a drain, he noticed had never been gone for long as far as the others were concerned. But he always had a deep-seated feeling that there was more work to do back in the other world, that he had to get back and continue his plan of first altering the stories, and then, once he'd found a connection, of making them gone – permanently.

It was getting harder to get back in to this other world, though, and he had to come up with myriad ways to get himself sent to hospital and somehow hope they would do something else that might send him over. Certain prescriptions helped, if they were the wrong level or the wrong combination – something to create a reaction and he would fall back to the grass and be able to restart his journey of gently, (oh, so gently, because these were a people who did not react well to harshness or anger from anyone outside their own lives), moving them about and watching the tales disappear.

Sometimes he had to resort to violence, but he quickly discovered that if a creature was *supposed* to die, another would just take its place; yet he found that if one of the things they were supposed to be *dealing* with was removed, then it worked. They had nothing to keep them tied to the storyline and therefore they found something else. But some of the creatures had strong memories. And for them to stay could allow them to start the process again. He'd seen it happen and could recognise the types. They were dealt with swiftly. Like the little dog. And the candy woman. She remembered too much, would continue to do so and he needed no one to point a finger his way when he had made himself so simple. So innocuous. So *not* memorable. Even Danni had all but forgotten him until he had jogged her memory.

But now, everything was falling into place. It was all going to work out this time, this last time, he knew it was to be the last, he knew he might not get another chance to come back. With Danni's help he would get it completed, regardless of the boy, maybe even because of the boy. After all, the boy was just that, a child. He could stay a step ahead of a mere child. And children were never really heard in these stories. Not until the end. And by then, Simon was certain there would be no real end, only discord and milling about and something akin to life like where he came from. He would keep an eye on this Doyle. He would be watchful. And diligent. And simple.

"Here's the roasted corn..." he called out to Danni. The mouse giggled in anticipation. "Is there anything else you would like, Danni?"

She considered the collection of fruits he had already gathered, the fresh vegetables, the sausages and bread, what a feast they had planned. She looked at the cart sign and sounded, "Ku... oh... err... nnn..." before asking "That says 'corn'?"

Simon looked at the sign and kept a simple demeanour while he felt every nerve tense. "Why yes it does!" he congratulated, looking with a smile at the mouse. She puffed with pride, happy to let him in on her growing ability. "Danni, I didn't know you could read!"

"Well," she said shyly. "I'm only just learning..."

"And doing quite well, I must say. How did you pick this up?" The mouse did learn things at a very fast pace. He wasn't sure if this would work for him or against him.

"Doyle," she piped cheerfully.

Simon knew it. "Really?" he smiled.

Danni nodded. "He has a book of stories and he's been reading to us. I didn't know that words could be put on paper and looked at to tell a story!" she effused.

"It's pretty amazing, isn't it?" Simon asked. "Well that saves me teaching you!" Her eyes grew wide.

"You would have?" she asked.

"Certainly, Danni."

"Because there is still a lot I don't know... Oh, I would appreciate the help, Simon!"

"Of course I will!" he assured the mouse and bought a few ears of roasted corn.

As they turned to walk from the stall, they saw a boy, about Doyle's age, but smaller in build and uncertain of his gait, on a path leading to the fayre. The boy was leading a cow behind him. He was listening to a man, an older fellow in a dirtied apron proffering the boy a small bag. Simon took in a slight breath at the possibility. He continued to chat with Danni about reading as he wandered in the direction of the boy, not absentmindedly, until he found himself almost directly in front of the boy and man.

The man droned on: "… their value is so great, I should not want to part with them all, for they are worth much more than this sad beast, but as you are in want…" he drifted off, looking over to Simon hesitantly.

"Good evening…" Simon said, "please don't mind us… just showing my little friend around," and he indicated Danni on his shoulder.

As he had hoped, the boy looked at the mouse with a broad smile. "Is he tame?" he asked.

"If you mean 'do I bite?', no," Danni interjected, "and I'm a she."

"A talking mouse?" both the boy and the man were attentive now.

The man looked at Simon and started to hold up his bag: "You wouldn't be wanting to sell the darling creature, would you?" he drawled. Simon wanted to hit the man right there and then, but he just smiled.

"I'm no one's to be sold!" Danni exclaimed, but her curiosity was aroused. "What is it you have in there?" she asked, pointing to the bag.

"Oh," interrupted the guileless boy, "He wants me to sell my cow for his bag of beans, and he says they are of great value…"

"Oh, he did, did he?" Danni intoned. "And what were you *planning* to do with the cow?" she asked the boy.

"My mother sent me to sell it for a good price as she has not been well and we need the money or will surely starve."

"Beans?" Danni asked.

"Of great value," the man inserted.

Danni turned her stare on the man. "Oh, so they'll grow tomorrow and be ripe and ready to eat? When these poor people need it? While you take this cow off and kill it to make many meals for other people to buy so you can have money hand over fist while this little boy and his mother starve? I mean, you *are* a butcher, aren't you?"

"Well, yes…" the man said, "but the…"

"And instead of *paying* him for the cow, you're going to trade him beans?" Danni demanded.

The man stopped and looked at the bag. He looked back at Danni. "Of great value…"

Danni made a noise of disgust and turned to the boy. "Look, what's your name?"

"J… Jack…" he stammered.

"There is a big paddock down that way, Jack," Danni pointed. "I saw it earlier with another friend of mine and people are buying and selling animals there. Your mother asked you to do something that made sense. Go do it."

Jack pondered this for only a moment. The mouse was talking to him. This sort of thing obviously didn't happen every day so he knew he ought to listen.

He nodded. "I will…" he said, "I will!"

"And don't let anyone try to give you anything but money! Listen to your mother!" the mouse admonished and Jack started down towards the animal paddocks with renewed purpose. Danni turned to the butcher. "And you should be ashamed!"

The butcher took on an indignant look. "A woman bade me offer these to the boy for the cow, the idea was not mine," he sulked.

Danni snorted. "You probably hoped that boy was not all there and didn't consider what … and I …" and she stopped for a moment.

Boy. Beans? That seems familiar, somehow…

But her thoughts were interrupted as Simon took up the cause. "How right you are Danni! Go on," he chided the man. "I think you've caused enough trouble…" And with a sniff, the butcher left them. "Danni, I really don't get these people around here. What was that boy thinking? Beans for a cow!"

Danni was pulled completely out of her thoughts, and nodded, but she was quieter when she spoke. "Maybe we should go back now…"

"I think you are very right," Simon agreed, and kept up the banter as they headed back towards the cart and Doyle and Leo. Soon enough, Danni was caught up again in the chatter and even sooner, the boy Jack had fled from her mind.

Chapter 20
Backward, Go Forward –
Make Now Become Then

Doyle was busily attending to the cart when Simon and Danni came along the path to meet them. Leo had been sitting on the little seat and Danni saw him move closer to Doyle who nodded, looked up from his work and gave a wave.

Simon held up his parcels of food as Danni was waving back. Once close enough, she made a little leap for one of the handles, skittered along it to the seat and settled in close to Leo. "Simon's got a feast!" she proclaimed.

"Sounds grand," Doyle said, "but maybe we ought to move the cart to the other site before we eat?"

The man nodded. "Very wise," he concurred. "We don't want to be so far in the back that we can't see everything going on at the Festival, do we? I heard there were going to be fireworks!"

"Really?" Doyle asked, grabbing onto the handles.

Another nod from Simon, falling in beside the lad as they made their way across the field. "Danni tells me you have a book of stories…?" Doyle didn't flinch.

"I read some more words, Doyle," Danni explained, "and Simon wondered where I had learned so I told him about your book of stories… Do you think you can get it out now…?"

"Well, Danni," Doyle thought quickly, "maybe later. You see, I packed it away in the cart and it really isn't easy to get to… I figured with all the excitement of the fayre and now the Festival, we would put aside reading for the evening…"

"Oh…" came the mouse's disappointed reply.

Doyle turned a smile back to Danni. "Don't worry… we'll get back to it…" he assured. The mouse gave a grin and nodded, still staying close to Leo. Doyle began to wonder what had happened between Danni and Simon.

"That's pretty amazing," Simon was saying, "Her picking it up like that…"

"Well, I guess you know first-hand just how smart she is." Doyle tried not to sound sharp but knew it had come out a little that way. He tried a smile at Simon. "I think I am getting hungry... my mum can always tell when I'm the hungriest because that's when I become the most cross..."

Simon smiled back, his eyes searching. He indicated the bags he was carrying, "Well, here's hoping this'll put you into a better humour..." he offered and Doyle nodded.

They found a space close enough to the fire ring without being too much in the way of the other carts. There were two large rocks nearby they could use as seats. And they soon discovered this was not only a spot for overflow people staying the night but also the rendezvous area for people from the nearby town as well. There were a few with families but many were simple town folk out for an evening's enjoyment. It became clear that once the festivities had drawn to a close there would be very few people staying the night. Doyle placed the cart to his liking and brought out his cushioned mat and pillow, then took up his blanket and spread it on the ground between the two rocks. Simon then laid out the bags of food as Doyle was bringing out some dishes and utensils.

Leo was making the best of the time by giving himself a little clean and noticed that Danni hadn't moved from her spot beside him. With his leg pointing at an angle in the air and his mouth ready to dive into a spot by his thigh, he looked at the mouse carefully. She was staring off towards the paddocks of larger animals.

Checking carefully to see that Doyle and Simon were working, Leo asked, "Are you all right, Danni?"

The mouse looked up at him thoughtfully. "I was hoping Doyle would have his book handy..." she said, though Leo thought that this time, her voice was filled more with apprehension than disappointment.

"Well, he said he'd bring it out again later for reading, Danni, I wouldn't be too worried..." the cat tried, hoping Danni would continue. He was not disappointed.

"That's not it..." her voice dropped. "I think I did something..." Leo casually looked over to the two people. Still busy.

"What do you mean...?" he asked. The little mouse looked at him, her eyes fighting back tears and her little body quivering with a deep-seated anxiety.

"You know how Doyle was talking about the stories that were missing? And how it seemed like some of the people I had talked to might have been part of them...?"

"Y... yes..." the cat stammered. He really wanted Doyle to be in on this...

"I'm afraid I may have done another one!" she admitted. "But I'm not sure! I need to ask him if there is a story about something like I came across, but I don't want to do it in front of Simon..."

Leo's eyes widened. Was she having second thoughts about him? Before he could ask, she continued. "I mean, I don't want Simon to be disappointed in me... this can't be a good thing, really, can it? And here he's so excited about me trying to read... and wants to help me learn more!" she all but effused, only to find herself almost shaking again, "And if what

133

I've done *is* bad... I... don't know what I'll do, Leo... or what he's going to think of me..."

The cat nodded his great head, thankful that he hadn't blurted out his own concerns. "Can you tell me a little about it?" he asked, "That way if one or the other of us is alone with Doyle, we can ask. Someone is bound to get up and move around..."

Danni thought about this. It made sense. She nodded and leaned in to the cat, who leaned down and let her whisper in his ear about the lad and the cow and the man with the beans.

Finally she asked, "Do you have that...?" Slowly, Leo nodded. "And you won't say anything to Simon?"

"That's a promise," the cat smiled.

"Hey, you two!" Simon called, "Dinner's on!" Danni skittered down the side of the cart as Leo delicately leapt from his perch. "Thick as thieves, you two..." Simon smiled as the pair came to the blanket. "Do you have any cups, Doyle?" he asked, pulling a bottle from his pocket. Doyle looked over at him curiously. "Fresh apple juice," he informed. "Couldn't pass that up." Doyle went back to the cart and brought out two small metal cups and passed them to Simon. "Oh, and before I forget..." he handed over some coins to Doyle. "Your change, sir." He took the cork from the bottle and filled both cups, passing one to Doyle.

Doyle was looking at the coins. Ordinary. On one side, the face of an ordinary monarch – male on some and female on others – nothing too distinguishing about them, just a typical profile. On the other side was a blossoming flower of some sort. They were different sizes, but with no numbers. And no date.

Simon pushed his cup-filled hand more into Doyle's view, jarring him out of his thoughts. He smiled politely at the man. "Thank you, sir," he said softly, putting the coins in a pocket of his jacket, to keep them separate from his others, and taking the proffered cup.

"Did I use too much?" Simon asked solicitously.

Doyle looked down at the food before them and smiled. "Oh no, sir, I don't think so... not for all of this!"

"The fellow I gave it to do not quite know what to make of the number..." he smiled, "He thought that might be how much it was worth!" Doyle was uncertain how to respond to this. He was certain it just said one. One shilling, Simon was looking off, thoughtful, and continued, "One, nine, three, nine, was it?" he was remembering. Doyle felt his cheeks go hot. "I told him it was probably how many were made..." and he looked at Doyle. "Was that it? It certainly was an interesting coin..." Doyle took a sip of the juice but barely tasted it as it went down his suddenly dry throat.

"Actually, I got it here..." he lied, again. First to Danni, now to Simon – this was only making a tense situation worse!

"From one of the other vendors..." he continued, managing to look very contrite. "I'm sorry if it caused you any trouble..." and he turned his attention to the food before them. "But if it got us this, I think it's a grand

134

thing. Shall we?" Simon gave a nod and they filled their plates, Doyle carefully finding things for both Leo and Danni.

Simon attended to his food. The boy might be lying, he might not. Either way, Simon was going to keep an eye on him.

Chapter 21
Elegance in Moonlight

As the sky grew darker, Guards from the palace began to bring torches and set them up near where they had originally kept the cart and then all along the path to the enormous tent. The distance gave it a mystical quality, the light flickering, sometimes moving almost of its own volition when one couldn't see the Guards and footmen clearly. Light also began to ensconce the tent area where the festivities were to begin. A small orchestra had been set up and was now practicing a few bars of music here and there, sometimes all together, mostly as practice for the individual. Behind the tent, an area had been designated for making food, and even more glorious smells wafted through the trees and over to the observers by the fire ring. More servers from the castle came down carrying covered tray upon covered tray of unseen treats. Soon, magnificent coaches and glorious carriages began to drive up, led by beautiful horses, which were directed by the Guards where to drop off their passengers and then where the carriages ought to be stationed. As the finely dressed ladies and gentlemen moved into the tent, the music officially started. Then the light show began. This must have been for the benefit of the townspeople, as the people going into the tent paid little heed.

Fireworks exploded above them, in myriad shapes and colours and sounds. Danni covered her ears as the noise was practically deafening, but was awed by the splashes of colour that ignited the dark sky. The show didn't last long and they now saw the prince himself was arriving at the Festival and was coming down to the tent prepared in his honour. People around them ooh-ed and ah-ed at the sight of him, tall and sharp-jawed on his white stallion, and then they began to applaud and cheer. Leo, whose cat-eyes were very good, especially in the dark, took special note that this fellow was not The Prince they had met. He leant down to tell Danni, but the mouse was nodding.

"I don't think that's Rupert either…" she whispered. The cat smiled. A noise behind them made them both turn to see Simon rise.

"I'll be back," he assured.

"I could come with you…?" Danni half asked. Simon smiled down at the mouse. "Danni, some things people like to do in private. They've set a spot up behind that hedge over there..." he indicated, then looked at Doyle, "Passing the information on..." he said softly.

"Thank you..." Doyle shifted a little. Doyle watched Danni watch Simon depart, her sharp eyes watching him go over a small rise and behind a group of hedges. She blinked. "He will be back, Danni..." Doyle said gently. "He said he would." The mouse looked over at Doyle and tried a smile.

Leo sniffed loudly. "Personally, I am feeling very under-appreciated..." Danni's smile broadened and she clambered up his back and onto his neck before pushing her hands in and scratching for all her worth. The cat began to purr loudly, his head rocking back and forth. Doyle let loose his rumbling laugh and lay down so the cat and mouse were in front of his stomach and he let his hand drift over Leo's head and then let his finger trace over Danni's head. Then the three friends settled back to hear the music and listen to the observations of the crowd.

Finally, Leo said, "Danni... maybe you should tell Doyle before Simon gets back..." Doyle became very alert and sat up. Danni looked up at him, knowing she ought to tell him, but not pleased with how he would take it either. "Go on..." Leo encouraged.

The little mouse jumped from Leo's neck to Doyle's knee. Leo sprawled on the blanket, looking for all the world as if he were doing precious little but actually staring out intently to see if he could spot Simon making an appearance.

Danni looked down and then back up at Doyle again.

"Are you all right, Danni? Did something happen?" he asked.

She nodded slowly. "We had just gotten the roasted corn and were walking along, when we saw a young boy with a cow talking to a butcher... and Simon went over to them... and I started talking to them..." Danni paused and Doyle looked carefully at her.

Danni was shaking as she continued: "Well... then I remembered about the boy who traded his cow for beans... and after he left the butcher, I wondered... if it was a story and if I made it go away..."

Doyle took in a little breath. "Did he trade the cow...?" he asked, as gently as he could.

"Not for the beans..." Danni replied. "I didn't think it was a good idea and I told him and then Simon was saying how smart I was again, and then we talked about all sorts of things and I didn't really think about it until we got back to you two... and..." she took in a big gulp of air. "I just want to know if it was a story and have you check in your book to see if it's still there or not..."

Doyle didn't know what to do. Jack and the Beanstalk. Was *it* now gone? Was she logicalising these stories out of existence? He held his breath for a moment, not wanting to get mad at her as he knew she might either get defensive or shut down. And he didn't want to bring out the book even though it was just in his jacket pocket, he didn't want anyone thinking it was easily accessible at the moment.

"Danni is also afraid that if this is a bad thing, Simon might be disappointed and might not help her learn more about reading," Leo added, not really shifting from his laconic lookout position.

Danni shot a look over at him. "Leo!" she called out sharply.

The cat shrugged. "I just want Doyle to know what's what..." he yawned.

Danni turned to look sheepishly at Doyle. "He had said he would help me..." she admitted. Doyle felt a momentary pang of jealousy but knew he couldn't allow that to colour his actions. Finally he grinned.

"First off," he said gently. "It's a good idea to have other people help you learn, Danni. You do know that as long as you want me to, I'll try to help you as well, right?" The little mouse nodded. "As to the other matter, Danni, I'm sure it will be all right, but it doesn't change the fact that the book is still in the cart... and I really don't want to have to get it until later..." he saw the mouse's face cloud over and didn't know what to say next.

Leo came to his rescue. "Danni... if it were something of great import, you and I both know he'd be getting that book out to check no matter *where* it was! You saw how he was back on the path! I was getting nauseous for you just watching him bending and reaching and turning and..."

"I remember, Leo..." Danni said, not really wanting to recall the feeling but certainly recollected how imperative it seemed to Doyle to get to his book at that time.

"It might have just been someone who could have made a bad decision and you stopped them," Leo finished.

Danni's eyebrows rose. "I may have done a good thing?"

Doyle looked carefully at her. "Maybe," he said, he still wasn't really sure what was happening or what it all meant. "But worrying about it right now is not going to help. My mum has always told me that if there's nothing I can do about a problem at the moment I am faced with it, to put it out of my mind until I *could* do something about it. It will keep and most of the time a clear solution will make itself known. There's a saying... 'Clearer minds prevail'." He gave Danni a look. "Does that make sense?"

The mouse smiled. "If you think I should wait, Doyle, I'll wait."

Doyle nodded. "And until we know for sure, we'll keep it to ourselves," he promised.

Danni let out a sigh. "Thank you," she said, then looked back towards the hedges. Simon was nowhere to be seen. "Maybe I should go see if he's all right...?" she tried.

Doyle shrugged. He wasn't too sure how he felt about her venturing out on her own, but at the same time he did want to look at the book. "I'm sure he's fine, but... if you want to..."

Danni gave a perfunctory nod. She held up her paw to them, "I'll be right back," she said to the pair and tore off across the grass towards the hedges.

Once she was gone, Doyle nudged Leo, "Keep a close eye on her," he urged and reached into his jacket pocket, pulling out his book.

Leo let his mouth drop, "You said that was packed in the cart...?"

"Keep an eye on her, Leo!" he hissed and the cat let his eyes follow Danni as she skitter-stopped over the grass towards the hedges.

"She's almost there..." said Leo testily. And then, "You could have told me, you know..." he huffed.

"It's bad enough me lying, Leo, I didn't need you to do it, too..." his fingers flipped over the pages. "I hate not telling her... I don't like keeping things from those I care about and maybe she'll hate me for it later, but I just can't tell her what *might* be! Or that I *feel* something is wrong, you know how she is about that... when I let her know it will be when I am fairly positive and maybe she can use that good common sense of hers to help me become truly positive."

"She's past the hedges," Leo informed. "I can't see her now..." he looked at Doyle, who had stopped flipping pages. "It's not there?" the cat asked.

"Jack and the Beanstalk..." Doyle said and shook his head. "Gone." Quietly, he put the book back in his pocket. "It was a good thing you brought it up, Leo..." he told the cat, who nodded.

"How long do we give her before going to look?" Leo asked.

"Not long," he said.

And they both watched by the hedges.

******

Simon knew it would only be a matter of time before Danni would let her innate curiosity get the better of her and come after him. And he had made sure she watched him go over to the hedges so she would come the same way. Whether or not she would be with Doyle or Leo he was uncertain, but he would deal with that one way or the other if he had to. Of course, to have Danni work her magic, he would have only one option in handling anyone else who showed up, so he kept a firm thought that Danni would come alone.

And then he heard: "Simon...? Simon, are you all right...?"

He placed himself behind a hedge. "Danni?" he called back, "I'm fine but I'm still... well... indisposed..." He could hear the mouse moving back and forth. "Now don't be nervous... I shouldn't be too much longer... why don't you go over away from me near the last hedge... you can still see what's going on and I'll be there in a minute..." Danni stopped moving. "Go on, Danni... I promise..."

The little mouse sighed and began to walk slowly to the edge of the hedges. The moon was coming up almost full and light was cast brightly around, making the grass and shrubs take on a silver hue and for a moment Danni was mesmerised at its beauty. Before she got to the end of the hedge, she turned and saw a glorious figure in gold and silver seated before her.

Together, Danni and the woman took in a breath, both making a tiny squeak.

The woman was dazzling to see: her blonde hair taking on the silver light of the moon, cascading down her shoulders and falling onto the gown which almost seemed otherworldly. And on her feet, she wore shoes that were of such a finely spun silver they looked like glass. The woman was clasping and unclasping her long slender-fingered hands in an agitated manner and staring at the mouse, not knowing whether to faint, scream or run.

"I'm sorry…" Danni got out. And the woman released another little gasp. "I'm sorry, I can talk, too…" Danni explained. The woman still stared, her dark eyes fearful and questioning. She was so beautiful, so magnificent that Danni knew she was in the wrong place. "Don't you belong down there…?" Danni asked. A longer sigh escaped the woman's lips. The fear and question was replaced by sadness.

"I don't know where I belong, really…" she said softly. "I wanted to go to the Festival, so my stepmother gave me extra chores to do saying if I finished them all I could, which I did, with the help of my bird friends. Then she broke her promise: she forbade me, she said I was dirty and couldn't dance and would embarrass them all… my stepsisters teased me and laughed at me… my father did nothing…"

"That's awful," said Danni as the woman nodded. "You certainly don't look dirty… you look beautiful."

A surprised look seemed to cross over her face.

"Thank you," she said and smiled. Especially beautiful when she smiled, Danni thought. But the smile faded as quickly as it came.

"Before my mother died, she made me promise to be good and kind and devout and then I would always find help… but…" she stopped. "My father remarried and soon after I was made to clean and look after the house and care for my stepsisters… I…" she looked away and willed herself not to cry. "I'm still good and kind and devout… but…" she trailed off.

"It's getting harder…?" Danni tried.

The woman nodded. She leaned down slightly, after looking about with great caution. "I went to the Festival last night…" she whispered. "After the family had gone, I wished for a dress and beside my mother's grave over there, I found one… my bird friends, who always help me, showed it to me…" Danni nodded – somehow it was easy to accept that an animal would help her – as she continued: "…and I went and danced with the prince… and no one recognised me… then I went back home and became the servant again…" She paused and looked sadly off at the tent. "So I hoped I would go again tonight, and I asked my stepmother again, and again there were extra chores, and again in the end, forbidden… and after they had gone, when I wished for a dress, the birds led me to this one…" her voice faded again.

"You don't want to go…?" Danni asked.

"I'm afraid…" she replied.

"Afraid?" Danni asked.

"Afraid of being found out… that I am really just a scullery maid… that I'm not who he thinks me to be… that my family don't even want me… that he if he finds out he will be disappointed…"

Danni shuddered for a moment, she understood. "Is there no one else you can talk to…?" she asked. "Your father…?"

The woman let out a sad little laugh and Danni realised: *Since he hadn't been defending her from all the abuse being hurled at her for all these years, there was no reason to expect him to help her now!* Danni thought for a moment. "You say you look after the house?" she asked.

"Yes, every bit," she said, matter of factly. "I clean and do the laundry and feed the animals and help with the cooking and…"

Danni was clearly impressed. "You certainly are capable." The woman looked surprised. "Really?"

"Goodness, yes!" Danni enthused, how could she not realise! "Why, I have met some people who can barely make a decision regarding what's right or wrong, whether something is sensible or not and you can manage an entire household?" Danni shook her head.

Danni went on, "Where do you live?" A delicate finger pointed over some trees and Danni could see a lovely manor home. Her mouth dropped open. "Oh my," she got out. "You take care of that place?" The woman nodded. "That's huge. Well, I bet you could go anyplace else and… and… be appreciated and make something of yourself! That would certainly show them! See how well they got along without you."

The woman looked down at Danni. "I would like that…" she sighed. "I would like that a lot…" and she stood up.

"What…?" Danni asked, perplexed.

"To see how they get along without me…" She looked at Danni again. "Dancing and dancing and then running away like I did last night… I felt so free… I felt I hadn't a care in the world and no one knew… no one had a clue as to what I had done. I danced with a prince and he didn't want to dance with anyone else… and I ran home in the moonlight with him chasing me and hid away from him and got back home with no one the wiser."

Danni was captivated. How wonderful that must have felt. To have done something so astonishing and no one would know but you. Free.

"You weren't afraid…?" Danni asked.

She shook her head. "Not until a few minutes ago… I thought I heard someone saying what I was doing was wrong… that I was just a scullery maid… and… I stopped… I… doubted…"

"Oh, I think you can do anything," Danni sighed.

The woman smiled. "I do, too… now…" she said and she turned around, calling over her shoulder, "Good bye little mouse…" and started to run over the grass. Away from the tent. Away from her father's house.

"But where will you go…?" Danni called.

"Away!" she heard.

"But… the prince!" Danni called.

"Oh… if it is truly meant to be, he will find me!" and the woman was gone.

Danni stood there, transfixed. *Meant to be? Meant to be…* it went round in her head. She thought about what Leo had said. How could she still deny there was a 'meant to be' when the things that had happened over the last few days had, in fact, happened? It was dizzying, the whole idea, and the whole concept. How could it be? How was it supposed to 'be'?

These thoughts were interrupted by a soft call: "Danni…?" She turned sharply and saw Simon coming along the hedges. "Anyone here…?"

For a moment Danni wondered at what had just happened. Was it real or had it been a dream, a trick of the moonlight? And then, off in the distance, where the beautiful woman had run, she saw the glimmer of a finely spun silver shoe that looked like glass. She smiled and bounded over to Simon.

"I'm here, Simon! I'm here!" she called. He stopped and looked down at her, all but dancing on the grass.

"I thought I heard someone else. What, were you talking to yourself?" he asked, placing his hands on his hips.

"Oh, no… no… there was a beautiful woman… she was going to the Festival but…" she looked off. "She changed her mind…" Simon bent down and placed his hand before the mouse who, startled at first, climbed up and let herself be placed on his shoulder. She was suddenly very, very tired.

"We'd better get back to the others before they get worried…" he said gently and started down the rise and back towards the camp when he saw Doyle heading up the rise towards them. It was almost laughable how serious the kid looked. Simon smiled.

"Is everything all right?" Doyle all but demanded.

Simon looked at him, sizing him up and Doyle could feel it. He dropped his head slightly, but still looked at Simon. "Nature can't be rushed, boy," Simon told him.

Doyle nodded, his attention drawn to Danni, her body waving slightly on Simon's shoulder. Immediately concerned, he reached up and took her in his hands before Simon could do anything.

"Danni, are you all right?" he whispered to the mouse. Danni smiled up at him, her eyes half-lidded with sleep.

"I'm sleepy…" she sighed.

Doyle smiled down at her. "It is very late," he told her and started back down the rise to the campsite, Simon following close behind. And Simon began to feel sleepy himself.

"I had a *big* day…," added Danni.

"Several big days…" Doyle assured.

"I'd like a regular sized one, please?"

And Doyle let out a chuckle. "Well see…"

As they arrived at the campsite, Leo waiting impatiently on the pillow on his seat on the cart, Danni said: "You know, Doyle, Simon is very smart… maybe he can help you figure out how to get home, hmmm?" Simon's ears perked at this.

Doyle felt his face grow hot. "You don't worry about that, Danni, you just get some rest…" He saw Leo's concerned face and assured, "She's very tired," and he sat the mouse on the pillow next to the cat.

Leo helped her get comfortable and curled himself around her, snuggling his face into Danni's little body and giving her a small lick. Doyle smiled, then turned to arrange his sleeping cushion and blanket. The Festival was still going on, but there seemed a bit of disorder. He saw Simon setting up his own sleeping arrangements nearby. Maybe Simon hadn't heard Danni…

But Simon asked, "What did Danni mean, Doyle… how to get home?"

Doyle thought quickly. "Really, I'll have no problem," he said. "I just wanted to see them to town, you know, I think she's just concerned I won't be able to find my way back…"

"Will you?" Simon asked almost sharply, a taunting edge on the outside of the question.

"Of course," Doyle answered a little defensively. He looked over at the cat and mouse sleeping quietly. "I just want to be sure they're both all right…" he ventured.

He looked back at the Festival tent and changed the subject. "The woman hasn't come back," he said softly. Simon barely looked up, seeming intent on setting up his makeshift bed.

"Woman?" he asked cautiously.

"The Maiden in Gold," Doyle replied.

Simon looked him square in the eye. "I guess it was a one-night deal," he said. Then he narrowed his eyes. "What's this all about, kid?" he asked. "I can see you don't really like me and that's okay, I don't care much about you… but you are getting a little fixated on things going on around here that are really just every day occurrences. People come and people go, each and every day. Makes me wonder if you really *are* from around here… I mean… one would think you would *know* that… if you *were*…"

Doyle almost took a step back. Instead he lowered his eyes. The man was right. Maybe he was reading too much into things. Maybe these were every day occurrences. Maybe he did need to have a closer look around and see for himself. And maybe he had to keep his mouth closed about things with Simon and get over thinking he might trip the man up. He looked up and found Simon was laying himself out on his bedding.

"I'm sorry…" Doyle offered. Simon barely looked at him, he was beginning to feel very tired indeed and it was unnerving him. He had to stay. He had to stay longer to finish this, to see that it was all really going to come undone.

"No need…" Simon replied. "I think we could all use some shut-eye." Doyle nodded and settled himself onto his own cushioned mat. He took off his jacket and carefully folded it over to use as a pillow then pulled the blanket around him and set his head down. He could feel the books. He sighed.

And then his eyes flew open. There was a movie he had seen before the war, in his village with all the other children of the town. A western from America. Shut-eye. They had said 'shut-eye' and it was the first time Doyle had ever heard the expression. The head of the cattle herd had broken up a fight and told all the men they needed to bed down for the night as they were moving the cows a long way the next day. They needed some shut-eye. Doyle froze on his side, not wanting to breathe, not wanting to look over at Simon for fear the man would be able to tell that he knew. While the man didn't sound completely like the cowboy, he did have a similar accent: American. He was an American. No one else here sounded like him, no one Doyle had met so far, everyone either sounded like they were from England or had some other European accent.

Doyle was confused. Americans were allies of England… still… he didn't look like an American… well… like any of the pictures he had seen of them. The newspapers he'd read from time to time had articles about things that were happening over in America and he *had* seen some movies and then there were his history books, but even those pictures were from thirty some years before, still none of them had long hair and even fewer had the strange facial hair Simon had, a moustache and a beard that connected with the moustache but then only grew on his chin. It looked like the face of a billy goat, only better maintained.

His mother had always told him to trust his first instincts, not to make any snap judgments about people, but to always take note of his first reactions as they were usually right. And he knew now that he had been right. But he also realised that there was no way to trick him into admitting anything. He had been a little silly to think he could. He would just be as natural as he could and watch. He had uncovered this much, he could uncover more. He would. Somehow he knew he had to.

His mind racing about, Doyle finally allowed himself to be caught by sleep.

Chapter 22
A Turning of Tables, a Turning of Tides

The morning broke grey and somewhat overcast, as though the sky itself was not sure it wanted to wake up.

Danni woke to find herself curled up on the cart between Leo's front paws, his chin precariously close to her head, leaving just enough room for her to eye all around. It was odd to her how tired she had become the night before. It wasn't as if she had done *that* much, but she had slept deeply and, from all appearances, for a long time. From her vantage point she could see people milling about, some chatting with one another and she could also see Doyle at their fire circle, arranging wood and fanning the gradually building flames. Beside him was his pan, beside that, some wrapped items Danni imagined were left-overs from the night before.

She thought back for a moment to the night before – the woman in the moonlight. Her story was sad and yet inspiring. Danni barely said anything to her, in fact she had been hoping the woman would go down to the Festival and be pursued by the prince – anything to be rescued from where she was. It was sad the woman could not even rely on her own father. Even though Danni did not understand what her own Mother did, her Mother had been good to her and taken good care of her. And when Danni was smaller and her cousins would call her names, her Mother had protected and comforted Danni.

And, last night, Danni had really not done that much – the woman seemed to be making all the decisions on her own. But the woman's fear of being a disappointment, how it had mirrored Danni's own fears. "Oh, how could the prince or anybody be disappointed in her?" Danni thought. 'If it is meant to be, he will find me' she had said. And if he didn't, then that seemed to be all right with her as well. Danni thought about it. Maybe having been in such an unhappy situation with her stepsisters had made her this way, gave her the strength to move on without fear. Maybe she was afraid but was hiding it. Danni's eyes opened very wide.

The shoe! She had left a shoe! Danni smiled in spite of herself. She eased herself away from Leo's legs and stretched.

"You're awake?" the cat asked, causing Danni to jump and let out a squeak much like the one she had emitted the night before.

Doyle looked up from the fire ring, and seeing both Leo and Danni moving, he smiled. "Breakfast soon," he said and went back to it.

Danni looked up at Leo's golden eyes, "You could give a person warning…"

"What if you'd been asleep?" he countered. "I didn't want to wake you." There was truth to this and Danni continued to smile.

"Good morning sleepy heads…" Simon greeted, approaching the group from the fayre site.

Leo sniffed, "She was the sleepy one, I was merely keeping her warm…"

"So those little snores I heard earlier were from some other cat?" the man teased.

He seemed in a very pleasant mood and Danni was happy for this. There were a few moments the night before where she thought perhaps he had been thinking of leaving them, and Danni wasn't sure what she would have done. She thought of the beautiful woman and what she had said. 'If it was meant to be…'

Simon had moved over to Doyle and sat on the stone near the fire circle. "I've managed to secure some work around the fayre," he stated, "so I won't be readily available. But I should be easy enough to find if you need me."

Doyle looked at the man with a smile. "That's good to know…" he said, "You've really been very kind… I'm sorry if…," and he faded off.

Simon took on a grin. "No need, no need… I think everyone was pretty exhausted after yesterday."

It made Danni happy to see them chatting so and even with Simon going off to work, he was making it clear he would be easy to find.

Simon continued: "I'll be over at the animal corral first… then over at the saddler… and the tent with the tools… oh, and a couple of the food stalls so I might be paid in some tasty treats."

"Food?" Leo asked.

Simon held up his hands. "No promises, but sometimes these people would rather let go of a loaf of fresh bread or a cake or pie before they let go of a penny. And as that's what I would usually spend it on, the better for me!"

He was certainly in a jolly mood, Doyle thought as he smiled at Simon, who began to put his sleeping gear together. Simon had been gone when Doyle woke, but he knew Simon would be back for the bed things that were still on the ground. He had decided then to give every appearance of acceptance. He would not share or divulge anything that might bring the man any closer to him, but he would be polite and forthright. He felt his books in his pockets. He would be able to get to them after Simon had gone. Danni had to know about what was happening with the stories. He wasn't certain how to tell her yet, but he knew he had to let her know.

His thoughts were interrupted by a loud conversation going on nearby, and though Doyle preferred to stay out of other's business, it was hard not to hear.

"Oh he was in a right temper…" the one man was saying.

147

Judging by his clothing, Doyle recognised him as one of the Guards who had been around the tent the day before and more than likely one of the one's assigned last night.

"…Waited and waited. Finally he danced with some of the lovelies, what they came there for, wasn't it?"

The person he was sharing the story with let his head back and laughed; it was a piercing sound. "Is it true he knocked over the punch bowl?"

The Guard now laughed: "No, no, no… that was some nasty bit of work from over the hill… Seems her sister was finally having a dance with him and she got right jealous so when she was positioning herself to be at a better vantage point for the end of the dance and maybe be next up, well, wouldn't you know she just jostled the table and down came the bowl, crashing to the floor, drink everywhere… and what does she say? 'No worries, I'm all right,'" and he burst into laughter anew. "Instead of leaving as respectable folk would, they all stayed, proud as you please. But she never did get a dance with him. 'Cause he just took off out of the tent, went away over that rise. Some of the other men went after him, and his groomsman had his horse. Next thing you know… he's racing away, back up to the castle!"

"Will there be the last Festival tonight, then?" the listener asked.

"Dunno…" the Guard reported. "I wasn't up there last night, but I hear there was quite a row over his leaving like he did. Well… I best get back to it… seems nobody's in a very good one this morning…" he observed. "Cept maybe you and me, eh?" And again, laughter that grated down Doyle's spine like nails on a blackboard.

Cinderella hadn't come. If it was Cinderella. He would have to look and see.

Reheating some of the things from yesterday wasn't a large chore, and when they were about ready, in his periphery, Doyle saw Simon withdraw something from his shirt. Doyle didn't move sharply, but did reposition himself ever so slightly.

It was a book. A small book, thickset, with a deep red cover, but a book nonetheless. Doyle wondered for a moment if it was one of the blank ones like he'd just bought, but seeing the way Simon moved the pages and held it, he could tell there was print in it – and that it was old. Then Simon wrapped an elastic band around it and placed it back in his shirt. Doyle took the pan off the fire. "I hope you're all ready…" he called out.

Leo looked up from his requisite morning cleaning, which Danni had been observing with a cocked eyebrow. She knew the cat never got that dirty, but he would clean as if he had been dragged through mud. The farm cat had never been that fastidious and he was often more dirty. Maybe it had to do with Leo's tale. She opened her mouth to say something, but then remembered how hesitant Leo had been telling her in the first place. She wasn't about to tread on that. But before she could come up with any other topic, Leo jumped delicately down from the cart and made his way to Doyle. Danni skittered down the cart and did the same.

"I'm going to have to take mine with me, Doyle," Simon was saying, and he took up a slice of bread, placing it on some of the extra paper. And held it out for Doyle to place a sausage he had cut length-ways. He reached into another bag and pulled out an apple. "This ought to hold me," he said congenially and as an afterthought, "Oh, there's cherries in there as well!"

Doyle perked up: "Cherries? Oh I haven't had cherries in almost a year…" and then he abruptly stopped himself.

"Not in season where you live?" Simon asked casually.

Doyle looked up, innocently, "We don't have a tree," he smiled. "And none nearby. But this is a real treat, thank you, Simon."

Simon nodded. He took up his pack and his sleeping gear. "Do you mind if I put this on the cart, Doyle? Save me a bit of weight…"

Danni smiled. He was planning on coming back. That was a certainty.

"Sure…" the lad replied and got some food together for Leo and Danni.

Simon placed his sleeping gear on the cart and hoisted his pack on his back. "See you later, or see you around!" he called out and started off towards the fayre, whistling the same tune they had heard when he first appeared on the path.

"Happy little ditty," Leo observed and Doyle was finding it positively eerie how the cat could almost read his own thoughts, for when he looked at him – sure enough, Leo was gazing right up at him with his great golden eyes.

Doyle had sliced up some apple and cheese and set it before Danni, then he took a cherry out of the bag, looked it over and placed it before the mouse as well. "Have you had cherries before, Danni?" The mouse shook her head. "They can be very sweet and juicy… but there's a seed in the centre, so be careful…" With a nod, Danni took a bite. She smiled up at Doyle, a bit of juice on her mouth.

How old was the mouse? He wondered. If neither animal knew dates nor years it would be impossible to tell, but the fact that she hadn't had a cherry, if they were to be had here seasonally, could mean that she was not even a year old. He thought about that, but not really knowing the lifespan of a mouse, he felt ill-informed.

He knew that back home, many were taken off by birds of prey, others killed by cats and some even by dogs. He had no real idea how long Danni might live, and as he looked at her making a large dent in the cherry he had given her he was struck by how fond he had grown of her. And Leo. He knew cats lived fairly long lives… his grandmother's cat scoured her neighbourhood for almost eighteen years, or so he had been told. But mice were smaller.

The two of them seemed to live charmed lives here, not being bothered by other animals, no real threat from the birds above, and the people regarded them with, at most, a minimal amount of surprise. Still, some were non-plussed to hear them speak while others felt it was only due to their being 'magical' or a disguised fairy. This in itself gave Doyle every indication that he was, most certainly, in a totally different place and that the place he was in, somehow, was where all the fairy tales he had ever heard or read lived together in relative companionable ease. Thoughtfully, he took a bite of his food and wondered how he could ever explain all that to Leo and Danni and get them to understand. He also wondered about the disappearing stories. Were they only in his book? Was everything actually all right back home? If he could remember them was that still enough? Then he began to wonder if he actually could remember them all… for if he had indeed forgotten them, how was he to remember what he may have forgotten?

He became very quiet for a moment and took the time to listen inside himself. It was a trick his father had taught him, about being still and letting an answer come. It was not always a full sentence, it was sometimes a feeling or a word and it usually corresponded with an instinct he might have already had. Finally when he could listen without his ears, the only word he could come back with was 'Simon'. The only feeling was one of dread.

Still unclear as to how to proceed, he continued to eat his breakfast. Nearby, they heard a couple of people arguing. And it struck Doyle how since they had gotten to the fayre and even at the Festival the night before, there had been no cross words. Everyone had something kind to say to the other. There was laughter, gentle and happy. But today… between the gossiping of the Guard and now the angry tones of someone near… He thought of what Simon had said about every day occurrences and that maybe this was one of them. But if he was also to believe what he felt, then maybe this wasn't normal. He would have to set out and see which was true.

Mechanically, he had begun to clean while he pondered the situation, not really paying attention to anything around other than the task at hand and the thoughts going round in his head. He reached down for his shoes, putting one on and tying it then reaching for the other, careful to place the… he looked at his shoe. The tongue which had been hanging on a thread, the crucial bit of leather to keep the ties from binding his feet, was no longer there. He looked around where he had put his shoes and saw nothing. He checked under his bedding. Finally his eyes landed on Danni, who was trying to hide a smirk. He looked questioningly at the mouse.

"What's the matter, Doyle?" she asked, now trying not to laugh. "Cat got your tongue?" He turned around to the cart and saw Leo lying on his back with the soft leather piece between his front paws and partially in his mouth. The cat froze, staring upside down at Doyle. Slowly he took the piece from his mouth and held it up over himself towards Doyle. And a blink later he smiled his huge, disarming smile.

Doyle shook his head and rose, crossing to the cat with a sigh and taking the proffered piece of leather, shaking his head at the cat before going back by his mat and sitting back down. He looked at the tongue and where it belonged on his shoe. He couldn't remember if he had brought needle and thread or if that would really help.

Suddenly he missed his mother very badly.

Leo had edged over to him and looked at him with wide eyes. "I'm sorry, Doyle…" he whispered, "it… it's just so soft…" Doyle looked at the cat who really did look very apologetic and it was probably one of the funnier things the boy had ever seen. He took Leo up in his arms and held the cat, rubbing his face into his fur and laying his forehead against the cat's so that any bit of tears he had felt about to shed were truly gone and he smiled. Leo, for his own part, was too stunned to protest at the sudden show of affection before finding himself enjoying it. He gently placed a paw on Doyle's face.

Danni observed this from a distance. She didn't quite know what to make of it all, only that she suddenly felt very lonely. She then noticed a pair of golden eyes and a pair of blue eyes gazing at her.

The boy and the cat were smiling. "Are we going to have to come and get you or don't you want to be part of this?" Doyle asked.

She was across the grass and onto his leg in barely a moment, crawling up his arm and onto Leo as well. She let her nose touch Doyle's and then rubbed Leo's. The three friends sat that way for a few minutes, enjoying the feeling of being with each other.

Finally, Doyle said; "We should get all this cleaned up, don't you both want to look about the fayre some more?" He released Leo and the cat gave himself a shake allowing his ruffled hairs to fall back into place. Danni started to climb down and felt something beneath her feet in Doyle's jacket. She stopped for a second. She looked up at him questioningly.

"Doyle..." she hesitated. "What is this...? Did... did you get your book?"

For a moment, he wanted to say no, that it was his new book, he wanted to keep the feeling of happiness between the three of them for another moment longer. But, he knew he couldn't lie. Not anymore. "Yes," he said simply.

Danni searched his face. "Was there a story... about a boy and his cow?" Doyle nodded. "And... it's gone...?" Again, Doyle nodded.

"And a nursery rhyme..." he told her. "About a man being too long at the fayre..."

Danni's face screwed up sadly. "He was... buying ribbons...?" She began to cry in full force. "What have I done?" she wailed, "What have I done...?"

Doyle scooped her up and held her close, shushing her and rubbing her head as he had before. Leo stood close by, observing it all uneasily. It took some doing but it seemed to calm her again. After she had hiccoughed once and snuffled, she looked off, vacant.

"Danni..." Doyle said and she didn't shift. "Danni," he said a little more sharply. And she looked at him. "You've told me about certain things and we've only been able to tie them in with *some* of the missing stories, right?" After a moment, she nodded. "Well then, it isn't just you. Someone else is doing this. And there are lots of other empty sections, Danni, sections that I can't really remember myself, but you told me about *all* the things you may have done, right?"

She looked at him sadly. "I saw a beautiful woman on the path... when I told you I saw someone and thought they might be able to help you? Her name was Belle and she was running from a beast in a castle... I told her to go…" Doyle nodded, he had thought as much. Danni took in a breath, and continued, "And last night…" she whispered. "I saw the Maiden in Gold…" Doyle's mouth opened slightly.

"I didn't say much, really, Doyle… it was if she had already made up her mind. I told her I thought she was capable… and that it was so sad about how she was living… with people who didn't care about her… I said that I thought she was beautiful and could do anything… and she left. I tried to call her back, she had told me about the prince dancing with her and I thought it would be so lovely if they both fell in love and he took her away from that awful place… so I reminded her about the prince. She said something funny…"

"What?" Doyle asked.

"That if it was meant to be, he would find her. It was like something you would say, Leo, but I understood it. If being with her was right for him, he would look for her. And she left a shoe!"

"She what?" came Doyle's question quickly.

"She left a shoe…" Danni hesitated. Doyle set her on his knee and dug his book out of his pocket. He flipped the pages and saw the title page: "Cinderella". It was still there. He scanned the pages. The beginning, all seemed there and right… but the second night of the dance there appeared to be some changes. And the story didn't have an ending.

This story was being written as they sat there and talked about it!

What the Guard had said about the prince being angry the night before was there, and the stepsister upending the punch bowl after jealously watching her sister dance with the prince was there, and the prince going off with his men in close pursuit was also there…

The prince had found the slipper.

Doyle looked up at Danni with a smile of disbelief, "He found the shoe, Danni."

"It's all right? The story is all right?"

"It's not as I remember it, and it's not even all here, but Danni… it isn't completely gone either."

"But what does that mean?" she asked.

Doyle shook his head, "I don't know…"

"Do you think we should tell Simon…?" she ventured. Doyle looked at her seriously, "I'm afraid to, Danni."

"Do you think he'll be mad at me?"

"Danni, do you know how hard it's been for me to explain these stories to you and Leo?" Reluctantly the mouse nodded. "I don't know if I can try to explain it to someone else. Especially a person. And I know you care about Simon and all, but…" he took in a breath. "I think he's almost as judgemental as you've been."

Danni paused, taking in a breath, about to defend Simon when she realised what Doyle had said. "You don't think I am anymore?" she asked softly.

Doyle gave a wry smile, "Well. Not as much." He paused. "Danni, the minute you became concerned about Jack… that was when you started to,

152

well, delay your judgements, and instead, you began to think about the person. And you really did it with Cinderella. It's a big word, Danni... but you began to empathise with her. You started to understand her. You were sensitive to her. You didn't just tell her what to do..."

She recognised the truth of this. She didn't give the Maiden in Gold any advice. Instead she had tried to understand her. She was sad for her. And she really couldn't tell her what to do because, for the first time, she didn't actually know what she *should* do.

Suddenly, Danni wanted to take action. "So do we try to find her? Do we tell her the prince is looking for her? Do we tell her?" and looking into Doyle's face she saw the answer. She could do nothing. She *had* to do nothing. 'If it was meant to be, he would find her.' She understood it now. And she wanted to continue talking about it.

"You really don't think Simon would understand?"

"I'm afraid to risk it, Danni. We don't want to upset the balance any more than it already seems to be."

She thought about this and as much as she wanted to talk to Simon about it all, she could understand what Doyle was saying. Both she and Simon could be opinionated. Very opinionated. She would defer to Doyle for the time being. And so she nodded.

Doyle smiled back at her though he wanted to scream for joy as the tension left his body. He had skirted the issue so delicately and, while it wasn't the complete truth, he did get out some of his other chief fears – having to try and explain it all to someone else and that Simon might have issues in the judgement area. The fact that he knew Simon was lying about some things and that he might have something to do with the missing stories as well... Doyle didn't want to break Danni's heart with the former and until he had more proof of the latter, he felt it best to keep his own opinions to himself. Instead, "What shall we do today, then?" came from his mouth.

Danni didn't know how to react or what to say. Of course she wanted to go out, but now she was terrified that she might say or do something to upset some balance of which she wasn't aware. She wanted to find the beautiful woman and tell her everything would be all right but then she wondered if it really would be. She looked for inspiration from Leo, but she could immediately see that he had something else on his mind. Doyle saw it too.

"Leo...?" he asked.

"Doyle," said Leo, "would it be possible... maybe, do you think... would you please get me some yarn...?"

Doyle let out a big laugh and Danni joined in. Leo smiled. This was going to be a good day.

Chapter 23
The Story That Couldn't Go Away

Simon cursed under his breath as he walked along. It wasn't gone. The damned story wasn't gone. It wasn't finished either, but still, it wasn't gone! He couldn't just meander around looking for the Maiden in Gold, he had too much to do at the moment... he shouldn't have asked if there was work! But then, he knew it would look peculiar if he turned anything down and the last thing he wanted now was to have anyone point a finger at him and cry 'outsider', not if things might get difficult. No, he would leave that position for the boy. He knew people, he would be able to assimilate and, if need be, lead in the finger pointing. And even when they determined the boy had nothing to do with anything – if they got that far – Simon felt fairly sure he would be far enough away from the town and its impending upheaval. Hopefully, Cinderella was in enough disarray that the story would unravel and disappear... but he couldn't rely solely on hope, he knew that from the past.

He had to be certain, he had to see the outcome, the disappearance, or at least see the start of the transformation of this world, and the appearance of the kind of reality he was familiar with back home. Then he might be able to make things right. Then he might bring this world to a better place. A place where the weak are cast aside, so the strong can thrive; where fear is forbidden and boldness rewarded; where fairy stories exist no longer, because a head in the clouds never got anyone anywhere. A place of strong people. Rational people who understood that only the strong really did survive and worked to stay that way.

He knew he had to do something, he felt the balance beginning to teeter off; more people were arguing, they were gossiping more, getting others riled up in a way that was totally foreign and different from ways he had seen, and he knew that one or two things more would upset the apple cart well enough, and he would see it all fall out of place.

"... Leads the geese out every morning..." he heard and stopped. He leaned over and made to adjust his shoe... and listen.

An old woman holding court with another woman, not quite as old, but certainly not young and, with a stupid viciousness was bobbing her head at everything the old one was saying. "He's a good boy, you know, always does his chores, and watches the Old King's geese, well, that's a privilege he holds dear, you know? As does his family! Last night he comes home and says how the Old King has bade him take on a helper! He don't *need* one, you know? Seems the betrothed of his Prince brought a girl with her and wanted her to have a job, keep her out of trouble, don't you know, one of *those* sorts... so they puts her with *my* grandson! He says she's fair pretty enough, hair like night, but she won't friendly up to him! Said when he tried yesterday, his hat blew off and he spent quite a time looking for it... he just sat the rest of the time, over by the lake yonder, just wishing he had his job on his own. I tells you if this keeps up, he said he would tell the Old King to either make the girl gone, or him."

'The lake over yonder...' Simon had seen that lake. It was just on the other side of the fayre, and if one went directly across it, one would be in town. He knew he had to get over there and he knew it had to be today, because the next day, the Old King would be watching. Short. A quick fix. Checking the position of the sun in the sky, he knew he had enough time to do one of his jobs, make excuses for another and find Danni. He knew they would be walking about the fayre, her curiosity alone would not keep her still for long. And a quick trip back to the cart as well.

He stood up and hurried down the path.

******

The trio were enjoying themselves as they walked about the other side of the fayre. There were more games of chance here, more people parting with their money for the sheer joy of attempting. Some were more vocal about losing, but for the most part, amenable to getting a consolation prize. There were more children than the day before, or at least they were noticing more. Leo was fixated on the bird toy again, but was drawn away by the promise of yarn.

Everywhere they walked, people seemed to be enjoying themselves, but Doyle noted an undercurrent of quiet hostility. People reacted more to being accidentally jostled and some people actually seemed to jostle others on purpose. It was a rare occurrence, but one he noticed all the same.

Finally they approached a cart selling woollens. Doyle looked at the caps, considering getting one, but then, knowing it would make the rest of his clothes stand out more, he opted against it and instead, he lifted Leo to see the skeins of yarn laid out for purchase. The selection was not as varied and vast as the ribbon cart, but they were still of lovely colours. Finally, Leo turned a look up to Doyle which the lad thought meant put the cat down. This he did and knelt beside him.

"They all look very nice..." Leo started.

Doyle nodded. "Do you know which colour you'd like?"

"Well, you see that's just it, Doyle..." Leo informed. "I can't really see what you all call colour. Some of them are darker than the others, that I can make out... but..."

Danni stared at her friend. "But... how do you know what colour you are? I mean when people compliment your coat..."

Leo smiled at Danni. "Well I can tell when people are saying nice things, but then I have also heard what they say so I can remember that... And when I see something that someone names a certain colour I can usually remember what shade of dark or light... so..."

"I'm sorry, Leo..." Danni said.

"It's all right, Danni," the cat smiled, "I'm used to it..." and he looked up at Doyle, "but would you mind just picking one out for me...? I don't care about the colour... so long as it's soft..." and the thought of his impending ball of yarn was so thrilling to the cat, his paws kneaded the ground beneath him happily.

Doyle nodded and stood back up. He touched varying skeins, shutting his eyes while doing so. On one he stopped. He lifted it up. He and Danni turned a wry smile to each other when they discovered the yarn he had picked was grey. It had more of a bed shape to it, and the centre had been tied off, but he knew he could put this into goodly ball order in no time. He handed it to the woman in charge and paid her with some of the coins Simon had given him. There was no incident to this and Doyle knelt down to show his purchase to Leo. The cat nudged it with his nose then let his face be caressed by it. He nodded slowly. Soft.

"I'll keep it in the bag for now, Leo," Doyle said and the cat nodded, watching his new treasure become safely ensconced. They turned and started up the path only to see Simon striding over to them, a look of concern on his face.

"Thought I'd never find you," he breathed.

Danni furrowed her brows, "Is everything all right...?"

The man smiled at the mouse. "Nothing we can't handle, Danni, nothing we can't handle..." he assured and turned his attention to Doyle. "Seems we have to move the cart again," he told him, perplexed agitation reflecting through him. "I was going to do it myself, but figured if I couldn't find you before it was moved, and then you all tried to go back, well... that would be a worry I don't want to think about..."

Doyle found himself nodding. If he allowed himself, he could see where Simon could be quite affable and even charming. He was certainly being considerate here. "No, I appreciate that..." Doyle smiled. "Should we go now?"

The man rolled his eyes. "Well that's part of the problem... they want us over by the lake," he pointed and Doyle could barely make it out, "And people are starting to make a beeline. I thought I'd go scout out a place and you all could bring the cart."

"May I come with you?" Danni asked before she realised she had said it. Simon smiled at her. The mouse didn't disappoint.

"I'd like that very much, Danni!" he enthused. "With all this 'go here, go there, do this, do that,' well it's about ruined my good temper from this morning. It will be nice to have you with me, please..." and he reached out his hand to Doyle's shoulder. The mouse leapt on and was placed on

Simon's shoulder. Simon kept his hand on Doyle's shoulder, clasping it and looked at Doyle. "So we'll meet you at the lake?" he asked.

"As soon as we can," Doyle promised and he and Leo turned themselves in the direction of the cart.

Simon smiled again. It wouldn't be that soon. "Well, then my little Danni... let's be off." And they went the other direction, quickly heading for the lake.

Chapter 24
And a Grasshopper Shall Join Them

As much as he didn't like being separated from Danni, Doyle knew he couldn't put up much of a fuss without making it seem as though he didn't trust Simon. And as much as he didn't trust Simon, he knew he had to have a bit more to go on than a feeling and something he couldn't explain – they had never even heard of the movies, much less American Westerns. But he hurried along, not wanting to keep them waiting, and wanting to get back to Danni quickly. Leo was trotting along with him, when he heard:

"… She never came back from lunch and now she hasn't turned up this morning!"

He saw a woman holding a tray of candies, talking to another woman. Doyle also saw that he and Leo were passing by the candy stall where the woman had offered them a sampling and had spoken about Cinderella. He slowed slightly and Leo almost fell over himself trying to adjust to what was happening. He looked up at Doyle in mild consternation when the lad put his finger to his lips and indicated with a slight cock of his head that they should listen. Leo gave a vague nod and then set to looking bored. Doyle knelt beside him and made to look into the cat's fur.

"Mind you… she had some pretty pie in the sky ideas, this one did… mooning over the Festival and that woman what showed up all in gold… you think it was she herself going to the dance the way she went on… but still… she's not turned up and now I'm a pair of hands short!" The other woman clucked a sympathetic response and Doyle stood abruptly and started off.

Leo was again taken by surprise and hurried after him. "Really, Doyle, *some* indication of a stop or start *really* would be helpful to me…" he chastised.

"Sorry, Leo, but that woman was talking about the person we got the candy from yesterday…"

"*You* got the candy from…" the cat reminded.

Slicing hairs, Doyle wanted to say. "Yes, but we went to the cheese stall after that and Simon stayed to talk with her…"

"So?"

"She had been talking about the Maiden in Gold… Cinderella… and now she's disappeared."

Leo made a half-stop and then maintained his gait alongside Doyle. "That doesn't sound good." Doyle's mouth was set in a grim line. No. It didn't.

They got to the cart and made sure everything was secured. Doyle took up the handles and started to move it when he felt a shudder and stopped. Carefully setting the cart back down, he walked around it, examining the wheels. The third wheel showed him what he feared. The wheel pin was missing. Had he taken another step the wheel would have slid off the axel and who knows what kind of damage would have been done.

"What's wrong?" Leo asked.

"Wheel pin…" he replied. He pushed the wheel firmly into place and pointed. "Goes in this little hole…" He moved over to the fourth wheel to be certain it was all right and was pleased to see it was. Again he pointed. "Looks like this…" he indicated the pin to Leo. The cat nodded and began to look around the area, as did Doyle.

Abruptly Leo stopped and looked up at Doyle. "Do you think *he* did this?"

Doyle looked back at the cat. They didn't even need to say his name. Doyle nodded. "I have a spare pin… but Danni's still out there with him… and…" Suddenly, they were interrupted by:

"Danni! Danni? Looking for a mouse called Danni!! Anyone help here?" They both looked around feverishly for the small voice.

"Hello?" Doyle called, "About Danni? Who wants… hello?"

"I'm down here, giant boy."

Doyle looked to the ground, his eyes darting around until they lighted on a small grasshopper standing on one of the stones by the fire ring. Then, it sighed deeply.

"You better have made me stop for the right reason, kid…" Jon intoned, "Because I am cranky and more than a little bit tired."

Leo came up beside Doyle and looked at the bug. "Whoa!" Jon cried and took a jump back.

Doyle knelt down. "No, no, no, he won't hurt you…" he promised. "We're friends of Danni's… well… we think it's the same Danni…"

"Small, brown and opinionated? Not that there's anything wrong with that…" Jon eyed Leo as he said he last part. "Ran away from the Farm?" Both Doyle and Leo were nodding.

"You're the grasshopper!" Leo cried.

Jon looked up at Doyle. "Bright, isn't he? You must be proud."

"What about Danni?" Doyle prodded.

"Look, I've been travelling for a bit of time here… we had to take a vote on it all, I am really not so sure I like this group discussion thing, and it was decided that I go and find her… the little dog?"

"Arnie?" Leo asked.

Jon nodded. "He's dead."

Leo shook his head. "You came all this way to tell her that…?"

The grasshopper rolled his eyes heavenward. "He was killed, kitty. My friend and current employer thought it best that I come and tell Danni... I really hate being a messenger but I really had to get away from that assembly line attitude..."

"Killed..." Doyle breathed.

"Some tall man..." Jon explained. "Of course, every one of you is tall to me, but this one had been asking the dog questions about Danni and once Arnie told him he thought Danni was off to town..." he stopped. Jon didn't like thinking of that part. Even though he had a hard exterior, indignities and especially injustice were just wrong. He continued: "It was discussed and I was volunteered to come." He looked around. "Is she here?"

"Tall man...?" Doyle was white and Jon saw this.

Hesitating ever so slightly, Jon continued: "He's apparently been to the Farm before... sounded like he knew her... a repair man it seemed..." Doyle sat back on the ground. The cat didn't look too good either. "This seems to be worse news than I thought..." Jon ventured.

"We've got to get to the lake!" Doyle exclaimed.

"We have to move the cart!" Leo reminded.

"The pin..." and he rose to go to the tool kit he had in the back of the cart when he noticed. No one else was moving their carts. The few people who had stayed the night around them, their carts and caravans were all still there. One of the owners was heading up to his caravan and Doyle tried:

"Sir..." he called, "Sir..." The man turned, pointed to himself and after Doyle nodded he came over. "Were you told to move your cart? Over to the lake?" he asked.

The man looked curiously at Doyle. "No..." he said. "No, in fact I had asked the Guards in particular today, we was so upset having to leave our spot yesterday... they assured me no one was gonna be moved..."

"Thank you..." Doyle got out and the man went on his way.

"I can get there faster," Jon said. "Tell me which way." Doyle placed his hand down beside the grasshopper and he jumped on. He lifted him up and pointed in the distance.

"Over there..." he informed, pointing to the water beyond the trees. "But be careful, Jon... She's with the man you're talking about."

The grasshopper turned on Doyle. "Wha... she's what?!" he yelled.

Doyle levelled a stare at him. "I suggest you hurry. We'll be right behind you."

Jon had often wondered why he had wings. Now he knew. Stretching them out, he took to the sky. Doyle watched for a moment, then looked down at Leo. They nodded to each other and took off at a run.

******

The lake was calm and bright blue as they approached. For a moment, Danni remembered how Leo could not see colour and this saddened her

160

again for a moment, but he did seem to take it all in stride. She supposed that there was no real reason to be upset over something you never really had, but she was very happy to be able to recognise all the different shades of blue on the lake or in the sky, or the different shades of green between the grass and the trees.

The overcast had burned off and now the sun was beginning to shine again.

"You know, Danni," Simon said, "I was meaning to bring this up to you…" Attentive, the mouse cocked her head in his direction. "There's a boy up around here in danger of losing his position all because of some silly girl…"

"Losing his position?" Danni questioned.

"His job! His livelihood! The thing that makes him money and brings back food for his family…"

"Really?" Danni asked.

Simon nodded. "I was speaking to his grandma this morning. Seems the Old King has given this girl his same job and the two have to share it now…"

"That's awful!" Danni concurred. "So he's getting paid less…?"

"Well, I don't know about that… I expect as much… it wouldn't be so bad, but… he's been trying to make friends with her and she seems to be just too high and mighty for him… so much so that he just won't stand for it… seems he's going to tell the Old King that it's either him or her, someone's gotta go…"

"Well, if the Old King knows the boy, I'm sure he'll find something else for the girl to do…" but the she noticed that Simon was shaking his head.

"She came with the Princess who's supposed to marry to his son. I just know he'll keep the girl just to keep peace all around. Apparently there's nothing else for her to do…"

Danni's brows furrowed. "Oh that doesn't seem fair…"

"No," Simon intoned with a sense of finality. "No it does not. I knew you would see that! See, I told his grandma that I knew a terribly sensible mouse who had ways of making people see sense and fair play! I told her that you and I would be pleased to go and speak to them both, see if maybe we could strike a truce between them… at least get them to be friends. Do you think we could do that?"

"Oh, I would like to try," Danni nodded. "It just doesn't seem right that he might lose his job just because they don't see eye to eye…"

Simon looked over to the lake and took in a small breath. "There they are!" he said and pointed the two people standing on the long slope of grass, well off from the lake. The boy and girl were calling out and thrashing long sticks to guide some geese down to the lakeside where they would take to the water and find food or just sit along the shore, some tossing their beaks into the shallows to get bugs and others quite happy to have the mud cool along their breasts. Once the geese seemed settled, the boy and girl moved off a little and settled themselves.

Simon was getting close to them as well. "So you go on down and chat with her... and I'll talk to him... it's funny actually... because I think he really likes her..."

"What?" Danni asked as they came to a small wooden fence.

Simon took her from his shoulder and placed her there. "Well, his grandmother said he went on about how beautiful her hair was. That he just wanted a lock of it... but every time he's tried, the wind's come up and taken his hat for a wander and he spends all his time trying to catch it. Maybe if that happens I can go after his hat and you can get her to be a bit more amenable in understanding what he really wants..."

Danni's mouth opened slightly. Then she heard a song. Someone was singing so beautifully, clear like little bells, clear like the water, sweetly and earnestly and a sharp breeze came up suddenly as Danni looked over and saw that it was the girl singing. That she had let her hair down. That it looked like the night sky and the sun was dappling stars on it.

Simon sighed. "There he goes!" he called out and Danni saw that the boy had been making his way over to the girl and the wind now lifted up his hat and made to carry it off. With a sigh and a stamp of his foot he ran after it and the girl continued to sing her delicate song. "Okay Danni, you go chat with her and I'll go help the boy..."

"No..." Danni said softly. Simon stopped short. "What?"

The mouse looked at him, perplexed. "No..." she repeated, "I can't."

"But... but..." Simon spluttered, "But the boy will lose his job!"

"But she will lose her chance to be helped!" Simon froze and stared at the mouse. "If she lets him touch her hair, he won't complain to the King and the King won't come to see what the matter is! He won't see her talk to Falada, he won't hear what Falada has to say! Falada will have been killed in vain! And the girl... she won't regain her rightful place..."

She knew. She knew the story. She knew the damned story.

"But she's a stupid girl!" Simon yelled angrily. "Never standing up for herself, she *let* herself be put in that place!"

Danni stared up at him. "Because she was raised to be kind and modest and swore under an open sky not to tell a soul or she would have been killed!"

"All the better!" Simon was shouting. "At least, she would have died with dignity!"

"She was only doing what she was told! She's a good girl and should be rewarded! That other woman is a liar and needs to be found out and punished!" Danni shouted back.

Simon stepped away. She wasn't going to help. She wasn't going to help. He turned and looked for the boy. He could do something... Simon was certain he himself could still do something and he started running towards the boy.

"Danni!" they both heard.

It couldn't be them, Simon thought and stopped abruptly, they would be fixing the wheel or the axle. He spun around and saw no one. Then he noticed Danni was focusing on something else on the fence. Some... bug...? He looked at the boy, still scurrying after his hat, the girl still combing out her hair but getting close to finishing, and back at the fence where the mouse was now sitting on her haunches, her mouth dropped open in amazement. She turned to look at Simon and shook her head. Was she worried? Sad? Disappointed? – he couldn't tell. He took a few steps towards Danni.

"You killed Arnie?" Her voice was so small, so sad, so drained of everything that it almost hurt.

Simon could make out a grasshopper beside her. The bug was looking up at him with loathing. The Grasshopper and the Ants. Danni had made that one go away from his book. And here he was, ratting him out. "Simon...?" Danni tried.

The song finished.

Simon looked over his shoulder and sure enough, the girl had finished combing her hair and had it all back up in her cap and was seated near the shade of a tree. The boy was sitting nearby with his hat, sulky and pouting.

Simon, rage pouring through him, took his pack from his back and swung it with all his might at the fence and the grasshopper.

"Jon, look out!" Danni screamed as the pack hit the fence and shattered the old wood. Danni went flying with the reverberation and landed on the grass with a small thud. She shook her head to clear it and saw Jon on the ground near her. She looked about to find Simon and saw him tearing down the hill towards the lake. He was screaming something, words Danni had never heard before and with such anger it frightened her. She scurried over to her friend, she was so afraid he had been smashed, but the sturdy grasshopper appeared to be in one piece, yet wincing in pain. One of his front legs looked injured. "Oh Jon..." she breathed.

"Coulda been worse..." he intoned. "Coulda had bug guts all over and that would not have been a pretty sight..." He looked after Simon. "He didn't take that well... but your other friends should be here soon..." he said and winced again.

Danni shook her head and looked up. Simon had been *trying* to mess it up. He wanted to destroy the story. He knew what it had been about and he wanted the Goose Girl to never have her rightful place. He was the someone else Doyle had talked about. Danni set her jaw and began to run down the field to the lake.

There was a little dock and a small boat which Simon was now attempting to untie, his fury making his hands fumble. She noticed that both the boy and the Goose Girl were moving away, bringing their flock to shore, out of harm's way and away from the angry man now manning a boat. He had just shoved off when Danni careened from the dock and landed on the boat. Simon saw her and froze.

"Why, Simon?" She asked breathlessly.

A calm came over him, unearthly and sudden. "Whatever do you mean, Danni?" he asked as calmly and normally as he ever would.

"Making stories disappear... did you know that's what you were doing?" and then Danni thought: "*maybe he didn't, maybe he didn't know what was happening.*"

"Of course I knew," he said simply. "That's what I was sent here to do."

"Sent here?"

"I don't live *here*..." he spat out. "I live in a place called America. I live in a time so far away from when this place was even considered, that many people there barely even know of these stories, let alone think there's a place where they actually exist! Two Thousand and Five, Danni, that's where I come from. Way farther in the future than your little nosy friend."

"But..."

"But what? You thought I *liked* it here?" he snorted derisively. "I thought you *didn't* like it here. I thought *you* and I were going to take this place down. You see how they all are! You knew what they were all like! How stupid, how inane, and to what purpose? None. As soon as you could, you saw that their ways were wrong and you let everyone know it. I was going to take you with me... but your mom..." He gave her a level stare. "It didn't take much to rig the clock," he said.

Danni felt the air leave her.

But Simon continued: "They didn't know what they had with you! They thought you were an error, a mistake, when she brought you back in from the field, they thought she was crazy for doing it, oh, and they named you... 'Dummy'. You took so long to learn to speak, you didn't behave like the others, and you wouldn't do what you were told... 'Dummy'... She thought Danni sounded better..."

Her mother protecting her when her cousins called her names... just one name... "And I was going to help you see that the world could be as you saw it! Logical!

Right-thinking!"

Field? Had he said field? "Brought me from the field?"

Simon heaved a sigh. All that he was going to be able to do with her and that's what she latched onto. "Didn't you wonder why you had no brothers and sisters? Didn't you even notice that most animals give birth to more than one? She found you! Found you, brought you to the farmhouse, tried to raise you and didn't know what to do with you when you started displaying your talent for logic. I could have helped you, Danni... I could have shown you the right way..."

"Right way?!" the mouse exploded. "Ruining people's lives? Destroying the only things they know?"

164

"You didn't stop your cousins." Danni froze now. She hadn't. "You could have said something to them before they left that hole and were killed. No, but you felt *bad* about it… enough to destroy the clock and see to it no other mouse would run up it. You didn't blink about changing that grasshopper's life. The fox? He was going to give up on those grapes until you gave some to him and made him *promise not to judge!*" he spat the words out. "Then what else? The Prince looking for Briar Rose? Sleeping Beauty sleeps on… Hansel and Gretel will never know what it's like to be brave enough to defeat a witch… Jack will never go up to the clouds and reclaim what is rightfully his from the giant that took it from his father. Oh… and what about a pretty, pretty woman? You never told me how you managed to convince Beauty to leave the beast. She'll never know he was a bewitched man and will now die unloved." Danni flinched with each memory. "So don't go accusing me of destroying lives… I had help and I thank you very much."

She didn't know. She didn't know about what was really happening. She looked at him, his dark eyes wild, even though he remained terribly, terribly calm.

"I didn't know what I was doing, Simon, but you did!… Only now I do, and I won't do it anymore… and neither will you! I won't let you!"

"Danni," he said quietly, with a hint of ice that unnerved her: "have you heard the adage 'Don't rock the boat'? Do you know why? What that means?" The mouse was taken aback but had to think it through, it was her very nature.

"You'll tip the boat over…?"

"And fall off," he said without remorse. And with a simple sweep of his delicate hand he dashed her off and she flew over the water. He took up the oars and headed across the lake to the town. He paid no attention to the soft plop as he rowed.

******

Doyle had never known a cat to run as swiftly as Leo did now, careening down the grassy hill to the dock and the little boat now pushing across the lake. He was quite nimble for his size. He found he couldn't keep up and had begun to slow when he heard the young woman tending the geese cry out:

"That beastly man! He's pushed the little mouse into the water!"

Doyle found new energy and sailed down the hill after the cat. Leo flew off the bank, splaying his legs and paws in resolution and anguish, with equal parts of the hope of saving Danni and the terror of hitting the water.

Doyle quickly doffed his jacket and jumped in after the cat, who had submerged briefly and now was wildly pawing at the water. Doyle was grateful he hadn't dived, since the lake was shallow enough for him to stand easily, and he moved as quickly as he could to the flailing cat. Lifting him up as high as he could, he was surprised to see something in Leo's mouth. That something was Danni.

Once back on land, Leo rocked back and forth on his legs, partly as a reaction to the wet and partly in fear, which actually amounted to a double dose of fear, but for different things. He relinquished Danni's inert form to Doyle's hands and the lad looked the mouse over. She was warm, but not breathing. Cradling her in both his hands, locking his thumbs over to keep her there, he stood up and spread his legs then pulled his hands downward abruptly, swinging them between his legs. He did this two more times and noticed water come out of the mouse's mouth. With one thumb he massaged her little chest and then finally he put his mouth over her nose and mouth and gave a short, but very firm blow. It seemed an eternity to Doyle. It seemed a lifetime to Leo.

Danni coughed and more water flew from her mouth.

Doyle gave a short laugh, and held her so her nose pointed downward, she was coughing violently and drops of water continued to spray from her mouth and nose. Finally she settled and took in a few ragged breaths. Doyle let her lay straight in his palm. Her eyes opened and she looked at Doyle above her, then beside him she saw Leo, dripping, anxiously trying to peer into Doyle's palm to see. He placed an agitated paw on Doyle's hand so the lad was forced to kneel and allow Leo a good view. Danni sighed. A long, pained sigh. Doyle's smile faded.

"Danni...?" he called gently. She looked at him, but there was a vague quality about the look. "... Are you..."

"I'm cold, Doyle..." she said with a little rasp.

"Of course..." and he looked over to see the young woman standing near, holding his jacket, looking pensively at them. He moved over to her, cradling Danni in one hand, he took his jacket from her. "Thank you..." he said gratefully.

She smiled shyly and looked into his hand. "Is the little mouse all right...?" she asked.

Danni heard her and tried to sit up but was very light headed. Doyle angled his hand so she was in a position not unlike sitting.

Danni looked directly at the Goose Girl and breathed out: "You're unchanged! It's all right... You'll be all right... Be true to yourself and what you've been taught... you'll be all right..." and then slid back against Doyle's hand, closing her eyes.

The young woman took in a gasp. Doyle looked at her and saw beyond to a young boy watching over a flock of geese. *The Goose Girl.*

"Thank you," Doyle assured, "this little mouse'll be all right, too." He could feel Danni shiver in his hand so he took out his handkerchief from his jacket and began to dry her off with it. He heard a crinkling noise and looked to see Leo trying furiously to get the yarn, out of the bag which had fallen from Doyle's pocket.

The soaked cat looked up at Doyle with desperate eyes.

"Put her on it…" he cried. "It's soft…" he got out. "And warm…" and tears began to fall from his great golden eyes. Danni let out another cough and Doyle lay her on the skein of yarn, covering her with a series of threads. She shifted slightly and settled into the soft wool.

"She's going to be all right, Leo," he told the cat and put his hand on the cat's wet back. "You were so very brave."

The cat looked up at him, searching. "Was she… was she… dead…?" the cat asked, his huge eyes even larger with all his fur plastered down from the water.

"I don't know…" Doyle said softly. "I think so… she wasn't breathing. You saved her Leo," he told the cat.

Leo shook his head. "You saved her, Doyle, I wouldn't have known what to do…" Doyle drew the cat in closer to him. "We saved her," he said softly.

And in the distance they heard: "Still in a little pain up here…" and they looked up towards the broken bit of fence at the top of the hill.

They looked at one another for a second and cried: "Jon!" at the same time.

"So nice to be remembered…" the grasshopper muttered. Doyle, still carrying Danni carefully on the skein of wool, moved back up the hill with Leo.

"Jon…?" Doyle called out.

"Fence…" Jon replied "…the broken part." He had crawled onto the shattered wood so he would be a bit higher off the ground and away from any passing footfalls, and from there, he was gesturing awkwardly to them. "Is she all right?" he asked.

"Are *you* all right?" Doyle countered, looking at his twisted front leg.

"It's broken…" he admitted, "But still there. Coulda been much worse. I won't be able to play for a bit… unless I lean on something… but I think I'll be okay… What about Danni?"

Doyle nodded. "I think she's asleep…" he said. "She's breathing much easier…"

"She's *breathing*…" Leo interjected, "she wasn't…" Doyle nodded.

Jon nodded as well, "So who's carrying me?" he asked. Doyle sighed. "Can you get on my shoulder?"

"Can you bend down so I don't have to fly? Have you noticed my leg…?"

Doyle knelt down and the grasshopper leaned back and hopped onto his shoulder and said: "Thank you, so what're we going to do?" he asked. Doyle tried to look at him, but he was leaning against his shirt collar, "Do?"

"About the crazy man?" It had seemed an obvious question to Jon.

Doyle's jaw was set. "Right now, I want to take care of Danni…" he said softly. "Then we'll see about Simon."

"But he could be long gone!" Jon cried.

Doyle shook his head. "Oh no… he won't go far… he thinks he has work to do…" And they trotted along in silence, heading back to the cart.

Chapter 25
And the Dead Shall Live Again

"Is this normal?" Leo asked Doyle for what he thought was the thousandth time. They were back at the cart, it was the next morning, the sun was beginning to rise and Doyle had gotten the fire restarted.

"Really, Leo, nothing around here is normal to me so I don't think I'm the best judge on that topic... but I know she's breathing and seems to be resting comfortably. And I also know that when she wakes up she'll be hungry and thirsty..." Danni was still resting on the yarn, which had now been placed on Doyle's pillow, which was beside his sleeping mat, close to the fire circle. Both the lad and the cat had taken turns sleeping during the night with the mouse curled up between them. The lad had also replaced the wheel pin and done a number of other chores (including getting himself into another pair of trousers and letting the wet ones dry).

Leo had stayed beside Danni anytime Doyle was not. And even when he was. He hadn't eaten or drunk since they returned, nor had he cleaned himself and sections of his fur had dried awkwardly, matted in areas and dirty in others. Jon was resting on the cart, observing all. Finally, Doyle stood and went to the cart, returning with his canteen and the small bowl he had used for Leo's water. He poured some water into it now and placed it by the cat. Leo didn't move or flinch, but gazed intently at Danni's inert figure on the wool, her little chest going up and down with breath, her eyes moving underneath her eyelids and her limbs and tail twitching from time to time.

"Leo, you are not going to be any good to anyone if you don't at least drink," Doyle insisted. Grudgingly, the cat moved to the bowl in a way so he could still see Danni and he lapped at the cool water. It was very good and he began to realise how much he needed it. And other things. Once he finished drinking he began to shift nervously. Doyle shook his head. "You can go to the other side of the cart, Leo, you don't have to go far... you always clean up after yourself..."

"I hope you're not saying what I think you're saying because I'm over here..." Jon called out.

Leo looked up at Doyle and sighed. He was that obvious. "But what if..."

"Then I'll call you... don't worry..."

Very hesitantly the cat made his way to the far side of the cart for some moderate privacy. He waited for a bit and then finally, Doyle looked down at the mouse.

"I know you're awake…" he said softly. Danni opened her brown eyes and stared up at him. "Really, Danni, do you want to keep Leo this anxious?"

"I… I… don't know what to say, Doyle… part of me… wishes… oh, I've ruined everything…" she sighed and her eyes filled with tears.

Leo rushed over. "She's awake!" he cried, "She's crying! Why is she crying? Doyle, what did you do? Did you say something? Danni, Danni, please don't cry, you're all right, you're awake and you're all right, right?" Leo's backside was swaying back and forth, his tail swishing agitatedly.

Danni looked into Leo's great golden eyes. Was she all right? She didn't think so. She had loved and trusted someone who had used her and then killed her – would have killed her had it not been for Leo and Doyle, and she almost wished she had stayed dead. She had shifted the lives of so many without any regard as to why they might be doing what they were doing, and only because it didn't suit *her own* idea of what they should be doing. She had believed only in what was in front of her, what she could see, what was tangible, and now she found many of those things had been shaken. Simon was not a kindred spirit, she had all but allowed her cousins to get killed over a subliminally remembered slight, and her mother wasn't really her mother.

"Oh, Leo…" was all she could manage.

"You were dead…" Leo said simply. Danni nodded. She had been. She had been. "What did you see, Danni?" Leo asked.

"Nothing," she whispered.

"N… nothing…?" and his eyes narrowed.

"I can't… I… don't make me say, Leo…"

"Why…?" The mouse looked straight at the cat.

"Words will shrink it." Leo looked at her carefully, letting it settle. He sat down. And smiled. He leaned in and placed his nose onto Danni's head, and breathed out his warmth onto the mouse. Strangely, this comforted the mouse and she suddenly reached up to hold the cat's face, tears falling anew.

Doyle looked at them both for a time, then went back to the cart. "Sweet," Jon intoned.

"Yes…" Doyle agreed.

"I gotta get outta here…" the grasshopper said, shaking his head.

Doyle cocked his head at the bug. "This sort of stuff bother you that much?" he half smiled.

Jon was shaking his head. "No, no…" he said, gruffly, "Yeah… I just can't really participate, you know?"

Doyle shook his head. "Not really, I don't know…"

The grasshopper looked him over. "No… you wouldn't. Well, we're solitary things, you know, my kind… the only time you really see us as a group is when we're born and then we make a big deal of leaving, just pushing off... or, if we're swarming, and then we're just running on instinct. But, things like this... foreign to me. Not that I don't appreciate it... sort of... but..." He smiled. "As soon as it gets a little lighter, I can make my way easier – once all those early birds have filled up on worms... then I can more easily get around most of the things that hunger for this fine specimen of bug." And the smile faded. "Besides... Her Highness will be wanting a report."

"Doyle, do we have any more fruit?" Leo called, "Danni should eat something!"

"One minute..." the lad called back. "You'll say goodbye to her, won't you?" The grasshopper nodded. "She did the same for me," he replied.

Doyle got the bag of remaining food from the cart and went back to the fire ring. He reached in and felt the cherries. Maybe not a good idea. He pulled out an apple, "Shall I cut it?" he asked.

"I'm really not that hungry..." Danni sighed.

"Just bite off a piece, Doyle," Leo instructed. "Like before. She needs to eat."

Danni looked up into Leo's face and saw there was going to be no arguing with him. Had she done anything to Leo? Kept him from his appointed course? No wonder the cat believed there was a path to follow. If everyone was living out their lives as a story from a book, they all had to stay on course and not be changed... But Leo had spoken about forks in the road. Were there places in a story where the person could choose? Or if they did, was it always the right way? Her head swam. Doyle handed her a bit-off piece of apple.

"Doyle... are the stories always the same?" she asked.

"What do you mean? The same kind...?"

"No, each story individually... do they always stay the same when you read them?"

Doyle thought carefully about her words. He remembered reading the stories and how comforting it was that they always ended the same way – the good triumphing, the bad being punished. "I guess that's part of it, Danni... that you know what needs to be made right will be and that the bad things will be punished..." he faded out and thought again, how as he got older, certain things about the stories changed and that while their meaning was ultimately the same, how he interpreted them would change. He looked at the mouse. "But then... when you read them again... sometimes things are different..." he said. "I can't explain it, but sometimes you read something again and it seems as if you hadn't paid attention to it as much before because now you see other things..." he shrugged his shoulders. "Maybe they *do* change."

Danni wasn't sure how she felt about this, she wasn't sure how she felt about anything, but she couldn't stop her head from posing these questions. "I'm a monster..." she finally said.

Leo gasped, "What?" he snapped, and Doyle looked sharply at her.

"I'm a monster... I could have saved my cousins and I didn't... I believed a man when he told me I was doing good and right and he was evil so what I was doing was evil and I didn't even think about it... I just did it... the mouse I thought was my mother wasn't even my mother; she found me and brought me in, took me in and when she wouldn't let him take me he killed her... and I couldn't even show enough respect for her to take over her job, I just let it go so it disappeared as if she never existed..." The mouse wanted to cry again, but felt so drained of everything she just lay back on the yarn bed, barely moving.

"Eat your apple," Leo demanded.

"What?" she asked. After all she had to say, that was all she was going to get from him. No fork in the road, no placations, no swaying back and forth on his feet in agitation. The mouse looked at him. He was staring at her severely, his eyebrow cocked. Danni wasn't sure as she looked, but she thought Leo was actually angry.

"Eat your apple," he repeated, more forcefully. Instinctively, she put it in her mouth and took a bite, chewing slowly. After she swallowed she looked at the cat again but his demeanour hadn't changed. "Eat it all," he told her. She continued. Something in her told her not to cross the animal right now. "You're a monster, are you..." he said with an edge of disgust. "Someone comes along and shows you kindness and you find out later that he's trying to destroy everything you know, even you, and *you're* a monster? You could have saved your cousins? Not if they were doing what they were supposed to be doing. But then, they weren't really your cousins, were they?"

"They were all I knew..." Danni tried to inject.

"And that *other* mouse, the one who raised you, who brought you in from the cold and raised you, who *chose* you and then died for you... she wasn't your mother?"

"Stop it, Leo..." Danni tried weakly.

"No," the cat was adamant. "You are not getting off so easily."

"This is easy?" Danni demanded.

"I am not going to let you sit back and feel bad for yourself. You don't like what's happened? Then what are you going to do to fix it?"

The mouse sat up in defiance for a moment and then sat back. What could she do? "Nothing," she whispered.

"What?!" Leo all but yelled.

Doyle was starting to become a little concerned with the cat's attitude, now. "Come on, Leo, let it go..."

"No!" the cat hissed, and turned back to Danni. "You are going to do nothing? The mouse I know would not just lay here and feel sorry for herself! The mouse I know, who risked her life to pull a thorn from the paw of a cat when she didn't know if it would eat her or not, the mouse I know would pick herself up and do something!"

"What am I going to do, Leo? Huh? How can I beat him? He just tossed me off that boat as if I were nothing! *Nothing*! And you want me to *do* something to him?"

The cat wasn't fazed. "Did you need him to talk all those people and animals out of doing what they were supposed to do? Out of their stories?"

172

This was stupid, Danni thought. "Of course not, but..."

"Then talk them back in."

"What?"

"You heard me, talk them back in."

"Talk them... back...?"

"If you can talk them out of a story, you can certainly talk them back into one." Doyle found himself nodding, "He has a point Danni..."

"But how?" the mouse asked.

"Well how do I know?" the cat demanded. "Did you plan what you were going to say to them when you met them all? Did you sit down and think, ooh, how do I talk The Prince out of going to Sleeping Beauty?"

Danni shook her head, "Of course not but..."

"Then I guess you will have to think of a way as soon as you meet up with them. Come on, Doyle, let's get the cart moving..."

Without questioning, Doyle began to gather up everything and get it on the cart, Leo sitting beside Danni. When Doyle had completed his tasks, he came back to the two animals.

"Put her on the seat with me, please," Leo said to the lad as he went to the cart and leapt easily onto the seat. Doyle lifted the pillow with the wool and Danni and carried them over to Leo.

"Wait..." Danni started. "Wait, Doyle, you're just going to listen to *him*?"

Doyle shrugged. "Sorry, Danni. But *he* makes sense this time," and he lifted the handles and began towards the path.

Danni was flustered and beyond words. She was still a little weak and that added insult to injury. She looked up at Leo who still had an eyebrow cocked as he looked at her sideways.

"Don't mean to be a problem, here..." Danni wheeled around to see Jon sitting beside her.

"Oh, Jon..." she sighed. "Are you feeling better?"

"Well yeah, as long as I don't use the leg... but..." he looked at Danni. "I really have to be getting back."

The mouse's face fell. "You're gonna leave?"

Jon grinned at her. "You did, Danni..."

It felt so long ago. She thought she was going to help everyone solve their problems and set them on the right way to live. The sensible, logical way to live. Now, she was sorry she ever left the Farm.

"I know it doesn't matter, Danni..." Jon was still speaking, "But you really aren't a monster. Some of us *think* horrible things at different times. It's how we feel afterwards that determines if we are or are not horrible." Danni looked at him carefully. "Gotta go," he called, and unfurled his wings, "Don't be a stranger!" he cried, and took off.

How we feel afterwards...? Her head was swimming with what she had been told not only over the past few days but all of her life, and she could not really assess what was true and what was not. She sat quite still as the cart rolled on, noticing that Doyle was making a fair pace on the road. It was almost startling when he began to slow down but when she looked to her side, she could see the reason.

A crowd had begun to form off to the side of the path, near an area where a little stream babbled by, but was mostly hidden by an overgrowth of tree and shrubs. The King's Guards were pulling something from the area. A woman screamed and some in the crowd began moving their children away, with averted eyes.

"What...?" Doyle asked, not really to anyone, but one of the men departing with his child in his arms took it to be to him and shook his head.

"Woman. They found a woman in the stream..." and with a tone of utter disbelief he whispered, "dead..."

"It's her!" Doyle heard next, "Oh no, no, no, it's her..." and a sort of keening wail came next. When he looked over, he saw the owner of the candy stall clutching her hands to her face, then her chest, while a King's Guard was holding her back. "I thought she just took off... I thought she was being lazy... I... didn't... I didn't..."

Another Guard took a third Guard aside. "Go tell someone at the castle..." he urged. "This wasn't just no drowning... someone meant for this to happen..." The third Guard looked very stunned for only a moment, the full import of what was being said sinking in fast, then gave a terse nod and headed off towards the castle.

Doyle began to move again, not too quickly, but deliberately and forceful. Danni watched the Guard and the woman, and the people around the area. She saw someone place a blanket over a figure on the ground, then she noticed a pretty pink bonnet not quite covered by the blanket.

Leo tried not to stare. Danni gazed at the bonnet for a while, sensing its familiarity but not quite placing it. Only once they were well away from the scene did Danni realise that both Doyle and Leo had been holding their breath and they sighed out together. She looked from one to the other.

"What?" she asked, quietly.

Doyle looked back at Leo and the two exchanged a meaningful stare.

"Doyle... Leo... what is it...? Who was that back there... what did they mean...?"

Doyle nodded to Leo and continued walking. Leo looked down at the seat while he spoke. "That... woman... was the one giving candy samples... the lady who told Doyle and... Simon about... the Maiden in Gold..."

The bouncy pink bonnet. How eager she had been to talk. How Simon hadn't gone with them to the cheese monger because he wanted to talk to her...

The air left her lungs. She shook her head and drew in a ragged breath. "Did he...?" the question was left dangling.

"We don't have any proof, Danni," Doyle said tightly, "but if he killed your mother, and he killed Arnie and he tried to kill you..."

Again, Danni shook her head. She watched the road going by beneath her. Was there nothing he wouldn't do? What was he trying to achieve? Why did he hate it here so? And again, Danni felt her size deeply. She looked about her, at the tall trees, the vast expanse of sky, the long road ahead of them, the size of the cart even and she felt terribly, terribly small. What was it he had said? Where? Ah mera kah? Ah mare ekkah? "Ah... mar... eh... kah..." she tried softly.

Doyle stopped. He turned to look at her. "What did you say?" he asked.

Danni shook her head. "He said he was from someplace else, that he didn't like it here, he seemed happy to not be from here..."

"America?" Doyle asked.

Danni nodded emphatically. "He said he was from farther away than you, Doyle... Two Thousand and Five, does that mean anything?"

Doyle felt a chill. The future? That man was from the future? A future America? Not possible. No. He looked at Danni carefully and saw the question in her own eyes. "It does a little, Danni..." he said, carefully. "But I don't really know for sure... We'd better get into town." He looked at Leo and the cat nodded. He had no idea what was going to happen when they got there, but he truly could not see any other option. There was a low rumble in the distance like the sound of thunder.

He took up the handles and began to walk.

Chapter 26
Clever Ella

They saw a small inn down the path from them, just outside of town. It was a one-level building with several opened windows, a goodly amount of space for horses or the odd cart to one side, and another, smaller building, set behind the first. There was also a barn and a small vegetable patch to the side. Trees surrounded the back lodging, but the front was clear of them and a sign hung on the front door displaying the words: "Burnie Bee Inn". Doyle sighed and nodded. He pulled into the side area, moving past the few horses and alongside another cart.

"What are we doing?" Danni asked.

"I need something to drink…" Doyle tried.

"Haven't we anymore water?" Leo inquired.

"I guess I want something else…" Doyle said, and offered his hand to Danni. The mouse looked at him.

"What are we doing here, Doyle?" she asked.

"There's someone we have to talk to Danni. Someone from the book." The mouse sagged visibly.

"*Another* story?" she was drained. She didn't want to talk to anyone else, didn't know what she would say or what good it would do.

"Not really…" Doyle replied. "But the only one that's writing itself right now, so the only one I know to go to and check out."

Now the mouse looked at him, her curiosity getting the better of her, she took a tentative step onto Doyle's hand.

"Will I have to say anything?"

"If I'm lucky, someone else might do most of the talking." And with a resigned sigh, the little mouse climbed up his hand and made her way onto his shoulder. Leo hopped down from his seat and trotted alongside Doyle and Danni to the front door which Doyle opened.

Inside was a well-lit establishment, the fire roaring but not making the room too hot. The windows allowed in much light, but they were also sparkling clean. The whole place was superiorly well-tended. The people who were there all seemed cheery and pleasant; some were at the bar, others at well-scrubbed tables playing dice games and cards. There was a dog at the fireplace who looked up when he saw the trio enter, then rose and walked casually over. Leo backed up slightly behind Doyle and, as the door hadn't yet been shut, was ready to bolt. The dog, a large wolfhound, with watery brown eyes assessed them congenially.

"Mind ye close the door…" he said gently to Doyle, who looked at Leo. "I'll nae be bothering yer friend, tush now, ya should know better," the last he said to Leo.

Doyle shut the door. The dog looked about at the tables. "Go where ya like… but the bar is where ya order…"

"I was wondering…" Doyle ventured. The dog turned to look back up at him. "Is Ella here…?" The dog all but smiled.

"Of course she is… you set yourselves down and I'll fetch her for ya…" and he trotted off to the side of the bar where two swinging doors stood above the floor. Ducking under slightly, the dog disappeared for a moment.

"Wot are you doin' *now*, dog?" came a bellow from behind the bar. A big man stood there with an apron across his large chest. He had a bald head and an air of stupidity clinging to him. This adverse appearance was compounded by the fact that he was also halfway over six feet tall and prone to violent outbursts. The dog poked his head back under the swinging doors. He indicated where Doyle was now sitting, and Leo curled about his feet. Danni was all but unseen on his shoulder.

"They're wantin' to see Miss Ella," the dog announced. This did not set well with the big man. He threw his rag to the bar in a fury.

"Wanting to see Miss Ella?" he cried. "Wanting to see Miss Ella?! She comes in here all high and mighty with her dog and her birds and cleans up and cooks, aye, a worker, she! And just whose establishment is this? Who is the one who owns this place, hm?" He was starting to walk down the bar to the doorway, eyeing Doyle murderously when the swinging doors were opened by the backside of a young woman who placed two steaming plates of food on the bar before reaching both hands up and squeezing the cheeks of the angry bar man.

'Oh everyone knows it's yours, Bull," she said with such sweetness that the man absolutely melted under the combined effect of her touch, gaze and voice, "But everyone here knows who runs it…" The remaining people, who up until that moment were hushed at the outburst, burst out laughing.

"She's got you there, Bull…" called out one.

"Sweetest thing ever…" said another.

"Best thing that's ever happened to this place was her walking through the doors…" The barman, Bull, rolled his eyes under a badly botched attempt to hide the smile that everyone had seen.

"Will you give these to Ben and Otto over there?" The lovely woman asked. She pushed a stray strand of long blonde hair back into her bonnet and turned around, surveying the room with her dark brown eyes and a happy smile. "Now, someone is looking for me…?"

Danni gasped.

The woman flexed her long, slender fingers delicately as she peered about at the familiar faces until she saw Doyle. Another happy smile crossed her face and she all but wafted over to him which was no mean feat as she was wearing clogs. As she drew nearer, Danni was transfixed, afraid to move and wanting to move at the same time and just as she was close enough to speak a greeting, the woman's dark eyes saw Danni on Doyle's shoulder. Her hands came together in a happy clap.

"Oh, little mouse!" her voice tinkled. She was not as majestic or stunning as she had been in the moonlight, but then, she had been dressed magnificently then and now she wore the clothes of a working woman, but her whole demeanour and her lovely voice let Danni know that she was in the presence of the same woman she had seen two nights before.

"Are you Ella?" Doyle asked, softly. Cinderella turned a smile to the lad and Doyle all but blushed.

"I am..." she replied. She was simply the personification of joy and happiness. "You're with the little mouse?" she asked.

"I'm Doyle and yes... this is Danni..." Doyle was suddenly aware that Leo was smacking his leg and that he was adding more nail to it with each hit. "And the feline assaulting my leg for want of an introduction is Leo."

Cinderella knelt deftly beside the cat and beamed a smile at him, scratching him under the chin with her slim fingers. "Why hello, Leo, aren't you handsome!" Still kneeling beside the cat, she looked up at Doyle. "Well you all must be famished! Would you like some food? Of course you would..."

Doyle hated to interrupt her but: "Actually, I don't know if I can pay..." he said softly. "My... money isn't all from here..."

"Well don't you worry about that one little bit!" she insisted. "I am happy to take care of you three..." She looked fondly at Danni. "Especially you!"

"Me?" Danni squeaked. Cinderella's eyes grew wide at the mouse's reaction. "Well of course!" she cried. "Look, Danni! Look around you. I take care of this place," her voice dropped to a whisper, "Oh you should have seen it yesterday," her eyes rolled heavenward, "but once a good cleaning was done and a few other changes made, well... Bull asked me if I would work here, and of course I said yes... it's so wonderful to be appreciated! Oh I know he looks mean and tough, but he's ever so grateful and so are all the people here..." she looked at Danni fondly. "And you did this..."

The mouse shrank back onto Doyle's shoulder.

Cinderella's smile faded as she saw the mouse practically deflate before her. "Why Danni... whatever is wrong?"

Danni tried hard not to cry. She looked into Cinderella's earnest face and blinked. "I've made a mess of everything..." she got out softly and began to tell Cinderella about her exploits. About leaving the Farm and giving advice and meeting up with Leo and Doyle and how she altered the paths of many people and how their stories were disappearing from Doyle's book. She mentioned Simon in short terms, not sure how much to tell, but ending up telling almost all, right up until her death. It took a surprisingly short time, and the mouse looked up at Cinderella carefully. "But your prince found your shoe..." Danni tried.

Cinderella smiled. "Danni, you have been through so much!" she admired.

"But you're not supposed to be here!" Danni cried, "Everybody is all messed up and I have to set it right but I don't know how! I don't know how to find everybody and what I would say to convince them to alter what they are doing to make the stories go back... and you love it here, but if the story is to go back to the way it's supposed to be, you'll have to go back and I can't... think... I can't..."

"You sound like you doubt yourself..." Cinderella said softly. Danni looked at her with wide, sad eyes and nodded. "And you're afraid..." Again, Danni nodded. And then Cinderella smiled. "Oh, Danni..." Cinderella sighed, "I think you can do anything." The mouse let her mouth fall open.

Cinderella stood up abruptly. "Let me go and get you some cheese and fruit and fresh grain bread that ought to hold you... I'll be right back!" and she whooshed off to the swinging doors.

Danni took in a breath. It was what she had said to Cinderella. It was a few simple words that had galvanised the woman and set her off on this adventure.

"Well someone really ought to do something!" she heard from a section of the room and her attention was drawn to the voice. "That thing is a beast! Comes down from the hills and attacks farm animals," the man's voice dropped to an edged whisper, "Interfering with sheep..." he shook his head.

Another man took up the cause. "You know that Old Woman in the shoe house? Her place was ransacked! All those children just tossed about, bruised and battered – looked over, she said, it was as if they had merely been looked over! And then it was off!" There was much nodding of heads and a general agreement of shared dismay.

"Someone ought do away with it... go up to that castle and kill the beast!" someone finally said. And Cinderella came through the doors with the plate promised for the newly admitted travellers. She admonished them all with a stare.

"Stop this instant!" she called out firmly. The room went quiet. "You know *he* doesn't like hearing about it..." and she indicated with her head to the far corner of the room to the man sitting in the dark. His white feathered hat lay on the table before a tankard. A shaking hand lifted up the tankard and took it to the dark, then returned it, shaking still, before withdrawing back into the dark with the rest of him. Cinderella put a finger to her lips and let all see it. There was more nodding of heads and a quiet began to fall again. She made her way back to the trio.

"What was that all about?" Doyle asked. She glanced over her shoulder and placed the dish down then sat in the chair opposite Doyle.

"I don't know the whole story, but he came here a few days ago... just a mess... he had a run-in with the beast they were talking about, he was trying to stop him... bothering the sheep... I don't know all what happened, he hasn't said much. Just sits back there nursing his tankard of ale... sad... He looks as though he is somebody important, though... his clothes are very well-made, and he has a goodly amount of money... and his horse is of good quality..."

"Horse?" Leo found himself asking.

Cinderella nodded. "We've been taking care of him, he's in the stable. Beautiful grey horse... his name is Rupert." All three jerked their heads in the direction of the darkened corner.

"Oh no..." Doyle breathed.

"It's..." Leo got out.

"The Prince," Danni finished and lowered her head.

Cinderella looked at them curiously. Then her eyes opened wide at the realisation that it wasn't the prince she had danced with they were referring to, but The Prince they had met on their travels. She stood up and placed her hand by Doyle's shoulder, palm up. "Come along, Danni." The mouse looked at her hand and shot a look up at Cinderella, a pleading, dreading look. Cinderella smiled serenely. "I know you can do this," she said gently. With the utmost hesitation, Danni climbed onto her hand. Giving Doyle and Leo another smile, Cinderella turned with the mouse and walked to the darkened corner, picking up a small lamp as she went. "We really could do with some light over here..." she said gently, setting the lamp down not too near the figure in the corner. His face was turned away but Danni recognised his clothes and his tumbling straight blond hair. It was dirty though, now, and unkempt. "Someone wanted to see you..." Cinderella spoke softly and gently.

The Prince turned his face towards her and she placed the mouse on the table. He looked at Danni for some time before he blinked in recognition. "... The fairy," he whispered. Danni shifted uncomfortably. Cinderella backed away. "Did you come to gloat, fairy...?" The Prince asked dryly.

"What?"

"I have failed," he said softly. "I have not found the castle... only a beast... who made short work of me... and now... here I am... content to linger in the company of those beneath me and become friends with the bottom of a tankard."

Danni stared at him. "You... you're giving up?" she asked, hollowly. The Prince looked at her sadly. "What else is there for me?"

Danni sat back. She understood. She felt that way. "I've failed, too..." Danni started. She looked at The Prince and knew what he must be feeling, how inadequate, how small. Beaten by a creature he never should have met. Had he known where he was to really go and find what he was really supposed to find, it would have been different. But if he had known, what would he have really gained? She looked at his sad face and realised it wasn't just sad... it was older... "You weren't ready..." she said softly.

He looked at her sideways. "What...?"

"How could you really get what you were meant to when you weren't ready to receive it?

There was a moment of reflection for The Prince before he cocked an eyebrow at the mouse, "... Go on."

"Those thorns would have torn you to pieces..." the mouse continued, "Unless you had felt a pain far deeper, far worse..."

The Prince looked away briefly, the back of his hand dragged harshly by his eyes and he took in a breath before he looked back at Danni. "...A test...?" he ventured, the tiniest bit of life sparking in his brown eyes.

"Your Princess has been asleep for so long..." Danni went on, not knowing where the words were really coming from, but knowing she had to say them. "She can't be awakened by a brash youth, bursting about without an ounce of caution. She must be awakened by someone who has known hurt... and wants to right it, gently..."

The Prince took in a deep breath, "I should..."

"A bath is ready for you, sir..." Cinderella had appeared near the table and was indicating through the swinging doors. The Prince nodded perfunctorily and stood. He took up his bedraggled hat. "And I'll give your things a good once over, sir, I'm sure you'll want to be on your way."

He handed his hat to Cinderella and gave her a small smile. "You have been too kind..."

"Oh... I don't think anyone can be *too* kind, sir, do you?" Cinderella smiled and she set her hand down for Danni to step onto.

The Prince looked at the mouse. "Thank you again, disguised fairy," he said softly.

"Don't thank me..." Danni stopped. "Just go and wake Briar Rose." Another perfunctory nod and he walked to the swinging doors.

Cinderella brought Danni up to her face where she could see her very close. "You see, little mouse? You can do anything."

"But... he might not find the castle..." Danni started, "What if..."

"If it is meant to be... and from what you have told me, it is..."

"But then... *you* can't stay here..." and a sadness swept through Danni.

"If I am supposed to be there... I will be. Right now, Danni, I don't want you to fret, I just want you to do what you are supposed to do." She was standing by Doyle now, who had risen.

"May we leave my cart here?" he asked. "I'm afraid we will be very easy for this other person to spot if we keep it... but I need to keep it somewhere safe..."

"Of course," Cinderella was happy to help. "Take it to the side of the barn. It should be safe and well out of the way."

"You must take care, too, miss..." Doyle said. "He might come looking for you..."

"Oh, but he already has," Cinderella admitted. The three friends all stared at her.

"He was here yesterday. Wondered if there was any work... he asked if I had been to the Festival..."

"What did you tell him?" Danni felt her throat constrict.

"That I had, but that I was working here now. He seemed to be happy with that. We didn't have any work for him so he went on."

"But..." Danni started, "... you might..."

"I didn't know then that I might have to leave, Danni… I didn't know then that the prince had found my shoe." She kissed the little mouse on the top of her head then smiled at her again. "I know what he looks like and I will be sure to be careful." She indicated the barman, "Bull may not be the smartest man… but he is a fierce protector."

They all looked at the fellow behind the bar who, seeing them stare, was momentarily disoriented and looked behind him, realising there was only a wall there, turned back and gave a small wave, and then continued to dry the glass he had been attending to.

There was another low rumble like the sound of thunder, but this time, it sounded more like it was coming from deep inside the earth. "There's that queer noise again…" Cinderella mused, then turned her attention back to the trio. "You go move your cart," she instructed. "We will keep it safe," and she walked them to the door. "And you all keep safe as well…" she offered, "I've not been to town in some time… but some of the people here have told me it has changed… so, do be careful." She looked at each of them individually with such a fond and deep gaze that they all felt warmed.

"We will…" Doyle spoke finally, and they walked out of the Inn.

Chapter 27
Little Thieves Steal No More

"But what do we do now?" Danni asked after they had hidden the cart behind the barn and started off on foot down the road to town.

"I'm not sure, Danni," Doyle confided. "I know we need to try and fix as much as we can… but…" he stopped and looked down the street into the town. It was *so* similar to the pictures of towns in his story books… the white stucco walls of some houses, the brick of others… thatched roofs and slate… fishmongers and cheesemongers… the cobble-stones of the streets, slick and uneven… the shuttered windows… he was really stunned.

There were people about, but they didn't have the same calm air as the ones back at the Inn. They looked sullen. They looked angry. Some looked frightened of their own shadow. They seemed like bitter versions of the way people were becoming back at the fayre. It was as if something wrong had taken root and spread and everyone had become affected by it.

"I don't like the look of this place…" Leo intoned and he moved sharply to one side as a person walked by and almost stepped on him.

"The carry offer still stands, Leo," Doyle reminded. The cat wasted no time in jumping into Doyle's arms. They stood for a moment, looking around. They had not been to the town before, so they really were not certain what they expected. But Cinderella had mentioned that there had been changes. They wondered if this was because of everything that had happened. And whether Simon had managed one or two more alterations…

"'Take this place down…'" Danni whispered. Doyle looked sharply at her. "What?" he asked.

"Simon. He had said how he thought he and I were going to 'take this place down'… What have I done…?" she said again.

"What you need to fix," Leo said sharply. She looked at the cat and saw that he was smiling. "You can do this, Danni."

The mouse worked her mouth for a moment. She nodded. "We have to find whoever I spoke to… Jack… Belle…" she shook her head, "We don't know where they are or if they're near… this could be…"

"Stop!" they heard someone yell. "Little thief!" Looking down the street they saw a young boy running for all his might around a corner and head towards them but before he could pass them, he turned down an unseen alleyway. A man came racing around the corner and towards the trio. "Did you see?" he demanded of Doyle. "Did you see a towheaded child

183

run this way? Come on boy, speak!" Dumbly, Doyle pointed past them, towards the way they had come. "Could have said so!" the man spat and was on his way without a word of thanks.

"Why did you…" Leo began and Doyle watched the man leave before going to the alleyway. Half-way down, they saw the boy by a barrel, a loaf of bread in one hand and he was pulling a sausage from his pocket with the other. Then they heard another voice, this one from the alley.

"Vy, zis iz gut!" the girl's voice sounded and she rose from behind the barrel. "Zis should fill us up…"

"But for how long?" Danni called out. Doyle stopped. He hadn't expected the mouse to say anything. Hansel and Gretel looked up with a gasp, Gretel had a sturdy piece of wood in her hand. They saw Doyle and the cat but froze when they saw the mouse.

"Za magic mouse…" the both sighed out together.

"I'm *not* magic…" Danni started.

"You're telling *us*?" Hansel cried.

"Ve came here and it's been nussing but trouble!" Gretel added.

"That sixpence didn't go too far, did it?" Danni asked sarcastically.

"No! Und nobody vant to give verk to children!" Hansel continued.

"Ve try begging… but after a vile, people start to be angry vis us for zis," Gretel explained.

"Of course," Danni said to Hansel "People will only give handouts for so long… but if the best you can do is steal…"

"Danni…" Doyle interrupted.

"No, Doyle, don't stop me… I just figured before that they weren't brave enough… now I see they're stealing…"

"Brave…?" Gretel asked hesitantly. "Vat has zat to do vis anysing?"

"Well, you ran away from the house… so…"

"But you told us to leave! You said it vas a trap!"

"*Might* be a trap. I am pretty certain I said might."

"You did say might, Danni…" Leo agreed.

Two pairs of blue eyes gawped at Leo. "A magic cat?" they asked together.

"NO!" Danni yelled. The children looked back at the mouse, but stole gazes at Leo. "That house is what's magic," Danni told them.

"*Vat*?!" they both cried.

The mouse nodded. "But you were both so scared I figured neither one of you would be able to figure out how to find the riches and defeat the witch."

"*Vitch*?!" was the stereo incredulous cry.

"Of course. Who else would have a magic house made of cake and candy?" Danni assumed an air of insouciance. "But you were so scared…"

"She vas scared!" Hansel pointed a finger at Gretel. Gretel hit him with her cudgel. "OW!" he cried.

"Who's scared now, huh?" she demanded.

"You are not going to get anywhere like this!" Danni called to both of them as they were readying to battle one another. They stopped and looked at her. "You have to work together! You have to remember that you are brother and sister and you are all the other has!" With this, the two children looked at each other and their wide blue eyes filled with tears. They threw their arms around one another and kissed each other's neck and cheeks. "Okay, okay…" Danni called out, "that's enough. And no more stealing! Never again! Now. Can you find your way back to the house from here? I mean… I know how you are with directions…" Hansel nodded excitedly

"I 'ave gotten better since ve came here und started stealing," his smile faded under Danni's glare "Vich ve von't be doing anymore… but if ve go back up za pass ve came ve can find it… it smells so good…"

Gretel also nodded. "Und I vill be brave…" she told Danni.

Hansel took her hand. "Und I vill help you," he told her and they looked fondly at one another.

"Is there a back way out of this alley?" Danni wondered aloud.

"Of course!" Hansel said.

"Then you two had better use it! And see that fellow whose sausage you stole doesn't see you!"

"Ve vill be careful, Magic Mouse," they said together.

Danni sighed. "I'm not…" she looked into the children's wide and eager blue eyes and stopped herself. "Good," she said instead. "Now go!" With a little bow from Hansel and a little curtsy from Gretel, the children darted down the alley and around another corner and were gone. Danni sighed then looked at Doyle.

"How did you know there was a witch?" he asked. Her mouth dropped open. "There's really a *witch*?"

Chapter 28
Easily Listened to, Easily Swayed

Simon had started out slowly once he left the lake. A few people at a time. Bringing their attention to the changes. The differences in people's behaviour, not doing what they usually did, not acting the way they usually would – something was going on. At first, people were a bit hesitant, but something would happen to draw their attention and they'd see what he was saying was right. There were strangers around, he would tell them, once he had ingratiated himself and gotten them to acknowledge his familiar face – even if he had never met them. Other people seemed to know him, and that was usually enough to give the impression of belonging. He had checked in on Cinderella and was content she was happy where she was. The story hadn't added anything of import so he set it aside and set about finishing the collapse.

When he heard the rumblings, he knew it was only a matter of time. The people would allow their fears to get the better of them, and with the well-placed people he had spoken to being on the alert, they would fan the fires of chaos. And he would step in, casually of course, and they would hear him. By that point they would want to hear someone who knew what was happening, that things were falling apart... he would give them something they could do about it. It would assuage them briefly. Then he would be gone. And so would they.

He knew that spreading the alert had a two-fold reason. The first was the simple and obvious prelude to destruction. The second... well, should the boy show up, he could fulfil the object of their fears nicely.

He had no clue as to whether or not Doyle would turn up. Now that the mouse was dead, that might put a damper on any further interference from the boy, but it might also make him step up his game. Not that he really had a "game" per se, but if he wanted to try and make trouble, Simon could and would do whatever was needed to get him out of the way.

Simon skirted around the town now, looking off to see where *it* would be coming from – the break, the opening – and then, just outside the westerly side of the town, he saw the hill. Easy enough to climb should he need to and something inside him told him he would need to – he could feel the pull, the almost-ache of having to leave, but he knew that even if an angel had asked him now if he wanted to leave, he would say no. He had to remain long enough to be sure it was all falling apart.

So much back home was depending on this. He had seen the people, weakened from too much being given, rewarded for nothing, so that people felt they were due, that their share did not require them to do anything, that they were entitled. Something for nothing, was it now? Not as it had started out – a handout that was actually a hand, aid until you showed you were on your feet and if you couldn't, well... you found something else. It was a trickle down affect, though... when people in positions of power could get away with things and get a light slap on the wrist, well... even the lowest man on the totem pole was going to want a share of that. And why? Because they had been handed a load of crap. About how if they worked hard, and were loyal and honest and gave everything, they too could achieve anything. "Within reason" was never added. "For your social class" was never mentioned. And of course neither was "except for you" – which seemed to be happening more and more. Oh, wealthy people stayed wealthy, of course they did, they had the resources to maintain that, but more and more, people were backing down from hard work – why bother, when you could steal or lie or cheat your way into the hierarchy? There were no more people who would scrub a toilet to make ends meet, that was beneath them, they had been taught that, they had been sold that bill of goods, those stories assured them of it. Being "special" was your right! It was what you were due! And now there were so many who had been weakened by that thought, they had become a blight on the rest.

The stories were unrealistic at best... what kind of a world were they supposed to be talking about? How could any of them really aid in helping someone in the world he knew? How could mutilating a foot to fit into some crazy "glass" slipper really secure someone a place in the palace? These things were supposed to be a fulfilment of wishes, winning out over all competitors and the destruction of enemies. And *what* destruction! Eyes plucked out; dance to death; red hot shoes; a barrel filled with nails and spikes, the guilty party placed inside and rolled down a hill until dead... parents killed several times over, parents killing children – or having them killed...! These things just promoted the rampant violence he had seen and been a part of. He knew if that were to cease in this world, it would start to diminish back where he was from. He knew that if these stories hadn't introduced the violent context to begin with, a punishment for purported wrongdoers, people would not have resorted to it! Cain slew Abel. But even God would not let anyone kill Cain.

He knew he had killed. He knew. But he also knew it was something that had to be done and it would be looked upon as such later. The Crusades were a perfect parallel of what he had done. Rid yourself of the transgressors to allow the pure to thrive. It was weeding. They were weeds in the garden he had to till, that he had to set right. And what were they really? Parts of stories. Not even based in reality.

There was another rumble, still deep down but rising. He saw rocks begin to cascade down the side of the hill. A young red-headed man on the road stopped to watch as well.

Simon looked at him and shook his head. "What do you make of that?" he asked. The young man looked questioningly at Simon. "Didn't you hear the rumble?"

The fellow nodded, "The Mountain is in labour," he said simply. "Who told you that?" Simon disdained.

"The old woman under the hill," he replied, as if peace had met his heart. "And did she say what it would give birth to?" Simon asked.

This stopped the man. "What...?"

"If it's in labour, it is going to bring something forth. I tell you... I don't know if I'd want to be here to see what that will be..." There was a glimmer of fear in the man's eyes. That was better. "Too many things happening..." he went on, "did you notice there's been more stealing going on than ever?" The man gave a slight nod. "And tempers? People can't seem to hold onto them anymore..."

"What do you think it is...?" the man asked.

Simon looked at the hill. "Something's in there... that's for sure..." he looked back towards the town. "And something is in there... someone is doing this... someone we don't know... something is wrong..." He walked over to the man and congenially put out his hand. "Now I *know* I have met you... my name's Simon, but I'm horrible with names... You're...?"

"Tom..." the other said and shook the first's hand.

"The piper's son...?" Simon asked, his crooked smile all warm.

"Oh no, no, sir. Tucker."

"Ah... the singer..."

The man blushed and ran a hand through his red hair. "I've been told..."

"Are you going into town, Tom? I know I am and I'd love some company..."

"Sure," he acquiesced and the two started down the road.

"I heard there was all sorts of mischief at that fayre... did you go...?"

"No, no I didn't... what did you hear?"

Simon smiled again – sometimes it was just too easy.

Chapter 29
La Belle Dèsire

The trio walked into the square. There was a market going on, so all around the fountain, which was the centre and pride of the town, were stalls and carts and people monging their wares. Along the edge of the square were benches and patches of grass with lovely trees growing, so it was cool and shady. As they stopped to study their surroundings and assess, the door to one of the shops opened and a beautiful woman came out, adjusted her bonnet to hide her face and called:

"I'll just be on the bench outside. Take your time..." before she closed the door and walked to the nearest bench. Once under the shade of the tree, she readjusted her bonnet so that her amber eyes were shaded slightly, and she gazed off over the house-tops, over the trees, to a castle, tall and turreted, far away.

"I need to go to her, Doyle..." Danni said softly. Doyle looked at the mouse. "Beauty...?" he asked. "Belle..." she replied.

Doyle nodded. He walked carefully over to the woman, so as not to take her unawares, and stood before her, gently coughing to get her attention. She looked up at Doyle and he could see such sadness in her amber eyes that he wanted to cry himself.

"I'm sorry, miss, to bother you..."

She tried a smile, "No, no, it's perfectly all right, let me make some room..." and she moved to the edge of the bench.

"Oh no, miss, I don't mean to sit here..." Belle looked at him questioningly. "My friend wishes to speak to you... again..." and he placed his hand to the opposite shoulder so Danni could step onto it. Seeing the mouse, Belle took in a small gasp. "Do you want to be alone, Danni?" Doyle asked as he put the mouse on the arm of the bench near Belle.

The little mouse nodded. "Yes, please."

Doyle and Leo took several steps away and sat beneath a tree. There was an awkward silence. Finally, Danni asked, "Shopping?.."

"My sisters... one is getting married..."

"That's nice." Again the awkward pause. "You think about him still..."

The amber eyes turned to look at Danni so suddenly that Danni was about to jump away. "Every night! And every night there is the same dream... a lovely man appears and looks so sad... the same man I would see in my dreams when I was at the castle! He wants to know why I left... why I couldn't trust my heart over my eyes... and I... I wake in tears...

and…" She stopped and looked at her hands as they fidgeted on her lap. "What does it mean…?" she half asked, not expecting an answer.

"Belle…" Danni tried. "I don't know what your dream means… but I do know this much… I was wrong." Again, she turned abruptly to look at Danni, who jumped. "I'm sorry, but you're really frightening me with the turning so fast…"

"Wrong?" Belle urged.

The mouse got her thoughts back on track and looked up at Belle. "Yes. I shouldn't have told you what to do… no one should… only you can experience what is happening to you… People may tell you what to do, but it's how they would perceive it and your experience will never be identical to someone else's…"

"But… he was so angry…" and a beautiful tear slid down her lovely cheek, plopped on her blue dress, and made a small dark spot on the fabric.

"Because he isn't what he seems…" Danni said softly. She didn't want to give away too much, but she had to get Belle to go. "He just wants to know… that he deserves… that he has earned your love." Belle heaved a heavy sigh and looked towards the castle. Danni shook her head. "He's dying, Belle."

Belle drew her hand to her heart. "Oh no…"

"And he's been…" Danni needed to proceed with caution, "taking his anger out on the farms nearby… people aren't happy with him for doing that… they want to… stop him…"

"Kill him?" the woman whispered. Danni waited a moment then nodded. Belle looked up towards the castle. "I have to go to him," she breathed.

Danni was dumbstruck. "Do you remember the way… can you…?"

Belle stood and looked at Danni. "I remember it like my hand… I have played in my mind over and over how to get back… I could do it blindfolded. And I have a horse." She started toward a post where horses were tied off, and untied a handsome chestnut. She moved the horse to a little stair unit and climbed up the stairs to mount the animal easily.

"But… your family…?"

Belle smiled for the first time since Danni had seen her, and it was as if the sun came out from behind an enormous cloud. "Oh… my father will understand… my sisters… not so much… but I don't care! Thank you, Danni…"

"Good luck," Danni offered.

Belle nodded, reined in her horse then headed down the street at pace – to the annoyance of many of the shoppers who called out, but she didn't stop. And once she was out of the way of the foot traffic she urged her horse on down the road. Danni watched for as long as she could.

In the shade of the tree, Doyle kept an eye on the mouse but said to Leo: "I might have to separate from you two, Leo…" The cat sharply turned a stare up at the boy. "It's for her safety, Leo… a cat like you can travel unimpeded… you can slip away easily even with her on your back… there are many a crack and nook you could go in with her and keep someone from getting to you, finding you…"

The cat's eyes narrowed, "Simon…?" he asked, already knowing the answer. Doyle nodded, feeling a bit numb. Leo went on: "You're not planning on doing anything stupid are you, Doyle?"

Doyle shrugged his shoulders. He certainly didn't hope so. "Jack needs to be found, Leo," Doyle reminded the cat. "He might still be at the fayre. From what I remember, the cow was not exactly one he would be able to get rid of at the price his mother was hoping for. If we don't find each other before the sun goes down, we will meet at the cart."

Suddenly there was another rumbling, only this time the ground shifted slowly as well. People at the market screamed, the tied horses jumped back and shifted nervously, some fruit fell from a cart and a child tumbled onto the cobble-stoned street, releasing a pitiful wail even after his mother picked him up to soothe. But there was no soothing, as the mother's eyes were also wide with fear.

Danni had scurried over to them and Doyle stood up. "Danni, get on Leo…" he ordered.

The mouse balked. "But…"

"Now!" Doyle demanded.

"What's happening?" Danni cried.

"The mountain is in labour!" someone yelled from another entry to the town centre. A young-red haired man was making his way to the centre of the market and stood on a section of the fountain. "The old woman under the hill said it… it's in labour and it's going to spew forth something!"

"The old woman under the hill?" someone asked. "The wise woman," someone else cried.

"And there's been mischief about! You all know it!" the red-haired man called out.

"Did she say anything about that?" someone else called.

"Take her out of here, Leo, *now!*" Doyle hissed and Leo gathered Danni up carefully in his mouth, so suddenly that Danni had no time to protest and Leo hurried back in the direction they had come and away from the people who were swiftly being stirred up into a mob. 'Woman under the hill'… Doyle wondered. She must live somewhere back along the way the red-haired fellow had come.

And then he saw Simon. Standing near the young man, but not too near. Watching the young man carefully, but not too carefully. A study in nonchalant interest. Doyle looked about and saw a small alleyway between two businesses. He hoped it would have a back way out, like the one Hansel and Gretel had used.

Mostly, he really hoped Simon hadn't seen him.

Chapter 30
To Lead a Mob

Simon recognised the cap and the shock of dark hair of the boy darting away. He didn't need to see more. Where the boy was going was incidental to what was happening at that moment. He would find the boy. That would be simple enough because he knew the boy wanted to find him. He listened with one ear to Tucker go on about the mountain and how he had seen the rocks crashing down from the summit. They had rolled gently and there were only a few, but it was good to be a bit over the top. He saw what it did to the crowd: they were rapt.

"Tom…" he finally called gently, when the young man hit a lull. Tom looked at Simon and extended his hand to him. He called out to the crowd.

"This is Simon, you know him! I met him on the road by the mountain, he was braving it himself. Listen to what he has to say!"

He could not have asked for a better introduction. He stood on the fountain ledge and surveyed them all, their fearful eyes gazing up at him, waiting for solace, for some balm to be salved over them.

"Thank you, Tom…" he said with a nod to the fellow. "Now most of you know me…" he intoned, "and those of you who don't, well, you know someone who does…" he took in a timed breath. "That mountain is making way for something. And I don't think it's a coincidence that the way it's flaring up is like the way everyone and everything is flaring up around here. You know it; you've seen it. Some people stealing… others trying to make a penny without truly earning it… I've even heard that some of the costermongers have been making their scales heavier so as to make less food cost more money!"

Some of the people looked to the food sellers, who in turn looked shocked or a little sheepish, and some even began pointing fingers.

"I don't want to think it's anybody here, but… I have *heard* it! You all are feeling tense… angry… there's something going on here… and I think it's manifesting itself out there!" he gave a sweep of his arm off to the mountain. "We have to remember we are a town. We are all together! We all need to pull together and care for each other! Those tempers flaring? We need to put those down. Look at your neighbour. Go on!" and the people hesitantly gave sideways looks to the people beside them. "You *know* these people! You do!" The sideways looks gave way to full looks in the face, smiles began to emerge, a few people patted each other's shoulders, shook hands, took hands... "But be diligent! There are strangers! We don't know everyone and I believe there are some who are coming here, or are already here, to try and change things... change what we know and hold dear... and the mountain is trying to warn us. Think about what you do and say... and who you say it to. We must find the perpetrators and deal with them. We must also look inside ourselves and see what we may have done to have brought this on!"

There was a pause and he saw people nodding, he saw some looking at others with slight suspicion and some looking at others fondly. And from the far corner, he saw a King's Guard come in, flanked by two more. They looked at the scene before them with curiosity and their steps faltered slightly. "The King's Guard!" Simon called attention to them. "Make way for the King's Guard!" and he stood down as the Guard, now puffed with his own importance, made his way through the throng, the people separating for them as they came.

The Guard cleared his throat. "We've had... an incident at the fayre..." he said. Not used to public speaking, his voice didn't carry as well as Simon's but the words still brought a hush to the crowd: "A woman... has been... has met with... foul play... If anyone has information... please see us... We will have a tent set up just outside of town," and he made to move but Simon stopped him, calling out:

"What's happened?" and made to look as if someone else had said it. The Guard opened his mouth slightly.

"Yes!" someone else called, "Foul play, what's happened?"

"Who was it?" came a fearful question.

"Do you know who?"

"At the fayre!"

The Guard held up his hand and the growing din simmered, but still brewed. "She was the candy lady's assistant..."

"Was?!" someone cried. "Dead?" someone else asked.

The Guard was becoming agitated and held up his hands again.

"We will be at the tent if anyone has any information!" he yelled. "That is all I have to say on the matter!" and he made his way, with his men, back down the newly opened channel of people. But now, the crowd was becoming unruly. People clamoured closer to the King's Guard, asking frantic questions. There was fear again and the Guards said nothing, but only asked again for information. The people in charge didn't seem to know how to calm the town. The Guards made their way out of the square and the people started to chat up a frenzy.

Simon stepped back. And watched.

******

It was quite some time and quite a bit of yelling before Leo finally stopped but did not release the mouse.

"What are you *doing*, Leo? Why have we left Doyle? I demand an answer!" she was still screaming.

"Naht hutting yu dan dill I know yu won'd run ahay…" he tried to say with his mouth full of Danni.

The mouse stopped squirming. "What?" she asked.

"Naht thayin' agan…" he mumbled.

"I won't run away…" the mouse tried.

"Huromiss?"

Danni looked down, then back at the cat. "I promise…" she swore.

Leo lowered his head and placed her gently on the ground. He flexed his jaw from the cramp keeping his mouth just tight enough to hold the mouse and not hurt her.

"Now, what madness is this?!" Danni demanded.

"Oh, just the usual that seems to be piling up on us," Leo finally said. "Doyle wanted us to split up for a little. He thought we might get noticed, you saw how they were all getting. You know who must be behind it…"

"But…"

"Danni, you cannot do anything *there*, not right now!" the cat urged. "Doyle wants us to go find Jack."

The mouse sagged. "He's probably sold that cow…"

"Doyle doesn't seem to think so… are you a good judge of cow?" he asked. Danni shrugged. "What's to judge? They're big."

Leo rolled his eyes. "Well, Doyle is of the opinion that the cow wasn't going to fetch the price Jack's mother wanted, so…"

Danni perked up. "He might not have sold it!" Leo nodded, then the mouse was tense and stared back to the town. "But what about Doyle?" she asked.

Leo sighed. "I don't know right now, Danni… let's take this one step at a time, okay? We'll either find him, or he'll find us… or we meet at the cart by sundown. Now, wouldn't it be better if you got onto my neck?"

Danni didn't like it, leaving Doyle in the town where Simon might find him and then what would happen to him? She dreaded to think of it, but knew she had to do this as well. Finally, she nodded and climbed onto the cat's back, settling just at the back of his neck.

"Okay…" she offered.

"Hold on…" Leo warned, "I don't think we should walk…" and he took off at an easy run. "I didn't hurt you back there, did I? Didn't bite down too hard?"

"No, you were extremely gentle…"

Chapter 31
The Hill That Wanted to Be a Mountain
[and Other Such Nonsense]

Doyle couldn't keep himself from looking back to the town as he went down the road away from it. He had a strange feeling Simon might have seen him. He was fairly certain that Leo and Danni were out of the square before Simon came in and hoped they would not have too much trouble finding Jack. It was strange how easy it had been to find the characters who had been displaced... almost as if they too knew there were something amiss and were looking for answers themselves. Leo would certainly have something to say about that and by now, Danni might not even argue about it.

There was another rumble, the ground swaying gently beneath him, and he looked off at the mountain, where a few loose rocks were tumbling gracefully down. It was more of a hill, he decided, as he looked at it. Hill... Old Woman... He reached into his jacket pocket and withdrew his book and began to slip through the pages. There it was.

'There was an old woman Lived under a hill; and if she's not gone, She lives there still.'

He made a face at the book. He didn't see how that made her wise. He looked to one side of the hill and saw a sinuous line of set-in stones and trees making a sort of rugged pathway up to the top. He continued along the road from town and saw where some of the ground dipped incongruously, as if a giant had sliced a bit of the earth so the mountain couldn't meet the road. There were heavy stones here, as if it were a wall, and planks of timber were inlaid as well. He continued along and saw a gate jutting away from the stone and wood wall that swept down to the road. There was a patch of grass and some shade trees, with a bench under the trees. Just beyond the bench was a round wooden door, similar to some of the doors he had seen back home in Solihull, only it was round all the way. He wondered at how it was hinged and, without realising how he got there, he found himself standing right before the door. This was not the door to a house, though – it went directly into the hill.

"...'and if she's not gone'..." he mumbled and knocked on the door.

"I'm not in there," he heard behind him and he wheeled about.

She was small, with a wry grin and merry blue eyes that seemed small on her face. Her grey hair peeked out from under her white bonnet which featured a blue ribbon that matched her eyes. Her dress was also of blue, and atop that she wore a sharp white apron. Her lips were thin with wrinkles round them from sometimes being pinched together, but the lines along her eyes indicated she smiled a great deal as well. "But I am here still..." she said happily. Doyle smiled in spite of himself. "Hello, young man," she greeted.

"Good afternoon, ma'am... erm..." Doyle was disarmed by her demeanour. "Call me Grace," she smiled.

"Miss Grace..." and now she laughed.

"Oh, I am much too old to be a *Miss* anymore... but amiss I usually am..." and she looked up at him curiously, a little arch to her brow.

Doyle's brows furrowed. "You mean... mistaken...? Gone wrong...?"

"Or astray or faulty..." she finished. "Very good! It's not often people understand my word games and riddles. Sometimes I think their heads are full of sawdust! Or just too occupied with other things..." Again she looked up at him with an arched brow and sat on the bench.

He liked the word play, and joined in, "like their own business...?"

"Or lives..." she smiled. "Or stories..." Doyle looked at her sharply. "Don't you think everyone has a story to their lives?" she continued. I think so... I think yours must be fascinating."

Doyle blinked. Now he was a little lost. "I don't know..." he ventured, "I think I'm rather young..."

"Oh, but that's when all good stories begin! In the beginning...." She indicated a place on the bench for him to sit. Slowly he did.

"Do you know many stories?" he asked.

She laughed gently. "Of course I do, but I don't think you came here for a story." Doyle shook his head.

"No," he nodded, trying to stay on task, "No, I didn't... I'm Doyle, by the way."

"Of course you are," she replied as if everything were right with the world. "It's the hill, isn't it?" she asked. Again, Doyle nodded. She sighed, "I told Tommy Tucker, and didn't he say anything?"

Doyle wondered if that was the red-headed fellow. "That it's in labour?" She nodded as he continued, "... and that it is going to spew something forth and that there's mischief about." Her face darkened at this and her lips pinched slightly.

"I said nothing about that..." she said staccato. She did not seem like someone he wanted to see angry. Even for her small stature. "Goodness, what a silly young man, I suppose I ought to have put it to song, he would have remembered that..."

"Well then, what did you mean?" said Doyle, trying not to sound silly himself. "It's in labour!" she insisted. "Look at it for goodness sake!" and Doyle took a moment to look at the slope behind them. He turned back to her and stared blankly.

"Well it's a hill, you know…" she said, waiting for the penny to drop. "It's growing…"

Doyle tried to make sense of it: "So, the mountain… is in labour, and…"

"No, the *hill* is in labour! It's growing." And, noticing his confused expression, she continued, gently. "It wants to *be* a mountain, you know…"

"But, it's not because there's something wrong?"

"Oh, I never said that," and she picked up a basket beside the bench and withdrew her knitting. "Honestly, sometimes I wonder why I don't just go down there myself…"

"Maybe you ought…" Doyle offered.

She shook her head. "And tell them what to do? Oh, no… That's been tried before and they all just move about like ants without a soothing tune… next thing you know, no one is in the right place and everyone is just in a sorry state…"

"It's happened before?" Doyle asked sharply.

She nodded comfortably. "Nice fellow… a reverend, I believe… had fallen asleep under a tree, or had a fit of some sort I would imagine, and managed his way here… but he was even more confusing than I… wanting to make the egg human, of all things…"

"Make the egg…?" said Doyle, his blank stare returning.

"Well it couldn't be human, it was an egg! And that is why it is a true tragedy," She sighed. "It wanted to sit on the wall even though it knew it was an egg."

"…Humpty Dumpty?" Doyle said, triumphantly.

She nodded with satisfaction, "And therefore couldn't…"

"Sit on a wall…," but then Doyle stopped short: "But a tragedy is a medieval narrative poem or tale that describes the downfall of a great man…"

"Or…?" she prodded, gently.

"Excuse me?"

"An additional definition…?"

Doyle thought. "A serious drama?" he offered.

She made a sort of "Pah" sound and his blank stare returned.

"That typically describes…?" she led him.

His brain was reeling. School wasn't this challenging! "A conflict…"

She smiled, "…between…?…"

Doyle suddenly thought that the rhythm of this banter was a little like tennis, only with words, and he continued, "Between the protagonist…"

"Our egg…" she interjected and Doyle found himself giving a nod.

"And a superior force…" Doyle was really enjoying it now.

"Fate or destiny… or, in this case, his desire…"

"…. having a sorrowful or disastrous conclusion that elicits great pity or fear!" *Aha! That was surely the winning volley*, thought Doyle, smugly.

She looked at him. "Having a disastrous conclusion would have done it, dear Doyle – the rest is overkill, don't you think? Anyway, our egg knew he was an egg, but still he wanted to sit on the wall, to boldly go where no egg has gone before! – But… he fell. Now, if he were human, how would that have elicited the same kind of response? We are sitting. I don't see either one of us in any fear of rolling off…"

Doyle shook his head and suddenly latched onto something. "You said a reverend fell asleep or had a fit and managed his way here…"

She was tending to her knitting. "'The hart he loves the high wood, the hare she loves the hill; the knight he loves his bright sword, the lady…'"

"'Lady loves her will.'" Doyle finished with a smile. "My father used to say that to my mother… when she wanted something to go her way…" It felt so long ago.

"Did it?" Grace asked, interrupting his reverie.

"Did what?"

"Go her way…?"

Doyle smiled at the memory. It would already have done so. His father said it when he could see that his mother had made certain of it. Not in her dealings with his father, not always, but in little things, maybe with a neighbour or a worker.

He nodded. "Grace…" he started, but she held up her hand.

"Doyle, I cannot answer anything directly, not really. You know that, don't you?"

"So you can't tell me how he may have managed his way back…?"

She shook her head. "But I think we both know that he did." She looked at him pointedly. "He meant no malice…" she said, "He just wanted to make the love gift of a fairy tale."

"Fairy tale…" Doyle breathed.

"Love gift… wonderful way of putting it. Very comforting."

"You mean, you know…" began Doyle, but Grace was still talking:

"I would think that is one of their main purposes… to give comfort…"

"…About fairy tales?…" continued Doyle. It was the first time someone here had even mentioned the words.

"I don't think you're here to discuss that either, Doyle," she admonished gently. "You know about those already. What you don't know…"

"Is how to stop it."

"It?" she queried.

"Him."

"Ah," she smiled. "'For every evil under the sun, there is a remedy or there is none. If there be one, seek till you find it; if there be none, never mind it.'"

Doyle stood up, angry all at once. "Never mind it?" he cried. "But he's doing horrible things! I think he wants to put an end to all fairy tales! He's killed animals, a person… How can I not mind that? How can I not think about something that could affect so many?"

"I don't believe I said anything about thinking, Doyle…" He stopped and dropped his jaw. He looked at her as she quietly set to her knitting, the needles clicking away.

"'… If there be none…'" he whispered. "Is that because… because, the evil is still there… but the remedy may not be something *I* can mete out…?'"

She continued to knit, but he could see a small smile crinkle her cheeks.

He sat beside her again. He looked at her and tried to have her look at him directly. "Am I really here?"

"As real as real can be…" she answered. "Funny…" she said, and looked off. "Visitors who end up here look at the goings-on and wonder at them… sometimes two, three times in a year… they're amazed that these people can do such things…" She turned a look at Doyle: "…They can't find the logic in what they see… probably because there is no logic in what they *see*… but, it's about what happens after it's gone… in here…" She took a slightly boney finger and touched his head. "And how it resonates here…" and that finger moved to touch Doyle's chest and he felt his heart beat quicker.

"And *him*, is he really here? And the mountain, why now? I know he thinks the mountain signifies the end… people are getting scared… and I know people behave poorly when they get scared…"

She turned her attention back to her knitting. "'Tommy's tears and Mary's fears will make them old before their years.'"

"But that's not the worst of it… they can go mad! Already their tempers are flaring, people are angry and suspicious…" Doyle stopped. He stared at the woman who turned a placid gaze upon him that felt gentle and reassuring, but he was still maddened all the same. "You have no other words of advice?"

She shrugged slightly. "'Come when you're called, do as you're bid, shut the door after you, and never be chid.'"

Doyle looked down. "I try to never sound reproachful, Ma'am. I suppose you have told me more than I knew before…" He slowly looked up and saw her beaming a smile at him. Again, there was a reassurance that he could not understand pouring over him. "And probably some things that I won't know until later…"

At this, she nodded. There was another rumble and the ground swayed. She sat on the bench still with her knitting. "Aren't you concerned, Grace? I mean… your home…"

"I have lived here a very long time, Doyle. I have seen things come and go and change and reappear and leave only to come back again anew. My only concern… is that you manage your way back."

He felt fear for the first time since coming through the gate. "You don't think I can?" he whispered.

"Not that…" she all but laughed, and then fell serious for a moment. "*You* don't."

It was true. He didn't. He had begun to feel that he was to stay there forever. That he had to get this thing with Simon sorted or die trying, but then after that, he had no real clue… could he wish his way back? Wake himself up? Was he asleep? Was he dead?

"'A hill full, a hole full, yet you cannot catch a bowlful,'" she sing-songed. He gazed at her fondly, and she continued. "I suppose you can put that under 'something for later'." She put her knitting down and stood, taking him by the arm and walking him down the stone path. "You must be moving on, Doyle… you have some things to sort out…" She got him to the gate and pointed him back in the direction of town.

"But *you* could talk sense into them, couldn't you?" he asked, indicating the town. "They believe you to be wise…"

"Oh I'm sure they do, but I can't leave here, people might think I don't live here anymore and I really don't want anyone else moving in, you understand that…"

He didn't like it, but he did understand. He had learned not to mess about with life here. He had to be aware of his decisions, he knew every decision he made would have a reaction and he had to be aware of what would happen if he were responsible for anyone here doing something other than what they would normally do.

Suddenly, but not abruptly, she reached up and took his face in both her hands. She pulled him toward her and gently kissed his forehead. He wanted to cry from the kiss, from the gentle show of affection, but he felt oddly warm and rejuvenated and, odder still, he felt peaceful. They stared into each other's eyes for a moment, blue on blue. He placed his hands on hers, still holding his face.

"Thank you, Grace," he said and took her hands from his face and clasped them together. Then Doyle started down the path towards town. Above him a shadow passed and he stared up to watch a huge, beautiful white gander sail over, circle slightly and land on the grassy patch of the old woman's house. The old woman went to the creature, which was almost as big as she and patted it under its beak.

"Silly goose…" she chided gently, and looked back up at Doyle. With her other hand, she waved at him. He took a moment to also wave and then headed towards town.

Chapter 32
Reflecting for a Cow

So much of Danni's young life had been spent in criticism. She had felt her cousins, who actually weren't her cousins, had been very critical of her, though her Mother, who was not actually her mother, had been gentle. Danni could see that she, herself, must have been a challenge. But it had made her angry. And because of that criticism, she had begun to see what others did with a jaundiced eye.

And of course it couldn't make sense... to her. If she hadn't been born to the mother she thought of as her Mother, who had she been born to? And where *did* she come from? It would have made sense if she hadn't really come from this place of stories, as Doyle had made her come to believe it was; it would have made sense, then, for her to look at what had happened and question. Was she from the place that Doyle had come from? Or worse, Simon's place? She shook her head. Even if it was from one or the other, that did not determine the way she would live her life. She knew that would be her choice and that she would do as right as she could, considering everything, not just her idea of what should be right, but others' as well. Some of them were so simple in their wants and desires. Others were more complex, but seemed simple at first. She had to be careful how she spoke to any of them.

She shook her head and looked around. It felt as if they had been on the path for ages and had barely gone anywhere. Still, she had remembered passing the inn where Cinderella was and thought they ought to be getting close to the fayre by now. Then she noticed that they weren't on the main path, but an off-shoot.

"Leo..." she called, "we're not on the path!"

"I know that, Danni..." he said simply.

"But shouldn't we be? I mean, how can we keep track of everyone coming and going if we aren't on the path?"

"But we're *near* the path, Danni," Leo pointed out, "And I can keep track of everyone coming and going without anyone keeping track of us."

He was very proud of himself for that. If they were supposed to keep out of the way, he was going to take as many steps to see that through as he could. Danni almost smiled. It was a good idea. Leo was more sensible than Danni had given him credit for. In fact, she realised, she hadn't given the cat much credit for the intelligence he had shown at all. To Danni, Leo was still the silly cat with the thorn in his foot, mewling and howling away at the pain while blindly avowing a faith that could not be seen or be considered in any way tangible.

And it had served him well, she could see that now. Allowing himself that 'leap of faith' and trust had given him the capacity to continue regardless of the situation. True, he had become anxious on several occasions, but it was never regarding himself, it had usually been – she stopped as she realised it – it had usually been about her. His concern and compassion for her truly seemed boundless. Unconditional. And he had saved her. She had helped him, he had returned the favour and he was still with her, protecting her, guiding her when most would consider the debt paid. Unconditional. Danni threw herself onto Leo's neck and hugged with all her might. The cat stopped suddenly.

"Are you all right, Danni? Am I going too fast? Are you all right?"

From somewhere in his neck, buried into his golden neck, he heard a muffled voice: "I love you, Leo."

The cat's golden eyes filled with tears but the smile on his face was unmistakably happy. "I love you, too, Danni," he whispered and felt the mouse hold tighter. His smile faded slightly. "I don't mean to not give this moment its due..." he said softly, "But I need a drink..."

"The water's nearby, to the right..." and she tugged his fur in the direction opposite to the path they were following, "Can you hear it?"

And when the cat set to listen, he could. "How do you *do* that?" he marvelled, moving towards the sound.

"I have a friend who gets very thirsty. I like to think about him."

Then they saw before them a small rivulet, the perfect size for Leo. Ample space for him to stand and not get his feet damp, but easy enough for him to bend his great head down and lap up. Danni jumped off beside a stone so as to allow Leo more freedom of movement. There she found a small area that was easy for her to sip some water as well.

The plaintive "moo" sounding near made them both stop. Simultaneously and slowly they turned their heads in the direction of the sound and in the not-too-far distance they saw the large head of a cow staring at them. And before the cow, sitting on another rock, staring dejectedly at the forest floor, was Jack.

Leo asked softly, "That him?" Danni nodded. "You certainly have a way, Danni..."

Danni nodded again and skittered to a tree stump in front of Jack. "No one would buy her...?" she asked gently.

Sadly, the boy looked up and saw the mouse. The same mouse. He shook his head. "I've got to have something to give my mother..." he whispered. "I'm afraid to go home... I'm afraid to do anything..."

"That why you're here?" she asked.

He made a motion to the cow. "She likes the greens under the tree canopy best." He looked at Danni. "I don't know what to do..." he said softly. "I'm afraid to go home, my mother will be so angry... but I don't

203

want to just give the cow to that man for beans… I think you were right and I ought to wait for money…" He gazed at his cow. "Still, I might at least have had some beans to give my mother…"

Danni quickly latched onto what he had said. "Wait… the man still wants to give you the beans?" she demanded.

"Don't you get angry, now," he told the mouse, "I did listen to you, you made a good and valid point…"

"I was wrong!" Danni yelled.

"Excuse me?" the boy did not look too happy.

"I know you must be upset…"

"You were *wrong*?" he got louder.

"I didn't know it at the time…"

"I've been sitting here feeling sorry for myself and not knowing what was going to happen to me…"

"Is the man nearby?" Danni asked, looking about.

"…And you tell me you were wrong?!" Danni could see the anger growing in the boy as he stared venom at the mouse.

And then, suddenly: "She didn't have to come back to find you, you know." Leo had jumped up onto the stump and sat next to Danni. The boy shook his head and looked from cat to mouse and back again. "So instead of losing your temper, take your cow and find the man, make the trade and go home, plant the beans and in the morning… well… let's just say get ready for an adventure."

The boy looked sideways at the cat. The cat didn't flinch: "Oh sure, you don't have to believe me, I mean, you believed the mouse and look where it got you. But I look at it this way: That man is still trying to give you those beans. So it's either your cow, or it's the beans. Now, nobody else wanted that cow, so I'm thinking it's not the cow. And seeing as he doesn't seem to be offering those beans to anyone else, maybe it's you he's wanting to give the beans to."

Leo yawned to make his point. "Just an observation." And with one paw he nudged Danni, who climbed on his back. "Do with it what you will…" and with Danni on his back, he jumped down and started back the way they had come. He stopped for a moment to look back at the boy who was staring after them, slack-jawed. "I wouldn't be all day about it." And Leo slowly made his way back down the path from where they had come.

At this, the boy stood and gathered up his rope, then urged the cow to follow. Calmly, it did. The boy stared daggers at them: "If nothing happens by tomorrow, cat, I'll be coming to look for you *and* that mouse!" and he pushed passed them on to the little path and then to the main one.

"Leo," Danni started, "you were brilliant! That was marvellous!"

And the cat's knees buckled beneath him and he collapsed to the ground. Danni was lurched forward and slid off Leo's neck onto the soft ground.

She stared up at the cat in a panic, seeing his eyes wobble in his great head. "Leo! Are you all right?"

The cat blinked and panted slightly before looking directly at the mouse. "Don't let me do anything like that again," the cat whispered. "That was mad, that was... that boy coulda hurt us both... he..." The cat stopped and took in a deep breath.

"You were very logical, Leo," Danni admired.

"Scariest thing I've ever done..." the cat breathed out then looked at Danni again, "Really?" he asked. Danni nodded, bursting with pride. "Well, don't let me do it again..." He shook himself, allowing all his golden fur to right itself and gave a nod. "Climb aboard, Danni," he ordered. "Let's go see if we can find Doyle."

The mouse did as she was told and once back on the cat's neck, they started back down the side path, heading for the town square.

Chapter 33
In for a Penny, Out with the Town

As Doyle looked ahead of him, he began to seriously wonder how he was going to get into the town. There were King's Guards at one of the entrances and they were being more than a little rough with some of the people trying to pass through – people who looked like they were from the town: one on horseback, two on a donkey-pulled goods-cart, and a group of what appeared to be beggars, complete with barking dogs.

The Guards busied themselves with the man on horseback – bringing the post – and reluctantly let him through. As the Guards turned their impatience to the cart driver bringing bolts of cloth for the dress maker's shop as well as woollens for the specialty shop, Doyle decided to slide in with the beggars. They were an ill-looking lot, and their mean appearance made him think twice. If anyone was to be given trouble, he thought, surely it would be them. But what choice did he have?

"And why are you coming this way?" the Guard demanded of the hapless cart driver, "Weren't you at the fayre?"

"I already told you, my good man," the cart driver said in a monotone, "we are not for the fayre, we are for the town. These bolts are for the dressmaker who is working on a wedding dress and the woollens are to go to the Old Woman of Leeds Charity Shop. She must be knitting socks for the poor of the neighbouring area."

Dressmaker. Doyle saw his chance. It would either work or… well, he'd cross that bridge after he had burned it.

"Bolts of cloth?" he came forth and looked at the man who peered down his nose at the boy. "Would that be for Miss Belle's sister?" He gave the Guard a look of utmost courtesy and even more solicitousness, quick to remove his cap and fumble it up in his hands. "Her sister is getting married, soon, sir, I believe some of these bolts are for my lady's bridesmaid's gown…" He looked back up at the man on the cart, "My lady flew out of the courtyard and set off back home when all was not ready for her to see…"

The man on the cart looked resolutely at the Guard: "Do you see? You are keeping me from my appointed task, sir, I must tend to my work!" To Doyle he asked: "Will she be coming back?"

Doyle paused for a moment. "Oh I hope so, sir, but I was told to wait for you and see you to the dressmaker's in the square before setting off to fetch her."

The man on the cart again turned his attention to the Guard. "Oh, do let me through, my good man, Captain, is it?" This chuffed the Guard who was very low-ranking indeed, and he lifted his hand to let them pass. Doyle went up to the donkey and led him through the arched entry. Many thanks were thrown back as the beggars made their way to the Guard.

"Beggars, sir..." the tallest of them cried out. "Your town's turn." Without batting an eye, they were passed through. Doyle shook his head and then smiled. He would need to look over the Aesop's Fable about not judging by appearances. Still, he held onto the donkey's bridle and led him through the arch, heading to the town square.

******

Leo and Danni had just about gotten to the gates of the town when they saw before them a Donkey, a Dog, a Cat and a Rooster. The four animals looked surly and more the worse for wear. They eyed Danni and Leo briefly, then suddenly, the quartet moved as one towards them, the dog licking his mouth, the cat emitting a low hiss, the rooster scratching at the ground fiercely and the donkey kicking one hind leg as if it were a nervous twitch.

Without a word, Danni slid off Leo's neck. She slowly stepped before Leo and sat, stretching out her front paws as she stared at the four.

"You go ahead..." she said to Leo, with the utmost calm. "I've got this." The four creatures stopped their advancement.

"What...?" Leo whispered.

Again, not looking anywhere but at the four before her, Danni said: "I have this. You go ahead. I'll meet you just inside."

Leo took two steps back and then started for the gate, passing by the King's Guards as they intimidated three odd-looking women, one with an extremely large foot, another whose under lip jutted out awkwardly and the third with a grossly large thumb. Leo passed unnoticed and walked inside the town gates to a rain barrel near the entrance. Then his mouth dropped in shock.

What was he thinking, leaving Danni alone with those animals? If people were acting strangely, mightn't that affect the animals as well? At the fayre, Doyle had marvelled at how they were all getting along and now Leo was suddenly struck with a fear that even animals' demeanours could change. And those four had looked so terribly fierce and angry. He rocked back and forth on his feet for what seemed an eternity and was about to rush back when Danni appeared under the arch and looked about for Leo. Seeing him, she smiled and waved happily then ran over and made to climb the cat.

"Whoa, wait, not so fast... what just happened?" Leo demanded. Danni looked questioningly up at Leo.

"What? Them? Oh they left."

207

"Whatever possessed you to do such a thing?" he all but yelled. Then Leo stopped, "They just *left*?"

"They wanted to know if this was Bremen. I looked at the sign and sounded it out. It didn't say Bremen so I told them that. They thanked me and started off. A gander flying over told them it was farther down the path, but that they might find a nice cabin to rest in a few leagues into the forest." She gazed up at Leo. "What?"

Leo shook his great head. "No sense asking you not to do anything like that again, it probably won't happen, but I will ask you to kindly consider just running?"

Danni considered this. "If it will make you happy, Leo... But, it was perfectly safe. They wouldn't do anything to me, since I'm not part of their story, but you are a cat, so you could have been harmed."

The cat wasn't completely convinced. "Come on... up you go..." and Danni climbed up. "We will take a quick turn around here, back alleys and other ways that are out of sight, then if we don't find Doyle, we go back to the cart and wait for him there... all right?"

"All right, Leo..." she acknowledged, but she wished they would just keep looking around here until they found him. Things were moving fast.

Chapter 34
Doomed to Repeat It

Doyle led the donkey-cart towards the centre of town. The market had pretty much broken up; people were taking down their stalls and moving the pieces to nearby carts. Others were taking their goods into some of the buildings nearby. They were working in an orderly fashion, but there was still a tension and anxiety in the air. Doyle pointed out the dressmaker's shop.

"You know the way, sir?" he asked congenially.

"Yes, yes, of course!" the haberdasher snapped. The man's good humour had gone and he was anxious to get to the shop.

"Then I'll be off to fetch my lady..." Doyle said and scampered down an off-shoot of the square.

"But wait! Aren't you going the wrong way?" the man called. He shook his head: "I thought for sure he would go back the way he came..." then he shrugged and urged the donkey on towards the shop.

Doyle took off at an easy trot. He wasn't sure where he was going exactly – he wanted to have a moment to check in his book and see if Jack was back, but he knew that would have to wait a little longer. Up ahead was a set of arches that connected the houses on either side to one another; the main arch was for carts and people on horseback but there were side arches as well for foot-travellers. It was so long and dark underneath, that they seemed more like tunnels, but he went through anyway. As he got to the end of the archway, and was coming out into the light, he tripped over something he didn't remember seeing. He tumbled over and slammed into the cobblestones painfully, almost as if he had been pushed, the wind now totally knocked out of him. Before he could right himself, he was being hauled up by the back of his neck and pulled to a standing position.

Simon glared at him, with an incongruous smile on his lips. "Couldn't stay away?" he hissed. "Or can't get back?"

Doyle coughed and took in a ragged breath. "Not going anywhere until you're stopped," he got out.

"Oh and how are you going to do that, kid?" he demanded. "These people don't know you. As far as they're concerned, you're the enemy. And one or two choice words from me can make that a reality."

"Why?" Doyle asked finally.

"Because they believe me, kid... they know me... even the ones who don't know me believe they do..."

"No... why are you doing this? What do you hope to achieve?"

Simon pushed him back into the darkness, against the archway wall. "You're not where I'm from, boy... You have no clue what it's like... what it's become..."

"It's not very good where *I'm* from right now," countered the boy, "Thank you very much, but that doesn't answer my question."

"Fairy stories..." Simon said with disdain. "They seem innocuous enough, but they fill people with unrealistic ideas and dreams that won't ever come true." Doyle struggled a little beneath the man's grip. That didn't make sense. Not the stories he knew. Simon was continuing: "They breed fear... nightmares... doesn't matter how much people try to soften them up... what are they good for? People need to know to look to themselves! Their strength is what gets them through! The people who believe in this crap? Weak... weak people who believe that something will help them... some fairy or elf or witch... those people need to be weeded out... shown the way things really are or just be gotten rid of... But as long as *this* place exists... as long as these characters keep at it, over and over, stupidly reliving their fantasy lives, they will continually re-infect mine. The weak will be drawn to it..." He suddenly looked at Doyle with concern. He looked into him to see if he was comprehending. "You're a smart kid..." he tried. "You see what it's like here... you see what they are, what they do... It doesn't make sense..."

"You've never read them..." Doyle said softly.

Simon pushed him up harder against the wall. "Of course I have!" he shouted. "As soon as I knew there was a way of getting rid of them, I started reading them! You have to get close to your enemy, boy... you should know that where you're from... understand the enemy..."

"They don't breed fear and nightmares!" Doyle cried out. "They give hope... they comfort!"

"To all the weak and downtrodden... oh yeah... sure... they believe in all this and that they will be pushed up to the ranks on high... that's a load of crap and you know it!" He drew close to Doyle. "Look at them here, boy... they go where you tell them, change when you put even the smallest piece of logic in front of them, what the hell are they worth? Nothing! These stories are nothing, they do nothing but ruin it for people back where I'm from, where we are from! Which would you rather have, boy? Our world or theirs? You think it's bad in 1930-whatever, it's gotten a whole lot worse in the 21st Century. It's catastrophic. Listen, if something were to be destroying your life as you know it. If you could see there was something eating away at the fabric of your existence, wouldn't you try to eradicate it? Wouldn't you do everything in your power to make it go away?"

Doyle stared at him and his mouth dropped open. Sure, some of the people were silly, some of them inane, but many had good stories to tell and had meaningful outcomes, things that people could learn from and grow

211

from, but to blame these characters for the ills of a different world was just crazy.

"You're no better than Hitler…" Doyle whispered.

Simon stepped back. He drew his hand back and slapped the boy full on the face and Doyle fell to the cobblestones again. Simon kicked him in the stomach, then pushed him over onto his back and knelt beside him, one knee on Doyle's chest, his hands grabbing the collar of his jacket.

"Don't you say that… don't you ever say that!"

Doyle coughed and tasted blood in his mouth. "But isn't that what you're doing? Look at it! You want to destroy this whole place because you think it will better serve where you come from!"

"And you!" snarled Simon. "You, too! It's fitting! It's justice!"

"You're not talking justice, you're talking vengeance!"

"Same thing!"

And suddenly, it became clear to Doyle: "We won," he said softly. "We won the war… you wouldn't have reacted that way if we hadn't… you wouldn't have taken it as such an insult…"

Simon sneered at him. "Of course we won the war, once America got in it, of course we won it…"

"You're not an American… I don't believe it! I know what they did for my country before, and I know they will do it again and if you are from the future then you must be in one sorry little part of it because I believe the part that made that country, really made it, only *allows* your kind their time, because that's the kind of place it is… and when they tire of you and your whingeing, you'll go of your own volition… and they'll be happy to see you go…"

"You're just a boy, you know nothing of where I'm from…"

"And you've learned nothing from where I'm from…"

"What?"

"You can't do away with something you don't understand, Simon… people won't stand for it… they might seem to… they might go along because they've been scared into thinking it's the right thing… or been given one-sided logic to make them think it's the right thing… But once things look out of line… once people see the harm that's being done…"

"Those people don't matter!" Simon snapped.

"Oh, so it's all just for you? And *your* people? The rest of the world can go hang? You're going to do this because you think it will save your country? I don't believe America will go for that, Simon…"

"You'd be surprised…" Simon knew it was for the best, and once the rest of the world saw that, of course they would be grateful and want to fall in line with what he was doing… once everyone saw and understood…

"Oh I'm sure there are some people like you… small and sad little people who have been slighted… I'm sure there are people like that everywhere… and they might make a mighty noise… but I think you'll find the majority might not be so willing to go along…"

"This place is nothing… they won't miss it… no one will know…"

"I will. And I will raise holy hell to keep it."

"Not from where I stand, boy…" Simon spat out, threateningly.

"Is your name really even Simon…?" The man looked at Doyle sideways and a bit of a smile cracked on to his face. Doyle wished he could hit him, wished his hits would matter. "Any of your people come from England, Simon?"

"What?"

"If I'm from your past and you're from my future… who's to say our paths won't have crossed…?"

For a second, the man was stymied. Had any of his family been from England? Was there a tie to this child? Is that how he was able to get here, because the boy had been able to get here?

Doyle had no idea what he was saying, only that he knew he had to keep talking and keep Simon off balance. The man was mad. He was mad as a hatter and had to be stopped, but until Doyle could see a way, he needed to keep the man talking… maybe something would happen to let him slip away… maybe someone would come…

Simon shifted his knee slightly and felt it. In the jacket pocket. A book. The book the mouse talked about. The other story book. He had to have it.

The rumbling came again, much louder than before, and the ground lurched beneath them. Simon lost his grip and tumbled to the side and Doyle took the moment to roll awkwardly away and get to his knees. Again the ground shifted, and there was a creaking sound of timber: the houses were shifting as well, behind him he could hear a window shatter and the sound of things hitting the cobblestones, some slates from the roofs, maybe. Then it began to subside and Doyle rose. But Simon was up as well, staring at the boy, his eyes piercingly dark.

"None of it will matter if you're dead… Give me the book… or I'll take it!" and he leapt up at Doyle, who backed away sharply.

A King's Guard appeared from the other end of the archway and Doyle ran into his chest. The Guard placed an arm around him to hold him in place as he tried to struggle. The Guard tugged Doyle down the road towards the town square.

"That's him!" Doyle heard; it was the man from the donkey-cart. "He told me he was going to find her! I didn't think it was right! And no one at the shop even knew the woman had gone! Frantic, I tell you!"

"Wait!" Simon called out.

The Guard turned to him and recognised him as the one who had seemingly calmed the crowed earlier. Still, he owed him nothing. "I'll see to this now…" he said gruffly and pushed Doyle ahead of him, the man from the donkey-cart close behind.

Simon followed a safe distance away, his mind racing. He didn't understand, the boy didn't understand. But what could he expect? Child of a completely different era… and then he wondered about his own threat. Could he have killed him? Would he have died? Was he already dead where he came from? It wasn't lining up right. Things had always been so easy to assess, so simply set down; the stories were there in his book, he had always been able to locate the characters to do away with a story line. He had his set plan once he had gotten here, and was able to move through things swiftly, but he had never encountered another person from another time in reality – and was that really what it was where he was from – reality?

He knew that to come here, he had to put his body through some torturous times back there, he was never the same when he came to himself, not for some time. But he could assess the work he had done and see that things were righting themselves. Not that people were automatically or immediately behaving differently, but he could see a subtle change... people becoming less tolerant of the weak, not as concerned with them as they were with themselves or their own... the separation was beginning to take root. Certainly there were still those who wanted to fight for their bleeding-heart ideals, but they were being talked down more and more and seen for what they really were – a way to keep themselves in power, a way to threaten the stronger, those who would gain more strength were it not for this group wanting to pass strength on to those who had none nor seemed to have the wherewithal to have uncovered it within themselves to begin with.

People could be swayed, one way or the other, and he needed to be sure that the people here stayed with him. The boy had no proof, he had left nothing to chance there, and now it was just a case of making the people see the boy was the real cause. Yes. The boy was the cause. If he could get them to do that work for him, that would be another nail in the coffin... for they could not harm an innocent thing... that was not the way... and if they did... he smiled. It was on the brink of crumbling. This could help set it over. And the book... he had to have the other book. Once he saw things were truly falling about, he would destroy them both. There would be no order then and no way of getting it back.

He stayed near and waited for an opportunity. That's all it would take. A small opening. And then he realised. The boy had been bleeding. He upped his step slightly. He himself had never bled, and being a handy man, he had certainly had his share of attempts. And there had never been blood. The only blood he had really remembered was what had fallen from Snow White's mother's pricked finger... or the Old Queen in The Goose Girl... she had pricked her finger and placed the blood on a handkerchief for the girl to take for good luck... which she lost... but the boy was bleeding. He followed.

The Guard pushed Doyle ahead of him, but the boy was checking as often as he could to see if Simon was still following. He was. Not too far, but not near enough to be seen as a threat. The Guard was something of an oaf and oafs like these could prove particularly cumbersome if challenged. He wiped at his nose and found that it, too, had been bloodied. There was a knot on the side of his head from hitting the cobblestones as well. He was pretty certain he looked a mess and that might not help him.

Then, at the town square, he saw a small crowd gathering near the dressmaker's shop. Two young women, tall and coolly lovely, stood with an older gentleman who appeared quite perplexed. The two women appeared somewhat bored, actually, but still made small gestures to mollify the older man. Other people were talking amongst themselves in furtive tones, fearful that anything might come straight down from the skies to harm them. The beggars who had been so easily admitted were being chased by some young people about Doyle's age and they were making their way back down towards the gate to the town. People watching this were urging the children on, some encouraging them to throw stones. And suddenly, Doyle was brought before the older gentleman and the two lovely women, who looked down at him as if he smelled bad. The women brought up their fans and swished them before their faces. The Guard spoke to the gentleman.

"You know this boy?" he demanded.

The gentleman was taken aback by the brusqueness of the Guard's voice. He brought out a handkerchief and wiped his sweating forehead and under his chin. "I don't... I don't think so..." he stammered.

The man from the donkey-cart spoke up. "He's the one who brought me and my girl in to town, sir; he's the same one who said Miss Belle had left in a temper!"

The gentleman, who Doyle now took to be Belle's father, shook his head. "That is not my daughter's way," he admitted, "Belle is the personification of courtesy... she would never leave in a temper..." he looked at the two young women and Doyle knew these to be her sisters. Realising their father was looking at them, they put smiles on their faces. Doyle could also recognise that their father knew quite well that these two *did* have tempers. He looked back at Doyle. The poor lad's face was bloody and his lip looked a little swollen. What was happening around him? Everyone was acting so queerly, so mean... he looked at the Guard. "Did you do this to him?" he demanded.

The Guard looked at him in a surly fashion. "Didn't touch him except to bring him here... maybe the last labour pain knocked him over."

Doyle saw Simon lurking on the edge of the growing crowd. "He did it!" Doyle cried out, and pointed to Simon. People turned to see where he was pointing and even Simon took the moment to look behind him. "You!" Doyle cried out, "Simon! He knocked me down, slapped me..." The people practically turned as one and looked at Simon who was ready.

"I don't deny it!" Simon called back. "He's a stranger! He isn't from here and he was running away! I tried to stop him and he struggled! And now we find Miss Belle is missing? What did you do to her, boy?" Simon yelled back and the crowd as a unit went back to Doyle, some calling out the question as well, others calling out that they didn't know him, he *was* a stranger, calling attention to his mode of dress.

Belle's father looked about to weep or fall down dead. It was because of his promise. He knew it. He had broken his promise to the beast. When Belle came home he was overjoyed, he had been miserable without her and had almost convinced himself that he had sent his dearest daughter to her doom. When she spoke of escaping, part of him knew it was wrong, that a promise had been made and now was broken and something was going to happen. He had no idea it would reach so far as to affect the entire town.

But where was she? And who was this unfortunate boy the people seemed to want to rip apart? Did he have something to do with his daughter's disappearance?

"So he don't work for you?" the Guard asked. The man wanted to nod, but he looked at Doyle, seeing the fear growing in him as the crowd began to get angrier. Finally, he said, "Do you know where she has gone?"

Doyle nodded. "Back to the beast," he breathed. Belle's father gasped. "What did he say?" someone in the crowd asked.

"Look at the old man!" said another.

"Oh goodness, is he all right...?" another cried out fearfully.

"Did he kill her? Was he the one what killed the woman at the fayre?" another shouted.

"NO!" Belle's father cried out, "Be quiet!" and the people were brought to an uneven silence. "Let him go!" he demanded of the Guard who, taken by the man's forceful demeanour, dropped his arm from around Doyle. Belle's father took Doyle by the shoulder and looked into his eyes. "She what? What did you say?" he asked Doyle again.

Doyle blinked and licked his lips. "She's gone back to the beast..."

Simon took a step back. He looked up to the boy who was leaning in towards Belle's father.

Someone yelled out: "But what about the woman at the fayre? Did he kill her? What about..."

And Doyle looked out at the crowd and pointed to Simon. "He did!" he cried. "He didn't want anyone to know he had been talking to her about the Maiden in Gold!"

Some people knew about the incident, how a woman had come to the Festival and the prince would only dance with her. Many were certain she would be the one the prince would pick after the third day of the Festival, but she didn't come back the second night. Maybe the candy woman herself was the Maiden in Gold!

"How do you know that...?" someone shouted.

And Simon lazed a look at him, stepping forward through the crowd towards Doyle. "Yes, boy... where's your proof...?" he asked, still stepping closer.

"I don't have any proof, but I saw you talking to her... you were asking questions about the Maiden in Gold... you wanted to know all about her..."

"What...?" Someone murmured, "Eavesdropping, were you?"

"No!" Doyle cried out, "He was travelling with me... and my friends..."

"Couldn't have been Simon..." someone else shouted, "Gentle as anything... he wouldn't hurt a fly!"

"No? But he smashed in a dog's head." There was a general murmur of discontent. "Broke a grasshopper's leg... and tried to kill a mouse..." Simon, who had been shaking his head with a benign smile on his face, turned sharply and took in a ragged breath, a break in his veneer. Doyle saw it and reacted quickly. "Oh... you thought she was dead?" Doyle asked. Simon found he couldn't move. Of course she was dead. The boy was lying.

If he wasn't then where was she? Where was the mouse? He looked about sharply. "See!" Doyle called the crowd to attention, "He's looking for her! You left before you could see that we saved her! She wasn't as easy to kill as her mother! Who else, Simon? Who else have you killed?"

"None of you know him!" Simon got out, "Look at him! His style of dress, everything about him! He is not from here…"

"And neither are you, Simon!" Doyle yelled. "Where do you live? Where's your house?"

"I have no house… I travel by foot and make my way all around… I help people here… I always have…" and he looked encouragingly at people around him, braving a smile. Some of them weren't listening. Some of them were looking at him and realising they didn't really know him… It was true that they didn't know some people from the town or nearby… but, they had seen them all… they recognised them… this man… they hadn't seen him before… and even though he was known by some… and those had spoken for him today… but only today…

"I spoke to you all earlier," Simon said calmly. "I told you all that there were strangers in your midst…" he continued to move towards Doyle, but kept his back to him. "But I also told you to be kind to your neighbours. I think I spoke to you about a tolerance that you all seem to be lacking right now… and I will tell you truthfully, that I take responsibility for the creatures this boy said I hurt or killed… that poor woman… she fell to her own death and I was there… but I was frightened… frightened by what she had confessed to me. The lad here isn't being quite forthright in what he is telling you because… he doesn't come from here… but he has something… something that he's been using to keep track of you all and to be sure that the mountain will become nothing short of a volcano! To erupt and spill down wrath upon you! She told me of this! And in her fear, she started to run and fell… I knew I had to keep in contact with the boy and the creatures he had polluted into believing him and helping him rise up against you all! So I said nothing… but now…"

He was close to Doyle now and he turned swiftly around and reached for Doyle's jacket, ripping at the inside pocket and pulling out the book. He wheeled around to the crowd and held it up. Doyle made a grab for it but Simon pushed him back. "See? His book of shadows! Something in here about all of you! And he was seeing to it that it all disappears!"

"No!" Doyle shouted.

But Simon charged on, "And I can stop it! I can stop it if you'll let me!"

"What?" some called.

"How?" more tried.

"What will you do?" came from others.

"I will go to the mountain!" Simon was working the crowd masterfully. "I will find the crack in the mountain that *he* brought here and I will throw the book into it and bring an end to all the wrath he has brought down upon you!" There was murmuring in the crowd. "Come with me! Follow me to the mountain and watch!" The people weren't sure what to do. They looked amongst each other in confusion. Doyle turned to Belle's father, but even he was looking at Simon and considering what was being said.

And the rumbling came again, worse still, the statue in the middle of the fountain shifted and someone went to it to steady it.

"See?!" Simon called. "Any more delay and fire will rain down next!"

What was he trying to do, Doyle thought. Destroy the book...? What would that do? Unless... unless he still had his own book and he was going to throw that in as well... Would the books' destruction mean the end of the town? The surrounding areas? The whole land? Before he realised what he was doing, he cried: "No!"

Triumphant, Simon turned a stare at him. "And of course he does not want it to be..." he said, and raised the book high in his hand. "To the mountain!" he screamed and ran ahead of the people to the other side of town, to the path, the gate and to the mountain in labour.

"Bring the boy!" someone cried and the Guard wrapped his burly hand around Doyle's arm and pulled him from Belle's father. He turned to look the man in the face and saw question in the older man's eyes.

"He means harm..." Doyle said to him as he was jerked down the cobblestones to follow Simon and his crowd. He was being pulled harshly, and the people who were near sneered at him, some poked at him until another Guard joined up and held onto Doyle's other arm. This minimised people taking pot shots at him but his arms were being tugged at harshly, while his feet barely touched the cobblestones.

By the time they got to the gate and headed down the path towards the mountain, Doyle could see that it had grown larger, as Grace had said it would. He could also see Simon heading up the set-in stones on the tree-lined path that led to the top. He tried to lunge forward, but the Guards had a tight hold on him. The crowd was watching Simon make his way to the top of the mountain, he stumbled and the crowd reacted strongly for him to get up and keep on task. He would forge ahead, and they would cheer heartily. There were more rumblings, but the earth was not shifting beneath them as harshly. They stared and followed his progress, each one imagining it were him making his way up.

"I will be responsible for him...:" Doyle heard from behind him and turned to see Belle's father behind him. The Guards looked at each other and Belle's father handed over a nice-sized purse of gold, promising: "We won't leave..." The Guards smiled. The first took the purse and they both stepped aside to make room for Belle's father to stand beside Doyle. "How will this do harm, lad?" he asked quietly.

Doyle released a sigh. He was believed. "I'm not sure..." he admitted, "but he has a book of his own with the stories... the stories of all of your lives... and I think he means to throw it into the crevice to destroy the whole place." He saw a muscle tighten in the man's jaw and he looked to the Guards beside them.

"I said we wouldn't leave..." he mused. "I cannot go back on my word, not again..." Doyle could understand the man's hesitation. He looked up the hill at Simon, making his way further up.

"Looks like I missed a lot..." came a voice below him. He looked down and saw Leo looking up.

"Leo!" he cried and looked at the cat's neck. "Where's Danni?" Leo looked towards the crowd. Doyle reached down and picked up the cat quickly. "Where's Danni, Leo?" The cat looked to the mountain. Doyle scanned the area and sure enough, darting among the rocks and bushes and making her way swiftly up the mountain was the tiny figure of Danni. "What does she think she's doing?" Doyle sighed.

"Righting a wrong..." the cat said softly. Belle's father turned to Doyle, barely acknowledging the new addition of the cat.

"Do you really think that if he throws in both books...?"

"Books?" Leo questioned. He looked at Doyle. "He has your book?" the cat asked. "And a book of his own?"

"He had to keep track somehow..." Doyle started, "but..." The cat squirmed out of his arms, using his claws a little to get his point across. "Ouch, Leo..." Doyle cried as he released the cat, who hit the ground running.

Belle's father watched. "Oh, he does move swiftly for a cat his size..." he said, then he looked into Doyle's eyes. "You must stay here, lad... I see the prince has approached. I served his father well before, so I think he will listen to me..."

"I don't know if there's time," Doyle started.

"Well we will have to try quickly then," and he looked at the Guards. "I will be back. I am trusting you both to be certain no harm befalls him. I go to speak to the prince. It would not bode well for either one of you, should my request not be honoured."

The Guards looked to one another. With barely a hesitation, they both nodded and Belle's father pushed his way through the crowd towards the prince. Doyle looked back up the mountain. He could no longer see Danni, but then he was not sure where to look. But he did see a flash of golden fur and knew that Leo was quickly making his way up the mountain as well.

Chapter 35
The Mountain Gives Birth

Higher he climbed, almost out of breath, with a stitch building heavily in his side. He had to keep on. He had to get to the top. He felt both books inside his shirt. They had no clue. No clue at all. And they were even holding the boy back. All the better... The boy would remain here to further witness the great eradication. No vision. No sense of right. To have been living through a war of his own and not realise that some things just had to be eradicated to truly be stopped. The bombing of Hiroshima. Nagasaki. Of course he didn't know of those things, but that put an end to another aspect of the war. Sometimes people had to be put in their place. Had it stayed that way, who knows what kind of power the States would have had now... but no... they gave things back... they allowed... and it proved to be a lapse of judgment... now the other countries were getting stronger again and the people of his country were paying the price, though some were maintaining the status quo ... None of it was right... even he knew that those in power were there to keep others down... He knew that they too had their weaknesses and more and more of them were proving it each and every day... espousing a moral strength for the country, vilifying people with a weakness for drugs, speaking against those who cheated others for their own wealth... and then those same leaders... cheating on their wives or husbands, sometimes with the same sex, even after decrying the abomination that was same-sex relations... being found addicted to drugs themselves, these people who had believed abusers ought to be locked up permanently or killed ... They were certainly not taking a taste of their own medicine... and others, who hid their wealth away from the government, evading taxes or not declaring the illegal aliens working for them after they had gone on record that illegals were just that... It was a completely different set of rules and Simon saw it... Simon saw what they were doing and was about to embark on a new crusade when he returned to reality, when the fantasy had been lifted from their past and from their eyes, when the things of this place were no more, then he would have something to say and it would make sense and he would be heard and people would listen and it would change. It would all change as he saw fit.

He stopped for a moment to gather his breath and to push his fist into his side in an attempt to assuage the pain there. Up ahead he saw where the rocks had slid away and a section of a crevice could just be seen. It must be huge, he thought. He shook his head. He had thought it would be easy enough to climb the mountain, it seemed short enough and it was absurd to think it had grown in just a few short hours… He bent over and took in deep breaths, which only made the pain worse so he adjusted to smaller breaths. This seemed to work better and after a few more he stood straight and continued on toward the crevice. It was getting closer.

He smiled to himself. So close. He felt a pulling sensation, much like what he would feel when he would be taken back home. Not yet, he vowed, not until he had seen it start. No matter what condition he was in when he went back, it would be worth it to know he had accomplished what he had set out to do. The knowledge would make him strong again – he would regain all his strength and then some. And even if others had forgotten, he would not, he had left notes and writings about what he had set out to do, he had transcribed all sorts of information that would remind him, and should even he be struck by the great eradication and not recall. He would. He was certain. It was all coming together. Not far now. He would go to the ledge and…

The mouse stared at him. Even for so tiny a creature, the anger that spilled from her eyes was vast. For a moment, he couldn't move. A ghost? Or had the boy spoken the truth?

She saw that he had opened his mouth dumbly upon seeing her and she shook her head. He really thought he had killed her. Well. He had. But Leo and Doyle brought her back. And she would not let their actions be in vain. She had work to do.

"Whatever you're trying to do… it won't work," she said evenly and Simon felt a chill even though it was uncommonly hot on top of the hill. He placed his hand on his shirt and felt the books beneath. He could do this. He had gotten rid of her before… even temporarily was enough for him to get a handle on leading the townspeople to become a disorderly mob.

"Did you see them down there?" he asked. "Did you hear them?" Danni didn't move. Her glare was not shifting. "They have him. The boy. They believe he is responsible."

"Because you told them that, I'm sure. But I also know they will see and be sorry when they realise you were wrong."

"And how will they realise that?" he asked her sarcastically. "You gonna somehow broadcast it down there? And you think they'll believe *you*? A mouse? A mouse who has eradicated so much of their lives already?"

"Belle is with the beast now," she said softly. His brows furrowed slightly. "And The Prince has wakened Briar Rose by now, too… if you look to the castle, you can see the thorn-bush has gone. And I'm sure Hansel and Gretel are having their first meal in the Witch's cottage and getting ready for a first night's sleep before she takes the boy to the cage in the barn." Simon took a slight step back.

"Let's see… Jack's mother has probably scolded him horribly for the trade of his cow for a sack of beans but I'm sure he's planted them… come the morning there'll be a bean stalk over the valley. Cinderella knows the prince has found her slipper… we both know the Goose Girl has been observed by the King by now and is being put in her rightful place as the true bride. Have I missed anything, Simon? Anyone else my narrow-mindedness, my judgemental qualities might have turned off their pre-ordained paths? Any of the things I hadn't enough experience to see, needed to be worked out by the person involved. Or that even though I didn't understand it, made sense to them. *Have I?!*" she shouted.

There was a rumbling that shifted the earth and Simon was jerked to one side, falling to his knees. He caught himself with his hands, hitting the ground hard and cutting into his palms. He turned them up to inspect and saw no raw spots where they had grazed some broken rock. No blood was oozing. He had pain, he felt the pain but there was no blood. He looked up. Dust was lifting up, like smoke.

The mouse hadn't moved.

"You had such sensibility, Danni…" he started and wiped his hands on his trousers.

"I had the narrow-mindedness of a child!" she replied. She saw mud streak on the fabric.

"I was going to teach you so much…" He touched his shirt again, nervously.

"Were you? How to hate? How to kill? How to destroy? What else were you going to teach me? How to read? Read what? Read *what* when this is gone?"

"There are other stories, Danni…"

"That you approve of?"

"What's that supposed to mean?"

"You don't like it here… you hate it… why?"

The man didn't like the line of questioning. He didn't know why he couldn't just run over to her and kick her off the stone ledge she was standing on, step on her, stop her, why she hadn't been affected by the tremor that had knocked him off his feet.

"Because it's built on lies!" he called out. He still had the books. He would make his way to the crevice and toss in the books. He took a side step, angling away from the mouse, but still heading to the crevice. Another rumble from deep within the hill and the ground jerked beneath him again and he lost his footing, but he didn't fall this time. Still, things seemed to have shifted and he felt disorientated and the rising dust filled his nostrils and he coughed.

"Lies?" Danni asked, it was gentler now, he noticed a change in her tone.

This could be his chance. "Don't you realise what these stories are, Danni? What they want people to believe?"

The mouse looked at him, studied him. How dishevelled he was, how nervous and desperate. This wasn't the man she had met so long ago; he wasn't the man she thought he was. He seemed to have known everything. He had an opinion and if it wasn't completely like hers, it became hers. He had encouraged her to foster those beliefs when she could have been learning from her foster mother. Learning about what she called Faith. About what she believed would get her through her day. Learning why it was so important for her to climb the clock, that maybe somewhere inside she knew what she was doing was a rhyme that children were being taught somewhere else, as a way of understanding language, not that it made real sense, it was nonsense but a way for a mother to bond with her child or a way to teach them to read. And that maybe when Danni was a little older, maybe now, her Mother would have been able to explain things in a way she could have understood. Yes, her cousins had been mean, they had picked on her and belittled her, but she was protected by her Mother and then her Mother was taken away by someone who wanted to teach her his way... and she had embraced his way, because he listened to her, or at least he seemed to... he had paid attention to her, or he was taking note of her abilities... but he hadn't loved her. Of that she was very certain now.

"Tell me, Simon," she asked quietly, "what do they want me to believe?"

"That all your wishes will be fulfilled... that you will win out over all competitors... and that all your enemies will be destroyed."

"Really?" she asked.

"Of course not!" he snapped, "that's what they *want* you to believe!" he looked at the mouse and wanted to make her understand one more time, believe him one more time. "That doesn't happen! It can't happen. How can it? Bad things happen every day and the bad people don't get punished!"

"And who is it that thinks they are bad?"

"What?"

"Who is it that determines some people are bad over others?" she asked simply.

"You know who's bad!" he yelled, "The people who wrong you! Who won't let you attain what you have strived for! Who stop you from achieving!"

"That sounds like blame," she said evenly. "That sounds like not coming to grips with your own shortcomings."

"How can you say that?!"

"You taught me to judge, Simon, and based on what you've presented me, that's my judgement. But you know what I think? I think that this place has no real bearing on your world. Because it's *not* your world. What it does do is help you look at things differently... process things within yourself, learn how to deal with them... It makes you look at the better way to be... no... in your real world, you are not going to find a house made of candy and cake and then defeat a witch... or climb into the sky and meet giants... you're not going to be awakened by a prince, or love a real beast, but maybe you will learn how to grow away from your parents and be on your own... you'll learn to be able to determine for yourself how to proceed with a problem... you might know better how to choose the people to love... be ready for them so you can recognise them when they arrive... So no... There is no useful information for what is out there... but inside? Inside where you think things through for yourself? That's where the wishes come true. That's where you win. That's where any enemy would be destroyed, because unless you let them, they will not be allowed to enter."

Simon stared at her. What was she saying? Where did she get this from? Had she read the same stories he had? Sleeping Beauty, for all their attempts at protecting her, her parents couldn't save her. And then she did nothing. She slept. The Prince just appeared when the time was up. Beauty saw the animal and dreamed of a man. Only when she thought he was dying did she feel love for him out of pity. Jack tricked the giantess and killed the giant who had killed his father, how did that make him right? Hansel and Gretel were pushed away by their parents, left to die and when they gain riches, they take it back to the family that had deserted them? What was she talking about?

"You don't see..." he said. "You don't know..." And he stood up straight. "For me, Danni... I wish this would all disappear! Be taken away! Blown away! Destroyed! That's what I wish for me!"

"Then maybe you're too old to wish properly, Simon, because I wish it to stay, and be here always... for everyone who has been touched by it and will be touched by it."

"*Not for me!*" he screamed and he pulled the books from his shirt, one in each hand. He started towards the crevice, saw how deep it dropped as he got closer and had a momentary feeling of vertigo as he looked down. The mouse moved slightly, dodging out of his reach but not at all certain what he was attempting to achieve... books? Doyle's book! One of those was Doyle's book! If he destroyed the books would that make everything...

Simon screamed again, but this time there were no words, just a guttural utterance that came from pain and he reached for his lower back, fumbling as he was still clutching the books and was not about to release them yet, not until he was ready to see them into the crevice. He turned slightly, still aiming for his lower back and Danni could see Leo clinging to Simon's back, climbing it until he could dig his sharp claws into Simon's head and sink his needle teeth into the man's neck. With a mighty swing, Simon knocked Leo off and the cat tumbled away and out of view. Simon stood triumphant. He turned to Danni and raised the books over his head as the mountain rumbled yet again and some of the rock beneath him gave way. Dirt flew up like a plume. The triumph on his face slowly turned to fear as he saw himself falling, as he saw the crevice open and pull him in. Wait, it wasn't supposed to be like this... he could stop it by force of will, he only had to concentrate. It seemed an eternity, but finally he felt himself being pulled up, out of the crevice... then, farther and farther and faster and faster *away* from the crevice, away from the rumbling, away from the little mouse on the edge of the mountain.

Far away, further than Danni could even imagine possible, in a hospital where incessant beeps acknowledged life to still be coursing through the man's body as the doctors worked on him, continued to work on him, had been working on him since he was brought in, the man suddenly shuddered, his eyes flying open to survey all around him, and the doctors there believed for a moment there might be a chance as they stared at eyes that surveyed the room with a mixture of rage and sadness, then clouded over and one long beep began, unceasing, insistent, fervently determined, over-zealous... until the plug was pulled and time truly called.

Danni stared down after him. Where she thought he had gone, where it appeared he had gone. Somewhere into a deep hole, the bottom of which she could not make out. And Leo... was Leo down there? Her eyes began to well with tears.

"I guess it's truly not for him, just for the rest of us, eh...?" she heard from beside her and turned to see the golden cat also staring down into the crevice.

"Leo!" she cried and rushed to him. "Are you all right? Are you hurt?"

"I'm fine, but I couldn't get Doyle's book!" the cat admonished himself.

"What will that do?" Danni asked. She looked over her shoulder. All seemed quiet. She skittered over the rocks and looked down, desperately wanting to see that the town was still there. And what about Doyle?

Chapter 36
Consolation Is Good for the Soul...

Down below, the sudden silence was appalling. People turned to one another but said nothing. The last rumble had been the worst by far, and the keening cry was bone-chilling. They stared up the mountain – for a mountain was indeed what it was – at the dust rising like smoke from a blacksmith's forge. And slowly it began to settle. And at the top-most part of the mountain, where a bit of rock jutted out, giving the mountain almost a forehead, the people saw movement. They looked closer and saw...

A Mouse.

Nervous laughter began to rise. And then the humour of the situation began to hit each of them. All that noise... all that commotion and shaking... what were they expecting? The mountain to tumble around them? A monster to climb out over the edge? And there it was... a mouse.

"Well..." said the prince to Belle's father. "Wasn't that much ado about nothing." Serenely, he arched a brow and looked over at the townspeople who had heard the prince and were laughing more. "I think we have some work to do here," he called out. "Our little development seems to have still made quite a mess about the town. Who will head up a group to see to the damage?" One of the Guards raised his hand and called that he would. "Good man!"

And suddenly many of the townspeople called out the same. It was, after all, their town. And the sooner they got to straightening it up, the better it would be for all involved. The prince was pleased as he looked back at the people. "It's best we get this work completed... for I know many of you wish to return to the fayre... And some of you are still to come to the Festival!" There was a general uproar of delight. The prince feigned shock for a moment and looked at his attire. "I suppose I ought to get myself going as well, eh? Seems I am supposed to find a wife!" Another uproar of delight, some shouts of luck and a sprinkling of "here heres."

The prince turned his horse and began to lead them back to town. Doyle stared at the people as they began chatting with each other. Talking animatedly about what could be done and who would be best at what, and what sort of goodies were to be made, because a full stomach would make the work go faster, and they all set about getting it done, because the fayre was waiting and the Festival was sumptuous and they began moving back through the gates. Soon, they were all gone, happily ensconced in their happy little town.

Doyle stared after them. He blinked. No one had spoken to him. No one seemed to even recall that he was there. That he had been awaiting certain death. He shook his head. He could hear the people still in the distance, going about their work. He knew that tools were being brought out, bins located in which to place broken things and then taken away, and there was something else, something he hadn't heard for what seemed like a very long time: laughter. Real laughter. A cloud seemed to have lifted. Even with the sun lowering in the distance, everything seemed lighter.

Danni!

He turned back to the mountain and looked to the top. Nothing. He scanned the mountain carefully and saw, closer and getting closer still, Leo trotting along, his golden coat shining in the lowering sun and on his neck, Doyle could make out a bit of brown. Danni was waving.

He took off at a run to meet them, falling before them and gathering them up into his arms. But both were shaking him off.

"What's happened?" Danni asked.

"Where have all the people gone?"

"Did we fail?"

"The books, Doyle, I couldn't get your book!" Leo mewled. His book.

Doyle shook his head and reached into his other jacket pocket. And withdrew his slightly worn, very loved story book. "Not to worry, Leo, he took the one we got at the fayre…"

"But the people!" Danni cried.

"… Are all in town, cleaning up and getting ready to go back to the fayre *and* the Festival!" Doyle exclaimed. "The prince, well, not *The Prince*, I believe he must be Cinderella's prince, he was here and asked everyone to clean up the town and to go to the fayre and that the Festival would be tonight!"

"Does Cinderella know?" Danni squeaked.

"We have to see her!" Leo topped and Doyle nodded, his smile so wide it actually ached his face.

"Everything is fine!" he told them. "Everything is all set to rights!"

But Danni looked at him and a sadness filled her eyes. "But Doyle… *you're* still here…"

He nodded and still smiled. "Yes, Danni… but I haven't tried to go!" The mouse cheered at this.

Leo, however, remained dour. "I don't know if I want you to, Doyle…" the cat whispered. Danni suddenly realised the true implication and she stared up at Doyle.

The lad, touched and fighting back his own emotions, looked at his two friends. He scratched Leo under the chin and rubbed the top of Danni's head. "Let's burn that bridge when we've crossed it, eh? Let's get the cart and see if Cinderella is still there!" and he set his hand down for Danni to climb up and then moved her to his shoulder. With a look at Leo, they headed to the entrance of the town.

Danni grasped onto his collar and leaned in closely to his ear. "I love you, Doyle," she whispered. "No matter what... thank you for being so patient with me..."

The lad's steps staggered slightly and this time his eyes misted with tears which he carelessly brushed away. Then he placed a finger up towards the mouse and gently rubbed her head and her back. She grabbed his finger for a moment in a tight, swift hug and released. Placing his finger to his lip, he took in a soft breath. The trio entered the town.

******

It wasn't as if nothing had happened: there was some damage about, things had fallen, some windows were broken, a door or two appeared to have been shaken from their hinges, but everyone was helping one another, genially, with more than a smile. Shop keepers lingered outside of their doorways to chat with people. Even the animals were in a better humour.

Doyle looked about and saw the place as he had always believed it was: content and happy, the perfect place for dreams and wishes to come true. He saw a cart nearby in the town square, at a shop. Two men were struggling with a purchase; it looked to be a grandfather's clock. A woman was following them, watching carefully and directing the fellows though they truly didn't need it. In the cart, he saw a little dog. It was laughing.

"Danni..." he called hesitantly and pointed.

The mouse angled a look in the direction and dropped her jaw. The Farmer's Wife! And the Farmer! They were having a new clock loaded onto their cart. Then as she looked closer, she could not believe her eyes.

Arnie? Was it Arnie? She couldn't move. She was fixed and rigid on Doyle's shoulder and shaking her head.

"But... Jon said..." and the little dog caught her eye. And winked. "Arnie...?" she called tentatively.

"Miserable head ache..." the dog laughed in her direction, "but you certainly look well, Danni... I see you have more friends!" Danni was stunned and could only nod.

He laughed still. "But... what's so funny this time, Arnie?" The dog raised his eyebrows as the men got the clock onto the cart and tied it off. With a jerk of his head he motioned to the top of the clock. Danni peered at the clock and when she saw the top she noticed a small hole right at the top, in a position that might be missed were anyone not looking for it. It was almost identical to the hole in the top of the old clock. She wondered for a moment... she pondered leaping off Doyle's shoulder and skittering up the cart wheel and going into the hole. She smiled thinking how proud her Mother would be. She felt her claws tighten at the desire to jump. And then

228

she sat back. She looked around at the town, at Doyle's profile and especially at Leo, who she saw was gazing up at her with wonder. She smiled down at him reassuringly and the cat smiled. She looked back at the clock as she heard Arnie laugh again – and she saw it.

Peeping cautiously out of the hole in the clock was a small brown mouse. It looked about with caution, its nose shaking as it took in the air. And as quickly as it had appeared, it was gone, hidden back in the clock.

"Doyle…" Danni got out, patting his neck.

He already had his book out, had opened a page and was pointing, "'Hickory, Dickory Dock…'" he read, pointing to each word carefully. "'The Mouse ran up…'"

She patted his neck again, gently. "Thank you, Doyle," she said. "That's enough… thank you…" And Doyle was grateful she had stopped him, for the lump forming in his throat was about to make reading the rest impossible.

They continued through the town, marvelling at the happy bustling, Doyle noticing some of the rhymes he had loved as a child right there before him, true to life – come to life before him. They passed people who greeted them kindly, offered those samples of treats and showed their wares to them proudly.

Soon they were out the other entry to the town and looked down the road before them. Other people were there, making their way to the fayre, and others still with blankets and cooking kits, going up to the Festival. The road twisted gently as they walked among the happy throng. Up ahead, they saw the Burnie Bee and out in front, waving the people on, was Bull, a smile on his face, clapping some people on the back or the shoulder, giving a welcome smile to those stopping by to come in for a quick pint.

He saw Doyle and his smile grew. "I was wondering where you lot had gotten to!" he called. "Began to wonder if you was ever comin' back for your cart!" He clapped Doyle on the shoulder and placed a meaty finger up to Danni and gave a little wiggle to her. He bent down and gave Leo a scratch.

"Is she here?" Danni asked.

"Hmm?" Bull grunted, standing back up to gaze down at the mouse. "Ella… is she here?" Bull shook his head only a little sadly.

"Had to let her go, I did…" he sighed. "What else could I do? Specially when a prince comes by saying all eligible maidens are expected at the Festival. Well, I couldn't keep a eligible maiden here workin' when the prince has said she needs to be there… Left a shoe he did…"

"He did?" Danni asked.

Bull reached into his apron pocket. "And herself asked that I give it to you…" and he brought out the delicate spun silver slipper.

Danni gasped and Leo's great eyes became larger still. Doyle had never seen anything so beautiful. Gingerly, he held out his hand and Bull placed it there. It was almost feather-light and looked like glass. The trio looked up at Bull in disbelief.

The man just grinned. "It's all right. She said she knows where to get another complete pair. Now go get your cart! The fayre is still going on and the Festival will commence once the sun has gone down and that shan't be long from now."

They hadn't really noticed it before, but the sun was beginning to sink lower in the west. It would be dark soon. After tucking the shoe into his jacket pocket, Doyle led the others to the barn and brought the cart out from hiding. Leo was delighted to leap back up on his seat and Doyle actually found that his arms had missed pulling on the handles and feeling the weight of the cart behind him. With another wave to Bull, they got back on the path and continued along towards the fayre. They passed the lake silently, trying to remember only that the Goose Girl was safe and moved on without discussing anything else.

The fayre was a riot of colour and noise ahead of them. People milled about happily, children played with joyous abandon and sellers were parading about with trays of their wares.

"Sampling?" Doyle heard behind him and turned so quickly that Danni was almost knocked over. The pink bonnet, the merry face, the tray of sweets before her: the candy woman. The candy woman! She cocked her head to indicate behind her. "You can buy them over there..." Doyle was dumbstruck. Taking his silence as refusal, the woman smiled and shook her head. "Suit yourself, then..." and she moved off to another passerby, the pink bonnet bobbing with the movement.

"Now, Doyle, did you really think I could allow any kind of disagreeable feeling to last?" he heard behind him.

This time he turned slowly and saw Grace down the path a little ways. He gathered up the handles of the cart and rushed over to her. "Grace..." he started.

"Doyle, I think you know as well as I that the sole purpose of a fairy tale is to take one on a fantastical journey and bring them home again, safe and happy." She raised her eyebrows just slightly. "And maybe learn a little something on the way."

Doyle shook his head in wonder, a smile creeping across his face. "Danni, Leo... this is Grace... the Old Woman Under the Hill."

Grace let her merry blue eyes light on both the cat and the mouse, lingering a little on Danni. "Hello you brave souls..." she greeted. Danni gave a little nod and Leo gave a smile. "I should think you've been through quite a lot." They all recognised the truth in the statement and nodded as a unit. "And we are all very grateful for it," she finished a little quieter. "So Doyle..." she spoke up again, "have you thought at all about my last riddle?"

To be honest, he hadn't. He had flown from one situation to the next since seeing her and hadn't even considered it. But he remembered it.

"'A hill full, a hole full yet you cannot fill a bowl full…'" he recited.

She indicated a path that they had not seen before. Or else it hadn't been there. It led down a ways and then began to rise up. A short ways up, there was a low-lying fog that obstructed the view of the path for some ways but above that, he saw a spire that looked very familiar to him. St. Nicholas Church! His heart burst with the recognition of it. He wouldn't be far from home once he got up that hill. He looked at Grace with a smile a mile wide. She was returning it wider still.

"Mist," he cried out, and turned to smile at the beauty of the grey before him. "Thank you, Grace," he said, turning to her again. She gave a nod. A question suddenly furrowed Doyle's brow and, still smiling, he asked; "But why have you left your Hill?"

"Oh," she tushed, "I knew I wouldn't be long…"

"But it's quite a walk back, what if someone should come to see if you're there?"

"Oh Doyle, don't be tiresome. I have my gander, of course," and she moved to the huge thing which they just now noticed had been sitting a slight bit away from them.

Delicately mounting the bird, Grace held on to a ribbon hanging round the creature's neck and in an instant, it swooped up into the air, taking wing and making a full circle so that Grace might gaze happily down at Doyle and give one last wave before sailing off into the fading light of the day, back to her house under the hill.

Doyle shook his head in wonder. Still in a daze, he began up the path, set on his destination when…

"Doyle…?"

He stopped. It was Danni. She had leapt from his shoulder and was standing beside Leo on the little seat. Both of them gazed at the boy. He looked over his shoulder and saw the top of the church spire beckoning. He gazed back at the pair.

"Are you going, then…?" Leo ventured. Danni made a little hiccough and Doyle knew she was about to cry. He didn't know what to do. He knew he wanted to get home but he certainly didn't want to cause any more troubles here. He looked back at the pair.

"I don't know what to do…" he admitted. "Everything here… it needs to stay balanced… and I'm not part of that balance…"

Sagely, Leo nodded. But Danni looked down. "I know I don't belong here…" she started, "That I'm probably not even from here… maybe I'm from out there too… maybe that's why it took me so long to talk and do the things mice do here…"

Leo sighed. "Well, I *know* I'm from here…" he began, "but I certainly don't seem to be slipping into anything else, except this seat here…"

Doyle shook his head. "But what if it changes you? What if you get over there and you can't talk? Can't reason? Can't let me know when you want water, hm?"

Danni and Leo looked at each other, then Danni said: "I guess we're just going to have to take a leap of Faith."

Doyle felt his eyes well up with tears: "Oh, Danni..." he sighed.

"Well, there's one sure way to find out..." Danni continued.

"Oh?" Doyle bit.

"When we get there, you could just ask us."

"Personally, I know I am an excellent accent to almost any piece of furniture," Leo proclaimed.

Doyle couldn't help laughing. He looked up and saw Grace still circling on her gander; she dived down a bit closer.

"I think you three had better get going, don't you?" she called out. His heart soared up higher than the gander and the woman on it. He took off his cap and waved it to her, before looking back at his friends.

"Shall we?" he asked.

"Another adventure!" Leo cried.

Danni didn't care. She really didn't care if she had another adventure or if she never spoke another word. She climbed on the handle of the cart and then over to Doyle and leapt up onto his jacket, skittering up the sleeve to his shoulder and then down the front to the jacket's chest pocket. She burrowed into the pocket and peeked her head out. She didn't care. She had Doyle and she had Leo.

Doyle looked at the little mouse in his pocket as she gazed happily up at him. He gave a glance to Leo who threw up his paw as if to say move on, and Doyle took up the handles and made his way up the path to the mist before him. Danni let out a sigh from his pocket.

And somehow, she just knew that everything would turn out fine.

"Danni..." Doyle asked before they were engulfed by the mist. "Does the cow really jump over the moon?"

"Of course she does..." Danni replied, "when it's rising."

******

Index

References to Fairy Tales, Mother Goose and Aesop's Fables

Chapter 1

Hey Diddle Diddle - Mother Goose
Three Blind Mice - Mother Goose
Hickory Dickory Dock - Mother Goose
Georgy Porgy - Mother Goose
Wee Willie - Mother Goose
Hole in the Bucket - Traditional Song

Chapter 2

The Grasshopper and the Ants - Aesop's Fables

Chapter 4

The Lion and the Mouse [Also, The Lion and the Slave] - Aesop's Fables
The Three Children of Fortune - Fairy Tale
Jack and the Beanstalk - Fairy Tale

Chapter 5

The Crooked Man [and Simple Simon] Mother Goose

Chapter 6

Wee Sleekit Cowering Timorous Beastie - Robert Burns
Alice in Wonderland - Lewis Carroll
The Elves and the Shoemaker - Fairy Tale
[Revisit Georgy Porgy and Wee Willie]

Chapter 7

The Fox and the Grapes - Aesop's Fables

Chapter 9

Pat a Cake - Mother Goose
Ring Around the Rosie - Mother Goose
Rockabye - Mother Goose
One, Two, Buckle My Shoe - Mother Goose
Mary, Mary, Quite Contrary - Mother Goose
Bessy Bell and Mary Grey - Mother Goose
[Revisit Three Blind Mice - Mother Goose]

Chapter 10

Pussy Cat and the Queen - Mother Goose
Beauty and The Beast - Fairy Tale

Chapter 11

Sleeping Beauty - Fairy Tale

Chapter 12

The Gate of the Year - Minnie Louise Haskins
[Revisit Hey Diddle Diddle and Hickory Dickory Dock]

Chapter 14

The Goose Girl - Fairy Tale

Chapter 15

Dame Trot and Her Cat - Mother Goose
[Revisit Crooked Man]
There Was An Old Woman - Mother Goose
Hansel and Gretel - Fairy Tale

Chapter 17

[Revisit Simple Simon]
Cinderella - Fairy Tale [alluded to]
The Kilkenny Cats - Mother Goose
The Lion and The Unicorn - Mother Goose
The Bunch of Blue Ribbons - Mother Goose

Chapter 19

Jack and the Beanstalk - Fairy Tale

Chapter 21

Cinderella - Fairy Tale

Chapter 23

[Revisit Goose Girl]

Chapter 26

Burnie Bee - Mother Goose
Old Woman Who Lived in a Shoe - Mother Goose

Chapter 27

[Revisit Hansel and Gretel]

Chapter 28

The Mountain In Labour - Aesop's Fables
The Old Woman Under the Hill - Mother Goose
Little Tom Tucker - Mother Goose

Chapter 29

[Revisit Beauty and The Beast]

Chapter 31

[Revisit The Mountain in Labour]
Humpty Dumpty - Mother Goose
The Hart - Mother Goose
For Every Evil - Mother Goose
Fears and Tears - Mother Goose
Good Advice - Mother Goose
Mist - Mother Goose

Chapter 32

[Revisit Jack and the Beanstalk]
The Old Woman of Leeds - Mother Goose
Hark Hark - Mother Goose
The Bremen Town Musicians - Fairy Tale
The Three Spinning Fairies - Fairy Tale